ATHENS, AMERICA

A Novel By
Larry Baker

FIRST COAST BOOKS

ISBN 0-9755724-0-X
LCCN 2004108565

First Edition: March 2005

For
Tom Scott

"Opposition to power, and suspicion of government
as the most dangerous embodiment of power, are the central
themes of American political thought."

"The arrogance of power was superseded
by the arrogance of morality."
-*Samuel Huntington*-

"All politics is local."
-*Tip O'Neill*-

"All local politics is personal."
-*Joseph Holly*-

"There was a time that you curled up in my lap,
Like a child you'd cling to me smiling,
Your eyes wide and wild,
Now you slip through my arms, wave a passing hello,
Twist away and toss a kiss, laughing as you go.

I'm a tangled up puppet,
Spinning round in knots,
And the more I see what used to be,
The less of you I've got."

-Harry and Sandy Chapin-

Advice for readers in Athens

Do I need to say the obvious: This is a work of fiction. It's not real. It never happened. Any resemblance....you know the drill. If you think you see yourself in this book, you're wrong. Get over yourself. Sue me; my brilliant attorney is licking his chops. Of course, if you think you see some praiseworthy and wonderful person in this story who reminds you of yourself....then it is you. Absolutely. It is you. And I did that intentionally. And, yes, many real people are mentioned by name. But here's the un-ironic truth....if you see your name in this book it's because I like you, I respect you, and I want you to know that. If you don't see your name in this story, it doesn't mean that I don't like or respect you. It simply means that I had to keep the book under 400 pages.

Acknowledgements

First, my family. For their love and patience. If you had to put up with me, you'd understand how wonderful they are, and one of these days I'm going to write a book about them. This is their official warning.

Patty Friedmann, the best writer in New Orleans, and a wonderful friend. She read the first draft of ATHENS, and she was honest enough to tell me that she hated it. I still like her.

Mike Lankford: writer, friend, and confidante. If you want to read the best book ever written about life as a musician on the road, look for Mike's LIFE IN DOUBLE TIME.

And a partial list of those who have encouraged me when I was down, advised me when I was clueless, or endured me at my worst: Michael Wilt, Karin Franklin, Matt Lage, Jacquelyn Mitchard, Mitch Kaplan, Alan Roberts, Jean Norville, Daniel Bernstein, Ralph Berry, Asya Muchnick, Vrinda Condillac, David Press, Rona Brinlee, Angie Christensen, Dennis Johnson, Ashley Warlick, Barbara Moss, Elizabeth Robinson, and Peter Wyman.

ATHENS, AMERICA

Begin with three: a driver, a runner, and a cop. The cop is chasing the driver, and the runner is waiting for them at the corner of First and Court.

The driver is young, a teenager, and you would not want him living near you. He sells drugs and steals without hesitation. He is often high, and he is more often angry than calm. He has dark black skin and dresses in code. A few seconds before he dies, he is reaching for a gun on the seat next to him.

The white cop is also young, a few years under thirty, but he has been old all his life. Old in the sense of having always known what he wanted to be, even as a child. He was always the cop, never the robber. There had been no other cops in his family, and his parents were mystified as to why he had chosen this career. But they loved their son, and they were proud of him when he graduated from the police academy. They were immensely relieved when he got his first job in their town, where he had grown up. He did not tell them, but that was part of his plan too. When he was thirty, he had told himself, he would think about marriage. Everything in order, under control. But his parents died in a plane crash, and his sense of control died with them.

The runner is the youngest of the three. She is black and white, and she is running toward her home when she sees the flashing red lights and hears the sirens. She stops to see what happens. A few seconds later, as the driver's car rolls toward her, she steps to her right. It is the wrong direction.

The cop and the driver have a history. On this warm evening, that history comes to an end. For months, the cop has been cruising the driver's neighborhood. For months, the driver has taunted the cop. But the cop is not innocent. He has gone out of his way to look for the driver. He would drive slowly behind him, and he has given the driver two tickets for minor traffic violations. A rolling stop, failing

1

to give a signal. If you had asked the cop—why _this_ driver?—he would not have had a satisfactory answer.

The driver is an outsider, from a bigger city to the east, and he brought the big city's problems into the cop's small hometown. It is not that simple, not that clear, but the cop is not able to get beyond his feeling that his role in his hometown is to protect it from the driver.

The cop has worked eight straight days, filling in for other cops. He began his shift this morning going to a domestic disturbance in the driver's neighborhood. The husband had been warned. He was pounding on the door when the cop arrived. He resisted arrest, and the cop had to call for back-up. The husband took a swing at the cop and tried to get his gun, but the cop had him on the ground before things got out of control. As the cop put the husband in his patrol car, the driver cruised by and almost raised his middle finger toward him. A small gesture.

In the seven hours before the chase, the cop has answered a dozen calls, backed-up other cops, checked car tags, arrested a drunk downtown who had too much to drink at Happy Hour, and, a half hour before seeing the driver again, broken up a knife fight between two other drunks in an alley downtown. His uniform shirtsleeve had been ripped. The dispatcher tells him to call it a day, but the cop wants to swing through the driver's neighborhood one more time. He has begun the day already exhausted, but when he sees the driver run the stop sign he has a profoundly satisfying surge of energy.

It is supposed to be the same routine. The cop will stop the driver, and the driver will either smirk or sit sullenly while he is being lectured. But this warm evening, the driver does not stop. He keeps a steady speed, ignores the flashing lights, and then they reach First Avenue. The cop is talking to the dispatcher just as the driver begins accelerating. The driver has a minute to live. The cop will be gone *from his hometown in twenty-four hours. The runner is waiting at the corner.*

The cop thinks that he knows why the driver is racing away. This time, there is something in the car that the driver cannot be caught with. The driver will finally be sent away for a long time.

Fifty miles an hour in a twenty-five zone, then sixty. Through red lights and stop signs in a straight line. Other cars swerving for self-preservation. The cop's window is open, and he feels the air swirl and roar inside his patrol car. He starts to scream at the driver ahead of him, and his screams drown out the other voice in the car with him, a static-laced voice calmly telling him to break off the chase. But the cop knows where the driver is headed—through the next stop sign and out to the highway, where he has no jurisdiction. Beyond his control.

The driver looks back, then looks forward to the next stop sign, but his brain is crossing wires, and two contradictory impulses collide. Get rid of the gun and turn the car, but he cannot do both. He does not see the runner.

The cop sees it all in slow motion. The driver's car lurches to the left at First and Court, the rear starting to spin faster than the front, and then the driver's side of the car begins rising so that the cop sees the black underside. Like a movie stunt, the car rolls once and then slides on its roof to rest on the green slope beyond the curb. The cop sees it all, but he does not see the runner.

He has two minutes alone. Other patrol cars are already coming. He is out of his car and over to the driver's car, but the driver is pulpy and red and no longer human. Then he sees another form further up the slope, almost like it was sleeping. It is at this moment that the cop sees his own life go away. He kneels beside the sleeping runner and touches her crooked neck. Where did she come from?

The cop looks around for help, but he is still alone. He starts

3

CPR, *but he knows it is useless. The runner is dead. Who is she? The cop hears sirens, and he sits beside the sleeping runner, holding her hand. He knows that he has done something terribly wrong, and he will pay. He will go away from his hometown and never come back. And, until the end of his life, he will keep two things to himself about this moment.*

As a small child he had always dreamed about angels, in those dreams the angels had this girl's face. That was one thing, a feeling that might even be understandable if he ever chose to share it.

But the other memory will never be shared. As he sits there on that slope with the sleeping girl, he looks up to see an enormous blood red deer standing over him, looking down at him and the girl.

Jack Hamilton began every morning with a ritual. He was not paying homage to his wife's god. He was merely paying the daily tithe needed to redeem his body from a night of bad sleep. From his neck to his ankles, most of his joints reminded him how much he had abused his body as a young man. From junior high until his second year as a linebacker for the Chicago Bears, when his right knee could no longer be patched together, Hamilton had thrown himself at other muscular bodies and usually hurt them more. His teams might have lost, but Jack Hamilton never had a bad game.

First, he simply sat on the edge of the bed, staring in the dark at the red glowing numbers on his clock, rolling his shoulders and neck, reaching down to touch his toes, which he could not do when standing. He got up at 5:00 every morning except Sunday. After standing and stretching, arms out and upper torso slowly turning at a right angle to his legs, he would put on his cotton sweat pants and pullover, go into the kitchen, turn on the coffee-maker, put his hands on the edge of the table and slowly do deep knee bends. Not many, just enough to get limber. After his coffee, he would go for a walk around the block.

Even in the coldest of Iowa winters, Jack Hamilton walked around his block three times, a fast clip, but never running. Too hard on his knees. As he walked this late May morning, he reviewed plans for his day. Monday through Friday, those plans had to include his daughter Rebecca, getting her to and from school, taking her to a flute lesson or to her volunteer job at Mercy Hospital, or a dozen other spontaneous "events" of her teenage life. He called her "Becka" because she could never pronounce her own name as a child, and it always sounded like Becka when she told someone else her name. As soon as she entered high school, she began to insist that her parents call her Becky, not Becka, but Hamilton and his wife had not mastered the change.

Three laps around the block done, he went home to wake his wife Marcie. He would sit on the edge of the bed next to her, lean down and kiss her. Usually, she would act like she was still asleep, and he would kiss her again, usually. But this particular morning came after an argument the night before. They seldom argued, so making up was not a natural act for either of them. The night before, the argument had been about money for their daughter. Marcie wanted to increase Becka's allowance. Jack thought she was getting enough. The argument ended with him being exasperated because, as he told her, "You're going to give it to her anyway, no matter what I say, so why did you even bother asking me." As he walked that morning, he knew he had been wrong the night before. But he resented being put in a situation that made him look like the bad cop in a good cop/bad cop drama. It had happened before, and usually about money.

Hamilton and his wife both worked. He was a clerk at the post office. She was a fifth grade teacher at Regina Elementary. Solid middle-class homeowners in Athens, Iowa, with health insurance and a retirement program at his job so that she could continue to work at the Catholic school even though the public schools paid more and had better benefits.

With their two jobs, they lived a better life than their own parents had led. But Jack Hamilton could never shake the fear of being poor. He grew up in Chicago, raised by an unwed mother, sharing his bed with a younger brother in a room with two other brothers. A football scholarship got him out of Chicago to the University of Iowa. Four years later, he had gone un-drafted by the NFL, but he walked into the Bears training camp and stayed until his knees, as he told his older brothers, "turned to shit."

His wife woke up with a single kiss this morning. "How was your walk?" she mumbled, reaching out to pat his hand. Hamilton knew she was trying to make-up after last night's argument. She always took the first step. "Still cold out there," he whispered back, "Feels like we might just skip summer and fall this year, go right to winter."

The birth of his daughter was the second miracle in Jack Hamilton's life. The first was meeting Marcie Sturdevant. He was a college freshman on a football scholarship who could not read or write. Marcie was a senior, hired by the athletic department to tutor a dozen black athletes like Hamilton. Her instructions were simple: keep them eligible, whatever it took. If that meant that she did some of their assignments, so be it. She was a devout Catholic, but she compromised. She told her friends that the idea of a "student-athlete" was a bad joke, especially for the football program. Eligibility was the goal, not education, not even graduation. But of all the tutors, her groups actually always had more athletes get a degree of some sort. She went beyond teaching them basic skills. She also arranged their schedules, mediated disputes with instructors, and made it possible for them to continue living their dream of going professional. College was simply a farm system for the NFL. A few succeeded, most did not, but they always remembered Marcie Sturdevant.

Jack Hamilton was different from the others. Marcie knew that after meeting him. At first, she thought he would be a lost cause. On paper, he was illiterate to the point of seeming retarded. He had a "conditional admission," meaning that he was athletically good but not good enough to be guaranteed a scholarship regardless of his high school transcript. But then she talked to him. He spoke clearly, was even articulate, and he was absolutely focused on his goals, and those goals went beyond a pro career. He practiced harder, went to class religiously, attended her study halls without fail. For the first few weeks, however, he made no progress in reading or writing. No amount of revision seemed to help. Marcie then realized that Hamilton had more wrong with him than just a bad public school education. She literally took his hand and walked him to the university testing center. At the end of the day, they both listened to a mannish woman

7

explain how he was suffering from a combination of learning disorders that had never been diagnosed before. He could overcome them, he was told, but it would not be easy, and he would have to work against those problems for the rest of his life.

When she told her Iowa, descended from German stock, parents that she was marrying a six foot three inch black man from Chicago, she could only repeat what she had told her friends earlier. "Something happened that day in that office as he looked over at me, a look on his face like I was something precious he had lost and then found. He made me feel like I was holy."

Hamilton's family was not upset that he married a white woman. But his brothers and friends were astonished in his particular choice. "Man, is that the best you could do?" his oldest brother teased him. "Other brothers are bagging pretty white women. Why you gotta get the ugly one? And you ain't the handsomest nigger in the field. You two have some babies, you're compounding ugliness. Double ugly, you're gonna scare the nurses to death."

Jack Hamilton was not handsome. Marcie Sturdevant was not pretty. Their daughter Rebecca was gorgeous, even as a newborn, more and more as she got older. The greatest pleasure of their married life was when they would introduce their daughter to someone who had never seen her before. Always the look of "You're kidding me, right? This is your daughter?" And then the smile on that person's face, a smile that a confrontation with beauty always provoked. Turn the corner of any museum and see a classic work of art for the first time. You might be disappointed if you met the artist, perhaps a miserable human being, but the art gave you pleasure that you could not resist. You stop and marvel. That was Rebecca Pearl Hamilton.

As his wife showered, Hamilton read the morning paper. He usually started with the sports page, especially when the football season began, but this particular morning he went right to the lead story on

8

the front page. The Athens City Council had a long meeting the night before. Another public hearing had disintegrated into a shouting match. What should be done about all the deer running wild in the city limits? Hamilton had seen them in his own backyard many times at night, so he and Marcie had decided to put up a fence to keep them out. They were destroying most of the vegetation that she had cultivated for years. The Council was considering a plan to hire someone to thin the herds by shooting them. Deer lovers on one side of the Council chambers, aggrieved neighbors on the other side. The newspaper account made it seem like a circus.

He walked to the bathroom door, coffee cup in hand, and talked to Marcie. "Another wild night at City Hall. Suppose we should start watching those meetings on TV?"

Marcie talked over the streaming water, "You're the one with all the free time. You watch."

"Point taken," Hamilton replied. It was true. He did not have to bring his job home with him at night. Marcie was always working on papers or projects for her class. "Maybe I'll run for office." He looked at his wife's outline through the steamed-over glass door.

Sticking her head out from behind the door, she said, "Just make sure the divorce is final first, okay."

Hamilton laughed. It was an old joke between them. He would sometimes mention running for the City Council, and Marcie would always tell him to "get the divorce first, because I don't want be married to a fool." And he would always nod in agreement, "Right, a man's got to be crazy to want that job." The argument from the night before was fading.

By 6:30 they had both showered and finished their coffee. It was time to wake their daughter. She had a second floor bedroom, so her mother usually made the trip up. His legs did not like stairs. He would be cooking breakfast by the time Becka and her mother descended. It was the best moment of the day for Hamilton, to turn around and see his daughter and wife at the table.

Becka was in a foul mood this morning. She was fifteen, beautiful, talented, and mad at her father.

"How you want your eggs this morning?" he asked.

"How do I want them every morning, daddy? I DON'T want them. Eggs are bad for you," she snapped.

"Oh, I forgot," he apologized insincerely. He knew she did not want eggs. He looked at Marcie, who mouthed silently back at him, "Why do you keep doing this?"

"Yeh, right," Becka said.

"Becka, tell your father what…,"

"Becky, my name is Becky, please."

It was the last part of the morning ritual, teasing his daughter until she finally laughed. Still, as he and his wife had to admit, and as other parents had told them, teenage girls were sometimes not a pleasant chore.

This morning took longer, but Becka finally surrendered. As she left with her mother for school, she shouted at her father, always her last words until seeing him that night, "See you later, gator." And he would always respond, "Not if I see you first."

Wife and daughter gone, Jack Hamilton cleaned up the kitchen. With his house in order, he went to work.

Until the girl died, I had always thought that life was a joke. Not always funny, mostly never, but certainly not something to be taken seriously. If you took it too seriously, you had to go crazy. Too many things that made no sense to someone like me, who always wanted to believe in God but who kept getting proof to the contrary. My first baby dies in her sleep. My second, my boy, is born well and grows like a flower but now seems mindless. My wife is slowly killing herself with grief and rage and booze right in front of my eyes. Wouldn't I have to be ironic? Wouldn't you? Where's the sense in all this? So it must be a joke, right? Then I get a call telling me that a fifteen year old black girl is dead, a girl from another world, and a week later I go to one of those lunatic council meetings and listen to a mob scream that I killed her. That my hand was on the wheel of the car that propelled young Becky Hamilton into the hands of a god that does not exist.

I live in Athens, Iowa, a town that doesn't really exist either, except as a moral lesson in mass hysteria. North Carolina has Chapel Hill, the Athens of the South. Georgia has Athens, the Athens of Georgia. I have Athens, Iowa, the Athens of the Midwest. Iowa, more pigs than people, corn capital of the universe. The Heartland of America. Like all college towns, an island of art and intellect and tax-supported affluence, a world safe from the crime and poverty and shameless hucksterism of the rest of America. Or so we tell ourselves. We're different. We're better. We live the life of the mind. Athens, a world of perpetual adolescence, a world in which half the population is engaged in preparing the other half for their future. Give us your young, we tell those nervous and loving mothers and fathers who want their children's lives to be happier and more comfortable than their own. Give us your sons and daughters, their hopes and fears, their insecurities and their student loans. Wrap them in an ACT or SAT score and pack them off to Athens.

I love this town. I really do. I fell in love with Julie here, buried my first child here, and had always assumed I would die here. I just wish I had been able to save it from itself. Instead, here I am, turning all of us into a morality play. Changing the names to protect the guilty as well as the innocent. Don't misunderstand me. This isn't a story about academics or academia, about classroom politics or angst-ridden professors chasing firm-fleshed coeds, seeking the meaning of life as they realize that education guarantees neither intelligence nor happiness. Stories about "college" are a dime a dozen, full of sound and furious Francinian prose, signifying nothing. I went to college in Athens. I met Julie in a classroom. She was my teacher even though I was older than her. But this is not about college. This is about trying to make sense out of tragedy. Trying not to take myself too seriously because, after all, life's a joke, right? This is a story with villains like Ken Rumble but not enough heroes, not even me, who should have been braver when I needed to be brave. Come down to it, this is just a story about my divinely precious son Danny, and my wife, whose breathing I study every night as she sleeps, afraid she'll just will herself into stopping. A story about my town and my family, and how I lost one.

I should start from the beginning. I was a teenage Southern Baptist lay preacher, channeling Jesus in a hundred tent sermons. Or even younger, growing up with an absent father and smothering mother, but the real beginning was when I shook John Kennedy's hand the day he died.

I was sixteen, going to high school in Fort Worth, and JFK had spent the night of November 21st at the Hotel Texas downtown. Friday morning, the 22nd, I was in the crowd waiting out front, thinking I might see him get in his limousine for the drive to the airport to fly over to Dallas. I got there early and was in the front line behind a rope. He came out like he had all the time in the world, and the crowd started to push forward, squeezing me against the ropes. He walked down the line shaking hands, and I knew he was headed my way when I got this feeling like I had when I first thought I had found Jesus.

I made eye contact with him, and I swear that his eyes never left mine as he moved up to me, like we were in slow motion, and then he stuck out his right hand. I reached for him and felt his hand wrap itself around mine. Then, out of nowhere, I asked him the most profound question I've ever asked anybody, and I almost had to yell to get myself heard above all the noise around us. "Where's Jackie?" I asked, like she had been my girlfriend first, not his, as if I was his best friend now. His eyes brightened and he laughed out loud, throwing his head back, and then, my hand still clasped in his as his other hand reached around my shoulder to pull me closer to him, he leaned down to whisper in my ear, "She's upstairs picking out a dress for Dallas."

"Upstairs picking out a dress for Dallas." I hear that line all the time in my memory. He's dead, she's dead, I'm alive. That line dies with me.

Why begin my story with that story? I could tell you about nearly dying from pneumonia when I was a baby, or losing a kidney when I was twelve, or being introduced to my father for the first time. That would mean something, I suppose, me meeting my father. Perhaps explain something about me. He was in the Army, then the Air Force, and he was always gone. I slept with my mother, me the younger of her two boys, and the sickly child. Her bed was mine. Approach that bit of biography with caution. When my mother died, I refused to go look at her in the coffin. My brother paid his respects, but I stood on the other side of the viewing room for two hours, shaking hands with relatives, accepting condolences, but not going near her. All this stuff keeps coming back to me more and more ever since that Hamilton girl died. About my parents, about my past.

I had been at a friend's house all morning, that day in 1951 when I met my father. I came home and my mother met me at the kitchen door with, "Your father's home." She took my hand and led me toward her bedroom, to the door at the end of a long unlit hallway. It was almost noon, I remember that much, a scorching day in Texas. The door to the bedroom was at the very end, so as you entered you had to turn right, but until you made that turn you were in the room without actually seeing anything. So, I saw him, the man who was my father, sitting in the bed I shared with my mother, sitting there with his back propped against a pile of pillows, the bedcovers up to his waist, bare-chested. Weird enough, this strange man in bed in the middle of the day, in a room with all the curtains open and blinds up. Of course, I had surely seen him countless times before then, I must have, but this is my earliest memory of him. But there's more, and he denied this ever happened, but he's wrong. It happened. He was sitting there in that bed, bare-chested, and he had a pair of binoculars hanging from around his neck. There's no punch line to this story, not even an explanation. With my father now dead from Alzheimer's, there's not even another witness. I'm in my fifties, but I remember his first words to me as he stuck out his hand, as he sat in the bed I shared with my mother, "Come here, Joseph, and let me show you something." That's all I remember from that day.

Why start with Kennedy? You're probably thinking that I'm a cynic, but the truth is much different. Kennedy was my bridge from church to state, but it wasn't even him. Before that morning, I knew squat about politics. But I knew a lot about God and Jesus and the Bible and Satan and Sin. Sometimes it comes back to me, a passage I used to be able to pull out and quote verbatim. But something was happening to me that morning in Fort Worth, a process that had begun months earlier. At the beginning of this story, I said that God doesn't exist. But he did, a long time ago. For me he was as real as my breath, as present in my life as the air around me.

I'm a Catholic now. If my mother were alive she would roll over in her grave. The son she prayed over, the son she baptized twice in different towns, the son whose naked fevered body she washed with alcohol for hour after hour as he almost died of nephritis. Joseph Holly, her most devout, now a pagan Catholic.

I was fourteen when I saw Jesus at a Crusade at the Fort Worth Coliseum. Billy Graham was waving all of us sinners down front as the choir sang "Just As I Am." Standing on the ground under Graham's podium, Jesus beckoned to me. I began walking toward him, hearing Cliff Barrows and George Beverly Shea sing as Graham spoke softly. When I reached him, Jesus took me by the hand and led me to the front of the line of people being saved. They stepped aside, not seeing who I was with, but knowing there was something different about me. I went to the Richland Hills Baptist Church the Sunday after that and told Brother Bailey I wanted to speak to the congregation. A week later I was in a tent in front of a crowd that had come to see just me. Just me and Jesus.

When I heard that John Kennedy had been shot, I looked at my hand, the hand he had touched. I had forgotten what Jesus felt like. I'm simplifying here, trying to get to all the other things I need to tell you. I'll try to come back to it, all the reasons I was drifting away from Jesus even before I met Kennedy. All the church hypocrisy, my mother's apron strings I was trying to cut, the warm skin of Wanda Sue Kidd, the retirement of my father and him coming to live with us full-time. Enough for a book, but not now. It's the connection between my two lives, between religion and politics. That's the point. In both lives, I felt like I was doing something good for other people. That Joseph Holly, all by himself, made a positive difference. That I was a good person.

Kennedy's death was all I needed to leave the church. Of course, I was sixteen and basically shallow. I resented Lyndon Johnson. He was no John Kennedy. So my first real political campaign was to work for Barry Goldwater in 1964. Joseph Holly——a Young Republican. Did I really understand any of the issues? Not a chance in hell. I wanted to punish LBJ, whose heart was closer to mine than any President of the twentieth century, but whose voice and style were an insult to a teenage boy who had been touched by John Kennedy.

So it all began with Kennedy. Coming to my senses in 1968 and working on the campaign of every Democrat running for office since then, all the grunt work of planting yard signs, licking envelopes, and those god-awful phone calls the night before every election, interrupting people's dinner and asking them, reminding them, begging them to go vote the next day.

Through all those years, as I operated theatres and worked my way through college, I dreamed of taking some oath of office myself someday, finishing something that began with John Kennedy.

The only trouble with my dream was—me. I turned my personal life into a paradigm of self-indulgence and self-destruction. As I humped past thirty, I accepted the fact that the public was probably not going to elect a man who had cheated on his first wife, had sex as often as possible with sixteen year old girls who worked for him, lived in sin with a girl not old enough to vote, was arrested by the FBI but turned state's evidence to have his record expunged, and established the film obscenity standards for the state of Oklahoma. Not to mention the drugs. If dope had been legal in the Seventies, I would have single-handedly been Pfizer's profit margin for the decade.

But then I met Julie, and, like the worst of clichés, a good woman turned me around. I had sold my theatre in Oklahoma, made more money by simply selling the building to my competitor than I had made in all the years I had fought him. I took the money and moved to Athens to go to graduate school. I knew nobody, was in a new town, and simply erased my past. Don't ask, don't tell. I was out of show business.

I've been here twenty years, and I've fooled everybody but Julie. And I've been happy, that's the strangest thing. It's true, you get smarter as you get older. If you're lucky, you fall in love, like I did, and you make peace with your demons, like I did. I was handling everything okay until that girl died. Right before a campaign to get re-elected to an office that I didn't care about anymore, running for the worst of reasons, because I actually needed the paltry salary to pay my bills, I was still okay.

From Kennedy's handshake to that morning when I was at Oakland Cemetery, like I am the first day of every month for the past fifteen years, after Julie has gone to work, after Danny has gone to school, standing over my baby girl's grave and talking to her, when I saw that other girl's father. He was on his knees, resting on his heels, rocking back and forth, a hundred feet away from me, but I was invisible and he was absolutely alone. One continuous thread.

Jack Hamilton always hated Press Day the first week of football season. Surrounded by reporters and photographers, he avoided speaking in clichÈs. The reporters' complained that he did not speak enough. After a close game, however, they always went to him first because he was able to analyze the turning points as well as any coach, and without praising Jesus or simply crediting luck. Everyone assumed he would end up as a head coach after retiring, but Hamilton walked away from professional football and never looked back.

If he ever coached, he told himself, it would eventually be in high school, so ending up in Athens as a postal clerk surprised him as much as anyone else, except his wife, who understood him better than he understood himself. After his knees forced him out of pro football, and before anyone offered him a job, his wife asked him if she could accept a teaching job in Athens. They would have to move back to Iowa, to a smaller town than even Iowa City, where they had met. Her salary would not be much, but their savings from two seasons of an NFL salary would tide them over for several years until he found something he wanted to do. Perhaps one of the high schools would have an opening. His wife knew that he would not say no to her request. He knew it was important to her, would make her happy, and Jack Hamilton adored his wife. She would have done anything for him, gone anywhere and put her own plans on hold, if he had asked first. But she asked him first.

Marcie had come to understand that her husband was the kindest man she had ever known. He had always been a kind man, even as a struggling student who seemed angry to most other people. When he told her that he was quitting pro football, she felt something that not even he recognized. His knees were an excuse. With the latest state-of-the-art surgery, a year to recover and rehabilitate himself, Hamilton could go back to football and be better than most linebackers, although not as good as he had been. But his anger was gone.

18

He had escaped Chicago, made a name for himself, come back to Chicago as a hometown hero, but he had never been happy. Marcie liked to think that she and Becka were the reason he changed, but she would never know for sure. That would be too simple, too romantic. All she had to do was ask him why he was so happy now, but she knew he would not talk about it. Her parents had been impressed by seeing that Jack Hamilton was not falsely humble, and he never had to tell them that he loved their daughter. It was obvious. Their granddaughter was simply more proof.

Hamilton took the civil service exam, but he never knew for sure whether it was his score or his color, or even his football reputation, that got him his job. A year later, he stopped wondering about it. He liked his job, especially after he worked his way up the system, from delivery to working behind the counter. None of the other clerks knew about his reading problems, how much he had to constantly work against them, or how much his legs hurt those first few years he had to go mailbox to mailbox. All they saw was a former football star who did not talk about football. Nor was Hamilton an example of what was wrong with affirmative action. In Athens, there were few black people in general. In the Athens post-office, there was only one. Hamilton worked diligently, learned all the routines, and he advanced up the chain of postal command faster than other men and women who had been there longer. But no one resented his success. They recognized, and appreciated, his ability to maneuver all the bureaucratic hoops that frustrated them. None of the petty rules and petty supervisors seemed to bother him. Most of all, they liked him because he seemed to like them.

Hamilton liked his salary, and the work was actually easy. He seldom missed a day, and his annual sick leave allotment was never used up. The thing he liked the most about his job, however, was something he only told his wife. Put simply: He never took his job home with him. Eight hours, and then his real life began. Hamilton never told his co-workers that as soon as he left the building he did not think about them or their work again until he came back the next day. He looked forward to his life with Marcie and Becka, and he liked the time he went to his study and read books and magazines. He liked going to movies and to Becka's school events.

He was not a deep thinker, he would admit. When he went to work the morning his daughter had snapped at him about breakfast, he wished he knew more about adolescent psychology. Usually, he let his wife explain their daughter's behavior to him later. Marcie was around young children all day, and she had always seemed to have some sort of feminine understanding about young people as a group and their daughter as an individual. Hamilton's own mother had also seemed to have the same insight. As he arranged his cash drawer that morning at the post-office, Hamilton told himself to ask Marcie to recommend a book for him to read that would help him deal with Becka.

His daughter seemed to be pushing him away more than usual, sometimes to the point of being hostile. Of course, much of it was typical female teenage behavior. Sometimes when Becka would start criticizing him, his wife would yell at her, "Get your own husband. This one is mine." Recently, Hamilton had been questioning his own behavior. Was he pushing her too hard in the direction of sports? Was he unreasonable about her not going on dates so young? Becka was five feet eight inches tall, and only fifteen years old. She was obviously gifted. She played basketball, volleyball, ran track and cross-country. She had already set school records for her grade. At first glance, she did not appear muscular. But Hamilton liked to tell others, over and over, you did not notice her broad shoulders or her lean and perfectly proportioned legs because all you noticed was her face. In his worst moments of parental insecurity, Hamilton wondered if he *would love his daughter as much if she had been as unattractive as her parents. His wife was just as guilty. They would always joke about catching the other just stare at Becka when she was not aware.*

My town and my family, and how I lost one, remember? My story. I saw Athens first, but Julie was more precious.

I remember sitting in the back of the room, my first class at Iowa Arts, the oldest grad student in a nineteenth century American lit and culture class, and in walked Julie, who I thought was just another grad student. But she walked up to the front and started handing out copies of the syllabus. She was wearing baggy jeans and a sweatshirt with a University of Alabama logo. She had one of those dykey short haircuts, and her glasses——her lenses had the circumference and thickness of the bottom of a Coca-Cola bottle. I pegged her right away: a humorless dull feminist who had a testosterone chip on her shoulder. I was Joseph Holly, a brilliant judge of character, and I knew I was going to be bored. Then she spoke, and I thought that not only was she going to be a boring man-hater, she was from another planet and English was obviously her second language. Her southern accent was as alien to me as algebra, and I was hunkering down for a long semester, but then something strange happened. I paid attention to her.

First words out of her mouth, absolutely deadpanned,

"Look around you. The college has done alumni surveys, and they found out that most graduates of this school met their future spouses in an English class. Chances are, you'll marry somebody in this room." Ka-plang went the cymbal that nobody heard. She kept that straight face and handed out more papers. All of us, me too, we immediately looked around. I noticed a semi-attractive blond who looked like a stripper I had dated once, wondering to myself why I hadn't noticed her when I walked in the room, and then I looked back at Julie. We all did, but I was the first. She was standing there like she had eaten our dessert when we were praying. A tiny smile on her face. I was hooked. Absolutely hooked.

She talked for fifty minutes, and I just stared. She had that class in the palm of her hand. Her accent was like one of those foreign languages you learn soon enough, then you master, and you wish you had spoken it all your life. Almost like French, but without all those French people who don't deserve their own language. Actually, that was Julie's line, once when we were drunk together:

"Only thing wrong with French is the frogs who speak it." You see, I had waited all my life for a smart funny woman, and Julie was the smartest woman and the funniest—person—I had ever met. Soon enough, she was also the prettiest.

As class ended that day, I stopped to tell her how much I was looking forward to the semester. I hadn't been that much of a brown-noser in years, but how else to introduce myself? Standing close to her, I stared some more at her face close-up. Not very subtle.

"Stare much?" she asked me. I fumbled something about being sorry, feeling like I was twelve. But there was something about her face. I started to imagine her with long hair and contact lenses, so her eyes would shine from a distance like they did when you saw them up close.

"I'm Joseph Holly," I said.

"Oh, I know who you are," she smiled, "I've heard all about you."

What did THAT mean? I felt another hook sink in. I thought nobody knew about me, but there she was telling me that I had no secrets. Of course, later she told me that she was kidding. But at that moment I felt like a dog rolling over on its back begging for mercy.

At the end of that first week, we were drunk together, but so were thirty other people. It was the first department party, and grad students were invited. Soon enough, there were two parties going on at the same time. One was inside the Chair's house, with serious discussions, solemn and grammatically correct, politically correct, complete sentence exchanges about tenure and Derrida, all maintained with a glass of wine in the hand. The other was on the patio, with the beer keg and everyone trying to get laid. Julie and I met at the beer keg. I had been looking for the blond. Julie, she confessed later, had been looking for me.

"I need a joint," were my suave first words.

"I need some vodka," were her's.

It was early September in Iowa, still warm, and she was wearing shorts, the last hook. Julie Knight had drop dead gorgeous killer legs, and if the flesh creeping out the bottom of her shorts was any indication, she also had a rump that would turn professional lechers like me into stone. How could I be so lucky, to fall in love with a woman for the right reasons, and then discover she had a perfect body. I just wish I had paid more attention to that line about vodka.

"You should let your hair grow out longer," I said.

"You should grow a beard," she said, pumping the keg handle. "Not a long one, just enough."

"Just enough?" I asked.

"Look, you have three reasons to grow some hair on your face."

I was about to ask the obvious question, but she cut me off, "Your chin is two of those reasons."

It took me a second, but I caught the meaning, my shoulders tightening because she had nailed my own self-image complaint. I was past thirty, and my father's chin was catching up to me.

"And the third?" I asked, wishing I was someplace else, self-conscious about my flawed appearance again.

"Because I think you will look handsome with a beard," Julie said, handing me a plastic cup of beer. Somebody was murdering a guitar out in the dark backyard. "You grow a beard, I'll let my hair grow. Deal?"

I can tell you a hundred things about Julie, why I loved her, but I can't tell you a thing about what she saw in me. She did, that's all

24

that matters. We saw each other everyday for the rest of the semester, and in that first three months I learned everything I would need to know about her. Smart? She had her PhD at twenty-six and was on a fast tenure track with her first job. She was twenty-eight that first day I saw her. More than smart, she was wise. I learned to withhold judgment about any new person I met until she met them. That was why she was on the department hiring committee from her very first year. She smelled rats and frauds like they were burning toast. She got fooled only once, I was told by another one of my professors— when she married me. The bastard. I pointed out to him that he had been hired before Julie was there, so he had gotten lucky himself. But I wouldn't admit that I sometimes felt the same way, that I had fooled Julie, that I wasn't the person she loved. But I wasn't about to disabuse her of the notion that I was a prince turned frog waiting for a kiss.

Funny? She was more than funny. She was brilliantly comic, and it was all so natural. She couldn't tell a joke and get a laugh if her life depended on it. Everything was situational, context was everything, and it was always spontaneous. I had never seen anybody do what she did. Remember Gilda Radner, from Saturday Night Live? Radner was funny with all those characters, but she had writers and time to rehearse. Julie's supreme talent was her ability to mimic anybody or anything. Get a drink in her, and I would just sit back as she performed, mimicking the rest of the department, her students, people on television. Dead-on voices and mannerisms, but taken to the next logically absurd level. But she only did it among people she trusted and liked, and stories would start circulating, the "Have you seen Julie Knight when she's wired?" stories. People who never saw her never understood. Other men who had seen her envied me. In her particular department, a bastion of political correctness, she sometimes irritated her colleagues, especially other women. She once proposed a law that would prohibit women from being announcers or commentators for men's sporting events. She was asked to apologize at a faculty meeting, by some sort of man-hating Andrea Dworkin feminist, and Julie upped the ante: female flight attendants should retire at age 45. The Dworkin actually tried to jump her. I wish I had been there.

Her supreme talent? Not only could she mimic people, she also created voices for animals or inanimate objects, and then she would carry on conversations between the voices. She would talk to our dog Roo and he would "talk" back to her, and his "voice" seemed like, if he could have talked, it seemed like what he would sound like. It was a dumb voice, and our dog was certainly dumb. The best? How about the night before she had to go get a mammogram? She gave each of her breasts a voice and then had them talk to each other about their past experiences and what they expected the next day. We were at the kitchen table, and even Danny was mesmerized, though I'm sure he didn't have a clue about why it was so funny.

Other things I found out about her, good things, like how genuinely considerate she was of other people, how sweet, and how moral. The exact opposite of me, and sometimes a cause of our worst arguments. Except for the Dworkins, most people loved Julie. But she married me.

We've been together over twenty years, and if I had to give one explanation for why she made me happy, beyond the humor and wisdom, and perfect body, it would be for this reason: She is the only person in my life who ever made me feel calm. Hard to describe, but I was like one of those lines on a lie detector graph that was jumping up and down all over the paper, feeling like I lied about every question ever asked me, even the simple ones like what was my name. Julie made me happy, and I calmed down.

So, everything should be okay, right? But I know something else about Julie that nobody believes when I tell them, but which explains everything else about her. My wife is absolutely, certifiably, completely insane. I'll tell you a hundred times—I'm not talking in metaphors here. She's not "crazy" like her friends describe her. I told you how she creates voices. I finally figured out that she actually hears those voices, those she mimics, and others she never utters but only hears. And not all those voices are funny. When she's not aware of me, which happens a lot lately, I can see her lips moving but no sound coming out. She's having another one of those conversations, and her body seems to be reacting to some invisible thing in the room. She clenches her fists, points, and her face goes from anger to fear to some ineffable version of—bliss. Sometimes she will walk right past me, as if she's looking for something or somebody in another room.

Because of Julie, I became a Catholic, and we've gone to mass every Sunday since 1981. It meant a lot to her, so I did it, but I always figured she was one of those educated Catholics who probably believed in some sort of God, and the Catholic church had a lot of ritual and history, so if you're going to express that sort of vague belief, why not go with the original church and ignore the knock-off brands like the Episcopalians and Presbyterians. And the Baptists, like I was, you had to avoid them like the plague. But when I believed in God, I believed in him, or it, or whatever, I believed that God was GOD. The God that Julie worshipped was something else, something more frightening. Her God was too human.

I once asked her who she was talking to, all those times her lips were moving in church or when she was almost crying when she thought she was alone but I was watching. "Sometimes I'm talking to God," she said. "Sometimes I'm talking to you. Sometimes I'm just listening to the two of you argue."

How would it have been if Kathy had not died? Me and Julie. Our life? This year we would have been helping Kathy get ready for

27

her first date. A thousand other moments frozen on film or in our memory. And Julie would be okay, I'm sure.

I was in the room when our daughter died, but I was asleep. Julie and I had been taking turns watching Kathy because we had seen her roll over too often and sleep face down. SIDS had not gotten the publicity back then that it has now, but we had talked to the pediatrician because Julie's niece had died from it the year before, and we were looking for clues on how to prevent it. The doctor had said that the only sure thing was to literally watch your baby sleep and be right there if she stopped breathing. But, he laughed, "no parent can be there 24 hours a day." Julie and I tried. We took turns. We both had some flexibility in our jobs. When she was teaching, I was home. When I was in class, she was home. Late at night, we alternated staying awake, Kathy's crib in our bedroom. We were exhausted, and we were grumpy toward other people. Too many times we found Kathy on her stomach, her face too far into the bedcovers or mattress, and we turned her over, and over, and over again.

Then one night, after Julie and I had two drinks, she went to bed and I sat by the crib trying to read. I went to sleep. How long was it, I don't know, but I woke up suddenly and looked for Kathy. She had stopped breathing. Six hours later, after the ambulance and police had come, and we had gone to the hospital and then come home, after Julie was drugged into unconsciousness, it was then that I stopped drinking forever, when I heard music across the street, and I started a conversation with my daughter.

There is this numbness that comes when you lose your child. Julie was in a void that night after we came back from the hospital. I watched as she lay motionless on the couch, then I went into our bedroom and folded the blanket that had been in Kathy's crib. I held it up to my face and smelled all her baby smells. All the formula and drool and urine and powder. The only thing left of her that was still alive. I found a clear plastic laundry bag and sealed the blanket in it, trapping the fabric that had felt her last breath. I wasn't thinking anything profound at that moment, but I do remember that each of my senses seemed to be acting independently of the others. One part of me smelled that blanket. My eyes saw her baby pictures on the wall, but smell and sight could not come together. I was two people, Kathy was two children, not the same. I felt the hard edge of the crib, a third me, a different child. And then I heard the music. Another world, but one that didn't belong in the world of my daughter. I went across the street and asked the two boys to turn off their stereo. They laughed at me. I went back to my garage and got a baseball bat, walked slowly back to the music, but the boys saw me coming and called the police. By the time the cops arrived, I was handing those trembling boys a check to pay for their smashed speakers, calmly telling them that if I ever heard them again I would be back. So I'm told, but I don't remember. I just remember folding that blanket.

Julie and I both needed help, and we did all the things that parents were supposed to do when they lose a child. We talked about it, we went to grief counselors, we took a trip to get away, and we finally put the crib in the basement. And we stopped having sex for a year.

I told the therapist about us not sleeping together, and she acted surprised. Julie had told her in a private session that she and I were doing fine in the bedroom. I should have been more forceful, should have told her that Julie was lying. But all I could do was shake my head and mutter, "Well, not like before."

First rule of therapy: Don't spend your money unless you're willing to tell the truth. When I asked Julie why she had said that to the therapist, she smiled and said, "You mean, that wasn't you?"

Julie was gone. I was living with some other voice inside her. We stopped going to the counselor because, as she said, "I've done as much as I can. Your wife seems to be recovering the best we can expect. In fact, I think she has a better grip on the situation than you do. You should consider continuing with my partner. You might be more comfortable with another man."

How could I explain to that woman that the Julie who had that "grip" was not the Julie I lived with.

Life goes on. I found an empty space downtown and opened the Hollywood Theatre. Nothing to compete with all the other screens in town, whose idea of innovation was to take a perfectly good old theatre and put a wall down the middle and call it a twin. I knew my niche. College towns need a theatre that shows art and foreign films, all the independent films that never get exposure, avant guard stuff. Sixteen-millimeter films. The trick was keeping your overhead down. I sold tickets, ran the projectors, had a limited concession inventory, and cleaned up afterwards. Julie even helped on the weekends. As Danny got older, it was him and me, the two musketeers. In his world, simple tasks were essential. Sweeping was his favorite. And, god bless him, blood of my blood, the boy loves the movies.

Joseph Holly, owner/operator of the Hollywood Theatre, next door to the great Prairie Schooner bookstore. Everyday, I would wander through the Schooner for a few minutes. I loved looking at book covers.

I went through graduate school, took the exams for the PhD in English, and dropped out. I had found a home. Julie's income and mine were enough, barely, to keep us comfortable. I became a pillar of the community.

"You watch the city fathers last night, Jack?"

Jack Hamilton was eating lunch with George Singleton and Rodney Christensen, his two regular noon companions. They always met on Wednesdays and Fridays, and after football and their complaints about the Athens Postmaster, they often critiqued the City Council. Singleton and Christensen deferred to Hamilton about football, Singleton was the expert on the Postmaster and was always frustrated when Hamilton would not agree with him about their supervisor's incompetence, and Christensen was the only one who watched every Council meeting.

"I read the morning paper, just before my daughter let me know how worthless I was," Hamilton said.

"Then you don't know shit about what happened," Christensen grunted.

"I'm telling you guys, there's nothing more entertaining than those idiots."

"A bunch of over-paid bureaucrats," Singleton chimed in.

Christensen rolled his eyes, "Not those idiots, I'm talking about the damn fools in the audience. Our fellow......... citizens."

"Brownstein there again last night?" Hamilton asked, offering him another straight line. Christensen was fixated on John Brownstein, a regular at the Council meetings, and the source of infinite entertainment for him and most other cable viewers. For Christensen, Brownstein was Brownstain.

"There, as predictable as pee in the morning. Only, get this, he was wearing deer antlers, telling the Council that they ought to use 'birth control' on those deer instead of killing them. That there was a more 'humane' way to cut down on the Bambi population. All I can say is thank god for Al Baroli being on that Council. Al nailed old Brownstain, told him that the Council would give him a hundred deer condoms and let him go out there and show them how to use 'em."

31

"And our fellow citizens..." Singleton started to say.

"Were either laughing at Brownstain or hooting at Al,"
Christensen interrupted. "You should have seen the orange hunting
caps. And I'm betting some of those guys were packing guns under
all those plaid hunting jackets. Half the crowd was those PETA nuts,
the other half NRA. And the Council just sits up there and lets 'em
yell at each other like they had nothing better to do, like find a way to
cut our damn property taxes."

Hamilton tuned out Christensen, letting him and Singleton rant
at each other. Singleton was trying to work the Postmaster into a
conversation about "bureaucrats" who were two levels above their
abilities, making postmasters and city council-members synonymous.

Hamilton had not told either man that he was thinking about
applying for one of the city commissions. Athens had two dozen
government boards and commissions, and the Council was always
advertising for volunteers. He knew he would not have a chance to
get on the Zoning Commission or Board of Adjustment. Too many
people wanted on those, and he had no real background for them.
But there was an opening on the Human Rights Commission, another
on the Library Board, one on the Parks and Recreation Commission,
and he knew a lot of the Recreation people.

He had asked Marcie if she had a problem with him doing one
of those, and she had looked at him skeptically. "You're not thinking
about anything beyond that, are you?" she wanted to know. He had
told her, "Absolutely not," and she had believed him, not knowing
that most of the present Council had first served on a board or
commission as preparation. Hamilton had thought about it more than
he admitted. Not soon, but perhaps eventually. First, he wanted to
get Becka out of high school and into a good college. First things
first, he told himself. He had won Marcie over when he pointed out
that the Recreation Commission only met once a month, unlike the

Council which seemed to meet three times a week, and the Rec meetings never lasted as long as those marathon Council meetings.

Hamilton never told Christensen or Singleton, when the Council was mentioned, that he did indeed watch the meetings. Not when they were broadcast live on Tuesday nights, but every-time he could not sleep, which happened more and more as he got older, he would go into his den to read or watch television. The Council meetings were taped and re-broadcast every night at midnight on the local government channel. He did not watch all of them. But he watched enough to know that Rodney Christensen was as wrong about the meetings as the morning paper seemed to be.

He tried to explain it to Marcie one morning, but she was adamant: She was not interested. So he watched alone and came to the conclusion that, "I could do that." He knew that he was not as smart as Ken Rumble or Joseph Holly or Bernadette Huss, that strange woman who sat next to Holly, but he could hold his own with the rest. Something about the dynamics of the group fascinated him, and he knew that he would have to go to all their meetings to understand it. But he was not that interested. When he imagined himself on the Council, it was always in the future, and all the people there now would surely be gone.

Still, it was an odd group. Hamilton and his companions agreed that, of the seven, the mayor was the least impressive. How could that happen, they all wondered. Rumble, Holly, and Huss were all more intelligent and articulate, had more forceful personalities than the mayor; especially Rumble, who dominated the meetings even without being mayor. But sitting in the middle was Steve Nash, a downtown retailer who could not control a meeting, who never knew when to bang the gavel, who seemed to stumble through the agenda. It was a mystery: In all of Athens, why was Steve Nash the mayor? The Council picked the mayor, Hamilton understood that. But, Nash?

Christensen had an explanation for why Steve Nash was mayor, and he spoke for a lot of council-watchers. "If Steve Nash was a good mayor, the meetings would be dull as dirt. Somebody upstairs did us all a favor when the rest of those jokers went brain dead and elected Nash as mayor. It's like they're in a speedboat and nobody's at the wheel. No other boats in the water, luckily, nobody gets hurt, and it sure is fun watching them fly all over the place."

Hamilton did not have an explanation, but he was not as entertained as Christensen and others seemed to be about their City Council's performance. If he were ever on the Council, he told himself, he would not want to be with this group. From his point of view, it was not funny. He thought Athens could do better. But if he thought too long, he always pulled back and criticized himself. "I'm here writing a speech in my mind that I'll never deliver," he would say to himself. "And I'm not up there with them now. Maybe it's not so simple."

So many parts to understand, to make sense of this story. I can talk about me and Julie and Danny. All that's easy. It's the town itself that I can't pin down. Athens? How to make it real?

I liked Athens as soon as I drove off I-80, down Dubuque Street past some giant trees along the ridges, and into downtown. My Camaro was farting blue smoke out its tailpipe and then sputtered dead in front of the public library. I was free, white, and thirty-three years old. Reagan was about to beat Carter, and I was looking forward to grad school and sleeping with coeds, just like I had done at Oklahoma when I was a TA in the English department.

How do you know you "like" a town even before you pay your first month's rent? When I ran for City Council the first time, I had to go back and learn all I could about this place just to deflect the obvious and legitimate charge that I was a carpet-bagging southerner. "Who are you, Rhett, to come up here and tell us how to run our town. You ain't been here long enough." All true, but all irrelevant. I had been like a lost tribe of Israel. Army base housing, trailer parks off base. I went to eighteen different schools by the time I graduated from high school. I called no place home. But I always had this image of what my home was, even if it was part Mayberry, part Naked City, part Paris.

Like love at first sight, I saw the surface first. A real downtown, with buildings from the 1870's and 80's, but also one of those pedestrian walking malls, where they had closed off some streets and bricked it over and then planted trees and shrubs. I arrived on a Friday evening in August, and the streets were swarming with people, most of them downtown for the weekly outdoor concert on the ped mall. Young and old, mostly white, but cosmopolitan. I heard conversations in German and French and even some Asian languages.

I fell in love with the skin, the look. A silly reason, I know, but if I had the talent I would have been an architect. I loved old buildings, but physics and engineering were foreign languages to me, so I had come to Athens to get my PhD in English and then move on. But I stayed, and I never wrote my dissertation. Academia did not notice its loss.

Athens was settled in 1845, but it had remained a small town until 1965, when the Iowa legislature, busting a budget gut with excess money, decided the state needed one more state university, but a very special place. Not another University of Iowa or an Iowa State University, but a small liberal arts college with high standards and a small enrollment. The plan was to establish elite programs in music, art, drama, and writing. Sleepy Athens seemed like such a logical spot for the school, especially since the Speaker of the Iowa House was from there.

A new school in an old town? And I like old buildings? Here's what stunned me as I drove up Washington Street and turned left on Linn to park in front of the library. Whoever planned the college in 1965 had convinced the Board of Regents to make the campus look like it had been there as long as the town had been. All the new buildings were designed like an old college, with Greek and Roman and Victorian and Gothic styles competing for attention. The western boundary of downtown was Clinton Street. The new Iowa Arts University was plopped down across that street, so the campus was simply an extension of the downtown. Old and new mingled, town and gown lying down in some sort of peaceable kingdom.

The créme de la créme of Iowa talent, that was the goal. Best and the brightest. That is, until Franklin Prose wasn't admitted. Little Frank, whose father was running for governor. A legend in his own mind, who thought he could write but whose SAT scores and writing sample were spectacularly average, Frank was not admitted. Suddenly, Iowa Arts went from the crown in the state educational system to the thorn in candidate James Prose's paw, and Big Jim Prose suddenly grew populist roots. I hadn't heard the BJ stories until after I was admitted to Iowa Arts, and by then it was too late. In the first two years I was there, enrollment went from 5000 to 8000.

BJ had lost his election, but he won a seat in the legislature two years later, and his crusade was to "Open Iowa's schools to ALL Iowans." Franklin Prose had already gone elsewhere, but his father never forgave Athens, so here's the first rule of politics: little people can make big things happen.

Standards were dumbed down, but the budget went up to hire more faculty. Money was found for more buildings, but money is not the same thing as aesthetic vision, so those imposing original buildings were soon sharing parking lots with some ugly piles of modernist steel and concrete. But the real problem, the one that began to change Athens forever, made before I arrived but whose consequences I had to deal with for two terms on the Council, that problem was social, not aesthetic.

Cash for classrooms and teachers, but not a dime for new dormitories. "A function of the private sector," James Prose said ad nauseum until lightning hit him on a golf course and he disintegrated. "We're not in the housing business. We're in the school business," was another one of my favorite Prose truisms. The housing business? That was for Dutch and Donald Prose, Big Jim's younger twin brothers, one of whom owned a lumberyard and construction company in Athens. The other was a plumbing supply wholesaler. I could never tell which one of those guys would never speak to me as we passed on the street. All I knew, even if a corpse ran against me, Prose money was on its contributor list.

Athens was flooded with fresh-faced teenagers with no place to live…except for my neighborhood. That's why I ran for the Council, my past be damned. Actually, my past be gone.

Julie and I had bought our first house on Dodge Street, walking distance from downtown and the campus; a street lined with Victorian houses and hundred year old trees. Not a big house, we still didn't have our first child yet, and what was kindly described in the real estate multiple listing as a "Handy-man Special." As Julie told me at the closing, "You're not handy, but you are special, sort of, and you are a man. I'll do the work. You do the dishes."

First rule of buying a house: Always check the zoning. If you want peace and quiet and a safe neighborhood to raise your kids, don't buy a single-family home in an area zoned for high-density apartments. Forget how it looks. Forget the Beaver-Cleaver charm. Check the zoning, especially in a town just recently flooded with 3000 young bodies looking for sex, booze, and a diploma. Let me suggest: Check your zoning.

Julie and I had worked a year scraping paint off old woodwork, re-sodding and fencing our yard, replacing the roof, pulling carpet off hardwood floors and polishing them, repairing windows that had not opened in decades, and we had our first baby. In each case, Julie did most of the work.

We walked to school one morning and came home that afternoon to find a pile of rubble across the street from us, where a white wide-porched house had stood before. A pile of debris, like a bomb had hit dead center, a hole in the ground where the basement had been. A bulldozer was pushing the rubble into a pile for a front-loader to scoop up and dump into a truck to be hauled away. Julie started crying, and I started making phone calls. Six weeks later, a mansard roofed six-unit apartment building opened its doors. You know what a mansard roof is? One is a novelty, two an eyesore, anything beyond that and your culture collapses. Sometimes I wondered to myself, would I have been outraged if the Athens' developers had better design taste? But there it was, the first of a half dozen to follow in the months to come, all of them within a block of us.

Beyond my neighborhood, like a cancer, those damnable mansards spread as lots were cleared during the night. Most of them were identical to the monstrosity across from me. Six units, three bedrooms each, with an average of four students per unit, with twelve parking places where the backyard used to be. Twenty-four future Rhodes Scholars, I was sure, in a space formerly occupied by a retired couple who had been to ashamed to tell us that they had sold their family home to Dutch Prose.

Trust me, I was young once. I went to college too. I partied until I puked. But I went to college in the stone ages, when stereo equipment did not have the power to move houses off foundations and render insects deaf and sterile. Nor did I, would I, ever, tell a man, who had walked across the street and asked me to turn off my stereo so he and his wife could rest, to "go to hell cause it's a free country, asshole" just six hours after that man had found his baby daughter dead in her crib.

Here's a fact: Athens is the most educated city in America. A lot of college towns are educated, but not like us. Some people in Athens make the illogical leap from education to intelligence, and pomposity is seldom in short supply here, but being schooled does have its advantages. In our case, our education also indicates wealth. A steady economy, untouched by national trends, and don't shed any tears for under-paid college professors. You want to give somebody a pay raise? Put it into your public schools, or pay those TA's more money. College teachers are doing fine. Athens has the highest per capita income of anywhere in Iowa. So, mix brains and money, throw in the cultural life of a college town, and you have the closest thing to an ideal place to live in America as you can get.

We read and we think, Broadway road shows grace our stages, ballet troupes spend the summers here, and we have free symphonies from a university orchestra every month. As much as me or Julie, Athens is a character in the drama of Becky Hamilton's death.

Facts, damnable facts. Athens is also a white-bread world. More Asians than blacks live here, but not your poor tired huddled masses of Asians. Smart kids with bright futures ahead for most of them, those who jump through all the hoops of American graduate school. Since Iowa Arts doesn't have an athletic program, we don't have many black students. Does it really matter? For this story, does it matter?

Becky Hamilton——her death matters. But two young black kids were killed that night. I don't know what Becky was thinking the moment before she died, but I can imagine how seventeen-year old Anheseur Hampton felt. The poor kid was screaming at the top of his lungs as he sped down First Avenue, his heart pumping in overdrive and his brain frying from too much crack, left hand on the wheel, right hand throwing bags of dope out the window, and then that right hand reaching for the gun next to him as the left hand tried to turn the corner at First and Court, racing through the stop sign, and, as the car started to float off the pavement and then roll over, he must have, he MUST, have seen Becky standing there. For Anheseur Hampton's soul, I hope to God that, at that moment, he at least begged for Becky Hamilton's forgiveness.

I'm not a true Catholic, but I go through the motions for Julie. I eat the body and drink the blood, but I taste nothing. In twenty years, I've been to Confession only once. After I first saw Becky's father kneeling at her grave, I asked Father West to hear me. I told him the ugliest truth I knew about myself: I didn't care that Anheseur Hampton had died. Worse, I was glad. Everything I had learned about him in the weeks after his death, it all told me that Anheseur Lionel Hampton was a sorry piece of human garbage. A criminal record five pages long, a petty thief and thug who was headed for murder and rape and a life behind the walls of the state prison at Anamosa. And stupid. All he had to do was stop when the Athens cop turned on his siren and flashing lights, take the lecture for a rolling stop on Muscatine Avenue, hide the gun under the seat, maintain his composure for five minutes. But he was stupid, drug stupid for sure, but stupid his whole life. I've seen the videotape he and his gang buddies made the week before, all their posturing, their vulgar bravado, and the face of the girl who was being handed from one lap to another. Hampton waved his gun at the camera and told the world to go screw itself. Born in Chicago, dead in Athens, a martyr in the hands of Ken Rumble. But in the universe that mattered to me, on the scale of value in my heart, Anheseur Hampton did not register.

A lifetime ago, after I smashed those boys' stereo, I became a neighborhood hero. I was angry, I was numb, and I did what a lot of people wanted to do. I called the police department every night. I went to my first Council meeting to complain about how neighborhoods were being destroyed. I might as well have gone to the Homebuilders Association meeting, or so I thought at the time. All I heard was, "no laws are being broken and we have to respect everyone's property rights." The only councilman who sympathized with me called after my first appearance and suggested I run for a spot in the upcoming election. Only later did I realize how desperate he was. I had been in Athens for less than two years.

How do you run for office in a small town? It helps to understand the issues, and more than just the issue that got you involved in the first place. It helps to have help. It helps if you understand that voters are intuitive rather than intellectual, even in Athens. I got my 189 signatures on a nominating petition, as did eight other men and one woman. I looked at my opposition. I was smarter than any of them, more articulate, had angels on my side, and I deserved to win. Ten candidates in the at-large race required a primary to pick the final

41

four for the general election. Top two finishers in the general get a seat. A piece of cake, I told myself. I came in fifth. The woman, who had trouble reading her notes and knowing where the microphone was, came in fourth and went on to win a seat. Was I bitter? More stunned than bitter, more confused than stunned. But I learned.

During the primary, I met Ted Stanton, the campaign manager for the other winner in the general election. Ted is one of my heroes. A long-time resident, bosses a gravel company, and never had one of his candidates lose a race. After the election, he was appointed to the Zoning Commission. Three months later, I was appointed. I served two years, and then he managed my campaign in the next election. In that two years, the commission, mostly Ted, completely re-wrote the zoning ordinance, putting all sorts of plugs in the wall to protect neighborhoods. The smartest man in city politics, too smart to ever run for office himself. But a lot of people owed Ted Stanton favors. One of the chips he cashed was getting four votes on the Council to get me appointed to the Zoning Commission. He assured the conservative majority that I wasn't really the bomb throwing lefty I appeared to be. Funny thing, I thought I was a bomb throwing lefty, but working with Ted taught me otherwise. If anybody was a lefty in the political closet, it was red headed Ted Stanton.

If democracy is supposed to work, Athens should be the place. The irony of college town politics, however, is that it truly is the essence of democracy. Those who vote are those who care, liberal or conservative, about their town, who see themselves as owners of the town. Students? Eight thousand students in Athens, all over 18, and about 500 vote in a local election. In Athens, the old-timers always voted in local elections, and the newcomers eventually stayed around long enough to become old-timers. Radicals? Full-moon lefties? Until Ken Rumble came along, they thought globally but never acted locally.

Athens has a city manager/council form of government. You

want real power, get a degree in Governmental Administration, become a city manager like the one we have in Athens, Harry Hopkins. I was on the Council that hired Harry. Seven bland interviews done, he was the eighth person we grilled, and he dissected the old organization chart and personnel like he was doing a civic autopsy, exposing all the tumors and blocked colons of the budget. Then, going from coroner to surgeon, he offered immediate relief and long-term recovery. An hour later we were offering him the money he wanted <u>and</u> a city car. He was that impressive, and in the next ten years I discovered that Harry was a better politician than any elected official in the state. You need to remember my definition of politics: The acquisition of power, the exercise and expansion of power, and the preservation of power. For us council-members, we each kept power by keeping about 3000 voters happy. Harry just had to keep four council-members happy. Four out of seven, that's all he needed, and he usually had six in his pocket. Harry is a model administrator, and to this day I still don't know what he really thinks of me. All I know, if you went in his office with a question, Harry made you walk out feeling like you were the only competent person on the council. He loved telling me, "Joe, my job is to make the Council look good." And I would always say, "Harry, you ain't that smart."

Details, the smallest details, that was the power of Harry Hopkins. My favorite game with him was to take the monthly list of city expenditures, usually about 30 pages of single-spaced abbreviations for every dime we spent, and each followed by a specific amount. I'd flip open a page and pick an item without looking at it. Harry had the details. He also prepared the hundred million dollar city budget. That was his show, walking us through each department every January, us nodding and asking big questions. When Harry was hired, we had less than a million in the reserve fund. In five years we had almost three million dollars sitting there and our bond rating had gone up to AAA, the best in the country. Trouble was, the only person in Athens who really understood the budget was Harry. Knowing the details, he sucked up power like a vacuum. You want a pet project but don't know where the money's coming from? Harry loved those problems. "You get three other votes, I'll get the money," he would say.

When we interviewed Harry, asking the necessary questions about his personal life because when you hire a city manager you also hire his wife, he was a happily married man. When he came to Athens a month later, he was separated, soon to be divorced. Handsome in a Cary Grant's brother sort of way, in his forties, with an eighty thousand dollar salary and the most powerful position in town, supervising hundreds of women. Soon enough, some of us expected trouble, wondered if we had been fooled. We suddenly noticed his five hundred dollar suits and the fact that his hair was never out of place. Me especially, I assumed there was dirt to be discovered. But Harry never disappointed us. You could see him out to dinner with an attractive woman, but never anybody who ever worked for the city. His biggest fault? He was not a humble man. Nothing he ever said, but there was something about his ramrod posture at council meetings, the way he would flip that swivel microphone around in front of him when he had to speak and then flip it back away from his face when he was finished, as if his time was more valuable than the question. Never to the Council, of course, but when somebody at a public meeting asked him a question or criticized him from the floor podium he would give them the barest, albeit complete and factual, answer possible. Harry did not suffer fools easily, and he ticked off a lot of people when he seemed to dismiss them and their grievance. So, let me amend what I said about him being the best politician in the state. Harry was the best institutional—bureaucratic—politician I've ever seen. He had shit for subtlety when it came to dealing with the public. When the mob came for us that first meeting after Becky Hamilton died, Harry was the embodiment of everything wrong with the system.

How does someone like me get elected to any office? I'm a cynic with a foul mouth. I've been a teenage preacher in Texas who lost his faith, the master-of-ceremonies at a strip club in San Antonio, a pornographer in Oklahoma, a skirt-chasing drug abuser, and I had cooked the books in my theatres for years. But Ted Stanton taught me something about local politics: There are no background checks the lower your goal, and City Council was about the lowest you could shoot for. I had no track record in Athens except that of neighborhood preservationist. Tabula Rasa. I put on a coat and tie, trimmed my beard, and curbed my language. I also learned Ted's second rule of local politics: In a race between two similar candidates, make sure you're more likeable than the other guy.

Ted and I worked together for two years on the Zoning Commission. Half the Council's eventual agenda had to come through the Zoning Commission first. After two years, I finally understood something Ted had been telling me all along.

"Half the people in this town get paid by the state. It's easy to be a liberal when you know you got a paycheck coming every week," he said over and over, especially when we went out drinking with other commission members. I would sit there nursing my Coca-Cola and suffering all the second hand smoke, Ted's student. "The other half go to bed scared to death every night worrying about a job for next month. Paying taxes so state employees can get paid. And you got all those faculty types and grad students who think they have all the answers about how everyone else should live. Hell, the only liberal I respect is a union carpenter."

"Ted..." I would interrupt, getting nods from everyone else at

45

the table, "...you're a Bolshevik yourself. If you had the power. . ."

"Be a helluva lot better town," he would snap, pointing his finger at me. "Same with you. Trouble is, we both might be totally full of shit."

A two-year apprenticeship behind me, I announced I was running for Council. Ted told me to make up my mind early and tell everybody. Show any potential opponent that I was prepared to fight a serious campaign, and, his finger pointed at me again, "Make sure everybody understands that I'm your campaign manager."

I knew the issues, I could talk, and I had a talent, which Ted liked. I liked to win an argument. I was not genteel. But I also had a secret weakness, and Ted kept harping at me about it. "You like to win, Joe, but you're so damn insecure you also want people to love you. Hell, you were born a politician."

So, WHY I became a small time politician was the question that came to fascinate me.

Over the years I went to dozens of conferences of local officials. All the usual workshops and glossy brochures, but after the day meetings, over dinner or at a bar at night, as they drank and I talked, I always found that most of them agreed with me: Winning an election is better than sex. It was our secret, and the comparison only makes sense if you've done it. A strained analogy? The campaign is courtship. You do you best to make the other person like you. Ted would say, "to love you." The nearer you get to Election Day, the more intense the foreplay. All this is metaphor so far, but every person who ever won an election will tell you about the literal part, the physical pleasure. Campaigns are exhausting, even in a small pond like Athens, but in the final twenty-four hours something very sensual happens. There is nothing else you can do that last day, Election Day. Sure, you hear about candidates making all those last minute get-out-the-vote phone calls, but those are window dressing games, irrelevant to the real outcome. Now, this thing about sex only works if you WIN. You lose, forget it. One vote or a million, you win or lose. If you lose, it's like a divorce that your spouse wanted and you didn't.

But winning? Every city council member I've ever talked to will tell you about election day, about that strange sensation of knowing that all over your town thousands of people are looking at a ballot with two names on it, and they choose…you. I thought I was going to win my first election, but I lost. I <u>knew</u> I was going to win the second time. But the pleasure was just as intense as an upset. You get the call from your campaign manager, or you watch the returns on television. Even in tiny Athens, the results are broadcast on a cable channel just as they are tabulated. The moment it sinks in, when all the slings and arrows of every petty injustice and major disappointment of your life disappear—your body floats, your brain disconnects from reality, endorphins race through your blood—they want YOU. The embrace is consummated.

Winning an election in your own town is better than winning at any other level because the consummation lasts for days, not seconds. Forget about being President or Senator. For days after my first victory, I would invent reasons to walk around downtown, or go shopping at the Hy-Vee grocery store. I knew what would happen. People stop you and congratulate you. They shake your hand. The embrace continues. You know that some of them probably voted for the other guy, but you won, and they have to court you now. It's the local thing, the idea that the voters are not some nebulous mass out there. You've seen their faces, shook their hands as you went door to door, touched their flesh, and they chose YOU.

After the election, I started running matinees at my theatre downtown. Not much extra income, especially after I paid the electric bill, but people knew I was there. They would come by to talk, to complain, and to ask for help. And that feeling grows inside of you,

47

like you're an extension of them, like you're finally accepted. Sure, some people run for local office out of a sense of civic responsibility, probably all of us start that way. A lot of people have civic pride, but very few run for office. Those who do, we're egoists and insecure at the same time. Blame our parents. I certainly blamed mine.

How can I say that winning an election is better than sex? Ask somebody who has done it; make them tell you the truth. If they were given a choice: One month to live, you can either have sex one last time or win an election one last time. Winning beats sex every time. Like Ted told me the night I won, "Joe, winning is sex."

So I'm like all the rest of them, the people you vote for, the ones who win. And I'm still me, who weaved through a crowd of campaign workers in my kitchen, all celebrating the results, accepting backslaps and handshakes, declining the "about a little matter." I was searching my own home, looking for one more vote.

I found her in the den, her eyes as bright as burning diamonds, a drink in her hand, smiling as I got closer, reaching for me like the first time, wrapping her arms around me, sighing into my ear, "I'm very proud of you."

At that moment, as she started to cry, I told her the truest fact I knew, "I love you." I could feel her heart beating, her arms trembling. I put my hand on the back of her head and started to stroke her hair.

"Can you make these people go away?" she finally whispered. "Please."

Jack Hamilton had a list of errands that his wife had given him. The Post Office was a block away from the center of Athens, so he took a half hour of "personal time" and walked downtown. Marcie had described a music box she wanted for her parents, and Hamilton thought he knew where he could find it. But when he got to Buc's, a gift shop that had been there for thirty years, he found the window front covered with brown paper on the inside, and a sign that announced: MOVED TO NEW LOCATION IN CORAL RIDGE. COMING SOON——BAILEY'S BAR AND GRILL.

Coral Ridge was a small town just across the river from Athens. It had just gotten its own zip code the year before, but it was a boomtown for development. Hamilton had noticed more and more retail stores moving from downtown Athens to Coral Ridge, replaced by more bars and restaurants to accommodate the increase in students. Marcie had stopped shopping for clothes downtown a year ago. "Nobody sells clothes for <u>women</u>," she would say. "At least, not for mature women with mature sizes. Not all of us are a size six."

Shopping was not an avocation for Jack Hamilton like it was for his wife, but he had also begun to be bothered by a creeping blandness that seemed to be overtaking Athens. He did not drink in smoky bars, and he disliked loud restaurants, but he did like to read. So he was satisfied enough with the downtown as long as the Prairie Schooner bookstore was still there. He also liked movies, but all that was left downtown was a theatre next to Prairie Schooner that seemed to only book movies with subtitles or in black and white.

Unable to find a music box, he went into Hudson River Gifts, one of the few remaining shops with a local owner who actually worked in the store. He had gotten in the habit of going to Hudson's when Nick Hotek, the owner, was mayor. The two men would only talk for a few minutes, most often when Hamilton would want

49

something clarified that had happened the night before at a Council meeting. Hamilton seldom actually bought any of the leather products that Hudson's was famous for, but Hotek was a patient man. Years of face-to-face soft selling had required it. He also knew Hamilton's wife, who had bought several gifts over the years. This particular afternoon, Hotek enjoyed talking because he had just sold Marcie Hamilton an expensive leather toilet kit that was intended as a surprise birthday present for her husband. Jack Hamilton was turning forty in a week.

"You miss being on the Council?" Hamilton asked, knowing that Hotek kept track of the current Council's reputation, and had served with some of them in the past.

"Not very often," Hotek replied, his wink an understatement. "You thinking about running? They always need good people."

Hamilton hesitated. He wondered if Hotek meant that he was one of the "good people" that the Council needed. "Only if my wife never finds out," he finally said.

Hotek laughed, "I guess my wife has been talking to yours."

"Actually, I was thinking about that open spot on the rec commission, and I was wondering if you could give me some advice," Hamilton smiled as he spoke, running his finger across the glass counter between the two men.

Hotek smiled back. He had known about Jack Hamilton long before he met him. "Tell you what. You come see me early some morning, before 8:00, and we'll grab some coffee. I'll invite Fred Riddle, the rec chair. He's always wanted to meet you anyway. If Fred likes you… and I know he will… you've got the spot if you want it."

Hamilton walked out of Hudson's a happy man, and then he remembered his original mission from Marcie—the music box. He walked further into town, but there was no place that sold music boxes. He thought about Sears, but that would mean a trip to a mall on the edge of town. Then he remembered another gift that he and Marcie had agreed on—a cell phone for Becka. She was taking driver's ed this fall and would have her license in the spring. He wanted her used to having a cell phone with her anytime she was out of the house. No excuse for being out of contact. Even without a car, Becka was starting to be gone from the house a lot more than she had last year, especially with her sports and club activities. Marcie and Jack Hamilton, like most considerate adults, disliked cell phones in general, and they had agreed to drill Becka over and over about when NOT to use the phone. But they were also parents. In discussions with other parents, all about how their adolescence was safer and saner than their children's, and how computers were over-rated and Sony Walkmans were a long-term curse as well as a short-term blessing, they also agreed that the cell phone was the best technological apron string ever invented.

Unlike his quest for a music box, finding a cell phone in downtown Athens took Jack Hamilton five minutes. He had already done his research about various calling "plans," so he walked into a store, had a rate plan and number confirmed, and was out in time to call Marcie on the new phone before she left Regina.

"Guess where I am," he asked her, quickly realizing that he did not have to talk so loud to be heard.

"Under the First National Bank clock, downtown Athens, USA."

"Jack, look up, darling," she said, her voice clearer than he expected.

"Where you think you're standing doesn't exist anymore."

Hamilton looked up. He had forgotten that First National, the first Athens bank, had been sold to Mercantile, which became Firstar, which was sold to USBank. The logo on the clock had changed the month before. "Touché, dear, but _I'm_ still here and I'm speaking to you on the phone our daughter doesn't know is coming. You want to eat out tonight, since Becka is too busy to sit down for dinner with us this week?"

As he listened to his wife go through a list of possible restaurants, Hamilton noticed a crowd of people running toward the ped mall across the street. Then he heard shouting, and for a moment he thought he was dreaming.

Floating over the red and brown bricks, through the manicured shrubs and around the dozens of neatly groomed trees, like a slow motion vision, was the largest deer Jack Hamilton had ever seen. A giant buck with antlers rising out of its head like a fiery halo, but it was the muscles in its shoulders that Hamilton noticed most. How could those spindly legs support such power? He stood there under the bank sign as the deer bounded through the ped mall, chased by a pack of college boys who were trying to corner it.

"As if..." he thought to himself, "As if that buck couldn't kick their pasty pale butts all over town. As if."

The deer froze at the corner. Marcie Hamilton could hear sirens in the background as Jack told her about the scene, and then his quick intake of breath right before he screamed, "Don't do that!"

Hamilton had been shouting to the deer as it first looked back over its massive shoulder toward the young crowd pouring toward him, and then it leaped into the street.

Three good years, that's what I had after I won that election. Three years of happiness. Julie seemed to snap back, and I ignored any evidence to the contrary. Business at the Hollywood finally started picking up, so Julie didn't have to work with me as much, giving her more time to work on a book she was writing. She had already had her dissertation published, and enough articles to pad any vita, but , as much as she ridiculed her own work, she still had another university press contract signed even before she finished her second book. Tenure decisions were around the corner.

We stopped the counseling and started healing ourselves, talking to each other like the old days. We would sit down after she got home and before I went back to the Hollywood. She would have two drinks, always prepared by me, and tell me about her day in the mondo bizarro world of university life, and I would tell her city business. Sometimes, she would come visit me at the theatre; sometimes I would surprise her on campus, like we were falling in love again.

The first Christmas Eve after the election, we got stoned for the first time since we had dated years earlier. Something about booze, I had a mental block, but I missed being high. The dope was Julie's present to me, and I didn't ask her where she got it. Unlike my graduate days in Oklahoma, when dynamite grass was ten dollars a bag and considered a proper gift for weddings and house-warmings, getting stoned in Iowa academic circles was considered politically incorrect. That night, as snow fell outside, surrounded by our glittery-wrapped presents, a frosted tree in the corner, warmed by the fireplace in our living room, we ate ourselves silly and enjoyed the guilty pleasure of listening to Karen Carpenter.

If you've ever been a stoner, you'll know how sometimes it makes you say and do stupid things. You play stupid games; ask stupid questions you think are profound. Julie and I were sitting on the floor across from each other, the soles of our bare feet flush with each other, my back against the couch, her back against a leather recliner which had been my surprise gift to her. We had been gossiping about her department, who was sleeping with who, who thought too much of themselves, who was a dick or a princess, the new Chair of Queer Studies, and she had the voices for all of them. At that perfect moment, I totally screw up. We had been asking each other all sorts of general "truth" questions, like who was the worst lay of your life or who was the best kisser and what was the dumbest thing you've ever done, and then we would talk about our responses. But then, out of nowhere, when it's my turn again, I ask, "What's the worst thing that's ever happened to you?"

The words came out of my mouth like I was just asking the time of day or whether she thought it was going to rain. I couldn't shut my mouth fast enough, even though I heard the words coming out of my brain before they get loose. It was a cruel dumb dope-inspired question, and I was an asshole for forgetting about Kathy. But Julie saved me.

She looked down at our Siamese-twin feet, shook her head, and I would have offered up every vote I had gotten the month before, would have given my hands and feet, forsaken my already worthless soul, anything to get that question back. She looked back at me and smiled a crooked smile, and said, "It hasn't happened yet."

I sat there like an idiot, utterly lost in a world that made sense to everyone but me. I would still be sitting there today if she hadn't pushed her toes hard against mine, as if they were fingers wrapping themselves around my fingers, an amazing trick, squeezing my toes with hers, rubbing her soft flesh over the hard sole of my foot. Her shoulders leaned forward, then her whole upper body seemed to sway, and her face was asking me to respond, to ask her the obvious question: "Not yet?" But I was clueless. So she answered the question I should have asked.

"You, Joe.........you. If you ever go away, that's the worst thing that could ever happen to me."

If you're a cynic, you could say it was the dope talking. That she was jerking my chain, or hiding the hurt I had caused her when I asked the first question. Playing games with me. But if you believe that, then you can go straight to hell. You don't deserve to know any more about her. But if you understand her, if you ever felt that same thing for someone else, then you'll believe me when I tell you that I cried like a baby when she told me that, cried as she crawled over and put her arms around me, whispering to me in her real voice, "You better never die, you bastard."

That was the night we made Danny. Maybe not, but that's what I believe. Two months later, she told me, "I think I'm pregnant."

I was scared to death. Julie had been on the pill. We didn't talk about it, but we had this implicit deal: We weren't going to be parents again. "You're sure?" were my first supportive wise words to her. "I thought you were taking…"

"I was, I think I was," she stammered. "But I might have missed a few days."

"Days! Julie, that doesn't make sense."

"Or a few months," she said.

You ever have those moments when you're looking at someone and trying to read their mind? Like you want to jump inside their brain and cut through all the mixed or misleading signals and get to some truth. When Julie had told me about being pregnant with Kathy, she was happier than I was, but as soon as Kathy was born I fell in love with my daughter, fell off a cliff like a rock that would never hit bottom. Back then, I had just assumed that Julie would be more of a parent than I was. After all, I told her, look at my parents. My father, who my mother once explained to me, "Joseph, you must remember that your father is not comfortable around children." I had screamed at her, "Mother, I'm not children. I'm his son." All I knew from my parents about parenting was that it was a thankless joyless job, to be avoided by men and endured by women. But Julie and Kathy changed all that. So I looked at Julie and wondered how she really felt, afraid to admit to her that I missed being a father and had always wanted a second chance, but I had always assumed that it would be too hard on her, going through all that again, remembering Kathy.

"So, if you are, what do you want to do?" I asked. That's when I looked hard at her, trying to get past the outer limits. Cards on the table, that's what I was after, show me the cards and let's see how this hand plays.

"I just want to be happy," she said.

I suppose I could have gotten angry then, told her to stop being so cryptic, to stop acting like I was happier than her, that we had a serious decision to make. I looked at her as she stood in our kitchen, noticing strands of gray hair on her head for the first time. Instead, I asked her, "You wanna go out for dinner?"

We didn't talk about her being pregnant, not at first. She told me stories about her parents and her brother. I had met them years ago. Like being in some sort of television sitcom. But she loved them all. At dinner that night, the first time since Kathy died that I had seen her eat without a glass of wine, Julie told me more stories about her childhood.

After two hours, with dessert pushed away, and the restaurant thinning out, I decided to tell her what I thought about having another baby. "You're going to do all the work, Julie, I know that, but I hope you want another baby. If you don't—I'll understand."

"I might not be pregnant," she said, avoiding the real issue.

"Go to a doctor tomorrow. Forget those home tests. Go to a doctor and get a definite answer," I said, reaching for her hand, but she kept it to herself.

"I just want to be happy," she said, and then she cocked her head as if she were overhearing a conversation at the empty table next to us. "I'm happy now. I don't want that to change. Tell me, Joe, are you happy?"

I leaned back in my chair and stared at her. She was starting to go away again. "I have everything I want," I told her, not quite the truth, "Except for you being as happy as you were in the beginning."

A week later we were arguing about names for the baby. She was definitely two months pregnant, and I thought we were okay. She talked about moving to a bigger house, which was totally unnecessary. She then talked about adding a room to our present house. At first, I told her that wasn't necessary either. But I slowly realized that for as long as she was pregnant, I was going to have to interpret everything she said and see if the real issue was hidden behind some sort of displaced concern. We had plenty of room, three bedrooms, but one of those had been Kathy's. Even if she had seldom slept there alone, it was still the space she first claimed. I had turned it into a study and reading room six months after she died, and Julie had helped me. The third bedroom, which had been the study, became a seldom-used guest bedroom. It would have been easy to turn that guest room into a baby's room, but it soon made sense to me, after understanding Julie without her saying it, that she wanted this new baby to have a completely new "space" in our home. I agreed to the addition, figuring we could find the money later. I might even have to jack up ticket prices.

When Kathy had been born, I had been in a hospital waiting room, reading month old magazines, wondering how I had ended up an imminent father. But with Danny I was right there in the delivery room with Julie, standing next to her, rubbing her shoulders and kissing her forehead, helping her push like Sisyphus. So there was a weird equality the moment Danny appeared. Julie had done all the work, sure, but we saw him together at the same time. She and I both looked down through her upturned legs and saw Danny raised up in a nurse's hands for our inspection. I started to cry.

The nurse cleaned him up and handed him to me, and I handed him to Julie. She sang the song that was so obvious, sang it in a whisper, "Oh, Danny boy..."

Daniel Lloyd Holly was named after my father. It was Julie's idea. I was just thankful that we had done that test to determine the sex of the baby before it was born. I was hoping it was not a girl. So when we knew it was a boy we attacked the name game, but Julie wouldn't let me get away from her choice. I suggested some combination of her father and brother, but she insisted, "You've got to start unpacking that baggage you've been carrying about your father. He's got maybe five good years left before his brain is gone. Let him love his grandson even if he never loved you."

She had been too optimistic about how long my father had before his Alzheimer's turned him into the living dead. By the time Danny had been diagnosed, my father had gone from living alone to living in a nursing home. But I had done what Julie wanted. For a short time, my father got to see himself in the flesh of his son's son. Julie had been right. My father loved Danny as the holiest of grandparents loved their grandchildren.

My father had not read a book in fifty years. He looked at the sports section and threw away the rest of the newspaper, watched football and basketball and boxing and even yacht racing on television, and he had never voted in his life. He was not an introspective man, I thought. But he kissed his dead wife's picture every might before going to sleep. "A sentimental sap, just like you, Joe," Julie had always kidded me. "But without your charm." The first time my father saw Danny, he insisted that I let him hold his grandson and feed him while they watched a Dallas Cowboys game. Julie had been right. I liked my father for the first time in my life as I sat there watching him hold my son. Two years later, both Danny and his grandfather seldom spoke.

Danny was incredibly handsome the older he got, more like his grandfather than me. That look that certain children have, the look of being little grown ups. Julie and I had both noticed how handsome he was, especially after we took turns watching him sleep at night. A year passed, and we thought we were safe. Julie drank less. She got happier. We would put Danny in his stroller and parade him around town like he was a new car. He was quiet, but he was walking at thirteen months, talking a few months after that. And he loved music, loved his mother singing to him, his father dancing with him. Julie published more and more. My Hollywood made more money than ever, and I even reported all my business income to the IRS. I joined the downtown merchant association. Julie even considered having another baby.

It was a Saturday night, the last time we ever heard Danny say a complete sentence for a long time. We had put him to bed in his own room, but he wanted a story from me, a song from his mother. "Aktil's Big Swim"—that was the story. A young English mouse named Aktil sneaks out of his house late at night and swims across the English Channel, helped by some sea gulls. Danny had heard it a hundred times. Julie sang "Fly Me to the Moon" and added her own lyrics; I mangled "Danny Boy." Then we kissed him goodnight. As we turned to leave, he said, "I want to go to France sometime, okay?"

"I want to go to France sometime, okay?"—In my world, it's the only competition to "She's upstairs picking out a dress for Dallas."

The next morning, I was in the kitchen when I heard Danny scream as Julie picked him up out of bed. Then another scream, and then Julie's voice seemed to moan, "Joe, I need you."

It took six months, and a lot of doctors, until we had a definite diagnosis: Danny was autistic. He had not spoken in all that time. Julie and I took him home, expecting the worst, but in a cruel way we were lucky. Danny was not as badly afflicted as many other autistic children, but neither would he ever get better. I read all the books and articles about autism I could find. Knowledge wasn't power. Knowledge didn't tell me how to pick Danny up without him struggling to get away from me. Knowledge didn't keep Julie from sleeping alone. Knowledge was worthless.

Near the end of my first term on the Council, I called Ted Stanton and told him I wasn't running for re-election. He was not surprised, "If you did, I was going to work against you, Joe, just to make sure you lost. You're doing the right thing. Take care of your boy and Julie. This damn town will have to get along without you."

I called the **TELEGRAM**, did some interviews, recruited my last batch of commission appointments, including Ken Rumble, got a plaque at my last meeting and an editorial from the **TELEGRAM** thanking me for my four years of community service, my "calm and thoughtful presence," and then I went home.

Ted Stanton called me as soon as he read the editorial. "Is this the calm and thoughtful Joseph Holly?" he yelled at me over the phone. "Jesus Christ, Joe, I told you to hire a press agent! Those morons down at the **TELEGRAM** wouldn't know a thought if it crawled up their butts. And calling you 'calm' is like calling Ted Bundy sensitive."

But I <u>had</u> been calm. Ted knew me in private. In public I was as calm and considerate and as conciliatory as I had always wanted other officeholders to be. Ted still insisted that I had "gone out with a whimper, not a bang," but he also knew that Danny and Julie were the real reason I wasn't running for re-election, and he cut me a lot of slack for that.

I quit and went home to Julie and Danny. To be precise, I should have said that I went back to the house we lived in, but it wasn't a home. House—home. Words matter. Meaning matters. I still hope so.

When I decided not to run again after my first term, I thought I would miss being on the Council, miss being that medium-size fish in a small pond. But I was wrong. At least, wrong for the first few years.

The first thing I did was take Julie and Danny on a long vacation. I had immersed myself in all the books and magazine articles about autism that I could, but all I discovered was that nobody knew exactly where it came from or exactly how to treat it. How much we didn't know—that was what I wanted to talk to Julie about as we sat on the beach in Florida, sat there as Danny used his plastic shovel to bury his parents' feet with the damp sand. Julie seemed genuinely interested in all the information I had gathered, and she nodded and smiled when I told her all about the stories of families that had managed to get through the worst episodes and how some autistic children responded to specific treatments or medication better than other children.

My favorite picture of Danny and me was taken that day on the beach. The bright sunlight bouncing off the ocean had been hurting his eyes, so he was wearing some Mickey Mouse sunglasses we had bought at a local gift shop. He and I were both wearing flowery baggy swimsuits, and I was holding his hand as we walked on the beach. Julie took the picture as we walked away, our backs to her, my head tilted down looking at him, his face looking up at me, both of us with the palest of mid-western skins, prime flesh for a burn if not for the #60 sunscreen we had lathered all over ourselves. Danny was so tiny, and I was so thin. I have a copy of that picture on my desk at home and in my office at the Hollywood, and I had a big poster made of it to hang in Danny's room for his sixth birthday. He's marked all over it with crayons and felt pens, putting a hat on me and wings on himself, lots of black dots on my back, that sort of thing, but he's never taken it down.

I talk about me and Danny a lot, but I don't want you to think that Julie is a bad mother, that she ignores him, or anything like that. She's a wonderful mother, but when we're all in public she always seems to keep her distance from Danny. With just the three of us, she never leaves him alone. I tell people that, and they always tell me how lucky Danny is to have me and Julie as parents, but they're not sincere, I know that. So I tell them things that Julie does for him, but I lie sometimes. I tell them about Julie singing to Danny every night, but I don't tell them that she is really singing to herself as Danny and I listen. Danny doesn't know the difference, that's all that counts. Let's face it; even in the best of circumstances, autistic kids can be hard to love. The older he gets, the more I wish he'd let me touch him, put my arms around him, but there's that world he lives in that Julie and I can't get into, and Julie started going away to her own world more and more the older Danny got.

As soon as Danny got old enough to go to special ed classes in the public schools, and Julie was at work in the mornings, I would sleep until noon. But that was usually because I seldom went to bed before three or four in the morning. With Danny and Julie in bed, I would watch Letterman, talking back to the television and telling him that he had been stealing my act for years. Or I would channel surf, punching the remote button every few minutes until I found something to keep me entertained for an hour or two. From the end of my first term on the Council until I ran that second time, I gained thirty pounds.

With Julie home in the afternoon, Danny and I would sit in the kitchen and watch her cook dinner. She was usually good about not drinking until after five o'clock. After dinner, she would read or grade papers while Danny and I watched television. The truth is, I'll admit now, the truth is that I somehow "willed" myself into believing she didn't drink before five o'clock, just like I willed myself into believing that Danny's autism wasn't as bad as it really was, just like I willed myself into believing that my father had come to love me in his old age before the Alzheimer's erased his son and his wife.

You total up your life, the good and bad, you want more good. Sometimes you want to forget the bad, as if it never happened. You tell yourself that you were a "different" person back then, and your friends laugh with you, remembering the sins of their own youth. The line is always: "Thank God you didn't know me then." You want to go back in time and watch yourself, like some lab experiment. Sometimes you want to go back and just slap yourself silly. "You damn fool," you want to yell at yourself. "How can you be so stupid and so cruel!"

The worst thing I ever did to Danny was wanting him to be something he wasn't. If he has to be autistic, I thought, why can't he at least be some sort of idiot savant genius, some sort of stunning mysterious cipher. There was this moment years ago. I was alone with him in the Hollywood, cleaning an old popcorn popper, and I heard him singing. You know anything about autism, you know that getting a complete sentence out of your child is something to be thankful for. There I was, hearing him sing the song that had been sung to him almost every night since he was born. Pitch perfect in his six-year-old voice, acapella words and melody, singing to another Danny boy about the pipes calling him home. I sucked in my breath and held it as long as I could, afraid to make a sound as he sang. This was some sort of textbook "breakthrough" I was sure. He sang the whole song, and then I waited, but he stayed quiet. "Danny boy?" I said. "You like that song?" But he didn't respond.

I told Julie about it that night, almost gushing, and she destroyed me, and something between us. "Oh, sure, he's a wonderful singer.

I've heard him a few times," she said matter-of-factly.

"And you never told me?" I said, getting angry, raising my voice, standing up. "You never told me that!"

"I'm sorry, Joe. I thought you knew. I just assumed you had heard him before since you spend so much time with him. I just thought…" she said, stopping in mid-sentence to look up at me, her voice trailing off to a whisper, "…but it's no big deal is it, really. It doesn't mean anything." Then she turned toward Danny, who was sitting on the couch watching some television show about animal babies, "Isn't that right, Danny, no big deal. Just an old song, right?"

Danny never turned around. And I chose to ignore the obvious problem with Julie. If I didn't acknowledge it, I didn't have to deal with it.

In the next few weeks I thought I did the right thing. I wanted Danny to sing for me again. I collected recordings of "Danny Boy" and transferred them to two cassette tapes. I scavenged the used record shops, called radio stations, bought new CDs, which had any version of that song. On one tape I put all the instrumental versions I could find: Glenn Miller to Henry Mancini. On another tape I put all the vocal renditions: Frank Sinatra to Harry Connick Jr. Four hours of that song, and I gave the two tapes to Danny, along with a new tape player, but he didn't cooperate. He would listen to the tapes all the time, but there was no pattern to when he would sing. Sometimes I would hear him in his room alone, sometimes with me at the Hollywood. And only that song. I knew he liked it when Julie or I would sing "Fly Me To The Moon" for him, so I made tapes of as many versions of that song as I could find. He liked listening to them as well, and sometimes I thought I could catch him humming the melody, but he never sang the words.

I gave up eventually. Danny was not a musical savant. He sang a song with his name in it, that was all. When he was nine years old, the tape frayed and was unplayable, but he didn't seem to notice. I threw it in the trash. That was the moment, the worst and lowest moment, when I screamed at him, "Can't you do <u>anything</u>? Can't you <u>be</u> anything?" I wanted to take him by the shoulders and shake him until he acknowledged me, but all I did was yell until he started crying. Then I was on my knees, crying myself, asking him to forgive me, begging him to let me hold him, but he pushed me away, hitting my shoulders with one tiny clenched fist and himself with the other until I could take both his hands in mine and stop him. He started to kick at me, so all I could do was get off my knees and lift him up as I rose, pulling him tight against me as I danced around the room, spinning in circles out of the kitchen and into the backyard, whirling around until we both dropped to the thick grass, and I set him free. I was alone, I told myself. I was miserably alone.

I didn't think about running for Council again until Harry Hopkins called me. Ken Rumble had been elected after I got off, and he had turned himself into an Athens legend, with his followers listening to just one radio station in their minds: KWOW——Ken Walks On Water. Harry was worried. Lots of openings in the upcoming elections, incumbents dropping like flies, some resigning early in their terms simply because Ken had worn them out. "Joe, the town needs you," Harry had told me.

I called Ted Stanton. He confirmed Harry's concerns, and then he asked if I was really sure I wanted to get back in politics. "Things are different now, Joe. A lot of meanness out there, and the lefties aren't taking prisoners."

"Ted, I thought we were the lefties," I said.

"That was then, six years ago, this is now. Liberal's not good enough for these people. We can win this thing, but you better have a thicker skin than you did last time around," he said.

Marcie Hamilton thought that May was the best month of the year in Iowa. Not yet hot, but consistently warm enough so that her heavy wool coats could be put in mothballs. Sometimes the nights would turn chilly, and last year there had been record low temperatures for a whole week in May. But May was the real beginning of spring in Iowa. April was always unpredictable. Sometimes winter refused to go away, and snow was not uncommon for April. So May was the month that her neighbors came out of their houses after a bone-cold winter's hibernation and worked in their backyards.

Marcie had pampered her gardens and grass ever since they had moved into their house on Court Street. Jack Hamilton had always been amused by his wife's obsession with their yard. But he helped her on the weekends. She had initially resented his lack of enthusiasm, his failure to "volunteer" to help her, but she finally accepted the fact that Jack Hamilton was not, as she told her parents, "a dirt person." A dirt person loved the black Iowa soil, soil so rich that even Jack had to admit that "if you just spit on that dirt you'll get a crop of sky-high corn."

Marcie was not interested in corn, but she did raise tomatoes, carrots, peppers, and dozens of varieties of flowers. When she worked in her yard, her husband would often carry things for her, bring her a tool or hose, but he usually just sat in his patio chair and read a book, always there if she needed him, always there when she stood up to stretch the knots out of her neck and shoulders.

As soon as their daughter was born, Marcie Hamilton made a conscious effort to make Becka a "dirt person." The playpen was set up on the grass while she worked in her garden, and she always gave Becka flower petals to play with, until Becka started eating them. Instead of nurse kits or Mattel kitchen appliances, she bought Becka tiny plastic garden toys, showing her how to dig furrows and plant seeds for her own section of the gardens. The indoctrination had been successful, and, by the time Becka was ten, she and her mother were side by side on their knees every warm weekend, laughing with each other about Jack Hamilton's spectator role. As a teenager, Becka often feigned opposition to her mother's weekend ritual, citing a hundred adolescent obligations to be with her friends or practice her running or flute, any excuse to "keep from getting my nails dirty." Then that opposition became genuine. Marcie stopped asking after awhile. When her father suggested to Becka that she spend more time with her mother, she had snapped at him, "Daddy, just leave me alone. Nobody I know works in the dirt."

Hamilton had gone to his wife and told her about his efforts, but she had only shrugged and said, "She'll come back. She just needs to grow up. I know I pushed my parents away from me when I was her age."

Hamilton had backed down grudgingly, "All I know is that letting her get away with so much because she's 'at that age' —— well, that gets old after awhile."

The May afternoon that Hamilton had called Marcie and told her about the deer running free downtown, she reminded him about how right they had been to install a fence around the backyard. She was not impressed with deer as cute and harmless forest animals, with as much right to roam in town as they had in the woods. She had had to re-plant a large section of her garden once already this spring. She did not want to do it again.

"But you should have seen it," Jack told her at dinner that night. "It was gorgeous."

They had gone back downtown to the Atlas Restaurant, where they had eaten once a month ever since they moved to Athens. One of their many routines: dinner on a Friday night, then a walk around the downtown, a stop for the live outdoor music in the spring and summer. Perhaps a movie, until all the old downtown theatres closed, and neither of them liked the movies that showed at the Hollywood.

"For a person who doesn't like camping, hunting, fishing, gardening, and even mowing the lawn, you seem a little too impressed by some dumb animal who took a wrong turn into town," she teased him.

"Yeh, you're right, probably right," he admitted, handing the menu back to the waitress before ordering. "But all I know is that I was glad to see it get away."

Hamilton did not tell his wife how he had laughed as three cars ran into each other as they tried to avoid hitting the deer, how he had literally applauded, along with dozens of other pedestrians, when the deer bounded between two cars and then stopped suddenly in the path of another car. A hundred thousand dollars worth of automotive metal and technology—reduced in value by half as they tried to avoid a deer, only to hit each other.

When their dinner arrived, Marcie Hamilton reminded her husband to eat slowly. It was his least attractive habit, she told him, and he agreed. He was very deliberate at first, but the more they talked the faster his fork reached his mouth. At one point, Marcie reached across the table and grabbed his hand. "Jack, I'm going to stop eating in public with you if you can't slow down. You're beginning to miss your mouth."

Hamilton put his fork down and took a deep breath. He knew his wife was right, he ate too fast. He could always rationalize it by pointing out how he had to fight for food at the table when he was growing up. But that was then, as Marcie always countered, this is now. "You're an adult, Jack, we have money and time, and it's no wonder that Becka doesn't want to have her friends over for dinner with us, or go out with us to restaurants," she said to him this evening. "And, like all teenagers, she's embarrassed by her parents in general, and your eating habits in particular."

They sat there in silence for a few minutes, until Hamilton grudgingly picked up his fork and self-consciously began stabbing at the food on his plate that no longer appealed to him." "I think we need to talk to Becka," he said, "We need to set some ground rules for this summer and next year in school."

"Rules?" Marcie asked, anticipating the same discussion they had had a dozen times in the past year.

"She's going to be sixteen this summer, old enough to drive, and...."

"And she's more mature than you give her credit for, Jack. You've got to loosen up. You can't expect her to be your little girl forever."

"You're right, of course," he said, and then lowered his voice almost to a whisper, "You're always right. I just think, just wish she wouldn't push me away so much."

"It's a phase, Jack, and it doesn't mean she doesn't love you. Don't take it so personal, especially when she won't go to a movie with you."

"Phase or not, I'm her father..."

"Jack," she interrupted him, "Listen to yourself, to the tone in your voice. You keep acting this way, you'll push her further away."

Hamilton nodded grimly, pushing his plate away from him.

"Another thing," Marcie continued, "She's going to ask you if she can spend a month in Iowa City this summer with her friend Jenny Baker, you know, her girlfriend who moved away last year. She and Jenny were best friends...."

"I know _that_," Hamilton snapped.

"Let's not ruin dinner, okay?" Marcie said patiently. "I told her that she had to ask your permission, but I didn't want her to spring it on you. So, when she gets home tonight, let her talk to you. I think she's bringing you a surprise, too. Something she made in art class at school. Jack, are you listening to me?"

Hamilton was beginning to feel a burning pain in his chest. His doctor had assured him that it was merely heartburn, a condition he was going to have to live with for the rest of his life. "So I'm guessing that she knows she's got your approval and I can either agree or I can be the villain...again," he said, rubbing his hand across his chest.

Marcie reached in her purse and retrieved a small orange plastic bottle, uncapped it and gave him two tablets. "She's staying after school this afternoon, but she promised to be home when we get there."

"You know I'll agree, don't you," he said, shaking his head as he looked down.

"Yes, I know, and so does Becka," she smiled.

All he could do was laugh.

I keep thinking that I should have been better prepared for what happened after Becky Hamilton died, that my first term on the council should have taught me something about Athens, some insight that would have helped, but I only put all the pieces together later. All the clues were there, big chunks of a communal personality, traits that hindsight focused. But I wasn't sharp enough to find the thread. That essence of Athens? How about pigeons and cemeteries?

Pigeon shit can be toxic. No doubt about it. Too many trees downtown that attract too many pigeons, and, if nothing else works, you remove the trees, tree-lovers be damned. You can always plant different trees somewhere else. That's a no-brainer. But Athens had a different pigeon problem.

Old Man Yokum lived on the edge of town and raised pigeons, like his father before him on the same lot in the nineteenth century. Racing pigeons, fifty of them. His father's land was originally in the county, but urban development is like a snake. It swallows land for lunch. Swallows it slowly, but fatally. It took a hundred years, but the Yokum land was finally surrounded by Athens, oozed over by sub-division after sub-division of modern homes. Old Man Yokum kept his home and pigeon coop, but sold most of his land decades ago. He eventually had neighbors. Him and his pigeons, I should say, they had neighbors.

Two women, partners for twenty years, co-founders of the local Women's Holistic Information Program, affectionately known as WHIP, bought the house next to Yokum. And then they sued him. Pigeons are a health risk. Air-borne germs, just ask any doctor. Doesn't matter that none of the previous neighbors had a problem, these two women did. One had bronchial problems. Windy days, they couldn't leave their house. Pigeon's fault, no other possible explanation. They sued, and they lost in court, twice. They went to the city council and asked that domestic pigeons be outlawed in Athens. They brought their friends, many of whom worked with Julie at Iowa Arts. They assumed I was on their side.

The council sent Jennifer Joslin, the animal control officer, out to inspect, and she came back and said—yep, lots of pigeons, but in a coop clean enough to birth babies and with a ventilation system and screen that mitigated a lot of the fumes. Joslin had always done a terrific job, with a droll sense of humor, a bit wacky about animal rights, but a person to be trusted. We asked her how big a problem the other pigeon coops were in town, and she informed us that Old Man Yokum had the only coop in the city limits. Still, she said, we ought to consider banning any future coops. Most people won't be as clean as Yokum. We asked her about the health complaint, and she said, "I do dogs and cats, an occasional ferret and python, but you gotta go somewhere else for an opinion about germs."

The pigeon-sufferers weren't happy about all this discussion. Their case, it was obvious to them, was clear. The council tried to be conciliatory, saying in so many words that this was an issue that had to be resolved between neighbors, and we tried to cut the baby in half. We would ban all future pigeon coops and grandfather in the Yokum coop. We spent a lot of time on this issue, over many meetings, trying to be fair to everyone. The best we could determine, Yokum's coop wasn't a problem, and he was there first, but why take chances on a future pigeon owner not being as fastidious. A crowd of Yokum supporters, all of them old-time Athens residents, who had lived there long before Iowa Arts was built, saw this as a grudging victory. The other half of the room, most of them affiliated with Iowa Arts, saw it as a crushing defeat, and Joseph Holly had led the opposition to their obviously reasonable request. The last of my liberal credentials were dissolving fast.

As the revised ordinance was being voted on, a liberal-wannabe requested that we remove the phrase "grand-father" and replace it with the more gender neutral "grand-parent." Fair enough, and necessary. Nouns and pronouns mattered. But I objected, and everybody in the chambers got quiet. For a split second, I told myself, "This is <u>not</u> that big of a deal, so why is everybody staring?" I went into my teacher/preacher mode, explaining that, sure, most of the old assumed masculine pronoun references needed to be changed, but "grand-father" had a specific reference in American civil rights history. Every-time we used "grand-father clause" in a debate, there was an implicit reference to some specific history, and I insisted, "that reference trumped political correctness."

I had created my own issue at that moment, and it was more important to me than the pigeon issue. That night, in front of old and new Athens, I refused to budge. I won the battle, lost the war. We kept the "grand-father" language, but all the **TELEGRAM** reported was my reference to political correctness. Somehow, in letters to the editor the week after, that attack became an attack on sexual equality. Go figure. Julie understood what I was trying to do, that's all that mattered.

The real issue that night had nothing to do with pigeons or language. As I sat there looking at that split crowd and remembered all their comments, I suddenly understood the real problem in Athens.

After the meeting, the liberal wannabe and another council member cornered me and started giving me hell about the pigeons and Old Man Yokum. They both agreed that the real problem was Old Man Yokum's open hostility to the women's sexual orientation. He was inflexible because he was homo-phobic. A reasonable, unbiased man would have been more considerate of his neighbors.

So I told them what I understood. Gender was irrelevant. This was a <u>class</u> issue. Old Man Yokum was blue-collar old Athens. The pigeon-sufferers were Iowa Arts gentry. They had the "experts" on their side, the medical journal articles, the articulate professional colleagues speaking about how "Mr. Yokum doesn't understand the dynamics of urban civility." Yokum and his friends had one argument: He was there first. It was the oldest town/gown fault-line. Pick any small college town, I told them, there's an Old Man Yokum there, slowly being pushed out. Diversity and pluralism for academics like the two women meant diverse people—neighbors—who were as smart as they were and as affluent. I told the two other council-members that when you scraped away the veneer of that night's meeting, you had a room full of rednecks on one side and snobs on the other, and the rednecks won. And that I'd rather be a redneck than a snob. Okay, so much for me saying that all our debates were high-level discourse that Athens could be proud of.

Two days after the meeting, one of two women confronted Julie in the English Department and told her to "tell your redneck husband that we'll remember him in the next election." One of the two council-members had gone straight to the WHIP women.

I asked Julie what she said to the woman who confronted her. We were at the Hollywood with Danny. Just the three of us. The greatest thing about owning your own movie theatre? You close the doors and watch any movie you want. I had a private copy of CINEMA PARADISO, that Italian movie about the kid growing up during WWII, working in the village theatre. My favorite foreign movie, and Danny's too. He loves the sub-titles, loves the projection room scenes. So Julie and I were sitting in the back row, Danny by himself in the front row, his favorite spot, wearing his earplugs, and she whispered to me, "Joe, you are a redneck. A Texas, Oklahoma redneck. An educated redneck, a funny redneck, a snobby redneck in your own way, but for damn sure a redneck."

"Is that what you told her?" I asked, pressing for details.

"Absolutely, and then I told her that you had a dick that would bring her over to the dark breeder side," she said, looking at the screen.

74

"You did NOT!" I said, raising my voice.

She took my hand and put the back of it up to her lips, saying, "Of course not," rubbing my hand across her face. "So, shut up. Your favorite scene is coming."

Up on the screen, looming over my son, a black and white collage of censored screen kisses began. Danny giggled, as usual. Julie kept holding my hand, but she turned her face away when I tried to kiss her.

Pigeons as moral lesson? Athens was two towns: two classes of people. Later, after Becky died, I added another split: two colors. Still, I had always thought I was on the right side of the issues for most people in Athens. I told Ted Stanton that, and he laughed.

"Joe, you have got to see a doctor about your memory problems. Have you forgotten all about the cemetery? Ken's people pigeonholed you years ago and haven't let you out of that box yet. Hell, he wasn't even on the council yet, but you were still politically incorrect."

A week after Danny was born, I had taken him to Oakland Cemetery to introduce him to his sister. Oakland is a special place for me. On my list of things and places in life that matter—like movies and books and old movie theatres, the ocean, popcorn, Gershwin, and Harry Chapin—high on that list are cemeteries, especially Oakland because I had helped keep it alive. As I sat there on a blanket next to Kathy's grave, with Danny lying there next to me, trying to fall asleep, I told him the story, the same story I had told Kathy years earlier.

In my first year on the Council, Oakland was running out of space. We had two choices: expand the cemetery by clearing out some trees in Hickory Hill Park, which abutted the cemetery, and landscaping the exposed hills; or we could buy some land and open a new cemetery across town.

Even before Kathy was buried there, I liked going to Oakland

and walking around. It was the quietest place in the city limits. But as soon as we even raised the possibility of cutting down one of the trees in Hickory Hill Park, you would have thought we had suggested rounding up the firstborn child of every Sierra Club member in Athens and throwing them into a mulching machine. At our first public meeting, I tried to explain how I felt that a cemetery was a park, that all the reasons people went to Hickory Hill were consistent with the experience of people going to Oakland. I started to talk about Frederick Law Olmsted when a future Ken Rumble apostle rushed to the public microphone and shouted that I was "murdering trees for the benefit of the dead and ignoring the wishes of the living." I was speechless. This was Athens, and this was a rational argument? The Mayor tried to point out that if we went to the other side of town we would have to pay premium prices for the land and then the development costs would be exorbitant, AND maintaining two separate cemeteries in the future would be cost prohibitive. But that was too rational, I realized. So I said something that I understood, and I didn't care if the young man in front of me understood or not. Someday, he would. I lowered my voice: "Cemeteries are not for the dead. They're for the living." Then I began to sense that the Council was about to back down, so I suggested we continue the discussion after some staff research on alternatives.

A week later, the City Attorney earned her salary. She discovered that half of Hickory Hill Park was originally part of land that had been willed to the City back in 1888 by the Russell family and was to be used explicitly for future cemetery expansion. So we had a rational and legal argument on our side. But the Council, remembering the previous meeting's heat, was flaming out like crippled Spitfires up against the entire Luftwaffe. A war metaphor seemed appropriate at that moment. When that legal background was announced at the next meeting, my smile was obvious, and that smile was seen as a smirk by the tree-lovers in the crowd, a smirk they never forgot or forgave. I became the enemy.

In the weeks that followed, as I worked the Council behind the scenes to expand Oakland, to do the right thing, to withstand the pressure, I learned another lesson about local politics. Just like national debates, any issue could be simplified and stripped of its complexity. Hickory Hill Park was more than a park. It was THE symbol of a way of life for a lot of people. A perceived threat to it was a threat to Nature itself, and a road or a house built near the park became more evidence that the wrong people controlled politics and business, proof that capitalism and greed were Mammon's soldiers in Athens, a testament to the trouble right here in River City, Iowa, America.

I thought I found a compromise. I started asking questions of the City Attorney in private. How binding was the original letter from the Russell family? I asked the Parks Director, who was also in charge of cemetery maintenance, how much land we needed for the next hundred years. The bottom line was clear: 40 acres was all we really needed, and the Council could then formally designate the rest of the Russell estate (after we got the descendants' permission) as inviolable parkland in perpetuity, or some legal mumbo jumbo like that. Something for both sides, a compromise.

We announced the "compromise" at the next meeting, all seven of us council-members very proud of ourselves. The first tree-hugger to the microphone raised his fist and slammed it down on the podium, sending the sign-in sheet flying, and enunciated his one sentence statement as if he were counting down the seconds before he pushed a button to demolish a building, "You (5) do (4) NOT (3) compromise (2) the (1) environment. (0) The crowd exploded, "NO COMPROMISE! NO COMPROMISE!"

The Mayor was in the middle of the Council as it faced the crowd. I sat next to him. As they chanted, he scribbled a note and slid it over to me: "Congratulations, Joe, you just became a tree-fucker."

I was too upset after that meeting to go straight home. I called Julie to ask if she wanted to go out, but she didn't answer the phone. So I went to Oakland by myself to talk to Kathy. I told her all about the meeting, just like I told Danny that afternoon when I introduced him to her. It was past midnight, but an almost full moon made it easy enough to find her spot. I had had too much coffee at the meeting, and I was talking too fast, I knew that. After awhile, I just stood there, listening to the wind shake the trees throughout the cemetery. Then I heard something else too. Something like horse hoofs pounding hard ground. I looked around, squinting toward where I thought the sound had come from. Seeing nothing, I was still getting spooked. Then, like a dream, I saw the dark outlines of animals racing through the cemetery, animals that became a herd of deer, deer that floated like ballerinas across the grass and around the tombstones, and then they were gone, all except one huge buck who stopped and turned toward me, as if wondering why I was there.

You ever see those ads for the Hartford Insurance Company, the ones with the big deer as a logo. This deer was like that, only bigger, as big as a Clydesdale, I swear it. And totally unafraid. It started walking toward me like I was trespassing on his territory, like I had better have a good explanation as to why I was there. Branches starting cracking in the trees at the edge of the cemetery, and the buck froze for a moment before his antlered head turned toward the sound, pausing, turning back to face me, then it bounded silently into the woods.

So when I took Danny to meet his sister, I told him about how I saved the cemetery from extinction, then I told him about Hartford. That's what I named that deer—Hartford. You think I'm telling you a story? You ask anybody in Athens. They'll tell you the same. Hartford has been seen by lots of people, alone or in crowds. He's not some Roswell UFO. We've got the pictures. News stations have filmed him. But I saw him first, and I named him.

Danny was totally unimpressed with my story when I told him. He was a week old, plenty of time for him to see Hartford for himself. All the time in the world. All the time in the world.

After dinner, Hamilton and his wife took their time going home. They walked around downtown Athens first. Window shopping, having a cup of coffee at the Java House, going to the Prairie Schooner Bookstore. They were in no hurry. At Prairie Schooner, they checked the calendar of visiting writers. Mary Pipher, who wrote books about teenage girls, was scheduled to be in Athens in a few days. Marcie wanted her husband to come with her to the reading.

After Prairie Schooner, they went past the box-office of the Hollywood Theatre next door. Staring at a poster in the window, they both knew what the other was thinking. A series of three foreign films— RED, WHITE, and BLUE—why can't they show something we want to see?

"You interested?" Hamilton asked his wife, already knowing the answer.

"You?" she said, looking over the top of her glasses.

"I'll wait for the videos," he laughed. "So I can go freeze frame 'em and go back and read the subtitles at my own pace. You know, enjoy the subtlety."

Marcie leaned into her husband, "That's why I married you…. your love of subtlety."

"Damn straight," he said, beginning to walk away as he took her hand in his. As they turned, Hamilton came face to face with Harry Hopkins who was swerving to avoid bumping into him.

"Excuse me," Hopkins said, reaching for the door handle with one hand and extending the other to make sure there was no physical contact between the two men, as if he were afraid that Hamilton would fall into him. Hopkins smiled, but it was obvious that he was in a hurry.

Hamilton had watched enough Council meetings to recognize the City Manager, but he still felt that vague pleasure that comes from seeing somebody on television in real life. He thought Hopkins' hand was extended for a handshake, as if the two men already knew each other, but, as Hamilton raised his own hand, Hopkins was already halfway through the door and Jack Hamilton was left in the awkward stance of a hand half raised as he said,' "Nice to…"

"You know him?" Marcie asked as the Hollywood door closed.

"That's Harry Hopkins, the City Manager," he said, staring through the plate glass front window to see Hopkins leaning down to shake hands with a small boy. Behind the boy was Joseph Holly. "He's a busy man."

"So that's the City Manager, eh?" Marcie said. "He sure doesn't look like he's a manager of anything. He's too…."

"Too good looking?" Hamilton interrupted, nudging her toward the store next door. Actually, he was surprised himself at how much better Hopkins looked in real life than he did on television. He had never seen him smile on camera.

"Well, I suppose I'd rather be paying a good looking man rather than…"

"Rather than a guy like me?" he interrupted again, in mock disappointment.

"Jack, you keep interrupting me, I'm going to make you a lot uglier," she said, poking him in the ribs.

"Now, get out your wallet and let's pick up Becka's picture."

Next door to the Hollywood was the Plane Geometry Frame Shop. They had given Ralph Berry, the owner, a collection of pictures of their daughter's various school activities and asked Berry to mat a collage and frame it. Inside the store, Hamilton immediately noticed that the shelves were half empty.

"You moving to Coral Ridge too?" he asked Berry after they had quibbled over the final charge, a ritual they had developed over the years. Berry always inflated his price for anything he did for the Hamiltons, and then he and Jack Hamilton would trade charges of

extortionist on one side and miser on the other. But both men knew it was a game, and the price always came down.

"Nope, but I am moving," Berry said as he handed over the framed collage. "I've got a deal out at Eastdale Plaza."

"Out near where we live?"

"Actually, the store here is closer. But out there I get two large rooms upstairs for my shop, and a separate room for a gallery where I can start showing some local artists. Lots of free parking out front, lower rent, and I don't have to clean the puke up every morning where some drunk college kid left his guts at my front door from the night before."

"Lower rent——that mean your prices are going down?" Hamilton joked.

"For everybody but you, Jack Hamilton. You've got the big civil service salary, so you pay premium prices for premium work," Berry shot back.

"Premium, my ass..."

"Jack Hamilton!!"

The two men looked at Marcie Hamilton and then winked at each other.

"Any idea what's coming into this space?" she asked, trying to elevate the conversation.

"Probably another bar," Berry said, scratching his trim red beard.

"Another reason not to come downtown," Hamilton muttered. Marcie and Ralph Berry nodded, but neither said a word. "And that's too damn bad," Hamilton continued, a little louder. "And nobody seems willing to fight it."

"Let's go home, Jack," Marcie said, and then, "Thanks, Ralph. We'll come see you at your new place."

"You're on my mailing list," Berry said as they left. "Remember, *if you want something done for Christmas, you need to get it to me by November."*

Walking through downtown, the Hamiltons looked at the new Firstar clock and realized they were late. It was past seven. Becka would be home, so they walked faster than usual down Washington Street past the College Green Park, regretting that they could not stop and listen to the band in the large gazebo. They walked past some new apartment buildings at the far end of Washington, then turned on Summit Street toward Court. At the corner of Court, they noticed a police car parked in front of their house, but it meant nothing to them. Probably just watching for speeders. As they walked past the car and turned on to the sidewalk which led to their front porch, they heard a car door open and slam, and then a woman's voice called to them, "Mr. and Mrs. Hamilton?"

It's all over now. The shouting, the late night phone calls calling me a murderer, the endless meetings, the sleepless nights, no more broken windows at the Hollywood. Becky Hamilton and that other kid are still dead. Harry is still running the city, but I'm not on the Council. Athens is still there, but I'm not.

Harry looks a lot older than he used to, older around the eyes especially. Sometimes we will look at each other and laugh about how naive we were that first day, thinking we could control things. Becky's death was the immediate problem, but not the only one, so we thought. An hour after he called to tell me about the car chase and the two deaths, he came to see me at the Hollywood.

"We've got some real liability on this one," he said as we stood in my small lobby. Danny was inside the theatre, watching a movie with sub-titles. He seemed to love those kinds of movies, fascinated with silent English words printed on the screen while some other alien words came out of the mouths of the actors.

"I've alerted everybody and told them to be careful about what they say. One of the families already has a lawyer calling us," Harry said.

"That's predictable," I said, "but so fast? Less than an hour?"

"Blood's in the water," he said. One of the secrets about Harry was the difference between the way he talked in private versus his public statements. The City Manager would never say "blood's in the water," but Harry Hopkins would. "They know it, we know it, and the truth is—we ARE responsible. We're going to pay. Trick is, don't make it worse. That's why I'm worried about Al, and even Steve. They say the wrong thing, people are going to get more riled up."

I couldn't help myself. I laughed, "Did you say 'riled up'? Harry, I'm from Texas and Oklahoma, and even I wouldn't say 'riled up'."

"Screw you," he said, smiling.

There it was, that exchange, proof that Harry and I had no idea what was in store for us. I was laughing with him, but I was also wondering about the parents of those kids, how they were feeling.

"Which parent was the lawyer calling for?" I asked, getting serious again.

"The kid driving, but I expect we'll hear from the others soon enough," Harry said. "I need some help on this, Joe. The city attorney will be working with the insurance company lawyers, and I'll take care of the cop involved, but you need to get the Council organized. Keep Al on a leash, tell Steve what to say, and if you can figure out where Ken is going with this, let me know."

"Take care of the cop?" I asked. "Is he pretty upset, I'm assuming."

"I don't care about him being upset," Harry snapped. "I told the chief to tell him that we wanted his resignation on my desk in the morning."

"So, what don't I know yet?"

"The chase was against department policy. He should have called it off after the first few blocks in that residential area. Plain and simple. Let the other units pick it up, and we've got witnesses that swear they were topping sixty miles an hour. In a school zone! I don't care if it <u>was</u> after five o'clock, it was a school zone. Doesn't matter that we told him to call off the chase, his actions made us liable."

"If he doesn't quit?" I asked. Like any good manager, Harry prided himself on getting rid of bad employees by having them resign, to avoid all the workman's comp and other legal issues.

"I fire him..."

"You're so sure on ..." I started to say, but Harry held up his hand, his fist clinched. He was more agitated than I had ever seen him, almost as if he were taking all this as a personal insult, a threat to his control of the city.

"The dispatcher told him to cease the pursuit. Told him to STOP the chase, two blocks before the kid ever turned that corner. Joe, there's something wrong with this picture, but I'm not waiting to get rid of this cop until I have it figured out. Resign or fired, he's gone in twelve hours. The police union can rant all they want to about due process, but the man is not on our payroll in the morning."

As he was about to speak again, we were interrupted by Danny. He had come back in the lobby without us noticing and was behind the concession stand getting some popcorn.

"Danny boy, you okay?" I called to him, but he didn't respond. He seldom did.

The interruption gave Harry and me a chance to compartmentalize. Police chases, fired cops, we also needed to talk about transit problems and property tax rollbacks mandated by the state legislature. In thirty minutes, we had outlined the agenda for the next meeting.

"You'll never guess what Vatican City is doing to us this week," Harry said, ending his list of things he needed to tell me about. Vatican City was his pet expression for Iowa Arts, the administration in particular. Their own little island, tax exempt, private security, untouched by the vagaries of capitalism, a religion all to itself. "You know how we asked them to build some new dorms to take the pressure off the neighborhoods. I got their answer today. They say they're adding a thousand rooms to the inventory."

Harry was rolling eyes too much for that to be the whole truth. I offered him a straight line, "And the catch is?"

"They're buying five old apartment buildings from the Prose brothers and renovating them," he said slowly, "which means that there are not really any <u>new</u> beds, just peas in a shell game, which means that two million dollars of private property is taken off the tax rolls, and we either raise taxes on everybody else or cut services to get the hundred thousand dollar property tax shortfall to balance <u>our</u>

budget," he finished with a flourish.

So it went that evening, me and Harry plotting strategy for the next six months, putting Becky Hamilton to one side, not anticipating the worst that could happen, not having a clue about the future.

An hour after he arrived, a few minutes before intermission, Harry returned to our immediate problem. "I've scheduled a news conference for Monday, me and the chief. We'll take the initial heat, and then you guys can have your meeting the next night, and there will probably be a lot of public discussion, but at least we'll have our proverbial ducks in a row. You and Bernie can prep Steve."

"Steve's the mayor," I said. "Don't you think he ought to be there on Monday?"

"You really want him under that spotlight?" Harry answered. "Me, I look at the Monday meeting as an administrative approach. You and Steve and the others are the political response. Make sense?"

Harry was not saying what I knew he was thinking. Steve Nash was an embarrassment. A well-meaning, reasonably intelligent, mild-mannered, totally ineffectual public speaker. Harry was right, better to keep Steve away from a microphone as much as possible. Let Harry and The Chief run interference for the Council. Me and Ken Rumble and Bernadette Huss would carry the load for the Council.

"Sure, Bernie and I will get with Steve and Ken and the rest this weekend," I finally said.

"One more thing, Joe," Harry was about out the door before he turned back. "You running for re-election in the fall?"

"Probably, one last time," I said, the music for the closing credits getting louder in the lobby as Danny opened the auditorium doors.

"Thank god for small favors," Harry said, waving at me as he left. "You probably won't even have an opponent. Even though," he added, "you <u>have</u> pissed off a lot of people. You smug bastard. You preach and you preach, and you have a lot less patience than you did a few years ago. You <u>can</u> be beaten, don't ever forget that."

"I ought to not run, just to piss <u>you</u> off," I said.

He was almost out the door, but he turned completely around. "I'll miss you, Joe, but I don't need you." Then, in another pivot, "Tell Julie hello for me, and remind her that if she ever dumps you...I want the first rebound."

I looked around, made sure that Danny was not watching, and then I pointed my middle finger at Harry, who promptly saluted and finally went out the door.

If you could pinpoint the break between the past and future, it was that conversation in my lobby with Harry. Sure, me and Harry, we're important, but we're not the stars. We get the Golden Globes for supporting performances in a category I call dramedy. Some hybrid of drama, comedy, tragedy, and farce.

Steve Nash was the mayor, sitting in the middle of the Council, with a toupee that made him look like a shorthaired George Washington. A good council member, Steve Nash was a lousy mayor. His monotone voice would make Jesus weep.

Sitting to Steve's right was Albert Baroli, fourth generation Italian, newly elected in the massacre that sent three incumbents home early. In the campaign he had been a joke, a hothead who labeled Ken Rumble as a "bullshit artist" at the first candidate forum. In a politically correct college town, Al made it clear that he had no patience for students in general, pedestrians and bicyclists in particular, pointy headed government bureaucrats, "plant sap sucking" environmentalists, and "nazi-fem" college professors. Al was the simplest person to understand because he was the least superficial of anyone on the council. Of all the council-members, he had the shortest fuse, but the truest heart. Get him away from the microphone, off camera, Al was the most decent among us. He had a beautiful and gracious wife he adored, straight-arrow children who made him proud, and ten percent of his income always went to charity, but he was not cut out for politics.

Steve Nash in the middle, Al to his right, Bernadette Huss to Al's right, with me on the corner. Ken was at the other corner, with two new women council-members between him and Steve. The women were handpicked by the Chamber of Commerce and managed to convey an image of responsible maturity.

Bernie Huss? Imagine Orrin Hatch and Gertrude Stein having a child. Bernie was a skinny lesbian whose political hero was the Senator from Utah. She dressed like him, complete with those high starched collars and tiepins. She also cut and combed her short hair in the same style. Bernie was the perfect candidate for Athens: former President of the League of Women Voters, a dean at Iowa Arts, a "woman" who owned a downtown clothing store that catered to fraternities and sororities. She owned rental property all over town and was a rock-ribbed economic libertarian. Through inheritance, investments, and skill, she was a rich woman in Athens. She also had Steve Nash in her back pocket. With the two new women, Bernie almost always had four votes.

Me and Harry, Al and Bernie, the others, we were just bit players on stage. More than minor, we were dwarfs in the shadow of the Athenian Colossus——Kenneth Rumble.

I criticize Ken in front of Ted Stanton, and he tells me, "Joe, you're right. Ken's a fraud. But that ain't the reason you hate him. You hate him because people loved him, and they never liked you. Deserve it or not, he had what you always wanted, their hearts."

When the Natural Resources commission was established by the Council, Ken was a charter member. He was knowledgeable and articulate. He was also ambitious, but that seemed to come later. To many people, Ken Rumble was a dinosaur from the Sixties. Too anticapitalist, too lovey-dovey, too politically correct. Ken had even led student demonstrations at the University of Iowa in his youth. That was my complaint about him, and my first advice to him. "You're too old to dress like that," I told him the first time we sat down for coffee. "Hell, you're as old as I am," I tried to joke, but then I discovered something about Ken that should have sent off alarm bells. He had no sense of humor, especially no sense of irony. Kenneth Rumble was deadly serious, a six foot four inch, Green Party, charismatic first-class debater, a competent carpenter, and a struggling folksinger. His singing had gotten him a locally produced CD and earned him the status of "artist." Al Baroli always added "bullshit" as an adjective.

You had to give Ken credit, however. He was Athens' first professional politician, and it took everybody else a long time to catch up. He took the part-time, advisory status of the Council and turned it into a career. Even after he got elected, he was always campaigning.

Ken finally got elected because he found the perfect campaign manager, a Canadian grad student at Iowa Arts named Buzz Mcfadden. You remember Lee Atwater, Bush's man in 1988, who came up with the Willie Horton ad that killed Dukakis? Well, Buzz McFadden was the Lee Atwater of Athens, but without Atwater's sense of ethics and fair play. It was McFadden who transformed Rumble's name from a joke to a catchy slogan on hundreds of yard signs:

"Are YOU Ready TO Rumble"

His opponents thought he was a political fluke, easily erased in the next election, but Ken thrived on people under-estimating him. He also thrived because he had the right enemies: other council-members not as bright as him, not as hardworking, not as committed to their goals as he was to his. He also had the perfect mantra for a town like Athens: PROCESS. The other council-members belittled him on camera, called him obstructionist, chided him for getting in the way of their own holy grail: ECONOMIC DEVELOPMENT.

Ken had changed all the rules, but the other council-members didn't adjust. He wanted to make the process of government a product of government. His own pet issues were dead on arrival. He had one vote and was pathologically incapable of forming alliances with any of the other six council-members, but he made them all look bad at the process of governing. And, damn, he looked good on camera.

"You wanna walk through the cemetery?" I asked Danny the night Becky Hamilton died. We had locked up the Hollywood and were headed home on foot. Julie had called to tell me that she was going to bed early, so Danny and I could take our time.

"Danny boy, the cemetery?" I repeated. "Look for spooks?" He nodded, but he didn't look at me.

It had been a warm day, but by ten o'clock that night it had turned cooler. As soon as we left the theatre I noticed him shivering. I put my arm across his shoulder and tried to pull him closer, but he pulled away. It had happened a thousand times before, but I had never gotten used to the fact that the only time I could hug my son was when he was asleep or very tired.

"You want my shirt?" I asked, and he nodded again. After he put it on, the sleeves covering his hands, he whispered, "Thanks, daddy."

You have an autistic child, you sometimes settle for those moments. You can be angry or sad or tired of trying to figure it all out, but you always settle. Or you go crazy. Me, I knew I was lucky. Some autistic kids are out of control. Danny was comparatively easy.

I tried to explain that to Julie once. I had kept going to a lot of the support group meetings for parents with autistic kids, kept going even after Julie stopped. I heard their horror stories. We were lucky, I told her. "Of course we are, Joe, of course we are. The luckiest people on earth," she had said. "Lucky in love, lucky in life, so wonderfully lucky."

"Let's go talk to your sister," I said to Danny, and off we went. Sometimes when Danny and I walked, I'd talk to him like an adult. Tell him about my day or some plans I had for the next day, stuff I used to tell Julie, but after awhile I got as much response from Danny as I did from her, and sometimes he seemed more interested than her. This night, I had a lot to tell him.

We stopped at Prairie Schooner next door before we went to Oakland. Paul Harris, the manager, was closing up, but he knew that when Danny was with me at the Hollywood we usually came by his place to get some hot chocolate at the coffee shop upstairs before we went home. Paul was a good guy, one of the few adults that Danny seemed to like, especially when Paul let him roam around Prairie Schooner and touch the book covers. Paul's first experience with Danny had not been so cordial. He had noticed a small boy re-arranging books in stacks that made no sense, and when he took a book out of Danny's hand—well, it was an ugly scene. But Paul learned, and he told his employees how to handle Danny when he was in the store.

"Hey, Dan, you taking your dad home?" Paul joked, handing Danny his cup of chocolate. Danny nodded, not looking up, as he slowly moved the cup back and forth under his nose, smelling his favorite smell.

"And you, Joe, seen any good movies lately?" he asked, his usual opening line to me because he was always giving me a hard time about the movies I showed next door.

"I'm going to do a Charlton Heston film festival next month,"

I said with a straight face. "All the ape movies, and then the Bible stuff. Finish up with SOYLENT GREEN."

"Do me a favor, give me the exact dates so I can close this store and take a vacation," he frowned. "If you want my advice, you'll take all the Council tapes and put them on the big screen and charge admission. I always love it when you guys don't know the camera is on you. His honor, da mayor, is blinking like crazy, you and Bernie are passing notes......"

"You can see <u>that</u> on camera!!" I stopped him.

"Cinema verite, Joe, we can hear Al ranting, or Ken Rumble musing, and you and Bernie are shuffling notes back and forth like a bad spy movie. Everybody I know would love to see those notes, find out what you guys are <u>really</u> thinking."

"Read my memoirs," I said, trying to act nonchalant, but I was telling myself to call Bernie and tell her that we needed to be more discreet.

"Well, if you ever do tell the truth about the past few years, I want you to do your first signing here, because it's going to be a bestseller."

I did my best Jack Nicholson imitation, "You want the truth? You can't handle the truth. You can't even handle Charlton Heston."

Danny was tugging on my hand, ready to go home.

"Well, I hope you guys can handle what's about to happen," Paul said as we were leaving.

"You've heard about the kids getting killed?" I said. Danny was yanking my hand harder. I knew I had about thirty seconds before he got upset.

"Joe, I've got contacts all over town. They've already called and told me they were getting off work next week so they can go to the Council meeting. Some sort of demonstration."

"Jesus Christ, Paul! Nobody knows what the hell happened

yet, all the details, and they're already locked and loaded?"

Danny jerked away from me and started to push open the door, but it was locked. Stymied, he began beating on the glass. I stepped away from Paul and grabbed Danny's hands, trying to make eye contact with him, finding myself squeezing harder than I needed to, quickly saying, "Sorry, Danny, but you ......," and then he began kicking the door.

Paul had the door open a few seconds later, and I let Danny storm out as I turned back to Paul and said, "Thanks for the heads-up. I'll keep you........."

Paul waved his hand and pointed past me, "Later... you better catch up to the Danster right now. And you might think about wearing more than a t-shirt. Just to maintain your tight-ass public image."

Danny was already at the corner before I stepped up next to him. "You in a hurry?" I said, but he was silent, intent on the traffic light changing. It was an odd form of self-control I had wondered about for years. He would get agitated, but he always seemed to know to stop at red lights when we were walking. Some autistic kids had trouble with colors, but not Danny.

Oakland was a mile away, an easy walk through the north side of town. From Oakland, home was only a few blocks. The more we walked, the more Danny calmed down. He especially liked walking at night.

We got to Oakland before the big orange lights were turned off, so it was easy to see where we were going. Danny's favorite spot in the cemetery was the Black Angel, a bronze monument with a drooping head and one wing raised as if it were a cape trying to shield the dead from the sun's morning glare. A nine foot tall angel on a three foot high base, the bronze blackened over the years, and you could see the Black Angel from anywhere in the cemetery. As long as the orange lights were on, it cast a shadow even at night. Danny loved the Black

Angel, and the mirror in his room had two of those Athens tourist bureau postcards, which had the Angel on one side. Kathy was buried in the baby section of Oakland, a hundred plots away, but I could still see the Angel when I went to visit her.

"Race you," I said as we came through the gate. He headed right for the Angel, and he always beat me. I know this is pathetic to admit, but him beating me was never a rigged race. I was in lousy shape. I tried to win, really, child self-esteem theories be damned, but after a hundred feet I was gasping for breath as he passed me.

Danny was waiting for me when I finally got to the Angel. He stuck out his hand for me to shake, one of our rituals after these races. "Get you next time," I heaved, and he was smiling happily. It was a good night. Cool, but no wind. No trees swaying, no music, no Ken Rumble or Al Baroli, just me and Danny and Kathy.

We walked over to visit his sister, and I told him all about my plans to run for re-election. Told him what I didn't tell Harry Hopkins—the truth. I wanted off the Council, but I needed the paltry five thousand dollar salary. The worst reason to be in politics if you had any integrity, I knew it. I was burned out. But I needed the money. Needed it more than I could tell Julie or Harry or anybody else. With Julie's salary at Iowa Arts and the Hollywood cash flow, we paid our bills. The Council salary was a cushion, and it made Danny's therapy, his school extras, those things which were not luxuries, it made those things easier to afford. Julie and I agreed. Danny's life was untouchable. We did what we had to do.

But there was another truth, one I didn't even tell Julie. Bernie Huss had told me that Iowa Arts was about to start its own campus film series, something called the Bijou Theatre, and the Bijou was going to show foreign and art films, like the Hollywood, but at a subsidized lower admission. The Hollywood monopoly was going to be busted. I had massaged it well enough in the past few years that I could afford to hire some help, so I had more time for Danny. But there was no way I could squeeze any more money out of it, and the Bijou would mean less. The Council salary was no longer a cushion. It was a necessity. Even with it, however, I'd probably have to go back to working more hours.

"So there you have it, Danny boy," I finished. "The future writ in green, money green. You and me are going to be spending more time downtown."

All the time I had been talking, I had assumed that Danny wasn't really absorbing anything I was saying. But when I mentioned more time downtown, he looked up as if he was going to say something. Sometimes he got that look when I was talking to him, sometimes when he thought he was alone, but it was a look that had to originate from his mother's blood, not mine. He was hearing something, listening to something, and it had nothing to do with me.

"You wanna go home?" I asked him. He shook his head. "You okay?" He was perfectly still. "You hear something?" He nodded vigorously.

I sat down on the grass, so he was taller than me. This was one of those razor moments I had with him more and more lately, as if he was bleeding away from me. He was his mother's son.

"Hear that?" he whispered softly, as if we were soldiers in enemy territory.

"Yes," I lied.

He kneeled down, forced my legs apart, and then he crawled between them and sat with his back pressed up against my chest, and he let me put my arms around him. We sat there for a few minutes, motionless, but all I heard was his breathing.

"Danny?" I whispered, nudging the back of his head with my chin.

"Time to go home," he whispered back, quickly enough to stop the tremor I was beginning to feel in my chest.

Thirty minutes later, he was asleep in his bed and I was walking around the house, turning off all the lights that Julie had left on. On the front of the refrigerator was a note: *Ken Rumble called, wants you to call him. You also got a call from your father's nursing home. Nothing urgent, he's fine, but I told them to call you tomorrow. Harry told me about the police thing. Sounds bad. Sorry about not waiting up. I'm beat. Be sure to get the cat inside before you come to bed.*

I went to the den and sat down at my computer in the corner. Soon enough, the only light in the house was from the screen. I sat there, wishing we still had a cat.

Jack Hamilton turned around and looked at the female police officer, and he knew something was wrong. He felt Marcie squeeze his right forearm. Weeks after this moment, he would still feel her hand tightening around him.

"Mr. and Mrs. Hamilton?" the officer repeated. But then she seemed to change the tone in her voice. Sergeant Polly Brotherton suddenly remembered the black and white couple in front of her. She had been their daughter's D. A. R. E. instructor five years earlier. When she had gotten the call tonight she had not connected the dead girl's name with the beautiful tall fifth grader she had known before. She had gone on to become the Athens Community Relations Liaison Officer, a nice title and more challenging position, and she had had to make this same visit a few other times, but seeing Jack and Marcie she now saw that fifth grader again, and for a few seconds she forgot all her training.

"What's wrong?" Hamilton asked her, but she could not speak immediately.

"We tried to call you, but...." Brotherton finally began, but it was not the protocol opening she was supposed to make. She took another deep breath, but she was feeling herself lose control. Her eyes were watery, but she forced herself to start over, "I'm very sorry to have to tell you this, but there's been an accident and your daughter.........."

As long as he lived, Jack Hamilton knew later, he would not remember the rest of that sentence. He would not even remember what he and Marcie said to each other those first few minutes. Silent or not, the visual memory was very precise. A young woman in a black uniform was telling him that Becka had been involved in an accident. Becka was dead. Just like that. Words from a woman in a uniform and his daughter was dead.

It was not completely dark yet, but the woman's uniform seemed to blend into the background so there was only a face. Marcie was a limp weight next to him, and he had to hold her up. He was having trouble focusing his eyes, and his knees hurt worse than they had in years. He wanted to sit down, but the two women around him were both crying and he had to help them. He must have asked the police officer if she was okay because she muttered something about thanking him.

Even though Brotherton was also crying, she took Marcie's arm and helped Jack Hamilton walk his wife into the house. The phone was ringing when they came through the door. Hamilton walked over, picked up the receiver and put it back down. The answering machine was blinking. Polly told him that two of the four messages were probably from her. He erased all of them, and then he left the two women in the living room, went to the kitchen and sat down alone. A minute later he was vomiting into the sink.

He kept leaning over the sink, his elbows supporting him on the counter edge, and wept for the first time. Trying to stifle it so they would not hear him in the other room, he only made his stomach convulse more intensely. He started moaning, and then his knees finally collapsed.

The next thing he remembered, he was back in the chair, with Marcie holding a cold cloth on his neck. Brotherton was holding his hand and rubbing it. The two women were no longer crying.

"Is there anybody you want me to call?" Brotherton asked. "I called Father West earlier. I knew you...." Nodding toward Marcie, "...taught at Regina."

Marcie smiled and nodded back at Brotherton, "Alan teaches with me. He's a friend too, as well as my priest. Thank you for thinking to do that."

Hamilton was still dizzy, but he was fascinated by how his wife and the woman in the uniform had seemingly become almost intimate.

He listened to them discuss what had to be done next. He felt useless because he had no idea how to get out of the chair, much less what needed to be done to take care of Becka.

"I'll call Mike Lensing," Marcie said, when asked about funeral arrangements. "He and Vicki are friends of mine. They're the ones who should do that. Don't you think so, Jack?"

But Hamilton had another, more important question. "Was she hurt badly? I mean, was there much…"

Before he could finish, Marcie had closed her eyes and slumped back in her chair, the damp cloth in her hand dropping to the floor. Brotherton answered quickly, reaching to hold Marcie's hand.

"I was at the scene very soon after it happened," she said, but then she had her own flashback to that moment and was silent for a minute. Jack and Marcie waited for her to continue. "I'm sorry, very sorry…" she began again, "…I should have recognized her."

It was the wrong thing to say. She realized that immediately when the parents in front of her flinched, assuming something else. "No, no, I mean it's been five years, and she looked so much older, so much more beautiful tonight. Not the child from back then." Brotherton was starting to cry again. "I mean, there was hardly a mark on her tonight. I think it was her neck, it was broken, but you couldn't tell, really, and the EMT thought there were a lot of internal injuries." She stopped herself.

"She wasn't hurt badly?" Hamilton asked again quietly.

"No, she wasn't hurt," Brotherton said, not looking up, "It was instantaneous. There weren't a lot of marks."

"That's good," Marcie said, not knowing what else to say, looking at her husband, wanting him to look at her, but he was looking at the floor, nodding to himself.

The phone rang, but nobody got up to answer it. It kept ringing, but nobody moved. After four rings, the answering machine switched

100

on, and they heard a booming voice, "This is Donnie Mason, Anheuser Hampton's uncle. Brother Jack, we've got to stick together on this thing. Those men can't kill our children and get away with it. I know you're grieving now, but we need to talk, we need..."

Hamilton was out of his chair before Marcie and Brotherton could react. He had the answering machine cord ripped out of the phone and the machine thrown against the wall, all in one motion.

"Jack!" his wife screamed at first but then quickly calmed down. "Please, Jack...please come back to me. Please sit down."

"Do you know the Hampton's?" Brotherton asked, surprising herself because she knew the question was not as benign as it might seem to the Hamiltons. She had had her own run-ins with Anheuser Hampton. The police officer in her suddenly wanted to know if there was a possible link between the two teenagers, a link that Becka's parents might not want to acknowledge. It was a calculated and professional question, but she was personally glad to hear Marcie say, "No, I don't know those people, never heard of them."

"Would you daughter have known him?" Brotherton continued.

The two parents were silent, not because they knew or did not know the answer, but because they both realized that Brotherton was no longer in the circle formed earlier. She had a role to play in all this, but it was not to be a family member. Marcie looked at the young woman in the uniform and answered softly, "No, I'm sure she did not."

Sergeant Brotherton nodded, satisfied, knowing not to ask a follow-up question, and profoundly sad that she would never again be trusted by Becky's parents.

Jack Hamilton had not come back to sit down with his wife. He stood in the corner and leaned against the wall.

"Jack, we need to do some things. Make some preparations," Marcie said, motioning for him to come back to her. "And we should call that Hampton family tomorrow. We have to remember that they lost a child too."

Hamilton stared at his wife, then at the woman in uniform. "I don't care about them, Marcie. I don't care about that boy."

"Jack, you don't mean that. You're better than that," Marcie said, almost pleading with him, wishing that the woman in uniform was not there to hear them. "You hear me, you're better than that."

Jack Hamilton shook his head slowly, " No, I'm not, Marcie. I don't care about anybody else. I just care about Becka."

Julie had been wrong about my father. My brother Carl called and told me that I ought to come see my old man soon. Don't expect a lot of small talk, he said. Carl was always trying to reconcile me and my father. He took his role as older brother very seriously.

Athens is a two hour drive from Des Moines, long enough to prepare a conversation I would not have. Carl met me in the lobby of the nursing home, genuinely happy to see me. It had taken a lot of years and growing up, but I had finally come to love my brother. He was an overweight chiropractor, and when I saw him again I was reminded of how weak he looked. His heart was dying, but it was important to him that he outlive our father. A few years ago, Carl had taught me how to "pop" Julie's neck and hips. Strictly unprofessional, he had insisted, and he assumed no liability for my probable life-threatening incompetence, but Julie was forever grateful.

"You want an adjustment?," he said as we shook hands. "You're looking stiff, little brother."

"How's your diet?" I replied, our own ritual exchange. But this time Carl had a new line.

"I'll lose fifty pounds of this gut if you'll lose that cloud over your head."

Our hands were still clasped when he said it, and out of nowhere I pulled him closer to me and hugged him. He was as surprised as I was.

"You're not dying too, are you?" he tried to joke.

"Sorry, big brother, you and pops got that market cornered. I'm just glad to see you, that's all," I said.

As wheelchairs cruised around us, we talked about his wife and kids, he asked about Julie and Danny, and then he wanted to know more about the news from Athens. It had already made the Des Moines radio stations. I told him I had to get back home as soon as possible, as if my presence in Athens actually mattered in a crisis. Carl had always had an unrealistic opinion about the importance of a city councilman in a small college town. I was always flattered, and I seldom corrected him.

Small talk out of the way, we went to my father's room. Carl sat in a chair in a corner while I sat next to my father by the window. His nursing home was more like a hotel than one of those death-processing operations you always hear about. No stench of pine sol, no high school dropout orderlies, no vultures waiting around to scavenge for jewelry as soon as somebody keeled over. A generous military pension and my mother's foresight were cushioning my father's physical exit. Nothing could have saved his mind.

A second floor view from the back side of the building, we looked out at a rolling hill of Iowa corn, just a few inches out of the ground, so the black dirt seemed almost pin-striped in green. I sat there wondering if my father saw the same field I did. He had not acknowledged my presence. Carl would say something, trying to get his attention, but he just blinked, never turning in Carl's direction.

Carl had been right to ask me to come. My father was tissue thin, as if all his insides had been removed, and his skin was stretched over shrinking bones. I had an image come back to me, my father in my mother's bed, the first day I had seen him, bare-chested. But that man had been huge, his chest tan and muscled. I looked back at Carl. He was three of my father.

"Daddy, you okay?" I said softly to him, patting his leg to get his attention. He blinked and stared at me. "Daddy," I said louder, all the while looking at the small bandage on his forehead; another fall, another cut that seeped blood. When he finally spoke, I jerked my eyes down to meet his.

"Sonny, you want that jacket back?" he said, his hand reaching toward me. And then he was gone again. I tried to remember any story about any jacket, but I was clueless, and then Carl explained.

"Not you, Joe. The Sonny he means is his brother. Remember Uncle Sonny?"

"He died when I was still a kid. That Sonny?"

"Yep, it's daddy's favorite story. Sonny played tackle for the Chicago Cardinals in the thirties, a real mean butt-kicker. Daddy was wearing Sonny's Cardinal jacket the first time he met mother. She thought he had played pro ball. It was a year before he told her the truth. Uncle Sonny thought it was a hoot, but you know mother. She made daddy apologize in front of <u>her</u> mother and promise to never lie to her again. Daddy tried to tell her that he hadn't lied, that she had simply assumed. Anyway, mother never forgave him."

"I don't understand. This is one of his <u>favorite</u> stories?" I asked.

"Yeh, go figure," Carl laughed. "I heard it a dozen times since mother died." I looked back at my father. He was actually smiling. Carl nudged me along, "Go ahead and talk to him. He probably won't say anything, or understand much, but he's listening to you."

So I talked to my father, stories about me and Danny, about the Hollywood in Athens, but not about the Hamilton girl dying. I looked at him, then out the window at the corn, back to him. After awhile, I forgot about Carl being there as a witness, about the fact that I was slowly losing my eternal struggle with creditors, about the Hollywood finally getting some serious competition. Most of all, I talked about Julie.

I wanted her back. It was that simple. I wanted her happy again. I wanted to go back to the beach like we used to do, sit on the sand and watch the ocean. I wanted some sort of HG Wells time machine so I could go back and stop her drinking when I should have, at the beginning. Go through the house and throw out every bottle, force her to some sort of treatment. But the more I thought about all that, talking small talk out loud, the more I realized that booze was not Julie's biggest problem. Life was her problem. And I was part and parcel of the package.

"He's drifted off, Joe," Carl brought me back to my father's room.

My father's eyes were closed and his head was leaning back against his chair. I thought he was asleep, but Carl told me, "He does that a lot. Remember how we always thought he was ignoring us by walking away?" I nodded, remembering one of my father's less noble legacies, a not so passive aggression, perhaps indifference, to his family when Carl and I were boys. "Well, he can't walk too much, but he can close his eyes, act like a possum. But he's awake, trust me. Just shake him."

I reached over and nudged his arm. Then one more time. His eyes popped open, and I could swear I thought he was smiling. Hard to tell since he wasn't wearing his dentures. He looked at me and muttered, "Carl?"

Behind me, Carl laughed until he started coughing. I was flipping my attention back and forth between the two men, afraid that Carl was coughing himself into a heart attack, then slowly realizing that my father had just tricked me. Carl managed to sputter, "He's back for a few minutes, you better have that father/son moment while you can."

"How's your boy?" my father whispered. I had already given him a Danny update, but I did it again. Complete with photos. He tried to hold my wallet but dropped it as soon as I gave it to him. I picked it up and took the snapshots out of the plastic sleeves and held them up for him one at a time, telling a story with each one. Ten minutes of clarity, then a mild shudder passed through his wilting frame, and the moment was gone. Still, he did manage one line for me, the last I would get from him. "Joey, you gotta take care of your family."

He had said the same thing dozens of times in the past five years, and each time I was reduced to the most evil angel of my nature.

I was always the ironic petty son who never forgave his father's hypocrisy of telling me to take care of my family while he had ignored his own until his sons were grown and gone. But this time was different. Carl had forgiven our father years ago. It was my turn.

"I will, daddy, I will," I promised him. How I was going to do that, take care of my family, I still had to figure that out. All I had to do was go back to Athens and find an answer.

"You read the **BM FORUM** this morning?"

Bernie Huss was not in a good mood. I could always tell when she was about to vent. Her tenor voice was diving to baritone. It was especially noticeable over the phone.

"Ken is asking, just asking, for trouble," she said. "Call me back in an hour. I'm going to the gym."

The **BM FORUM** was an internet website/chat-room combination, Buzz McFadden's brainchild. I was a subscriber, as were Bernie and Harry, but we never contributed our own voices. We just listened. McFadden had set it up as soon as Ken got elected, and every Sunday night the debates began. He would offer the "news" about local issues, and everyone else would offer their "views." Neither the news nor the views had to be grounded in reality.

I had a special animus toward the **BM FORUM**. Because I hadn't been "progressive" enough for the Rumble-ites, one of them had nicknamed me "Joseph Hollow." Soon enough, I was a caricature of that damn T. S. Eliot poem. It was a small universe, the **BM FORUM**, a few hundred regular readers, and being their whipping boy was no big deal. But then a reporter from the **Athens TELEGRAM** quoted some **FORUM** tirade against me for the paper, and some headline writer/page editor who was new to town saw the name Hollow and put it in the headline: *Hollow Opposes Rumble Plan to Reduce Capital Projects Budget.*

At the next televised council meeting, one of Ken's supporters came to the microphone and pleaded with "Mr. Hollow" to change his mind. The bastard never smiled. Harry and Bernie—they thought it was hilarious. Bernie didn't think it was funny the next week, however, when somebody from WHIP wrote in the **FORUM** that "Bernadette Hussy is a gender bending Benedict Arnold."

Two mornings after Becky Hamilton died, the **BM FORUM** was a call to arms. Dozens of voices were screaming for Harry to be fired, and it seemed like everyone had an Athens police horror story. Some harassment, some profiling, some verbal or physical abuse, no story so outrageous that it could not be topped by the next response. That the **BM FORUM** was a hotbed of mis-information and hysteria, that was no surprise. But there was something different about the views this time. There were names of people who had never contributed before, people who I thought were immune to Ken Rumble. A lot of professors from Iowa Arts, even some business owners I knew, none of them left-wing full mooners. But they were angry too. How could this have happened in Athens—that was their question. Who's in charge? Who was—responsible?

As I read the notes, other notes were added at the same time, as if I was reading a book that was writing itself as I read, as if it would never end. One of the first notes was from Ken Rumble, insisting that *"the people need to speak up about this tragedy. We need to hear from you, we need to see you at the next meeting."* Like a stone in water, his note set off the ripple notes that followed. Car pools were being organized. Babysitters were in demand. Blades were being sharpened.

I stopped reading after an hour and called Bernie. "You bringing a sleeping bag to the next meeting?" I tried to joke. "A book to read?"

"Very funny, Joe, so funny I forgot to laugh," she said.

"Bernie, I know how __not__ funny all this is, trust me. I'm just hoping that we can get through this without Al shooting us in the foot or Ken making us look like Nazis," I said.

"And I'm hoping that Steve Nash can handle the meeting," she said. "I wrote out a statement for him to deliver at the beginning of the meeting, something to express regret but without admitting so much that their lawyer uses it against us in court. But you and I both know that Steve Nash could make the Lord's Prayer sound like a laundry list. Now, I kick myself all the time for not supporting you for mayor. As smug as you are…"

"As smug as __I am__," I almost laughed. "Bernie, I'm a middleweight champ. You and Ken are the sumo super-heavyweights of…"

"Fair enough," she interrupted my interruption, "but my point is that we need somebody as mayor this week who can talk in public, and Steve Nash isn't that person. So I'm counting on you to step in as soon as Steve starts tripping over his tongue."

"And your role?"

"My role is to keep Al on the shortest leash I can. I've already gone to see him. He knows he's a hothead; I'll give him credit for that. He's promised to stay cool, even though he agrees with me about how it's our own fault that thugs like that Hampton kid are the chickens who've finally come home to roost in the housing program you and Ken are so proud of. As soon as this blows over, we're going to have a serious discussion about the housing program. This time I'll get my four votes."

"Bernie, you know as well as I do that the problem with the housing program is that it doesn't go far enough. Some job training programs, recreation programs, life-skills programs, more than roofs and doors is what's needed…" I stopped myself. "I'll fight that fight later…"

"And you'll lose, Joe. But for now, let's get through the meeting next week, okay?"

"Fair enough," I said. "In fact, I was thinking we should call a special meeting just to deal with this issue. A separate meeting to give people a chance to let off some steam, to show that we're not just crowding them into a business as usual agenda."

"That's sounds like a Rumble idea," she said, and the tone of her voice was clearly suspicious.

"The problem with you and the others is that you know that Ken is predictable. But you won't admit that he can be right sometimes. You beat him by ignoring him. This is my idea, this special meeting, but if I don't suggest it—Ken will."

"Now I remember why I didn't support you for mayor," she said dryly. "You've always been a Rumble wanna-be."

"Just talk to Steve, okay?" I said, wanting to get off the phone and downtown to the Hollywood to do a concession inventory. As Bernie was telling me again that it was a bad idea, that it would merely play into the hands of the Rumble supporters, I unfolded that morning's **TELEGRAM**. On the bottom half of the front page were side-by-side pictures of Anheuser Hampton and Becky Hamilton. I stopped listening to Bernie and just held the phone loosely against my ear, staring at the girl's picture.

The last thing Bernie asked had me that morning was, "Aren't you glad you came back for another term?"

I told her, "Yeh, like a man who re-marries his first wife." Not especially witty, not at all profound, but I was distracted. That girl was looking at me.

The dreams began the second night. The first night, Jack Hamilton did not sleep. He sat on the couch with Marcie, after they had gone to the hospital and funeral home, and kept his arm around her shoulder as she finally went to sleep. He sat up all night, his arm going numb after awhile, but he did not want to do anything to wake up Marcie, so he remained still as she slept. He sat there in the dark and thought about his daughter.

In the morning, he and Marcie went to Phil Reisetter's house next door to make phone calls. Reisetter had done some legal work for them in the past, and he was a good neighbor. He had seen the television truck pull up in front of the Hamilton house, and he knew the media circus was about to begin. So he went through his backyard and over to his neighbors, and he suggested that they use his house to make any calls they wanted. "You stay home; you won't have any peace and quiet. I'll be at my office all day, and my wife will be gone too," he said, "and nobody will know you're at our place."

As Marcie sat in the Reisetter study and made calls, Jack Hamilton watched the cars and trucks park in front of his house, the reporters coming and going, a few remaining for hours in their cars but finally giving up. He was fascinated by one reporter who actually went around the house looking in all the windows, pressing his face against the panes. At one point, he thought the reporter was actually going to climb through an open window. The man pushed up the window and stuck his head inside, obviously yelling into the house, and then raised his upper torso over the windowsill, his body half inside, his feet dangling. Hamilton surprised himself. He did nothing. The reporter finally backed out of the window and went back to knock on the front door. He then sat on a porch chair for an hour, greeting other reporters who came later. Eventually, he, too, went away. After he left, a television crew arrived and a young small woman in a red suit was filmed on the front porch, speaking into a camera, her intense body language conveying the right amount of weight to support her words. Arrival and departure, set-up and breakdown, took ten minutes.

Before noon, Hamilton had seen dozens of visitors, including Sergeant Brotherton and another man in uniform who arrived in a police car with her. After them, only a few minutes later, a silver Buick arrived, unloading an older black man and a young white woman carrying a briefcase. The older black man pounded on Hamilton's door, his voice loud enough to be heard through the open window of the Phil Reisetter's study. Hamilton recognized the voice as the one on his answering machine last night.

"Mr. Hamilton!" the man almost bellowed as he kept hitting the door. "I understand your grief. I understand why you would want to be alone at this tragic moment. But I want you to know that I am here to help you. I will leave you my card, and perhaps we can talk tonight. I am a man of God and a man of the law. I offer the aid of both."

Behind his neighbor's curtain, Jack Hamilton thought to himself, "Nobody talks like that in real life. Surely, this man is not real." He watched as the man motioned to the woman holding the briefcase. She pulled a small card out of the breast pocket of her dark jacket, then a roll of tape out of the briefcase, and the man scribbled something on the back of the card, handed it back to her, and she taped it to the front door. Every reporter who came after them looked at the card and made notes. The next day, three area newspapers reported that the Reverend Donald Mason, Attorney at Law, uncle to Anheuser Hampton, was representing the Hampton and Hamilton families.

Tired of watching his house, Hamilton studied his wife calling relatives. With her address book in her lap, she began each call with almost the same words, "We've got some very sad news…" and each time she would make eye contact with Hamilton, wanting him to just—be there. She had suggested that he call his side of the family, but he had begged off. He could not do it, not even to his own mother and brothers. Marcie intuitively understood that if he did not have to break the news to anyone, then he did not have to hear his own voice say that Becka was dead. She made the calls to Chicago, and she told the Hamiltons that Jack would call them later. "He needs some time," she said, looking directly at him as he nodded. She remembered a line from her mother years ago, the day Becka was born, a joke then, "Birth and death, men are too weak for either one." She wished her mother was still alive.

Hamilton was with his wife all day and into the night, doing everything she told him to do. But he seldom spoke. When she asked him about clothes for Becka to be buried in, he told her to make the decision. The services? She was the one who went to church every week, he reminded her, so he would let her handle those details. Flowers or charitable donations as a memorial? He did not care. There was only one point about which he was adamant. The casket would be closed for the visitation at the Donohue-Lensing Funeral Home. Marcie was puzzled.

"Jack, she's still beautiful. Mike and Vicki did everything right. She looks…" and she struggled for a word, settling for something that she knew was inadequate, "…she looks like an angel. Don't you want her to be remembered that way?"

"Except for me and you, I don't want anyone else to see her," he said, remembering the moment at two o'clock that morning when he and Marcie had gone to the funeral home to pick out a casket.

"Jack…" Marcie spoke with her head down, "…if the casket is closed, everyone will assume the worst, that she is…"

"I know, Marcie, I know," he said, reaching for her hand, "but I don't care what they think. I don't want anyone to see her except me and you. Can't you understand that? She doesn't belong to them.

113

She's our baby. Ours."

"We can do that, Jack, except for our families. We can have a private viewing before everyone else arrives, just your family and mine. Is that…"

"Oh my God!" Hamilton moaned and began convulsing, his numbness and postponed grief turning to open rage. "My God My God! Marcie, my God, you're right! They're part of this too. How can I be so selfish? How can I be so goddam selfish? Why am I this way? Who do I think I am?" He had stood up and Marcie could see his eyes blink furiously. "I don't know what to do, Marcie. I just want to wake up and someone tell me that Becka is going to come home. And she can yell at me or blame me for anything she wants. That's all I want," his voice getting louder. "I don't believe in angels, you know that. I don't want her to be one of your angels. I want her home! And I want the rest of the world to go away."

By ten o'clock that night, exhaustion put Jack Hamilton to sleep, and the dreams began. He was back in Chicago, in his old neighborhood. In the dream his house was next to Lake Michigan, not on the south side, but the Lake was more like an ocean, with towering waves and a sandy coastline that stretched for miles in either direction. Hamilton could not swim so he stayed on the beach staring as the surf pounded the shore. On the horizon, giant ships sailed back and forth, ships that were sometimes modern, sometimes old sailing ships. It was a clear day, but the sound of drums was everywhere, drums that sounded like thunder. In his dream, Hamilton wanted to get in the water but he knew he was too weak. The beach was crowded with other people, then empty, and cars were racing up and down the hard sand. Each receding wave left more and more jellyfish on the shore, so many that he had to watch where he walked. Then, like all dreams, everything changed. He was on one of those boats out in the ocean, looking back toward the Chicago skyline, but

114

the buildings were just large versions of the buildings in Athens. The old Jefferson Hotel, the new Sheraton, the Firstar clock clearly visible. Becka was on the boat with him, and she wanted to surf back to shore. She had one of those hard Styrofoam boards, covered with some sort of shiny cloth, barely large enough to stand on, but she insisted. Hamilton was no older than his daughter, in his dream. She was wearing a rubbery black bodysuit, her skin looking barely brown in contrast to the suit.

Becka dived overboard, waving at her teenage father as she stood on the board to catch the next swell. Hamilton looked around for Marcie, but all he saw on the deck were benches like the ones on the pedestrian mall of Athens. As soon as he sat down he was back on the beach waiting for Becka to come ashore. The sky was suddenly dark, but the ocean was full of a thousand green lights a few feet below the surface. As if the ocean were a sky with green stars. He was alone on the beach. Then he heard a high pitched squeaking noise, followed by a bass drum, and then far out in the ocean he could see a white glow that rose up out of the starry water and then went back in, rising with the squeaking whine, descending with the drum. In his dream, he knew it was a dolphin coming toward him, in that fluid motion of ascension and descent, white arcs coming toward him, but as the arc got closer he could see that it was the giant deer that he had seen on the ped mall in Athens. A huge blue deer, antlers blazing green flames, in and out of the water, swimming like a dolphin, until it took one last dive and then did not surface. That was when Jack Hamilton knew he had made a terrible mistake by letting Becka surf to shore. The ocean was full of sharks. He began screaming for her to come out of the water. Then he was flying over the water looking for her, but he was too close to see much more than the few waves directly under him, dark shapes twisting beneath the surface. He was terrified because he could sense the danger she was in, and he began to feel her terror as she realized that she was surrounded by sharks and they were closing in on her. In the dream, he became his daughter. He was falling into the ocean, his arms flailing, screaming with no sound coming out of his mouth, and as he hit the water he could see a pulsating blue flame coming up toward him from deep in the blackest depth of the of the ocean floor. Then he was awake.

That was the first dream. In the weeks to follow, there were others. Sometimes his daughter was not in them, sometimes the dreams were full of light and pleasant distortions of everyday reality, but the deer was always there. He never told Marcie.

The morning after the first dream, Hamilton got a call from Phil Reisetter. "Just a heads-up, Jack," he said, calling from his office. "I was just contacted by Donald Mason, the attorney for the Hampton family. He wanted to hire me to co-litigate."

Hamilton did not understand. "A lawyer wants to hire another lawyer?"

"Mason is not certified to practice in Iowa, and it makes sense to get some assistance if you're coming into a system where you don't know the judges or have a sense of the community. But that wasn't what he really wanted."

Hamilton still did not understand.

"Look, Jack, somehow he found out that I was your lawyer, and your neighbor, and he wanted me to bring you along for the Hampton's lawsuit. He wanted me to make a pitch to you to get you on board their train."

"Are you 'pitching' me now?" Hamilton asked.

"I told him to go to hell," Reisetter said. "Told him that in this situation I wanted to be your friend, not your lawyer. Told him to kiss my corn fed ass."

Hamilton felt a surge of tears, and he took a slow breath, but he did not speak.

"I'm here if you need me," Reisetter continued, "but not as a lawyer. You want free advice, you've got it, but not representation. If you want a list of names of good attorneys, I can give you that too. But let me tell you right now—stay away from Mason. He's a barracuda, and you'll smell his stink a long time after he's gone."

"He'll get me a lot of money?" Hamilton asked quietly.

Reisetter hesitated before answering, "If that's what you want."

"I want my daughter back, Phil. Can he get me enough money to bring her back?"

Reisetter sat in his office after he finished talking to Hamilton, muttering to himself, and to his neighbor across town, as he stared at the appointment calendar on his desk, "He's good, very good, Jack, but he's not _that_ good. Still, it'll be a great show."

You ever smell trouble? Smell something that makes your skin crawl, and every time that smell hits you then you look around for a place to hide? Betty Norris had that smell, and Betty Norris was trouble. A skinny woman, hair down to her waist, thick-lensed glasses, a missionary. Worst of all, she was a reporter for the **TELEGRAM**.

I had known her only as a byline name, the reporter who had the Iowa Arts College beat. Her stories were some of the best in the paper. Harry would send me a clipping sometimes, especially when Norris revealed something about the college he could not. Her best story was about travel expenses for the administration. Evidently, first class seating was the rule rather than an exception, all at taxpayer expense.

At the news conference that Harry and the Police Chief had arranged, I smelled her before I saw her. The **TELEGRAM** local government reporter was down front, asking some generic questions about when and where and all that, and Harry was knocking them out of the park. Then this smell behind me starting asking WHY it happened, WHY the cop did not stop the chase, meta-physical questions that only God could answer, and Harry went into his City Manager mode. I wanted to make eye contact with him, to somehow tell him to lighten up.

"Can you explain why you instructed Council member Baroli to not speak with the press, Mr. Hopkins?" Norris asked, and that's when everyone in the civic center pressroom turned to face her. I wondered if they all smelled the same thing.

Harry grimaced, but he spoke with the assurance of someone who thought he had truth on his side. "At no time did I tell Al Baroli or any other council member to not speak to the press. At no time."

Norris pulled a small tape recorder out of her giant cloth bag, punched a button, and a room full of press had a story. Al Baroli's voice was clear, "I can't talk to you. The City Manager told us to keep quiet. The damn lawyers are swimming around like sharks..." and then click.

Harry was momentarily stunned, but I thought I had an explanation, so I volunteered, "I think what Al was trying to say was that the City Manager urged all of us to be careful about what we said, that we needed to be precise in..."

Norris cut me off, "Mr. Holly, are you speaking for Al Baroli or the City Manager?" I was confused and fascinated at the same time. Why was this woman so angry? And why was she asking these questions when the **TELEGRAM** had obviously sent somebody else to cover the story.

"I'm speaking for myself," I started again, forever bonding her smell with some abstract concept of trouble. "I was merely...."

She punched the tape machine again, and a re-wound Al Baroli said the same thing, after which she added, "And Mr. Baroli was speaking for himself. I'm wondering now who is speaking for the Council. You, Mr. Holly...you, Mr. Hopkins? In other words, a lot of people want to know who is in charge. Who is responsible for these deaths?"

From bad to worse, from tragedy to conspiracy to cover-up. Harry's news conference was a disaster. He was as confused as I was. Even more confused was the Police Chief, who was asked only a few questions, and didn't know the answer to what seemed the simplest: What kind of car was the officer driving? The Chief blinked and said, "I'll have to get back to you." It was a straightforward answer, and perfectly understandable given the fact that the Athens police department drove three different kinds of cars. Not an efficient policy, but designed to spread city purchasing among three different local dealerships, so nobody could accuse "The City" of playing favorites. Each dealer charged the same, so it wasn't a question of money, just fairness, or so Harry had thought. But when one of those cars is involved in a chase that kills two kids, and the Police Chief doesn't know what kind of car was involved, then the story becomes more than conspiracy and cover-up, it now becomes a case of "competence." What kind of Chief can't answer a simple question? No wonder the department is "out of control."

The truth should matter, but if truth is too mushy, maybe the facts? The Chief didn't know what kind of car was driven. Was it a sign of some bigger problem? Harry didn't tell Al Baroli to keep quiet. He advised him the same as he had told all of us, to be careful what we said. But Al thought he was speaking to Betty Norris off the record, and he didn't know he was being recorded, and he said later that "that woman" had ticked him off anyway. And the comment about the sharks was his, not Harry's, so Al called the **TELEGRAM** the same afternoon of the press conference wanting "to clarify" his remarks before they went to press the next morning. The **TELEGRAM** accepted his version, but the **BM FORUM** was not so malleable. A few hundred subscribers to the internet news were convinced: *The deaths of two black teenagers are the logical culmination of a city government that has lost touch with the people. Thank god that Ken Rumble is still here.*

More facts became distorted or re-interpreted. Harry had said at the press conference that he had, indeed, talked to every council member as soon as he had the basic facts clear. The **BM FORUM** reported: *The City Manager called every council member EXCEPT for Kenneth Rumble. Why was the only progressive member of the council not privy to the information that the City Manager deemed to dole out. Why start a cover-up so soon? What is Hopkins hiding?*

Harry was on the phone with me an hour after that was posted. "Those bastards know I'm not going to get in a piss fight with them. They know I won't respond."

"Harry, you said you talked to all of us. So just call them up and demand a correction." I thought it would be simple, but Harry reminded me that the **BM FORUM** didn't have an editor to call. It was an open chat-room. To get a correction would require that he actually post his comments. He refused to step in that arena.

"I asked Ken to go on-line and correct it, but all he said was that I should do it myself, that I should not be afraid of public debate. He says that 'the people' don't feel connected to me because they didn't get to vote on me, some horseshit like that. Then he has the balls to tell me that the **BM FORUM** was 'technically correct.' That I did not call him, that he called me. A goddam distinction without a difference, I tell him, that I was calling the Council in alphabetical order, like I always do, and then you know what he says to me, Joe, the nerve of the guy! He tells me that he does not appreciate me using profanity around him."

I had to stop him, and I had to work hard not to laugh even though all of this was deadly serious. "Harry, you don't call us in alphabetical order. That's horseshit. You call the mayor first, then me, then Bernie, and then whoever else you want to, and I'd guess that you call Ken Rumble last every time. Right?"

"Of course I call him last! I wish I didn't have to call him at all, but it's part of my job. Jesus, this is getting messy and you guys haven't even had your meeting yet. All I know is that when this blows over, I'm using all my vacation time that I've never used. The Bahamas, and I might never come back. You guys will be on your own."

The wind didn't blow over. Not for a long time. Bernie thought so, Harry thought so, even I thought so. More like a hurricane, we were merely at the edges, getting closer to the eye, where the wind was most destructive. After that first press conference, two funerals. After the funerals, the Council's first public meeting since the chase. After the Council meeting, a mob downtown. After the mob, Hartford in the park. After Hartford, the calm eye. After the eye, a death in my family. After death, freedom. You have to bear with me. All I'm telling you, it's the dissertation I never wrote.

Anheuser Hampton was buried first. The day after Harry's debacle. I told the Mayor that the Council ought to be represented, but Steve Nash was afraid to go. Actually, not afraid. Just cautious, afraid his presence would be some sort of provocation. I called Bernie and asked her to go with me. Strange thing about a crisis, you learn things about people that surprise you. Two hours at the Broadway Baptist Church, in the back of a room with a hundred wailing black people, Bernie's eyes saw something different than mine. And I never saw her the same again.

I tried to be cynical and hypocritical. I was there to represent the Council, but I knew enough about Hampton to know that his death wasn't a loss to society. Next to me, Bernie kept quietly grunting every time another black woman stood up and cried out for Jesus. First week of June in Iowa, hot and more than humid. The air was liquid. It hadn't rained in a month, and the humidity had developed almost overnight, like being in labor too long, oppressive and exhausting, and Broadway Baptist didn't have air conditioning. Three huge ceiling fans turned slowly, hand-held fans were flapping like hummingbird wings, and all of us were sweating.

I was probably still a hypocrite, but I couldn't remain a cynic for long. Not even when Ken Rumble showed up and walked past me and Bernie to the front row to shake hands with the Reverend/Barrister right honorable Donald Mason, freeze-framing for a moment as a camera flashed. Following Rumble were his disciples, the only other white faces in the church except for me and Bernie. Then I smelled Betty Norris coming toward and then past us.

Bernie had explained the smell to me after I told her about the City Manager's press conference. "Betty is a true believer, well known in some of my circles, Joe. Doesn't shave her armpits or legs." Bernie had tightened her face as if somebody had eaten sulfur and then farted in her presence, "and her…body aroma…is fatal, so she tries to cover it up with some home grown organic perfume. Her sweat and that perfume, not a…success. But it is an effective test of friendship."

"You think this is all of them?" Bernie whispered to me as the choir began at Hampton's funeral.

"All of them?" I whispered back, thinking that she was referring to Ken and his group.

"Every African-American Negro in Athens?" she said, gently poking me in the side with her elbow. "You know, your core constituents."

I'm fifty-something. I'm a smart guy. I grew up in the south. I was six, I remember distinctly, when my father told me, "Joey, go ask that nigger in the red cap to come get these bags for us" as we got off a train in Shreveport, and I did it. I walked up to that old black man and said, "Nigger man, my daddy wants you to get our bags." The words meant nothing to me, and I thought it was natural when the old black man simply said, "Yessir, you just lead the way, little man." I remember all this because my father would tell the story over and over, and we would all laugh when he got to the part where he repeated how the old man had said, "little man."

When Bernie said "African-American Negro" it sounded like she was really saying nigger. At least, that's what I heard. The witty, socially liberal lesbian I thought I had known, she disappeared. For the next hour I was alone, even with her standing beside me.

I couldn't respond to Bernie at that moment because I heard "Amazing Grace" for the first time in forty years. You can tell me that it has become a movie and TV cliché, slapped into a plot anytime somebody wants to make some sort of spiritual statement. You're right. It's been pulverized into transparent vapor. But the first song of the Broadway Baptist congregation, to honor and mourn a drug-dealing teenage rapist, began as a single tremulous female voice and slowly swelled into a statement of true faith in the hearts of a hundred souls on a boiling day in Iowa. That was what I had not heard in forty years.

I was back in Fort Worth, seeing Jesus, preaching Jesus. And I understood again that Grace was amazing. I understood it, but I no longer believed it. I wanted to. I wanted Jesus to walk into the Broadway Baptist Church and raise that wretched Hampton boy up again. It would make more than his death tolerable.

If it happened that morning, Jesus there and lifting that boy up to heaven, if it happened, I didn't see it, but I could feel other people seeing it. Especially in the heart of a tiny black woman in the front row, ten feet away from a closed white coffin, Hampton's grandmother, who rocked and sang and wept and visioned her daughter's child taken to sit next to God the father.

Until Donald Mason stood up to preach, I was willing to suspend my disbelief in God, my belief in his absence. But Mason brought me back to the secular Athens. For the first fifteen minutes, I was impressed. The man could preach. He even made a special point of thanking "Ken Rumble here in front and his two brethren in the back for sharing our grief," cueing the congregation to turn around and see Bernie and me. Mason was better than I ever was, but something was wrong. He made the point, over and over, that although Hampton was a fallen child, a sinner, no mistake about that, he was also a gift of god, boilerplate language but poetry for those who needed it, and Mason shed tears as he said it. A gift of god, abused by a cruel world, Hampton was a victim of society, the "debris of society, a victim as much as that other poor child who met him at that crossroads."

I kept looking at Hampton's grandmother, wondering how she felt as Mason called her boy "debris" and "lost." The woman kept her head down, and she stopped rocking. Mason finally made his real point, resurrecting a name from history that still had power.

"You all remember Emmett Till, I know you do. You all remember his broken body in Mississippi and then brought home to Chicago…" and the congregation nodded amen, "…and how he was victimized, beaten and broken, and his mama made them look at what they had done to her boy."

That's when my stomach started churning. I thought to myself, "Surely, this sonuvabitch is not going to do what I think he's going to do." I whispered to Bernie, "I think we need to get out of here, soon!" But she seemed to be enjoying herself, as if everything around her was some sort of anthropology class.

"You all remember one of our first martyrs. I know you do." Mason was turning the congregation into a crowd. "I want you to remember this boy as well as you remember Emmett Till. I don't want you to ever forget **THIS BOY!**"

I grabbed Bernie's hand, but she jerked it away just as Mason stepped in front of Hampton's coffin, pounded his fist on the white lid, and then lifted it with one hand while his other hand was raised in the air as if calling down God. He slowly turned to face the crowd, his body blocking their view, and with his eyes glistening he intoned, "Do not forget THIS." Then he stepped aside.

Even from the back of the church, Bernie could see clearly. All she could do was gasp, "Oh my God!"

Becky Hamilton's service was the next day at St. Mary's, my church. I say it's my church because I go there every Sunday. I even go there sometimes in the afternoon during the week, when it is usually empty. My own metaphysical question: if I'm the only person there, is St. Mary's still empty? I go to St. Mary's because that's where Julie and I had started years earlier. I go because Kathy and Danny were christened there. I go there because it is quiet. I go there because, in that sort of medieval iconic way that the best Catholic churches are, it is inspiring. Stained glass, paintings, towering life-sized statues coming out of the walls marking the Stations of the Cross, high blue arching ceilings, all the aesthetics of faith and reverence. I go there, still reverent, but faithless.

St. Mary's was packed, probably close to a thousand mourners, almost all of them white. I didn't ask Bernie to go with me. I was still processing her, for lack of a better word, her "tone" from the day before. I asked Julie to go with me, but she begged off. I wanted Danny to go with me, but then I thought he might get too restless in such a long service. I went by myself after a night of almost no sleep, a pattern that would last until the election. For the next five months I would be getting by on three or four hours, tops, and I was always tired. Harry kept telling me, "You're getting too grumpy, Joe. You're going to snap somebody's head off one of these days."

I went early and got my regular seat on the right side. My first jolt was seeing the parents of Becky Hamilton as they entered to sit on the front row. Her white mother was a surprise, because she was white and also because I recognized her as a St. Mary's parishioner who was always at the same services I attended. But it was the father that really intrigued me. I knew him, that was the shock. Not by name, but by contact. I had gone to the Athens post-office for almost twenty years, and I had done business with the father hundreds of times. He was the only black clerk in the post-office, but I had never registered his name. He was just the big friendly black guy who sold me stamps or weighed my packages. I tried to remember precisely the image of the girl that had been on the front page of the paper. I stared at her father, then her mother. I didn't see either of them in the face I remembered.

Sitting to the father's left were two of the largest black men I had ever seen, large enough to be over-weight professional football linemen. Then a line of black women and children. To the mother's right were solid, pale Iowa men and women. In front of them, to their left, was Becky's casket, covered in a gray pall, topped by a small bouquet of white roses. From where I sat, I couldn't see the father's face clearly, especially since his head was always turned toward the casket. Even when Father West was speaking, the father kept staring at that casket.

Late that night, with Julie asleep on the couch, her head resting on my lap as I flipped channels trying to make myself tired enough to go to sleep, I re-played the most dramatic moment of the service. The entrance of Donald Mason and Ken Rumble. Before the initial processional, a beautiful Korean girl was playing flute up front, notes so pure and clear that you could hear them in heaven, I was sure. As the music ended, Mason and Rumble, and their entourage, entered St. Mary's, walked to the front, and began shaking hands with Hamilton's family line first, pausing to express condolences. Fair enough, and acceptable as part of the ritual, but, when Mason got to the father and extended his hand, Hamilton ignored him. Mason kept his hand extended, kept leaning down in the father's face, but the father was rigid as a stone. From my seat, I could see Mason's face beseeching Hamilton for a gesture of solidarity, black man to black man, us against them, but then Hamilton tilted his head slightly to one side. He must have said something to Mason because Mason's head snapped back and his eyes narrowed, but he withdrew his hand. It was only a split second of honesty, Mason's face at that moment, and then he was quickly back on message as he stepped over to the mother, who accepted his offer.

I was spellbound, watching Ken Rumble step up next, oblivious to what had just happened, extend his hand, to be rejected like Mason. I was trying to remember the father's name right then. It must have been in the **TELEGRAM,** but I didn't remember it. Who was this man, I wanted to know. How angry was he? How else to explain his refusal to shake hands? At my most petty, I was disappointed that Hamilton ignored all the other attempts to shake his hand, not just Mason and Rumble's. I wanted him to represent a rejection of <u>their</u> duplicity, but I also knew that he would have probably scorned my hand as well.

Unlike Broadway Baptist, the music in St. Mary's didn't transport me back to my past. Didn't really inspire me. The music at St. Mary's was always good. Short Patti McTaggart and tall Amy Kanellis sang acapella, and I was sure that their God was in their voices. The Athens High School choir was there, and hundreds of people wept as they sang "On Eagle's Wings." But I was immune. I was in my own church, concentrating on the large black man a few rows in front of me, wondering why I felt less emotional here than I did at Broadway. Then again, I had not felt any emotion in St. Mary's for years.

Father West was a large priest, a teacher at Regina High School. He didn't rant or rave. He seldom even raised his voice. I had come to St. Mary's for years and always looked forward to his homilies. West had christened my children, and I wondered if he had done the same for Becky Hamilton.

Becky's father was not listening to Father West. Only once did he seem aware of things around him. Only once did I see him almost lose control. Near the end, during a song that I had never heard in St. Mary's. Truth is, the Catholic Church has the worst taste in music. Calling it bland is too kind. It's the only thing I miss about the Baptists. But there I was, hearing a flute solo by that Korean girl, hearing the music before the Athens High choir filled St. Mary's with the words of "How Can I Keep From Singing?" I grabbed a songbook from the back of the pew in front of me. There it was, page 405, all the time an option but never chosen, a Quaker song. I watched Becky's father finally look up at the ceiling, then back and forth, and then put his massive arm across his wife's shoulders next to him. <u>How</u> could anyone keep from singing at <u>that</u> moment? I could have given a few reasons, but nobody was asking me. I guess I was the only person in St. Mary's who appreciated the irony.

Becky Hamilton was buried at Oakland Cemetery. Only a few dozen people from the St. Mary's service went to the gravesite. I wasn't going to, but as I sat there I kept wondering about that father.

The weather was surprisingly mild that afternoon, especially considering how hot and humid the day before had been. I walked to Oakland, getting there just as Father West was finishing. I had seen them from a distance, just as I came up over the rise of the last small hill. From there, I could see how close they were to the Black Angel, in a plot made possible by the expansion I engineered years earlier, and then I looked back toward Babyland. I went there instead of to Becky Hamilton's grave.

I could have found Kathy's grave if I were blind. I had gone there in the dark and in the day, and counted my footsteps a hundred times, knowing how many steps until a turn, what to avoid. I had even played a game with Danny, making him lead me like I was sightless, so I knew he could find it on his own one of these days. I was being optimistic about that, I knew, but it mattered.

I talked to Kathy for a long time. Told her all about her brother's latest drawing, her mother's new book, Hartford's latest sighting, but I didn't tell her about Becky Hamilton.

When Kathy was buried, there had been no trees around her, but fifteen years had provided shade. I talked for a long time, until my lack of sleep from the night before started to catch up with me. I told her I would be back with Danny, and perhaps her mother, soon. Then I walked back over the rise to see Becky Hamilton's grave, assuming everybody would be gone.

Under the tent next to her grave, her mother and father were still sitting there, surrounded by rows of empty chairs.

Do you have a favorite miracle? Water to wine? Death to life? Shadrach, Meschach, the other guy? My new favorite is the weather the day Becky Hamilton was buried. Out of nowhere, a perfect spring day. The day before, a sauna; the day after, a hotter sauna. Even Denny Frary, the television weatherman, raved about the "sudden downdraft of Canadian air" that cooled off Iowa for a day.

The day after the girl's funeral, Harry announced that The Cop— not a name anymore, just a role—The Cop was no longer employed by Athens. The Cop's attorney said that The Cop had left town. The Reverend Donald Mason's legal team filed a suit against the city, charging "wrongful death and racial discrimination." Al Baroli called me and wanted to know if I agreed with him that the suit was "total bullshit and we ought to counter-sue the bastards." The Hampton suit was a stretch, but the City Attorney sent a confidential memo urging us to meet in executive session soon and discuss a settlement. The Hamilton parents weren't heard from, but we assumed they were coming at us too.

Betty Norris announced that she had quit her job at the **TELEGRAM,** saying that she objected to its timid response to the mis-management by the Athens city government and the probable malfeasance of the City Manager. She was an instant celebrity.

Bernie wasn't impressed, "The phony had already given a month's notice before those kids even died. She was going back to school to get a master's. She had a week left on the job, but now she's a damn paragon of integrity." Bernie seldom cursed, especially on the phone.

Harry then called to let me know that the front window of the Hollywood had been vandalized, along with the front to Bernie's store.

"Whose side are you on?" had been spray-painted a dozen places downtown.

"And you'll love this, Joe," he said. "The **BM FORUM** is putting out a print edition, all over town, handed out like a fire-sale flyer. My picture, your picture...none too flattering, I might add...the whole Council, along with home and work numbers. And a call for a big turnout at tonight's meeting. Bring your coffee."

Danny and I walked downtown to scrape the paint off our windows. I had it easy. Somebody had painted the stone front of Bernie's store. She was going to have to pay for sandblasting. Everywhere I went that morning, I was stopped and asked how things were going. People who knew me also knew about Danny, so they didn't try to keep me long, but most people simply knew I was on the Council, and it was their constitutional right to yell at me—until Danny started yelling back at them.

The meeting was at seven that night. By six, the civic center was surrounded by hundreds of people. Ken was on the steps, telling them that they needed to let the Council know how they felt. He had a bullhorn, and Betty Norris stood under him handing out sheets of the latest **BM FORUM**. I had to admit it, Rumble looked good up there, his shirt soaked in sweat, his hair flowing around that handsome face of his. He could have been truly charismatic, but his voice was not meant for real life. He needed a debate forum, preferably on television, not a crowd to exhort. After a few minutes, even his supporters were visibly bored. They were angry and restless, and they didn't want to hear about Roberts' Rules of Order.

I watched the crowd from the corner, wondering if I should go to the side entrance, and then Al Baroli showed up, poked me in the back and blew cigar smoke past my head. "You know how pissed I am right now?" he said, offering me a contraband Cuban. I assumed he was talking about the crowd. "You know how arrogant the college kids are in this town?" I still assumed he meant the crowd. "I'm driving down here tonight. And they look right at you and then step out in the street, daring you to hit their sorry asses, as if a red light for them don't mean shit." I was used to hearing Al's profanity. "And if you don't yield to them they get all high and mighty, and worse." Worse? "Listen to me, Joe, they look right at you, step out in front of you, and then they start walking slower. Goddam it! Slower!"

I wondered how Al's students at Branstad Community College handled him. "Al, those kids are your bread and butter," I said, still keeping my eye on Rumble.

"My students are not like the artsy-fartsy crowd you got here in town, Joe. The world's not their oyster."

Al kept talking, but I kept trying to figure out why these people were here. It was not like any crowd I had ever seen at a council meeting. Two teenagers were dead, for sure. The Cop was responsible, for sure. But this crowd wanted something more than an explanation. Something more than an apology.

The heat was oppressive, and the air conditioning in the civic center was turned down too low, so all the front windows were blurred by condensation. Dozens of people were carrying signs. WHO'S IN CHARGE? WHO DO WE CHARGE? ATHENS = POLICE STATE? TWO DEAD AND A COP FREE? Variations on a theme. Everybody knew about the chase, The Cop's refusal to turn back, his resignation, Harry's press conference, The Chief's gaffes, Donald Mason's admonition to remember the Hampton boy. Then I saw the picture poster. It had been facing away from me, toward Rumble up front, and then it twirled around, connected to a hand that ascended from the crowd, a hand without a body, it seemed. A giant picture of Hampton in his coffin.

Those pictures of aborted fetuses that protesters wave at abortion clinics, this was worse. A recognizable human form, bludgeoned into a profane mush. You stare, and then you look away. Al saw it when I did, and I heard him whisper, "Oh, shit, this is going to be bad tonight."

The crowd was full of cell phones. You talk on a cell phone, your voice gets louder. And everybody wants to have their own unique ring, so that hot humid night in early June, my stomach was turning with the sight of a mangled black boy, the air was full of angry voices, competing bells and buzzers and chimes, and then I started to smile because I saw Ken up front, still talking, oblivious to the fact that the crowd wasn't listening. I smelled Betty Norris, but I didn't see her anywhere.

You have one of those moments? When you wonder how the hell you ended up where you are at that exact time and place? I had two of those moments that night. Out front, then inside. Out front, early, I was trying not to float away. I was tired, no sleep worth mentioning. Danny had been crying when I left the house, Julie holding him tight against her, telling him that she loved him, telling me to be careful.

Another picture poster floating above the crowd: Harry Hopkins' face. Then another: The Chief. More: a group shot of the Council. And then the inevitable: Becky Hamilton. The picture from her school yearbook. The picture that was in the newspaper. The only image Athens would ever see. I wanted to find whoever was holding that picture and take it away from them. To not let the girl be part of this moment. But I kept staring as the poster twirled around and around, her face disappearing and re-appearing. I was dizzy, and then I saw a deer walk through the crowd. Not the body, just the antlers, weaving through the crowd toward me.

But it wasn't a deer. That would be too much to understand. It was John Brownstein, wearing a set of giant plastic antlers on his head, handing out pamphlets. He saw me and waved like a child, happy and embarrassed at the same time, like being lost and seeing a parent.

Brownstein had come to every council meeting for the past six months and spoken against our plans to thin the deer herds in Athens by shooting them. Everybody thought he was a PETA nut, but John, I came to understand, just liked animals. His pamphlets this night were not about dead children and police incompetence. They were about how to reduce deer populations without killing them. Options we had looked at a dozen times but rejected as impractical and too limited. Athens had hundreds of deer in the city limits. Gardens and motorists weren't safe. Picture windows had been shattered. Deer were dancing in old ladies' parlors. For small town politics, it was a big issue. Until tonight.

"Big crowd tonight, eh, Mr. Holly?" John said as he stood beside me and Al Baroli. "You think I can get on the agenda. I've got some new ideas." John never had any new ideas. I knew that.

For some reason, John had always galled Al. I had tried to point out to Al that Brownstein was as mad as a wonderland hatter, that picking on him was like picking on the village idiot. It was too easy, and there was no glory in it. As soon as John walked up to us, Al humphred and walked a wedge though the crowd to go inside. He had always told me I was too nice to "Brownstain" and was wasting my time.

"I think I've got some more supporters tonight, Mr. Holly. I think you should listen to us," John said, his antlers slipping down his forehead. It was possible, I thought to myself. This crowd had a lot of people who had also spoken against the deer kill at previous meetings. But John was never going to be their leader.

"Looks like a busy night, Mr. Brownstein," I said, accepting his offer of a handshake. "You might have to wait a long time. But I'll make sure the Mayor gets to you. Right now, we better get inside."

John beamed, and, with a quick whirl around, he shouted in a booming voice to the crowd, "Time to go inside!" Then he bounded up the steps alone, his antlers bouncing. I think I loved him at that moment. The crowd had turned in his direction, suddenly mute, and as he went through the revolving doors we all followed him.

The council chambers had a hundred chairs for the public. They were filled immediately, and another hundred people stood along the side and back walls. John was in the front row. He was smarter than Al and others gave him credit for. He always sat in the same seat, to the left of the podium, so that that when anybody was speaking to the council, and the camera was on them, John could always be seen in the background. Antlers on his head that night made him impossible to miss.

As I sat next to Bernie on my left, with a grim-faced Harry seated on a lower stage to my right, I looked at the back wall. Over the heads of the standing crowd were a line of pictures looking back at me. Former mayors, former council group shots, some dating back to the 1800's. I had pointed out to Harry many times that there wasn't a single picture of a city manager.

For the first few minutes, we were all assuming our roles, council and crowd, while Bob Hardy, the government cable technician, checked lights and sound. He finally nodded to Steve Nash, and the Mayor began, "I would like to call this meeting of the Athens City Council to order........."

The crowd was restless before Steve finished. With his gavel pounded, Steve then skipped the usual opening agenda items to read a statement which had been written by Bernie Huss: *The City Council would like to offer its condolences to the friends and families of the two young people who were recent victims of a tragic accident involving a city employee. Our words cannot bring them back, but our hearts share this community's grief. Our goal is to make sure this never happens again. So we urge this community to come together and work toward a common goal. The Council needs your help, as the families need your prayers.*

The crowd wasn't happy, and neither was I. Steve wasn't a speaker. The words were good enough, but he could make the Gettysburg Address sound like a phone book. The only person in the audience who wasn't angry was John Brownstein. He was crying.

And then the people spoke.

The agenda that night had thirty-two items, a typical workload, and we could have done them in two hours, three tops. On a good night. At midnight this night, we were still on "Public Discussion," the first item on the agenda. This part of the agenda was for the public to talk to us, not for us to engage in a debate or argument with them. We had moved this item to the beginning of the meeting instead of the end, to encourage more public discussion about the issues. So we're supposed to listen to them and use their input to shape our future decisions. And we're supposed to be <u>deliberative</u>. Trouble is, if a crowd of people are yelling at you, pleading with you, cursing you, and you don't respond, then you can be accused of not listening to them. The day after this meeting, I watched the tape. I would have been mad at us too.

It took me about half an hour, but I finally figured out why they were there. It began with a police chase, and the first speakers were full of questions and complaints about that, but then speaker and speaker broadened the issues. The chase had killed two kids, ruined The Cop's career, but it was merely the straw for people whose backs had carried a lifetime of bad experiences with the police department in particular and city government in general. I began to hear stories that I thought couldn't be true, stories about police harassment and city incompetence. About alleged police corruption, rogue cops, crooked

136

building inspectors. You name it, their Athens was not the Athens I lived in. Trouble was, I listened to them, refuting them in my mind, but wave after wave shared one trait. They were absolutely sincere.

At one point, after two hours of discussion, Steve asked the council for a fifteen-minute recess so we could all take a break. At the podium, Betty Norris had finally gotten her turn at the microphone. Just as she was about to speak, Steve interrupted her, assuring her that she would be first at the microphone when we came back. She glared at him, and I could almost read her mind. Ken objected to the recess, saying that "the people here want to be, deserve to be, heard, and I for one am willing to listen to them." The crowd erupted, on its feet, cheering. Al started to raise his voice, but Steve grabbed his left hand and Bernie grabbed his right. And then the crowd shouted, "Let her speak! Let us all speak!"

Steve withdrew his suggestion for a recess, but Al got up anyway and walked out of the room. I knew where he was going. He had serious bladder problems. For the rest of the summer, however, his exit was the defining image for a lot of people in Athens. Al Baroli was the Council.

The strangest thing about that meeting? I talked to Bernie about this later, but she disagreed with me. She said she felt nothing like I felt. How did I feel? Like I had been wrong in all my assumptions. Like there was an Athens out there that was more real than the one I lived in. I was a medium size fish in a small pond, I had always joked, but at least I knew what was happening all over the pond.

I stopped listening to the people in front of me. In dozens of different stories, the message was the same. I had been oblivious to reality. I had scribbled notes to myself for two hours, but stopped that as well. I started writing questions for the staff, The Chief, everybody whose word I had simply accepted at face value, including Harry Hopkins.

I forgot I was on television. I forgot that Bob Hardy often had the cameras pan away from the crowd to focus on the council-members themselves. In a thousand homes across Athens that night, the other public saw a different council meeting than the one I was at. Steve was constantly haranguing speakers to hurry up, to be fair to others, but seeming rude himself. Al was constantly talking back to the speakers, not in reality, but his lips were moving. The two new women next to Ken seemed like deer in the headlights. Bernie had the tightest pucker on her face. Ken never looked away from the crowd, was constantly nodding his head in agreement, kept asking speakers to submit written statements as well. Harry kept repeating, "I'll look into that and get back to you."

Joseph Holly?

I was gone after the second hour. I was lost in the moment I told you about earlier, like the time out front, wondering how the hell I got there at that moment. All it took was a young black woman to talk about her brother Anheuser Hampton, and her loss, her thinking she knew enough about the white and well-fed Council in front of her, knowing enough to hate us. "You don't understand how my family feels!" she cried. Perhaps she was right. But then she said, "You've never lost a brother or sister or your child. You can't imagine the pain."

And I went away, wondering how I got there. I was tired. I had been called an accomplice to murder by one speaker. I wanted to go home. The people be damned. I wanted to go talk to Kathy. Go home to Danny and Julie. My being at that meeting was pointless.

I would have stayed away for the rest of the night, but I came back for the arrival of the Reverend Donald Mason. Ten o'clock, Ken had finally acquiesced to let the Council take a break. Half the crowd had gone home. Stretched and watered, the Council sat down again, and Mason entered the chambers.

He stood at the podium and signed the speaker sheet, cleared his throat and began quietly. "Mr. Mayor, council-members, I thank you for your willingness to let me speak here tonight at this momentous display of democracy in action. I applaud your patience, and your consideration. Your constituents are well served by you."

The crowd mumbled.

"I come here tonight in dual roles, but not in the role of your adversary. I am kin to a dead child. A nephew whose life, I am ashamed to admit, I had not counseled as I should have. My private grief."

The crowd was nodding, impressed by the flamboyant and nationally known attorney's humility. I was blinking my eyes. I had seen him a few days earlier at Broadway Baptist. I smelled Betty Norris at that moment, and looked around to see her in the front row corner, with empty space around her.

"But my other role is as a man of God, a role which shapes my thoughts at this moment. I come here tonight…"

The council knew that his team had filed a ten million dollar civil suit against the city at the county courthouse that morning.

"…simply to ask your help in the pursuit of what we all want. And that goal is…merely the truth."

The smell was stronger.

"Here in these secular halls, the wisdom of our Bible is most relevant. It says to seek the truth and the truth shall set you free. All I am asking you tonight is for each of you to seek that truth, a truth which will tear down the rising wall of distrust that I see being erected here tonight. My Bible tells me…"

I stopped him. It was the first extended comment I made all night, and I ignored my own advice to Al and the others. I refused to be silent, to let the public speak. I knew why I was there at that moment, not just how, but why I had come to this point. I lowered my voice, "Let me see if I understand you."

Mason gave me that look he gave Becky Hamilton's father when the man refused to shake his hand. Surprise, then analysis, then recovery. He started to speak again, but I stopped him again. "With all due respect, Reverend Mason, the essence of the Bible is not Truth. The Truth of the Bible, certainly the New Testament, is—Forgiveness."

Mason was not easily cowed. "With all due respect, of course, Mr. ..." pausing to look at the name plate in front of me, "...Mr. Holly, we must forgive our enemies..."

"As god forgave us for the crucifixion of his son," I interrupted again. "You forgive first, truth will follow." Mason opened his mouth, and I repeated, "Forgive first, truth later."

I realized too late that I might have been theologically correct, pulling out the last thread of the pre-historic Baptist lay preacher I used to be, but it was the wrong thing to say at that moment. The crowd was not there to forgive us, but I kept preaching until Bernie reached over and tapped my hand next to her's. The room was tomb quiet.

Mason had the last word. "Time will heal us, Mr. Holly, time will tell."

When I got home at two in the morning, Julie and Danny were still waiting up for me. They were playing cards at the kitchen table.

"You look like the devil, Joe," she said, shuffling the deck. Danny giggled, but it was probably because of the sound that the cards made. "But you're still the best looking person on the council. You ever consider a career in show business?"

"Acting?" I sighed as I sat down with them, a cup of warm tea waiting for me.

"I was thinking about some sort of tele-evangelism," she said deadpan. "As long as you let me screen the congregation."

"You watched the meeting, eh?" I said, stirring the tea. Julie usually never watched those meetings.

"Sure, I wasn't feeling bad enough about my life, so I thought I would borrow some of yours."

I was too tired to argue, to even do my usual "cheer up" routine. "How'd we do?" I said, not really caring.

"You're all in deep shit, husband. I just hope you've got the boots to get through."

"You mean six of us are in the shit, don't you. All of us except that damn Ken Rumble, whose shit don't stink, right?"

Julie turned to face me directly, shoving the cards over to Danny who kept flipping them over one by one. "I watched the whole thing, all five hours, and I turned off the sound after awhile. I could tell what everyone was saying. I watched your face, saw you drift off, and I knew when that black lawyer came in that you felt something and came back, even before you did your Billy Graham schtick. But you did fine, my hero, Mr. Smith goes to the Mount."

"I'm too tired for this, Julie," I said. I was finally ready to go to sleep.

"I know, I know, but I was serious. You <u>are</u> my hero. Things still matter to you. That's good."

"Go to bed?" I asked.

"Sure. I put a cot in our room. Danny wants to sleep with us. Right, Danny boy," she said, nudging him. Danny had laid his head on the table. He was asleep.

"Joe, one last thing," Julie said as I picked Danny up to carry him to our room. "Watch the tape. Look hard at Ken Rumble. The six of you seemed lost up there. Him, he was different."

"Yeh, he won the People's Choice Award," I said.

"No, Joe, look at the tape. Ken is scared to death. I can tell. He's absolutely petrified. You'll figure it out sooner or later. Right now, let's go to bed."

Jack Hamilton had been in St. Mary's many times in his life, going with his wife and daughter to mass. But less and less in recent years. "My mama's great disappointment," he would tell Marcie and Becka, "I never had her faith."

Not having faith, his daughter's death was not a test of God. He did not question God, was not disappointed in God, did not curse God, because he did not believe in God. He had never even wanted to believe. Still, he was glad that his wife had faith because it would help her live through the moments, stretching into days and weeks and months and future years, after she was told about Becka's death.

Becka's death did not lead her father to God. For solace or peace. Being raised by his Christian mother had not done it, being taken to the Baptist church every Sunday from birth to high school graduation, a lifetime of his believing brothers' good-natured lecturing, and after years of gentle persuasion by his wife, even after all of that, Hamilton was irrevocably immune to the mystery of God.

In the years before Becka's death, he had gone to St. Mary's and seldom paid attention to the service around him. Most of the time, it was an hour of enforced meditation. Nothing to do but sit there. Sort out the past, plan the future. He sometimes listened to Father West's homilies, learning a bit of history he had not known. But mostly he just looked around. He studied the windows and pictures, the statuary, the blue ceilings and dark red carpets. He counted the number of figures in the church, in all the forms, but once he got past forty-five he stopped counting. All of them a name from the Bible, plus angels and saints, a community he visited on Sundays.

But Becka's service provided a personal mystery for Jack Hamilton, and he wondered if he was the only person who noticed. Or if he was simply coming late to the obvious. As he sat there, staring at her coffin, sometimes reaching in his coat pocket to touch the cell phone he had bought her a few days earlier, a gift he never gave her,

Hamilton briefly looked beyond his daughter and saw Jesus for the first time. In all the years before, he must have seen the tiny crucifix hundreds of times, disproportionately small when compared to the other massive figures surrounding it in St. Mary's. The Stations of the Cross each had a life-sized Jesus hovering over the faithful along the sides of the church. Peter and Paul were huge and towered high above the crucifix. Mary and Joseph, all the supporting cast of the Passion, were easily seen.

But Christ on the Cross itself? Had he always been so small, Hamilton asked himself. Why had he never noticed? A cross less than eighteen inches high, a bone white dying Jesus probably only twelve inches tall, Christ and Cross the smallest art in St. Mary's. Hamilton recognized the contrast, thought about it, dismissed it, and then looked back at his daughter's coffin. He wanted it to be true, the story around him, for her sake, for the sake of his wife. But he did not believe it.

Sitting in the back of his brother's car that morning, being driven to St. Mary's, Hamilton and his wife had talked about Becka's first serious illness. She had been six, already a vision, and had pneumonia. Marcie remembered how she had prayed for her daughter's recovery. Hamilton remembered how he had called another doctor, who finally agreed with him that Becka needed to be in a hospital and not at home. Overhearing them as he drove, Hamilton's brother reminded them about how Becka had recovered and won her first race six months later. It was only a grade school picnic, but Becka had done more than win the race, she had stunned the crowd of parents, many of whom accused their own children of not trying to win. How else to explain the gap between the Hamilton girl and their sons and daughters. Hamilton's brother was almost jovial, "Hell, Jack, she was whipping my boys until they got into high school. Sorry, Marcie, about my language, but that girl was something to watch."

An hour later, Hamilton had gone through the memories of his

143

daughter's races, the ribbons and trophies, the pictures in the **TELEGRAM,** *and he remembered the first letter she had gotten from a college track coach, congratulating her on her success and wishing her well for the future, and, of course, that she would be hearing from them again. She had wanted to frame the letter, but Hamilton told her there would be a lot more like it to come, and he was right. He understood how recruiting worked.*

The hour was not enough time, he knew that. In the clearest moments before Becka's service, he wondered if he would ever stop re-living her life, even if only for a day. He wondered what would have happened if he and Marcie had had more children, if they would have absorbed his heart and mind and Becka would simply become a memory. Wasn't there a song for this, he thought, something about being "forever young." Other songs too, all of them meaning something different now.

Hamilton was sometimes aware of the service around him, especially when he heard little Jenny Baker's flute. Jenny and Becka had practiced together for hours until Jenny moved to Iowa City last year. But she came back for the service, wanting to play for Becka, promising not to cry. Hamilton had let his wife handle all the arrangements, but when Jenny asked him if he had a song he wanted her to play, he knew exactly what he wanted. "That song the two of you recorded for your parents? The one you played for your recital? Do you remember?" he had told her the day before. It was his only contribution. So when Jenny began "How Can I Keep From Singing?" Jack Hamilton closed his eyes and looked away from his daughter's casket, toward the ceiling, anywhere but where he had looked the hour before, and heard Becka's flute again. It was the only moment of the service in which he was not in pain.

Three hours after the music stopped, Hamilton and his wife sat under a tent at Oakland Cemetery. Mike Lensing had been the last person to leave them. He had stayed until his work was done. Lensing had picked up Becka's body from the hospital the night she died, and his funeral home had taken care of her from that moment until the last shovelful of dirt had covered her casket. In between, he had pulled a few strings to make sure that an autopsy was not required. It was not professional. He had disguised the coroner's work hundreds of times. It was personal. He knew Marcie, and his children knew Becka.

Lensing asked the Hamiltons if there was anything else he could do, but he already knew the answer. He left them alone.

Sitting next to Marcie, Hamilton let her do all the talking, about the service, how it had been beautiful, how the music had made her feel better, how Father West had been comforting, but Hamilton sensed that she did not believe herself. He patted her knee, and she began sobbing, her head resting on his shoulder. Except for her crying, Oakland was silent.

After awhile, after her eyes were dry, Marcie tried to start life over. She kidded Jack Hamilton about his behavior. "You were rude this morning, you know that don't you?" she said, but not harshly.

Hamilton was puzzled. "How so?" he asked.

"When you wouldn't shake hands," she said. "Those people were just trying to be nice, to do the right thing, and you ignored them."

Hamilton thought about it for a second, shook his head, and finally said, "I'm sorry, Marcie. I don't remember that. I don't remember anybody wanting to shake my hand. I just remember sitting there wishing I could talk to Becka one more time."

Ken Rumble can say things that I can't. He says the right things, things people want to hear, most of the time. He can say the word "soul" with a straight face and seem to mean it. He talks about downtown Athens being the "soul" of Athens, and every two years, during some campaign, all the candidates talk about what they would do to protect and enhance the "soul" of Athens. Ken is Plato. I'm Aristotle. He sees a spirit downtown. I see too many bars, too many student apartments and not enough adults living there. Ken thinks the big thoughts. I want to hire extra staff to keep the ped mall clean.

Three weeks after Becky Hamilton died, I was downtown with Julie and Danny for the Friday night concert. An Athens tradition during the summer. Usually some local musician, sometimes a good band for dancing, sometimes some jazz, and the closest I can come to feeling like Athens has a soul. On a good night, with the right band, thousands of people gather downtown to listen and mingle. You go enough, year after year, you get to know people who you see again and again, people you never see anywhere else. You relax, you joke, you gossip, you buy a gyro or snow cone from one of the ped mall vendors, a crystal at the Vortex store. Life is good, and Athens is the calm center of the universe.

That night was different. The air was too thick and warm, and it muffled the music, turned it into background noise. Julie and I had always liked to sit at the far end of the ped mall, near the intersection of Washington and Dubuque, away from the crowds, but we could still hear the music. We would talk, watch Danny, watch the town and gown flow around us, and she would mock and mimic the normalcy of Athens. I'd sit there and think I was the luckiest man in the world. With the music at my back, Julie beside me, shoulder to shoulder, whispering nonsense, Danny in front of us, and the Hollywood across the street, I was as happy as a man could be happy.

There was no breeze that night. The old buildings and ped mall bricks seemed to radiate heat. Only a few hundred people were there, but more cops than usual. Shops that were usually open to take advantage of the crowd were closed. And the music was bad. A salsa band had been scheduled but had to cancel at the last minute because their bus broke down. They had always been a favorite in the past, and they could always generate some dancing on the mall. As soon as it was obvious that a thrown-together folk trio was all they were going to hear, the crowd thinned out even more. The Kingston Trio—these guys were not.

Heat, fewer people, more cops, bad music, Julie in a foul mood, a broken window at the Hollywood—I wanted to cut my losses and go home, but Danny wanted to stay.

You ever see yourself—_you_—in your children? Strange, that night I saw myself and my father in Danny. Julie and I each had one of his hands and we started to go home, but he pulled away from us. He clapped his hands and pointed back toward the center of the ped mall, where the bad music was coming from. Julie looked at me for a translation.

"I think he wants to play in the fountain," I said.

"I'm tired, Joe," Julie sighed.

"For a little while, okay?" I said. "Let him run off some of this energy."

"You men go work it off. I've got papers to grade."

"Julie, the semester's over. School's out. Grades are in. You ain't teaching summer classes. You haven't got..." I was angrier than I should have been, "...you haven't got a damn thing to do tonight. So, cut me some slack, will you?"

She stared at me and then did the most surprising thing she could have done at that moment. She leaned into my face, kissing me softly on the lips, her tongue tracing a memory of our first kiss. How do I tell you what it did to me? I wanted us to be alone at home,

Danny asleep in his room, Athens gone.

"You better go get Danny," she whispered as she stepped away from me. And then she turned to walk home.

Danny had disappeared, but I knew where to find him. I watched Julie go away, and then I went to the fountain.

I have this photograph of my father when he was around Danny's age, at the beach wearing a baggy bathing suit and a cowboy hat. Back when he had a memory, he told me, "It was my big brother's suit. I always got the hand-me-downs. But it was my hat. I had it for years." In the picture, his right hand is on his hip, his elbow pointing slightly forward. There's also a picture of me when I was Danny's age. My father in his khaki army uniform, his two sons in front of him. My older brother Carl is wearing a khaki Boy Scout uniform. I'm in front of Carl, my right hand on my hip, my elbow pointing forward, wearing a cowboy hat. There's a picture of me and Danny at the downtown fountain in Athens. He's soaking wet, Adonis handsome child, wearing a cowboy hat, his right hand on his hip. Me, I look like my father.

It was meant to be Hallmark choreography. Julie had sorted family pictures after my mother died, and she put the three together and had them matted and framed, a present for my fiftieth birthday. It was too late for my father. I took Danny and the picture to visit him that evening, driving a hundred miles to Des Moines, where Carl lived. My brother remembered the second picture, but my father kept shaking his head. He didn't recognize himself.

Danny was waiting for me at the fountain, already soaked. He waved at me and ran back through the water arching out of the ground. I sat on a bench and watched. Every summer for the past five years, we had gone to the beach at St. Augustine, a week's vacation in a rented condo facing the Atlantic. Iowa is a great state, but it doesn't have a beach. As I sat watching Danny, I kept trying to juggle the dwindling money in my bank account, but there wasn't enough to take us back to the ocean this summer. The fountain would have to do.

Julie needed the beach more than Danny and me, I knew that, but she didn't seem too upset when I had told her that the money was simply not there this year. I suggested that we charge everything, but she knew I would lose even more sleep than I had been, obsessing about interest charges and how to get out of debt. She had said, "We can go next year, start saving now, go for two weeks instead of one. There's always next year." I didn't push the issue.

I was watching Danny stand right in front of the bad trio when I started to doze off. I was still having trouble sleeping, and I was catnapping away from home more and more, especially in my office at the Hollywood. I was on that bench, halfway between sleep and consciousness, when I smelled Betty Norris. I shook my head and looked around, but didn't see her. I looked back for Danny and he was gone. This happened a lot, but I always found him quickly. I wasn't worried. Scanning the ped area immediately around me, I quickly saw him over by the playground equipment. Norris was talking to him.

I was over there in two seconds. Norris saw me coming and turned to face me, her stench like some sort of Star-Trekian warp shield that slowed down my advance. I wasn't thinking in television metaphors at that moment. I saved that flourish for Harry later, who always had to have it explained to him. But if Norris had had her hands, as well as her odor, on my son at that moment she might have had a good lawsuit against me later. I was gearing up to tell her to stay the hell away from Danny, but before I could open my mouth I saw the expression on his face, his nose scrunched up like he had tripped over a dead skunk. I started laughing, giving Norris another reason to dislike me.

Danny saw me and started laughing too. I scooped him up over my shoulder and said to Norris at the same time, "How ya doing,

Betty? How's it going?"

"This is your son?" she asked, giving me a look like I might have been a pedophile she was confronting.

"Yep, this is my Danny boy," I said, flipping him upside down and acting like I was about to drop him, a game he loved, but which made Betty flinch. Danny squealed, and she visibly trembled. "Betty, it's okay," I said, no longer amused by her discomfort. "Seriously, it's okay. He's fine," putting him back on his feet.

Betty walked off without a word. How was I supposed to interpret that? Why was she even talking to Danny in the first place? I knew I would never get an answer from him. Why walk off? Was there a reason for <u>anything</u> that was happening in Athens? I took Danny's hand and started walking home. Throughout the ped mall, I recognized most of the cops by name. Fred Tymeson was new on the force, and he had apologized months ago when he gave me a ticket for a slow roll past a stop sign. His partner tonight was Andy Rocca. Both men were drop-dead handsome. That was Julie's view, and she always added, "Throw in a gun and a uniform, and those guys are heart-breakers." They nodded as I went by, but neither was as friendly as they had always been in the past. Had they watched the Council meeting when they and the other cops in Athens had suddenly become THE problem here—crime not the problem, but the crime-stoppers?

Something had happened since that meeting. I kept getting calls from people who had their own story to tell about police abuse or incompetence. People who did not want to go on record. People I had never heard from before or since. I asked them to send a letter, give us more details, and we would investigate each complaint. Some things were too unbelievable, like cops selling guns to drug dealers, or cops accepting bribes at every traffic stop. Still, these people seemed to believe the story even if it had not happened to them directly. Where did this paranoia come from? I see guys like Fred and Andy and I see

150

men doing a thankless job. But some of the stories were more than rumor. Looking for a burglar one night, a squad of cops, guns drawn, had charged into a laundry and knocked down—the owner. Young black men <u>were</u> roughed up in plain view of some white bystanders downtown as the bars were closing. Were they resisting arrest, like the cops said? The witnesses being drunk themselves didn't help their credibility, but why weren't the white drunks arrested too? Why were the traffic laws enforced more rigidly in the Broadway area than in my neighborhood? I could take all the rumors, all the facts I knew, throw in the death of Becky Hamilton and that other kid, but it still didn't explain the "cop-killer" or the "nazi-cop" graffiti all over buildings downtown. I had thought about all this ever since that first meeting, but I still didn't have a clue as I walked through the ped mall. Looking at Fred and Andy, I wondered if I had been wrong all this time, and the crowd that night had been right. Wondering if the problem had always been there, right in front of an indifferent or blind council, in front of a distracted Joseph Holly, and Becky's death merely brought it all to the surface. I was thinking about that, leading Danny home, because I was trying to <u>not</u> think about Julie.

"Mr. Holly, can I speak to you for a minute?"

I turned around to face a man I had never seen before. He was wearing an Iowa Arts t-shirt and khaki shorts. "About the last council meeting…" And then I recognized the voice. It was John Brownstein, without his antlers. "…I have some material I forgot to give you and the council that night. I was wondering…"

"John, I hope you're going to tell me something about the deer problem in this town," I said, wanting <u>that</u> to be the most serious problem we had to solve.

"You see, Mr. Holly, you keep insisting that it's a problem. I want us to see it as an opportunity…"

And he was off again, and I was thankful. No more Julie, no

151

more rogue cops, just whether to kill all the Bambis or simply supply them with condoms. Natural resource management. Danny and I kept walking, and Brownstein kept pace with us, holding up pamphlet after pamphlet as he talked, handing each to Danny after summarizing it. Danny loved pictures of deer.

Brownstein stayed with us all the way to the Hollywood. I hadn't planned on stopping in that night, but when I sensed that he would follow us all the way home, I asked him to excuse me while I went to work. A handshake, a wave, one final pamphlet, and he was gone. Danny and I were in the small Hollywood lobby, and my hired help was nowhere to be seen. In a less honest town, my cash drawer would have been empty.

Gary Sanders was my only paid employee. In my first city council race a million years ago, Gary had been one of my opponents. He called me a "carpet-bagger" at a forum, contrasting his own ten-year seniority as an Athens resident. We both lost that year, and a million years later he's one of the few ironic left-wingers I know. I hired him because he never seemed to keep a job with anybody else, usually because he was writing the OSHA people and reporting his employers. I hired him because he was scrupulously honest and dependable. I hired him because I knew he hated the movies I booked, so I never had to worry about him spending all his time slipping into the auditorium. I hired him because Danny liked him. And he was a political junkie like me. As soon as he flipped the projector switch, Gary would usually settle in behind the concession counter and read the latest **New York Times**, always keeping me informed about the obituaries, op-ed pieces, and point spreads.

"Gary?" I shouted as Danny and I stood in the lobby. "Gary!" shouted Danny, surprising me. "Gary," we shouted together.

The uni-sex bathroom door opened and Gary appeared, his shirt-tail half in, half out. "You men hold your horses," he said, his black plastic glasses almost falling off his nose. "I got a bladder problem...boss-man, something an old guy like you can understand...and you, Danny man, you'll understand soon enough. Just remember you heard it from me first."

"How's business?" I asked, letting Danny go get himself some popcorn.

"So far, we've made my exploitive minimum wage salary for the night, but the electric bill is still overdue. And I've spent most of my time answering the phone." Danny began throwing popcorn kernels at us. I knew he was about to lose control of himself. So did Gary, so he hurried up, "Your wife, Harry Hopkins—who said to call him tonight—the usual bomb threats. The only really interesting call was from one of my labor comrades who tells me that you're going to have a serious opponent this fall. Kenny-G has given them the green light. Green light...get it?"

"Should I worry?" I asked, shielding off more popcorn and ignoring Gary's admiration of his own humor.

"Depends on who comes out of the woodwork. You should win, all things being normal, but, boss, these are not normal times. I don't think you and the other Romanovs in the Duma really understand all the shit that's flying around this town. I'm losing friends just by keeping my job."

"Then they weren't your friends, Gary," I said, taking the textbook approach.

"Maybe not, but I've known them a lot longer than I've known you."

Danny was throwing handfuls of popcorn, and Gary went into his aggrieved employee routine, complete with his exaggerated southern accent, supposedly his imitation of me, "Dan'l Holy, you stop that, hare, youse know your daddy is gonna make me cleans up yore mess. You stop, yous hare me?"

Danny had his hand loaded and ready to fire, and then he got that look on his face when his mind went somewhere else entirely. He dropped the popcorn and ran past me and Gary and out the door.

"See you, Mr. DeMille," I heard Gary laugh as I followed Danny. Outside, he was frozen in mid-stride, his eyes darting back and forth, looking, or listening, for something.

Julie was still up when we got home, reading in bed. All the lights in the house were on. I had walked as fast as I could with Danny, hoping the pace would burn up some of his energy, making it easier to get him to bed. I was wrong. He wanted to watch television, so I left him in the kitchen and went to see Julie.

"You called the Hollywood?" I asked as I sat on the edge of the bed to take off my shoes.

"Your brother called. Your father fell again. That walker thing didn't seem to help. Said to call him tomorrow. Not an emergency," she spoke like she was reading from a note posted to the refrigerator, not looking up from her book.

I was thinking about that kiss she gave me right before she left me and Danny downtown. "You tired?" I said, as casually as I could.

Her shoulders slumped farther into the pillows. She then dog-eared the page she was reading and closed the book. "Exhausted," she sighed. "I've just been waiting for you to get home so I could go to sleep."

We looked at each other, and I wondered if I looked as old as she did at that moment. A few hours earlier she had been the woman I met two decades earlier. Not yet thirty, hair too short, but eyes and legs and a smile to die for. I took the book as she offered it to me, put it on the table next to my side of the bed, and said, "I'll stay up with Danny for awhile. You get some rest." I leaned down to kiss her forehead as she slid further under the covers. And then out of nowhere, I added, "I love you." She never opened her eyes, but she did reach

154

over and pat my hand.

I went into the bathroom and looked in the mirror, answering my own question. I was, indeed, as old as Julie. The thing we promised to do for each other when we got married, to grow old together...it was happening.

Jack Hamilton had not intended to be on his hands and knees, his hands in the dirt, helping his wife in her garden, but as he sat on his back porch in his usual spot, watching her, he had wanted to be closer to her, so he left his book on a small metal table and walked toward her. It was during that walk, perhaps twenty feet, perhaps ten seconds, that he noticed the deer droppings on the other side of their new fence.

He got down beside his wife and asked her, "Anything you want me to do?" She turned to look at him, initially shook her head, smiled, but finally said, "Spread some of this potting soil around those roses I just planted. And, Jack, you're going to _have_ to get your hands dirty."

Hamilton almost laughed. "That's okay. We've got lots of Ivory soap."

"And lots of dirt," Marcie replied, tossing a handful of the black Iowa soil at him.

Hamilton was far from a natural gardener, but he followed Marcie's directions faithfully for the next hour, asking for a break only when his knees started hurting him. She gave him a look of mock disgust, as if to tell him that his knees were no longer a believable excuse for avoiding work. So he stayed on the ground with her, sitting down instead of being on all fours.

"You want some water?" he asked her.

"You looking for a reason to go inside?" she answered.

"Nope, I'm just thirsty, thought you might be too."

Marcie stopped digging, and Hamilton studied her profile. Sweat dripped off the end of her nose. It was another hot and humid day, not a good day to be in the garden, certainly not in the early afternoon.

"That would be nice. With some ice, maybe?" she said.

"Why don't you take a break, come inside for awhile?" he asked as he struggled to get up, rolling to one side and using his arms to push himself up off the ground. Standing up, he extended his hand to her, offering to help her rise, but she just sat there.

"No, thank you, I want to finish this," she said quietly.

Hamilton looked around his yard, back toward his house, across to Phil Reisetter's house next door. It was a very cloudy day, low gray clouds, and the clouds were keeping the heat trapped close to the earth. He noticed the deer droppings again.

"Looks that the fence is keeping those deer out of the yard," he said, shading his eyes with one hand while he rubbed the back of his neck with the other hand. "We got our money's worth."

Marcie contradicted him, "Look again. That maple in the corner has lost a lot more leaves on the side closest to the fence. Some bark, too."

"How's that possible? There's no tracks on this side of the fence, and the crap is all on the other side," Hamilton said, walking toward the maple.

"I guess they're big enough to stick their heads over the fence and lean in," Marcie said.

Hamilton stood at the fence, measuring in his mind the distance between the top of the chain links and the closest branch of the maple. He had seen deer droppings many times, and he could recognize deer print divots in the grass on the other side. There was nothing unusual about the size of the droppings or the divots. He muttered to himself, "The bastards must have a damn long neck to reach that far. And you'd think there would be some fur or something along the top here."

"You say something?" Marcie asked from a distance.

"No, nothing..." he paused, "...I just wish they would leave the maple alone. They can have the rest of the garden."

They had planted the maple when their daughter was born. It was now the biggest tree in the yard.

Marcie slowly stood up, shaking dirt and grass off her garden

157

apron. She went to the fence and took her husband's hand, "I'll take you up on that offer. Let's go inside and rest."

In the kitchen, a pitcher of ice water on the table between them, Hamilton kept looking out the giant windows toward the corner of the yard. "I'm thinking that we can put some sort of extra fencing in that corner, add another couple of feet in height."

"I thought that six feet was as tall as the city would let us build, didn't you tell me that?" Marcie asked, seeing how distracted Hamilton was becoming.

"Something like that," he said. "We've got five already. Nobody will notice a few more. Phil won't care. He might even help. Sandy and Don, on the other side, they'll be okay with it too. They're all good people. They'll understand."

"Yes, they will, I know that. I was just wondering about..."

"About the CITY?" Hamilton interrupted, turning to look directly at his wife. "You think the CITY will object?" His voice was not conciliatory. "You think they will stop me?"

"Jack...."

"How about I start shooting the damn deer? Like they're doing! How about I buy a rifle and start shooting them? You think that would be okay with them? I get a gun and start shooting. Or I build a damn fence?"

Marcie reached across the table to hold his hand, but he jerked it away from her. Seeing her face, however, Hamilton leaned back toward his wife and offered his hand. "I just want to keep them away from the maple, that's all."

Athens has the biggest July Fourth fireworks display in this part of Iowa. Unlike the Friday night concerts downtown, which attracted locals only, the fireworks display in Weber Park drew thousands of people from all over southeast Iowa. Iowa City used to get those people, but for some dumb reason they switched the fireworks from their park to their airport. Who wants to sit on concrete?

Weber Park is two hundred acres of prime rolling woody real estate in north Athens. Like Central Park in New York, Weber has ponds and pools, tennis courts, softball fields, green expansive fields for picnics, all sorts of recreation stuff, an outdoor theatre for music and plays, and even a small carnival in the center. A ferris wheel, a miniature train that winds through the open areas, a merry-go-round, all operated by the same family for a hundred years. Summer nights—Weber is our own little theme park.

But the best thing about Weber is how it's surrounded on all four sides by a real forest. You go to Weber and it's like Athens disappears. Not just trees, an ocean of trees, a forest tall and old and thick, trees buffering the park from the interstate on one side, the river on another, and residential areas on the other two sides. Four entrances of narrow asphalt roads, not a problem except on the Fourth.

The Fourth of this year, I knew Weber was going to be packed more than usual. Sometimes you get these feelings. So did Harry, so he ordered extra police for crowd control and asked the county to assign some more deputies.

Athens had a perfect safety record with fireworks. But this year was different. Not the fireworks—the spectators. It was an edgy crowd. Lots of outsiders, but also lots of Rumble-ites walking through the crowd handing out leaflets urging everyone to come to the next council meeting.

Julie and I made a pact: one of us had Danny in sight at all times. Weber was going to be packed, so we went early, around six in

159

the afternoon, claimed our favorite spot near the porta-potties and concession stands, at the edge of the deep woods, with the best view of the fireworks which were launched from the other side of the park and aimed to come down over the river. We ate, and then Julie slept on the blanket as Danny and I walked all over the park, ending up together on the ferris wheel as sunset approached. It had been darkly overcast all day, hotter and more humid than usual. If I had had a muscle anywhere on my chest, I would have taken my shirt off to get cooler.

Danny loved ferris wheels, but he always kept his eyes closed when we got to the top. I would talk to him, my arm over his shoulders, and he would nod like a banshee. As soon as he could feel us going down again, he would open his eyes and look up at me. But he always wanted to buy another ticket and do it again. This Fourth, as I sat there with Danny at the top of the ferris wheel's arc, I looked straight up and thought I could touch the black bulging clouds overhead. If I had had a cell phone, I would have called Harry and told him to start the fireworks as soon as possible. It was finally going to rain.

Looking down, I could see the Weber grounds disappearing. An impending sunset, a cloudy sky, and smoke. Lots of smoke. Everybody down below must have found the cheapest sparklers and snake-twizzlers on the market. Rank stuff, that blazed brightly and then left nothing but smoke with a carbon half-life of a thousand years. Multiplied ten thousand times, with no breeze to force it through the trees, it was settling over the heads of everyone below. I could see the headlights of cars still coming into the park, but also headlights of cars leaving early. Sunshine patriots. Music from a dozen amplifiers was floating up out of the smoke. Neil Diamond was coming to America.

I wished I could have stayed on that ferris wheel to watch the fireworks. More than that, I wished I could have stayed on that wheel for the rest of my life. For the first time in weeks, I was falling asleep. The ascension, the descent, the circle, better than any drug. If I were alone, I could have laid down and stretched out on the seat of that oscillating car. But Danny was restless, and I knew Julie would be worried.

Back on the ground, getting back to Julie took longer than I expected because the crowd was harder to push through. Less penetrable than the past, more unforgiving. As I held Danny's hand and guided him back to his mother, I wondered if the father of that girl was there. Something, anything, to keep his mind off his daughter. Like Julie and I did for a while after Kathy died. We traveled, we went to movies, we sat in Weber Park and watched fireworks. But Kathy was still dead. That girl's father wouldn't have better luck, I knew that, but I still wished I could see him tonight. I would tell him to go ride the ferris wheel.

Julie was waiting for us, wide-awake, but visibly upset that the crowd had pushed itself too close to our own space. Too many people. We would have to stand up to see the fireworks.

A giant BOOM, and then another, signals that the fireworks were beginning. Through the gunpowder ground haze, we could see the first of the streaks go up and explode into a cascade that showered down. The crowd was fed. More and more, five minutes and then there was a BOOM but no fireworks. It was thunder, and then lightning, and after that all bets were off. Basic rule of lightning storms, get the hell out of the open and under some cover somewhere. But with four exits, ten thousand people, of whom probably a thousand were drunk, five hundred cars in the park itself—the rules didn't apply.

It was okay for the first few minutes. The rain hadn't started yet. The lightning was still in the distance. Julie and me and Danny had walked to the park, so we started looking around for somebody we knew so we could hitch a ride. The first familiar face I saw was

Gary Sanders, in the clutches of a pretty girl half his age. I yelled at him as he was about to disappear in the crowd, but all he did was wave and keep running. For a split second I had the sinking feeling that nobody was running the Hollywood, and then I remembered that I always closed for the Fourth. Why would I have thought it was open?

The crowd initially had its own sense of decorum, apologies were still offered for minor infractions of pushing and shoving. The Athens cops had traffic on the four roads flowing as smoothly as you could expect, maybe even better. We all might get wet, but we still had plenty of time to get home before the worst hit.

And then I heard the screaming. Heads were turning, looking for the source. More screams. I told Julie to hold on to Danny, forget the blanket and picnic basket. You get those feelings, right? Bad shit about to happen. For a second I smelled Betty Norris and there she was in the crowd, like the damn wicked witch of the east, but then she and her smell were gone again as she seemed to melt into the mass of people streaming toward the exits. I thought I saw Ken Rumble, but I could have been wrong. And more screams, "There it is! There it is!" So I thought tornado and started listening for the train coming, looking around for Julie and Danny and not seeing them.

Not a train, I heard drums, so I thought thunder, not tornadoes, just more thunder, but slow emphatic bass thunder. More screams of "There it is!" and I saw men with rifles arguing with cops with pistols, pointing to the crowd which was splitting like the Red Sea, falling all over itself to escape something.

Then, over the haze in the distance, I saw the antlers. Just those damn antlers, but bigger than I've ever seen them. I knew it was Hartford, but he wasn't the same. He was huge and getting bigger the closer he got to me, and I knew the sonuvabitch was coming for me.

162

He was walking through that crowd and coming to get me.

"Joe ..." I heard Julie's voice.

I turned around and saw her—alone. Danny was gone. I grabbed her and started screaming, "Where is he?" All she could do was point to the woods.

Thank god for Al Baroli. He was beside me without me seeing him come up. "I saw him go up through that path," he said, pointing. "You go get him. I'll stay here with Julie."

I turned back to face Hartford, but all I saw was the white patch of his tail as he walked into the woods, up the path that Al had pointed to.

It was like drowning, me pushing through that crowd to get to the path, like they're water and I was going down, so I pushed men and women out of my way, trying to get to the surface deep in the woods. "Out of my way, out of my way," I screamed, and then I stepped into the woods, and it was calmly quiet. No more crowd. No more thunder. No more drums. I could hear footsteps and breathing, but it was only me. I knew Danny was in there, so I kept walking.

Then I saw him, my son, standing with his back to me, and Hartford was right in front of him, towering over him, but with his head bowed so Danny could touch his antlers. I stopped myself. Hartford never wanted me. He wanted Danny.

"Danny," I whispered.

Hartford raised his head and looked over Danny toward me. Almost like the first time I saw him, face to face, in the dark. He tilted his head, examining me, and I wondered why those antlers seemed luminous, almost greenish, like the glow of a toy phosphorous stick, the kind you see at concerts around the necks of stoned teenagers. He looked at me, and then tilted his head back down for Danny, choosing to ignore my existence, just like Danny was doing.

"Danny," I whispered again. But then I remembered that he

was wearing his earplugs, so he couldn't hear a thing I was saying, especially since the wind was starting to shake all the trees around us.

Hartford raised his head again, but I wasn't scared anymore. I started talking to him, as if I talked to deer everyday of my life, "You've got to stop this. You've got to leave me alone, leave my boy, my family alone. You hear me?" As if, I thought to myself at that moment, "as if" that damn deer understood me, but he was all I had right then. And who knows why, but I was angry, and Hartford was all I had. "Look, you bastard, you stop this, go away and leave us all alone." I almost laughed at myself, knowing how stupid I must have looked at that moment. I started shaking my fist at Hartford. Why not lose it completely, I told myself, nobody in the woods but me and a giant deer and a boy who looked like me and my father. That's when Danny turned around, putting one finger up against his lips, shushing me, "You gotta be quiet, daddy. He's talking. You need to listen." Which is odd, because Danny hadn't spoken three complete and connected sentences to me or Julie in months.

"Danny, we have to go. Your mother's worried," I said to him, a little louder.

Hartford raised up on his hind legs, as high as the trees around us, his front legs stretching over Danny, and started to come down. Things were not working out like I had planned.

I grabbed Danny, kicking and squirming, and started running back to the center of the park. The closer I got to the path entrance, the more I could hear Hartford drumming behind me, the more I could see the smoke coming toward me. Danny kept fighting me until we broke free of the woods. Then, just as I was about to reach Julie and Al, just as I was about to lose my grip on Danny, some sort of cosmic fabric ripped and I saw lightning ripple across that black sky and hit the top of the ferris wheel, and all the red and yellow and blue light bulbs on the spokes of the wheel—they all exploded.

And it started to rain. Buckets, barrels, Exxon Valdez tankers full of water, rain stored up from the previous three months and dumped on Athens, like we were the first town downstream from a dynamited Hoover Dam. Thousands of tourists and townies were still in Weber Park, but, you know, the rain made them happy. So long without it, so much heat, so much withering corn and so many shrinking pigs, everybody stopped running, and I could see couples dancing, soaked to the bone, oohing and aahing every time the lightning cracked across the sky, like it was just part of another fireworks display, oblivious to the danger. Julie had Danny wrapped up and Al Baroli was leading us to his monstrous nine miles to the gallon All-American SUV, and all I could think of as we finally get inside Al's pride and joy is——has the entire state of Iowa gone fucking crazy? Everybody except me? I had just been talking to a giant deer, but I was the sanest person in Athens at that moment.

Al started the SUV with me next to him, Danny and Julie in the back. The rain was thudding on his roof, sounding like rapid-fire globs of mud hitting tin. At this profound moment of Zen, Al turned to me and said "Joe, something I've always wanted you to explain to me."

I stared at him, then looked back and saw Julie listening to us. We were all soaking wet, I wanted to go home and go to sleep, but I finally said, "The meaning of life?"

"Hell, no," Al laughed. "I just always wondered why you named your theatre Hollywood but you never show American movies. That never made sense to me."

I looked back at Julie, who smiled, kissed Danny's wet hair, and then said, "Joe, don't look at me. This one—you're on your own."

Jack Hamilton did not go back to the Post Office after his daughter's funeral. The Postmaster had called him and insisted that he take some time off. Hamilton had protested, but the Postmaster was adamant, "This won't even count against your vacation or sick leave or comp time. The guys down here will pick up the load, so take as much time as you want. As far as the USPS knows, you're on the job." The Postmaster was breaking rules, Hamilton knew that, and he was grateful. Unlike a lot of the other clerks, Hamilton had always respected his supervisor, and the Postmaster made his offer knowing that Jack Hamilton would not abuse the charity, that he would not take a day more than he needed.

School was out for Marcie, so she was already home during the day. It was a new experience for Hamilton. On vacations or weekends, his free time had still been controlled by the knowledge that he would be back at work at a specific day and time. But now there was no deadline. For the first few days, they spoke to each other in short sentences, functioning, and they ate out a lot, even for lunch, but not in Athens. They drove to Iowa City or Cedar Rapids, found a real Mexican restaurant in West Liberty, went to West Branch to one of those places where you could cook your own steaks. Marcie wrote a lot of letters, thanking friends and relatives for their kindness. She worked in her garden. Hamilton read two books that had been waiting for him on his desk for months. Summer was a slow season for sports, he did not care for baseball or golf, so he seldom watched television. He stopped reading the newspaper. He wanted no current events. He and Marcie both started to screen their phone calls through the answering machine. A visitor to their house was met by Marcie, but often ignored by Hamilton, who stayed in the den. The Reverend Donald Mason had come to see them twice. The second time, Marcie did not open the door. He attached his card to the mailbox.

The door to Becka's room stayed open, and one of her parents *would sometimes find the other alone in their daughter's room, sitting on her bed, touching the nightgown that she had thrown on the bed that last morning, worn the night before. They were well aware that they were not unique, not the only parents to lose a child, an only child.*

They talked a lot to each other the first week, less the second, and the third week was almost silent. Each found somewhere to go, even in their own house. The first week, they had talked about Becka. Marcie had filled boxes and boxes of Becka's life from the moment she was born. Too much, Hamilton had complained when Becka turned twelve. The basement was not that big, he would say, but he always helped find space when Marcie gave him another box to carry downstairs. Toys, clothes, games, report cards, pictures drawn by Becka, awards, ribbons, news stories about her, the crib, the plaster cast from a broken arm when she was thirteen, even secret love letters from her first elementary school crush, letters that Becka thought she had safely and discreetly thrown in the trash but which Marcie had found and saved, to surprise her daughter when she had a daughter, as Marcie assumed Becka would.

The pictures were kept in albums in the den. Late at night, three weeks after the funeral, after Marcie had gone to bed, Hamilton sat in the den and went through every album, counting. He did not focus on any single picture. He just counted. Fifteen years, almost two thousand pictures. After totaling them, he went back to the beginning. First album, first picture: light brown Becka in her pale mother's arms. Second picture: held by her black father. Hamilton had stared at that second picture, wondering who the man was. He knew, of course, but he wondered who he was anyway.

In the morning, Hamilton had told his wife what he did the night before. He also tried to explain something he felt when he saw that second picture. But he could not put it into words. He stopped talking, even though he knew what he wanted to say— the day after Becka died, he had stopped imagining the future. Always before, he could see himself all the way until the day he died. He could see him and Marcie retiring, see Becka grown up, married and a mother herself, him and Marcie as grandparents, even see how his grandchildren looked. Sometimes he visualized himself as a postmaster, or perhaps even having served on the city council in Athens. He could imagine those things. See all the places he and Marcie would go after he retired, places that had never seen before. Now, he could not see the future. Becka died, and Hamilton could not visualize his life the next day.

The next night, he went back to the albums, to the last picture. In the bedroom, Marcie woke up hearing her husband laughing. She looked at the clock next to their bed. Almost three in the morning. At first, she thought it might have been the television, but as her mind cleared she was sure it was him. She walked into the den quietly. He was on the couch, an album on his lap. "Jack, are you okay?' she asked.

He turned his head to face her, nodded, and then motioned for her to sit beside him. "Come here. Come see this."

Next to her husband, she looked at Becka's last picture. It had been taken by Hamilton in April. Marcie and Becka were both on their hands and knees in the garden, but Becka was looking back at her father.

Marcie looked at the picture and took a deep breath. "Oh yes, I remember that one." She almost started laughing too. "She was not a happy camper that day. I remember how she had argued all morning about not wanting to help me, saying she had better things to do with <u>her</u> time than—how'd she put it—'sweat like some future pork chop'— and she was really mad at you for taking that picture. Said it made her butt look too big, just like her mother's."

Hamilton was laughing again, "That's all true, but you're missing it, the thing I never noticed until now. You have to look again."

Marcie looked again. "You mean the smirk on her face. You're right, I never noticed it before."

Hamilton laughed louder. "No, Marcie, look at how she has her hand up in the air. When I took the picture I thought she was just waving at me. But look at her ring finger, her forefinger, look how they're ever so slightly bent. Our darling daughter..." and Marcie finally saw it too "...is telling her father to fuck off."

Marcie tried not to laugh, tried not to see her daughter's middle finger noticeably straighter than the others around it, but there it was, so she forgave her husband's profanity and started laughing with him.

Hours later, they were both still awake, sitting in their kitchen drinking coffee, the sun not yet up. "You got plans for today?" Marcie asked him.

Hamilton stood up and stretched. "Nothing in particular, but I do feel like taking a walk. You want to tag along? Morning's still fairly mild, so come with me. Only other people out will be the dog-walkers, and they don't care how you're dressed. Put on some shorts, those year old brand new jogging shoes I bought you, and come with me."

Marcie looked up at him and said, "Sure."

The question of Soul. I was beginning to think like Ken Rumble talked. This soul business. The big picture. I had given up on my own soul. Given up believing in it. But all this talk about the soul of Athens, how the downtown was the soul of this community? Sure, a soul of bars and morning puddles of puke and piss from the night before, of graffiti and kids with purple hair and silver-studded dog collars around their necks saying "fuck" to all the AARPs who lived in senior housing on the fringes of downtown. An ugly soul. But it was also the place where town and gown mingled during the day. Busy people engaged in the commerce of market and mind. Especially around noon, when the weather was good, I would see familiar faces like Gary Sanders, who worked for me, and Jim Clayton, who owned The Soap Opera, or Chuck Miller the poet, or John Hayek the brilliant attorney.

On Friday nights, before Becky Hamilton died, we would all come downtown and listen to music. Not a collective care in the world. Local bands, sometimes the high school jazz group, or a solitary singer like Dave Moore, who could sing circles around a B-list crooner like Ken Rumble, all of them performing in front of the fountain where children soaked themselves. Athens was full of great people, and maybe they each had a soul, but this communal Emersonian Over-Soul thing—where was it? And who were these "people" that Rumble and Betty Norris kept talking about? I was beginning to think "the people" were more abstract than our soul. Or were they the same thing? I probably need to go back to Alexis de Tocqueville, like everybody else seems to do when they need a quote about American democracy. Athens is in Iowa, in America, and Americans are religious secularists—they worship themselves. Is that it?

How to understand it? I would sit in the Hollywood box-office with Danny and try to understand a phone call from some woman in Lone Tree who told me that if I had any balls I would fire the City Manager and Police Chief. That Joseph Holly is "an apologist for

Fascist rogue cops." I'd sit there as Danny ate popcorn, and I'd start diving into my education and pulling out French aristocrats and American writers to explain what I was thinking.

People in Athens—lawyers and poets and soap sellers—little atoms of Athens, all part of the magnetic field that holds this town together. You can forget their names, but they exist, and thousands more like them. They're all part of my version of "the people" but somehow I'm not sure they are "the people" I keep hearing about.

Who do I blame for all this? Thomas Jefferson, that's who. Don't trust the government, a revolution every twenty years. Life, liberty, the pursuit of a high-speed Internet connection. In the beginning, I was on the inside looking out, trying to figure out why "the people" were so upset, and all I could finally think of was Jefferson.

Athens, Iowa, America—In the beginning, the whole world was America—John Locke said it. Jefferson and all those other enlightened fathers absorbed Locke, but Locke wanted to protect property, not pursue happiness. Monticello tinkered with the words, and we've been chasing happiness ever since, awe-struck by the fresh green breast of a new world. You want some more obscure allusions? Remember, I read all the books, but I never finished my dissertation.

"Joe, you're not going to believe this."

Harry stood in front of me as I was mopping the Hollywood lobby. Looking down, concentrating on the tile floor, I could see how shiny his shoes were as he shuffled his feet to avoid being splashed with a stray drop of sudsy water.

"Harry, my credulity level is a lot lower than it used to be. Try me."

"You want the good news first, or the bad?"

I opted for bad, hoping for some sort of compensating good.

"The County Attorney is not taking the case to a grand jury.

He's decided—no charges against the cop. His decision, his alone."

I stopped mopping. The Hollywood phone started ringing, but I let the answering machine get it. The mysteries were compounding themselves. Harry and I, most of us, had assumed that some sort of charges would be filed against the cop. Third degree criminal negligence, at the least; second degree manslaughter at the worst. Some sort of punishment. Of course, we also knew that a good defense lawyer could probably beat both of those charges, especially considering Anheuser Hampton's criminal record. But there would be a ritual of purification, another opportunity for an extension of the people—a jury—to pass judgment. Accountability in the halls of justice—who was responsible for the death of Becky Hamilton and that other kid? —closure for "the people."

The County Attorney had run for office un-opposed for twenty years. He had always been seen as Caesar's wife, impeccably ethical and politically savvy. But to some people now, he had slammed the door on justice. There would be no accountability. Harry had gotten The Cop off the city payroll and handed him to the County Attorney, but The Cop was out of town and now out of trouble.

I stood there with Harry, both of us knowing what was about to happen. The County Attorney didn't televise his office work. He didn't let the press into his staff meetings. "The People" had been quiet for a few weeks, letters to the **TELEGRAM** had dropped off, the **BM FORUM** hadn't distributed a handbill on the downtown plaza for a while. The Athens City Council had a meeting that night. We were open for business. The people would be there.

"And the good news?" I asked, motionless mop in hand.

"My sources tell me that the Hamilton girl's parents are not joining the Hampton lawsuit."

"Are they filing separately?"

"They're not filing at all," Harry said, looking at me like I had an explanation. We had always assumed the Hamiltons would hit us with a mega lawsuit, and we knew their case was a lot stronger than the Hampton boy's was. Their daughter was a blameless victim.

"For now, or never?" I asked.

"Never."

"How can you be sure?" I wondered. Harry's "sources" were always reliable, but there was something mysterious about the Hamiltons. Unlike the Hampton family and their attorney/uncle Mason, who had sent envoys to speak at every meeting to accuse us of malfeasance and cruelty, the Hamiltons had never spoken to the press, never sent anyone to a meeting, never been quoted by anyone. How they felt, we all thought we knew. What they were going to do, that was the mystery.

"Joe, they have a neighbor who's their attorney and their friend. He's my source. He told me that we would never hear from them. He guaranteed it. They don't want a dime."

I had wanted to tell Harry how I had gone to the post office everyday since that first meeting, more than a month earlier, just to see Becky's father. Not to talk to him, just to see him, but he was never there. Ever since the service at St. Mary's, since the moment I had seen him and his wife at their daughter's grave, I had thought I could figure something out. Jack Hamilton was the key. But if I told Harry all that, he would ask me <u>why</u> I went, <u>what</u> was I trying to figure out. And I didn't have a good answer.

Once, in an unguarded moment, I had told Bernie Huss about me going to Oakland Cemetery and talking to my Kathy. Bernie had been telling me about her dead brother, so I thought she would understand, but I was wrong. All she said was, "I think about my brother, Joe, but I don't talk to him." So I kept it all to myself from then on. After being with Bernie at the Hampton funeral, I knew I had been dumb to assume that she would have understood me. Harry might have been different. We had shared a lot of secrets over the years, and he had let his guard down in front of me lots of times. He trusted me. But Harry had no children. If he had, I might have done it, confessed to him about looking for Jack Hamilton, about Kathy, about me yelling at Hartford in the woods. But Harry was childless, he always slept well at night, and he always gave me one of those "I'm humoring you" looks whenever I mentioned Hartford.

We talked about the meeting that night for awhile, joking about flak jackets, but Harry also told me that he was going to have several plainclothes cops in the audience, just in case. Then, as he was about to leave, he dropped some more news on me, "I've been hearing rumors that you're going to have an opponent this fall."

I shrugged, "The Greens are pissed at me for not letting Ken run the city. I can deal with that."

Harry shook his head, "That's not a rumor. That's a fact. I'm hearing something else, something about a serious opponent for you, somebody with credentials. Somebody who won't upset the good citizens like you do."

"Is that part of the bad news, or the good?" I tried to joke, hiding my surprise.

"Ask me on November fifth," he said. The election was on the fourth.

At seven that night, the council chambers were packed, and the mayor called in sick. Steve Nash would have stumbled, but nobody could accuse him of being ungracious. The mayor pro-tem—Bernie—was efficient, articulate, but she was hell on a gavel. The first thing she did after calling the meeting to order was tell the crowd that "since the recent tragic events involving the Athens police department were currently in litigation, we are constrained by state law from discussing them tonight."

174

Since Bernie had moved into the mayor's chair in the middle, I was left alone on the corner, an empty chair between me and Al Baroli. I wasn't able to slip her a note, correcting her. Harry, whose flexible mike was always pointed away from his face, wasn't quick enough to swing it around and get her attention. The City Attorney and City Clerk, to the far left of Bernie, were each reaching for their microphones too. Ken Rumble, whose mike was never more than a few inches away from his face, pounced at the same moment several people down front rose from their chairs and started making a bee-line toward the public microphone, "Madam Mayor Pro-Tem, that is not true…"

I knew that Bernie realized her mistake immediately. Before she could amend herself, Ken continued, "We cannot discuss the details of the litigation, but the people here tonight can certainly express their views, and we, as representatives of the people, are obligated to hear them, and we can, indeed, discuss city policies in general and facts about this case that are already in the public domain."

Bernie knew that, but she had, as she tried to explain, "mis-spoke."

It was going to be a long meeting.

The first person to the microphone was Betty Norris, trailing yellow fumes and open space around her. "How is the council going to respond to the decision this afternoon to exonerate your police officer?" Bernie started to explain how The Cop was no longer employed by Athens, how we had no control over him. Norris started firing again, "You have control over his pension, don't you. Until he's more forthcoming, can't you hold that?"

Bernie looked over at me and then Harry. She didn't have an answer for that question because, although she didn't know it, the premise was totally bogus. Harry tried to explain, "The officer doesn't have a pension with us. He wasn't employed long enough to qualify for our plan." Harry's voice seemed to irritate most of the crowd. Norris continued, "That is not my understanding," the tone in her voice telling everyone in the audience that Harry was lying to them. Bernie was still processing, but Ken had been around long enough to know the truth. I waited for him to speak, but he was silent. Finally, I said, "The City Manager is right, Betty. We have no relationship with him now."

"Is that true, Mr. Rumble?" Norris asked, and the crowd turned to Ken for the truth. I was becoming intrigued. Ken didn't seem to want to answer. He knew the truth, but he was silent. I remembered what Julie said about him. I looked over at him, but he seemed the same old Ken Rumble, beacon of truth and beauty.

"Technically, the City Manager is right…" he finally said, and I avoided looking back at Harry, who was probably reaching stroke level. How brilliant, I thought, to support and damn the city manager at the same time. "Technically" was such a wonderful word, implying a self-serving interpretation of the union contract by Harry, saying that Harry was correct but still not telling the whole truth. I looked at Betty, and then back at Ken, then it hit me. This was all a set-up. Ken and Betty were a couple. Burns and Allen, one handing straight lines to the other. Ken was about to tell us how to get around all those irritating technicalities. "…but we can do some things. Rather than simply reacting to a situation, we need to be pro-active. Something this council has not done very well in the past."

Okay, now I was pissed. "Would you please tell us how the City Manager is wrong. The cop was off the payroll less than 24 hours after the accident. What else should we be doing?" I asked, my voice not yet shifting lower.

Before Ken could answer, somebody from the crowd shouted, "How about doing your jobs right?" An outburst which released others. "How about telling us the truth…how about listening to the people…how about firing the Police Chief…how about firing those other cops…"

Bernie started pounding her gavel, and I could see the two cops in the audience, Andy Rocca and Fred Tymeson, dressed in jeans and over-sized jackets, shift in their seats so that they could face the crowd. Then I swear I thought I heard a gunshot, and a scream, but it was just somebody who was so agitated that when he leaped out of his metal folding seat he knocked it over, but we all heard the same thing. Rocca and Tymeson were standing up in a split second, their guns just about out from under their jackets, their eyes computing everyone around them. Me, I was too stunned to think, but Harry stood up immediately, shouting at Rocca and Tymeson, "Andy, Fred………it's okay. It's OKAY!!"

The two cops spotted the guy who knocked over his own chair, and he looked like he just crapped in his pants. The guns never appeared. But it still took a few minutes to get all of us back to breathing regular. I noticed that a lot of the crowd had hit the exits, and I was beginning to think that the whole town had been getting less sleep than me.

A facsimile of order restored, Ken spoke again, "Joseph, you asked about what else we could do. For starters, I have a resolution I would like to introduce and have this council formally approve, so that we can go on record as a collective body, representing the will of this community." Another example of why nobody on the council trusted him. He came to this meeting with ten copies of a resolution he wanted us to pass, but didn't tell any of us ahead of time, so we sat looking like idiots while he set the agenda. And I knew that he knew that we would not pass it. Having us agree with him was not on his radar screen.

"It is a simple resolution, simply stating the council's desire that the County Attorney convene a grand jury to seek a criminal indictment in this matter."

Betty Norris was back at the podium, a copy of the resolution in her hands before a copy had even reached me at the end of the council table. The council and city staff hadn't even had a chance to read the damn thing, and Betty was already quoting it without looking down at her copy. "I would urge the council to follow council member Rumble's lead on this. If not, I would hope that each of you would explain to us why you don't want your officer held responsible."

Bernie started to respond, but Al Baroli wanted to be himself, as much as I told him before the meeting not to be. "We can't tell the County Attorney what to do. This is none of our damn business."

Norris leaped, "Justice is none of this council's business?" The crowd's decibel level started rising again.

I needed to get the attention away from Baroli. "Betty, each of us is entitled to an opinion on how the County Attorney is doing his job, and we can tell him that in person or in print, but this council, as a body, ought not to be telling him how to do his job. To be quite honest, this borders on..." and I paused, debating with myself how I was going to finish this thought, because I knew that what I wanted to honestly say would totally piss off this crowd, but I wanted them to hear it anyway, "...this resolution borders on being mere—institutional posturing."

Norris flinched, but she wasn't my intended audience. I waited for Ken, and he didn't disappoint me.

"Joseph, you seem to be missing the point. Posturing is hardly..."

"Kenneth, here's my point. I think the County Attorney made a mistake. So do a lot of us on the council. I see him at the Hy-Vee store, I'll tell him what I think. And he'll probably tell me to go to hell, and I can live with that. He does his job, we do ours. But, our job is not to tell him how to do his. I'm not a criminal attorney, neither are you, neither is our city attorney. For all I know, the County

Attorney might be exactly right. But you want us to put political pressure on him because of a legal decision he made. <u>That</u> is institutional posturing."

"Once again, Joseph, you miss my point. You are, in fact, twisting my point," Rumble said, and I heard Al mutter something under his breath about "twist on this" just loud enough for his own microphone to pick it up, so I had to jump in again before he became the issue.

"Kenneth, you feel this way, it's your opinion. For us to pass this resolution, we're posturing."

"Joseph, all of us posture. It is the nature of politics." As if I needed a lecture from him about politics.

My voice dropped to its lowest level of the night, and I turned my entire body so I would face him square on, "And some of us do it more often and better than the others."

I can't really describe how good it felt to say that to Ken at that moment. Him and his people be damned. I wish I could tell you that I turned him around, made him see the error of his ways, but he was beyond my healing touch.

"If you will not support my resolution, I have a second option. If you think that a criminal investigation is none of our—institutional—business, then perhaps you can support me when I request the city manager to expedite a settlement in the lawsuit against the city, to spare the families of the victims involved the anguish of a lengthy trial. Surely, we, as an—institution, do not want to prolong their grief."

I stared at Rumble. I blinked. Was I the only one on the council who knew what he had just done? Harry grabbed his microphone just as the city attorney got her's. Harry spoke first, with the attorney nodding vigorously. "I would strongly urge the council to not, I repeat, to not take a position on this matter in this public forum. We've got an executive session scheduled for the next meeting to discuss pending litigation."

Ken wasn't dumb. He knew that the city's insurance company was handling our defense, not us. We paid the first hundred thousand of any settlement, they paid the rest. They hired the attorneys. They defended <u>their</u> money. Ken had just publicly screwed them. That is, if we agreed with him. The two new council-members next to him were looking all over the room for help. Bernie was about to speak, so was I, but Al opened his mouth first, "That is the damn dumbest idea you've ever had, Kenny boy."

The crowd popped again. Bernie and I spent the next half hour trying to explain why we had to meet in a private session, why the law and common sense required it, but all we did was make ourselves look more and more out of touch with the people in front of us. Two kids were dead, our cop was responsible, and we didn't want to talk about it—that's all they heard. And just as we thought some of the steam was going out of the crowd, a young black woman came to the microphone and started to tell us how the cops on the accident scene that night laughed at her and refused to let her comfort her dying brother. What sort of animals did we have working for us, she wanted to know. That was too much for Andy Rocca, who went to the microphone and tried to tell us that he was one of the investigating officers that night and what the young woman had just described had not happened, that "Hampton was dead before anyone arrived at the scene." He was angry as he spoke. Angry at what he considered an unfair accusation. But at the podium, he was merely an angry man with a gun under his jacket, employed by Athens and supported by six council-members.

Another hour, more stories about the police department. A professor from Iowa Arts talked about how he had gotten calls over the past year about police brutality, how he had referred them to the state office of the ICLU, but that we needed to know about them now. I asked him if he had ever called the Chief or City Manager—no. Did the ICLU have a record of the calls—no. Did he have names, so we could contact them—no. But we "needed to know." I kept looking at him and remembering something Ted Stanton had said years ago, about the only left-winger worthy of genuine respect was a union carpenter. This professor and his wife were both employed by Iowa Arts, pulling down a hundred and fifty thousand taxpayer dollars between them. They were good citizens, good people, and protected by tenure.

Our third hour, I started to hope that Gary Sanders would phone in a bomb threat for the Civic Center. We were all caught up in some sort of Mobius strip debate about a Kafkaesque police state. I was running out of analogies and allusions, and I wanted to go home.

I drifted off. John Brownstein came into the chambers carrying a deerskin pelt, we made eye contact, and I hoped he could read my mind— "John, save me from all this. Jump in here and tell us not to kill any more deer. Tell us that that is our biggest sin." But John saw the crowd and knew he wouldn't get anywhere near the microphone that night, so he left. Near eleven o'clock, I thought I saw people in the chambers who weren't there an hour ago, as if the crowd was calling for re-enforcements. Some sort of cell-phone militia. I saw people reading magazines. Other people wearing Sony Walkman headsets, and I wanted to stop the meeting and tell them to either pay attention or get the hell out. Rocca and Tymeson had to go on duty, so they were replaced by two female cops. The council took another ten-minute break, and I pulled Bernie into the conference room and told her to cut off the discussion. She promised me another half hour and then we would go to agenda item number one. If Rumble didn't want to discuss everything on the short agenda, we should be out of there by midnight. Me and Al Baroli then went out back and I listened

181

to him tell me about his son's dissertation as he smoked a ten dollar cigar. I had to give him credit, he could compartmentalize better than any of us. He talked as if we had just met downtown outside the Hollywood. Not a care in the world.

Back inside, I poked Bernie in the back as she headed for her seat, reminding her about her promise. I looked at the crowd and saw too many cups of coffee in their hands. But I drifted again, zoning out, floating off, outside my body it seemed, and I started to look closer at the people in front of us. I knew a lot of them. Not always my fans, but as individuals they were all good people, educated, truly concerned citizens, but why were they so angry? I tried to be one of them, to look up at what they saw. Why were Bernie and me and Harry, the others, except for Rumble—why were we the enemy? These weren't anti-government nuts, the right wing full-mooners who would repeal every ordinance on the books. Athens had the best record in Iowa on the issues they cared about, and I doubted that very many of them had ever personally had a bad experience with the cops, but they all seemed to know somebody who had. I was tired. I wondered if they knew something about this town that I didn't. It was not a comfortable thought, to admit to myself that I might have my head in the sand. Did we even agree on the facts? An Athens cop had chased a drug-dealing black teenager, despite being told to cut off the chase. The kid's car went out of control, and him and Becky Hamilton were dead. The cop was off the payroll in less than 24 hours. Anger and concern—sure. But, hysteria? Steve Nash was a cold fish as he apologized in the name of the city. He was probably the same way when his kids were born and the nurse handed each one over to him. His cool style was offset by his genuine warm substance. But nobody saw that. The County Attorney didn't file charges. But that's not our decision. He's not one of us, and I'd bet that 90% of the crowd that night had voted for him the year before.

Harry had told me a few years earlier, "Things are different than your first term. People are harder to please, less trusting. Taxes are higher, services strained. You're going to have to make some hard decisions." So I was wondering that night if all the changes were outside of me, or was it just me? I started to blame Jefferson again: Government is the enemy. I blamed the Republicans, especially that smiling dunce Reagan. All part of the same history, Whiskey Rebellion farmers, John Calhoun Nullifiers, lefties from the Sixties, right-wing lug-nuts from the Eighties. And it had finally come to Athens. I was looking at the big picture, for sure—Athens, Iowa, America. Give me liberty or give me death. Live free or die. Yep, I was lining up with the John Winthrop, Alexander Hamilton, Teddy Roosevelt crowd. The common good, the common currency, the activist Big Brother government. Or, maybe not. I was tired, and I was riffing my own version of American history.

But there was one puzzle I still had to solve. Who the hell was Ken Rumble? And what did Julie know about him that I didn't? I was in that meeting connecting all the cosmic dots, and all the sudden somebody was at the microphone demanding that we create a Police Citizens Review Board. It's some guy who had not spoken all night, but I had noticed him squirming in his chair for hours, turning darker and darker. Then he was in our face.

"Nobody seems to know who's in charge in that department. None of you people up there seems to know anything. Other cities have review boards. Why not Athens? If you won't look out for the public interest, why not have somebody who's not a politician or bureaucrat doing it?"

I thought it was another set-up, especially when the crowd started nodding and murmuring in agreement, but I looked at Ken and there was a flash on his face that I had seldom seen. He wasn't prepared.

My first reaction was that a review board like this wasn't needed. We weren't New York City, with cops spraying bullets all over Harlem. We weren't Washington, with a crack smoking mayor. We were Athens, and there wasn't another city in Iowa that had a police review board. I knew that. But it might not be a bad idea. Sort through the devilish details, it might not be a bad idea.

"Why can't you tell us NOW that you'll create this board and start protecting us from the police department?" The man was angrier, and the crowd was shouting at us again. "Make a decision! Stop covering up! Stop protecting the cops!" I was almost too tired to argue, and I expected Ken to start badgering us to go along with the crowd, but he was silent. I looked at him again. He was thinking. He was a smart guy. He would know all the problems involved, the long process required to do it. He was thinking, but the crowd turned on him. His people.

"Ken Rumble, don't you agree with us?" the angry man said. The crowd shouted, "Ken, whose side are you on?"

"I think that is an idea with merit," he began to say, "...but we need to..."

The crowd interrupted him, "Whose side are you on!!"

There it was, just like Julie told me, but this time I could see it. Ken Rumble was scared of the people in front of him. The crowd was now a mob, and it was leading him. He hadn't prepared for this moment. He had cultivated his status for years, the lone wolf of integrity, the only one who listened to the people. Well, the people were speaking now and he had damn well better listen.

That night was the moment for Ken Rumble to achieve greatness. He had risen to iconic celebrity-hood on a record of making the council and city staff look bad, of pissing off developers, of being the "voice" of the people. At that moment, that night, he could have said, "You might be right, but we need to slow this down. You are asking us to make a split second decision, to do exactly what that officer did—to not think, to act viscerally, not thoughtfully. We need to make the right decision, not a quick decision."

Sure, he could have said that. Hell, I could have said that. But that crowd was not listening to me. I had no credibility with them. At that moment, Ken Rumble could have held up his hand and disappointed his own people, and Athens would have been spared a summer of rage.

He spoke, "Actually, I was preparing such a proposal to present to the council at a future meeting. But this is the right moment for this council to begin the process of healing this community. I would urge them to set a deadline for the establishment of such an oversight review commission. We can work out the details later, but we need to commit ourselves here tonight, in front of the people of Athens, to do this. I would like a show of hands from my fellow councilors. Who is in favor?"

The crowd applauded and stood. Bernie hit the gavel. Ken had his own hand in the air. The two women next to him started to raise their hands, but Bernie turned and glared at them. "Show us your hands," the crowd shouted. Bernie hit the gavel again. "Show us your bloody hands," the crowd shouted.

Harry Hopkins raised his hand.

The best moments of your life? All the pleasures? Your best meal, best sex, most uplifting music, you get that promotion, your team wins the Series, your mother holds you in her arms as you go to sleep? Sometimes they last a few minutes, a few seconds, but never forever. The chemical rush comes and goes. If you're lucky, the memory of it brings back a pale version of the past. For me, I'll always remember Harry raising his hand.

I've looked at the tape of that meeting, but it's not there. All the shouting can be heard, but the camera was on Bernie, and she didn't see Harry for a few seconds. By the time the camera swung around to him, he was merely explaining himself. Unless you were there like me, scanning the crowd in front and council to your left, you missed the big picture. The suspended animation. The stunned silence. The faces slowly turning toward Harry. The "what the hell does this mean" moment. After I absorbed the room, I turned back to Harry and listened, as fascinated as anyone else.

"I just need to remind the council that any such decision will not be a minor adjustment in city policy. You might want to reserve judgment until our special meeting next week in which we go over all the complaints that have been registered so far, and review current police policies. More importantly, such a board, to be truly effective, will have to have a budget and staff support, and that will require some serious reconsideration of the overall budget. The decision is yours, of course, and I'll do as directed, but you need to think about all the ramifications, and you might want to have some special meetings to get more public input about how to structure such a review board."

It took him about two minutes to finish, and another two seconds for the crowd to respond. They were more than angry. "Who's running the city?" they shouted. "Who's in charge?"

Bernie finally bit the bullet and banged her gavel for the last time, but it cost her another broken window at her store an hour later. "This meeting is adjourned. I'll call a special meeting for tomorrow afternoon to finish the other business on tonight's agenda. It's obvious we've all reached the end of our ropes right now. Some rest will do us all good."

"I object…" Ken Rumble began.

"Objection over-ruled. This meeting is over." And before Ken could respond, Bernie stood up and walked out of the room, trailed by the two new council-members and Al Baroli, who was muttering, "About time."

I just sat there. The crowd started leap-frogging all over itself, but in a few minutes it disappeared. It was then that I noticed Mike Wagner in the back of the room, standing next to a video camera on a tripod. Mike was the Athens reporter for the Cedar Rapids ABC station, a good guy. He waved at me and put his hand next to his ear, letting me know that he would call me. I kept sitting there.

"You going home?" I finally heard Harry say.

Except for Bob Hardy and his staff breaking down the government channel equipment and straightening chairs, Harry and I were alone.

"Hell of a meeting," I said. "Strange thing is, I'm not as tired as I was a while ago. Some sort of endorphins must have kicked in."

"Yeh, we should do this more often," he said.

"You're kidding, right?"

"Can't get anything past you, can I?" he said.

"Not a chance, Harry. I'm a college graduate."

"Joe, I've got bus drivers with PhDs. I've got the most educated staff in America. You're not the hot shit you think you are."

I laughed. "Still, a rough meeting, and just in case nobody else on council says it—thanks for slowing down the train."

"Just doing my job. You want a board like that, I just want you to do it right. That's all I was doing."

And, here's the moment I told you about, one of those singular moments that make life fun and worth living. Harry was telling me about "just doing" his job, and I'm staring at him, and he stops talking and looks right at me, and we look at each other, and I see the edges of his mouth start to curl down, but down in an odd sort of smile, and I read his mind.

"You were doing more than that, weren't you?" I said. "Sure, you were doing your job, but you know as well as I do that what you were really saying was, who you were really talking to, what you were actually saying was 'And fuck you, Kenny.' Just me and you, Harry, admit it."

I wouldn't want to play poker with Harry Hopkins.

"Just doing my job," he said, absolutely straight-faced. "And you've done your's. Now, take my advice. You look like hell. Go home. Go to bed. Rest up for the meeting tomorrow. You're not getting any younger."

Bob Hardy shouted from the back of the chambers, "Lights out in five minutes, gentlemen."

Jack Hamilton did not tell his wife about all the dreams. He described some, she shared her own, but he did not tell her about the ones that frightened him. Nor did he tell her about his daydreams, the thoughts he had when he was awake, when he should have been able to control his own mind, but failed.

Sometimes the deer was in his mind. Sometimes it was not a deer, but some version of the deer. Most often another animal, but always the same feeling of dread and wonder. The strangest dream was about football. He was back in Chicago, about to face Jim Brown. He would think about this dream afterwards, analyze it the most. Jim Brown had retired years before Jack Hamilton ever turned pro. But Brown had been his hero growing up, and Hamilton had always wanted to be a running back, like Brown. Hamilton was quick on his feet, but he was never fast enough to suit his coaches, never strong enough to break tackles until it was too late for a change. He was a linebacker. He always wondered how he would have done against Brown. He listened to some of the old retired Bears describe their own confrontations with Brown. Dread and wonder, dread and wonder, that was how Hamilton interpreted their feelings. And then Brown retired, in his prime, and the Bear veterans passed on stories. Hamilton had seen lots of film of Brown, him punishing the linebackers and safeties, him being gang tackled, piled on, slowly rising, limping back to the huddle, and then coming back on the next play like he had never been hit. The veterans agreed: seeing Brown on film and seeing him come at you in real time down on the field— not the same. Not even close.

Becka and Jim Brown were in the same dream more than once. Hamilton and his daughter would be on the grass on Soldier Field in Chicago, and Hamilton would be watching her run from one end of the field to the other, then back again, back and forth, never tiring, taunting her father to catch her. In the first dream, Hamilton heard the deer somewhere on the field, but he never saw it, then Jim Brown was running toward him and Becka, and he woke up. The worst part was him yelling at her, trying to warn her, but she was oblivious to the danger. Even as she passed close by her father, close enough for him to speak in a normal voice, she did not hear him. In another dream, Brown was running toward Hamilton. Becka was nowhere to be seen, so he at first thought that he was Brown's goal, but Brown flowed past him in a haze of motion, his cleated feet sounding like hooves on hard dirt. Brown did not even acknowledge Hamilton's existence. He was looking for Becka. Hamilton woke up.

It was the last dream that Hamilton finally described to Marcie, as if the others had never happened. He even lied to her about it, telling her that she was also in the dream when she was not, but he wanted her to be part of it, to see it as he had the night before. So he put his wife in the bleachers, himself beside her, and they watched their daughter run away from Jim Brown, run until she tired and Brown finally caught up with her.

At this point in his story, Hamilton could see that Marcie was getting upset. "No, no," he told her, "It all turns out fine."

Becka seems incredibly happy in the dream. She is unbeatable, but her parents see Brown coming closer and closer. At that moment in the dream, as Hamilton explains to Marcie, they can see Becka up close as she turns to see Brown almost upon her, and her face is beyond beautiful, laughing as Brown pulls up beside her, his muscled chest bare, his shoulders huge and parallel to the turf, and then Becka's parents are back in the bleachers watching her and Jim Brown run side by side, stride for stride. And the dream is over.

"That's it?" Marcie asks.

"That's all," Hamilton replies, and he sees Marcie smile.

"That's a good dream, Jack."

Hamilton was glad that he had changed some of the details.

Marcie felt better, and that made him feel better. The details he had exorcised from his dream, the darker details, he told himself, those were not important. Marcie did not need to know. Eventually, he told himself, he would not remember them either.

Alexis de Tocqueville was wrong. Richard Nixon was right. Not a happy thought, I know. In Athens, there wasn't a tyranny of the majority, but there was a Silent Majority. Tyranny of the Vocal Minority, that's what we had. Small cells of energy with the most audible volume, drowning out the other—people?

My problem? I was starting to think that the loudest people were right. Julie and Harry told me that that was my problem. I didn't possess the comfort of somebody like Ken, whose vision was described by Julie as "unhampered by competing interpretations of reality, whose ear drums weren't as tuned to the longer wave lengths of sound."

"I thought you had a PhD in English," I had told her. "Since when do you know so much about physics?"

"I'm a woman, a mother, and married to you, Joe. The triple whammy. I need all the help I can get."

For weeks after the meeting at which the review board was first mentioned, I immersed myself in the details of the police department. The council had three special public meetings about the department and the possibility of a commission to review it. Harry supplied us with reams of statistics about every possible category in which we could evaluate Athens in comparison to other cities in Iowa. Harry was good at that, supplying information, sometimes too much of it. After all, did it really matter if more police cars in Iowa were white than black? It did if you were Betty Norris, who used that fact as an analogy in one of her guest editorials to the **TELEGRAM**: *Is the Athens Police Department too white, just like its patrol cars?*

But if facts were truth, and perceptions could become the truth, I was beginning to understand something about the Athens department. It was nowhere near as bad as we had been told, as the comments at the meetings had seemed to lead us, but it was not as benign as I had thought either. Too many arrests for public drunkenness way out of proportion to the problem, too many complaints about arrogance from the young cops who grew up on television tough cop reality, who thought they were all Don Johnson or Dennis Franz, not enough cops on foot, some real problems. But the statistics showed that we had the fewest official complaints filed against the department than any other comparable city in Iowa. We had the most educated police force in Iowa, just like the town itself. A week after that long meeting, we also had the luckiest police department in Iowa.

Andy Rocca was patrolling the Broadway area, busted up a street fight, searched a suspect's car, and found the videotape of Anheuser Hampton.

The public meeting was just a formality to allow us to retire to executive session to discuss pending litigation, but I slipped Bernie a note as Steve Nash called the opening roll: My bet—we take a vote for the executive session—Ken objects—says we 'ought not to shut the people out'—votes against the session—he loses 6-1—then walks in with us behind closed doors.

Bernie shook her head and whispered, "You're right. He's getting predictable. We look like the Tories, he's Thomas Paine."

Al Baroli heard us and whispered loudly, "Thomas pain in the ass."

"Mr. Mayor, I was wondering why we could not keep this discussion…" Ken began.

Inside the conference room ten minutes later, Al sat beside me and folded his hands, very pleased with himself, leaning over to me, "Pain in the ass, Joe, worse than my hemorrhoids."

Harry was setting up the VCR when Ken started to speak, "I think we need to more seriously consider my proposal to settle these lawsuits. There is no reason to……"

With his back still toward Ken, Harry interrupted him, "We just got this. You might want to see it before we do anything else."

Then Harry turned around, with that downward curl smile of his, "For the record, there is only one lawsuit against us, and this tape will settle that case."

It was an ugly hour. The tape of Hampton and his friends passing the thirteen year old girl around among themselves, the guns waving, the drugs and money on the table, the camera recording every smirk and profanity, Hampton no worse than the others, but damning enough. A copy of the tape had been sent to our insurance company and would go to the Hampton lawyers soon enough. Ken said nothing as the rest of us agreed with Harry's proposal to offer a hundred thousand dollar settlement in exchange for the action going away. The tape and final settlement would be sealed. Hampton could still be a public martyr, but not a ten million dollar martyr.

Al Baroli didn't want to settle at all, thinking the tape would sway any juror against even a performer like Donald Mason. But he finally agreed with me that the longer we let the case drag, the longer the circus meetings at the council would continue. Public peace, I told him, was worth a hundred thousand dollars. I had looked at Ken, expecting him to disagree, but all he said was, "How soon will all this be finished?"

Harry said, "It might take a month, offers back and forth. Mason will not accept, try to bluff us, but when he realizes that we won't budge, he'll take the money and run. He has a dozen other cases working across the country right now. He'll declare this one a victory and make a strategic withdrawal."

An hour later, Harry and I were alone in the conference room. We both thought the worst was over. The Hamptons would settle. The Hamiltons weren't suing, weren't even speaking to the press. I told him that I was going to support the creation of the police review board. He shrugged, "I figured you would, but I think you're wrong. We don't need it, and you're nickel and diming the budget."

"Harry, the department's good, but it ought to be better," I said.

Harry wasn't impressed, "I don't need a review board to make that happen. Look, Joe, if you really think this is a good idea, all well and good, but don't do it just to be throwing a bone to those people."

I shook my head. "Harry, I'm not sure what the real issue is with everybody that's angry with us. But this thing let out whatever was always there. Health, safety, and welfare—that's our job. Nobody's <u>safe</u> in this town if people don't trust the police department. We've got to do more than make it better, we've got to make everybody think it's better. A citizen review board will help…"

"Save your speech for the public vote," he snapped at me.

I stopped talking, and we sat there a moment in silence. Then he said, "Look, you get a majority to see it your way, I'll make it happen. But you know that this thing has absorbed us for almost two months. It's not the only problem we've got, but we're being bled by this thing, all our time used up dealing with it. You do the board, fine, it won't get settled for another six months, and all you'll have me and the staff doing is do more research for you. I won't say this in public, but I'm tired, mind and body, tired of getting the abuse I've gotten all this time. I'm not the villain here. And I am tired of being in the cross-hairs."

"I'll do this as quickly as I can," I said. "I'll get Bernie and Steve lined up, and the new people. Ken will go along to begin with, but he'll eventually vote against the final version anyway, even after we've accommodated him on some of his ideas, saying it doesn't go far enough. Discrediting our work. I know that. And Al will vote against it. It will be a 5-2 vote. But I think I can make it happen before the election. Institutionally, it's a good idea. Politically, it tells the most alienated people out there that we're listening to them."

"You're speechifying again." Harry said, finally relaxing, "And politics is a bitch."

"Give me three months. We'll get this done by November, and then we can get back to sidewalks and sewers."

"If you win," he said quietly.

"The Greenies? You think they'll beat me? Hell, there's a big drop-off in their labor pool once you look past Ken. I'd love to face him one on one this fall, but you know as well as I do that he won't jump into my district. He'll send out some sacrificial lamb just to irritate me, and run himself at-large. Sorry, Harry, you're stuck with me for another four years."

"Maybe, maybe not. Just remember what I said. Politics is a bitch." He stood up and motioned for me to follow him back into the council chambers. "You've going to be on a crowded district ballot, Joe. Protect your flanks."

He led me to the back wall, where all the pictures of prior councils were hanging. Then he pointed to the yellowing picture of the 1961-63 council, seven white guys who looked like the board of directors for Ford Motors in 1930. I stared, finally saying, "Am I missing something here, or is there something in this picture I should see that I don't?"

"Your real opponent for this fall," Harry said, his finger under the man in the middle.

I looked again. Who the hell was Charles Firestone? I kept looking, thinking Harry must be joking. "The mayor from 1961? Is that who you're pointing to? I'm in the eighth grade and this guy is the mayor of Athens, and now we're running against each other?" I started laughing. "Harry, is this guy even still alive?"

Harry wasn't laughing with me.

Al Baroli flies his own plane, crashes a lot while landing, setting some sort of record for running out of gas on his final approach, but he keeps going back up. He took me up with him a year ago, before

Becky Hamilton died, with Julie and Danny waiting in our car at the Athens airport for me, as Julie said, "to come back in shock or in pieces." Al broke a few FAA rules, but he did what I asked him to do. I wanted to see Athens from the air.

You should do this if you live in a small town. Get in a plane and fly just high enough to see the city limits, to see where your town ends and the country begins. You can't do this if you live in New York or L. A. or places like that. The boundaries are too spread out, so you have to fly really high to see them, and then you can't really see anything. Al flew me over Athens and I could see my house and his, the civic center, Iowa Arts buildings, downtown, and each place was distinct. I could even see the new maple tree in my front yard, the kiosks downtown, the corner of First and Court, where Becky Hamilton would eventually die. But I was still high enough to see the corn and soybean fields around us. Two hundred years ago, Iowa was part of the West. Prairie grass as high as your chest, waves of open space. But now we're the heart of the mid-west, crisscrossed by I-35 and I-80, a farm state. Of course, Athens isn't a farm town. But, then again, America isn't a farm country anymore either. So, in a lot of ways, Athens is more American than Iowan. Commerce grounded in information and knowledge, not industry or agriculture.

Al flew me over Athens, and I thought I was looking at a Grant Wood painting, a small town of straight streets surrounded by a world of green and gold rolling fields. I could recognize places, see the whole town, but we weren't low enough to recognize the people. The last thing Al showed me was the open space between the Weber Park forest and the creeping Coral Ridge city limits. Two small towns drawing toward each other, and in between was a herd of deer that bounded in and out of the old trees. That was a year ago. John Brownstein is right, you won't see those deer today, nor the open space.

I have a game with Danny that he doesn't know I play. I tell him that somebody's name is Danny, like his, and he thinks that is the coolest thing. Sometimes it's easy, and the other person plays along, like the singer Dave Moore becoming Danny Moore for my Danny. Down the street from me and Julie is Dan's Short Stop, a convenience store. Not one of those chain stores, a local store, owned by Dan Glasgow, a good guy. Across the street from Regina High School, down the street from Athens High, Dan has the biggest selection of candy in town. You want sugar on a stick, you go to Dan's. My Danny and I walk up there all the time, and Dan has become another Danny. Why do I do this? My Danny doesn't talk much, but he seems to respond to anybody he thinks is also named Danny. And it has to be Danny, not Dan or Daniel. I can let Danny go up to Dan's Short Stop by himself, and he will come back with candy, usually a freebie from "Danny" Glasgow.

Me and Danny get our haircuts at the same time and place: Stan's Barbershop, near the library downtown, a guy place, not a salon, with Playboys hidden in the magazine stacks, and ads on the walls for pool cues. Stan Yoder has been there for years, but I introduced Stan to my Danny as Danny Yoder, and we've never had trouble getting his hair cut.

Does this all matter, my Danny stories? Of course it does. I tell you about Athens, about the crowd at the council meetings, about Ken Rumble, and you might think the whole town was like that, like it was some sort of political Wonderland, but it's more than that. For a few months after Becky Hamilton died, I forgot that. Forgot about Dan Glasgow and Stan Yoder and all the others who were not in front of me in the council chambers. For those months, Athens was Wonderland.

August in Athens, I was chasing white rabbits.

Harry warned me about Charles Firestone, but I thought Harry worried too much. I was at the Hollywood the next day, inventory done, and I called Firestone.

"Mr. Firestone," I began, self-conscious about the age difference.

"Who is this?"

"Joseph Holly, Mr. Firestone. You and I......"

"Joseph who?"

"Joseph Holly, sir. On the city council. I understand that you might be running against me, so I was wondering if perhaps we could......"

"Who are you?"

"Mr. Firestone, are you......"

"Call me Charlie, everybody calls me Charlie."

I paused, wondering if Charles Firestone had heard me. He was an old guy. Almost as old as my father. "Charlie......are you running for city council this fall?"

"Of course I am."

"Okay, you're running against me, and I was just wondering what you thought were the important issues, the things you're concerned about. Perhaps we have some common ground."

"Who are you?"

"Joseph Holly, sir. Your opponent," I said, enunciating too loudly.

"Why are you yelling at me?" Firestone asked indignantly.

"I'm sorry, sir. I was just wondering why you were running against me."

"I'm not running against anybody. They told me that I was unopposed."

"You're running in District-B, aren't you?"

"I'm running for the city council of Athens. I'm not running for some sort of district council. I'd appreciate your support. Thanks for calling."

He hung up on me. It was the last conversation I would have with Charlie Firestone for a long time. He never attended a candidate forum before the primary, only once after that. He never knocked on a door. He spent the rest of August on vacation in Colorado. His campaign spent sixteen thousand dollars, big for Athens. I spent four hundred and fifty dollars because Julie made me get some yard signs, and she picked out the colors: teal letters on a pink background. You could see them a mile away. I told the **TELEGRAM** that I expected to be judged on my record, that I assumed that the voters had been paying attention for the past four years.

A month after the election, as Julie and I sat on a warm beach in Florida, she pointed out the flaw in my strategy, "Joe, you assumed too much. Then again, maybe they <u>were</u> paying attention." I looked over at her, the afternoon sun and Atlantic waves making us both sleepy. Danny was laying on a towel in front of us, lathered in #60 sunscreen. "You want to go back to the room, smarty," I asked her. We both looked at Danny. He was asleep. "Can you carry him?" Julie asked, letting her fingers trace a line across my hand. I nodded. "Well, my hero, let's go take a nap," she smiled.

August in Athens, I was on the phone a lot. Everytime I thought we were ahead of the curve, I got a call asking me what I thought about the latest broadside in **BM FORUM** or the latest guest editorial in the **TELEGRAM**. The Hampton lawsuit hadn't been settled yet, and we were still fair game.

Harry called me about the latest Betty Norris guest editorial, accusing him and the Police Chief and the County Attorney of conspiring to keep the cop away from a trial: *The County Attorney needs the cooperation of the City Manager and Police Chief in order to insure a successful prosecution rate for his office. He owes them many favors. Is it unreasonable to ask these three men—what agreement did you reach that kept the public in the dark and justice from being served? What are you hiding?*

"Does she actually think the County Attorney gives a crap about my opinion in doing his job?" Harry barked at me.

Charlie Firestone's campaign manager, John Prose, called and suggested that I not run for re-election. Insisted that I was going to lose. Prose was a downtown businessman, a cousin of the infamous Prose brothers. He had an opinion about everything and wrote the council all the time to share his wisdom. Prissy and simplistic letters that made even his "friends" on the council cringe and want to gag, friends who were laughing at him behind his back. I asked Prose why Firestone was even running at all, much less against me. All Prose could say was, "This council's dysfunctional. We need a change, and Charlie will shake things up." Prose didn't appreciate it when I asked him who was going to keep Firestone awake at the meetings if he won.

I asked a lot of people why Firestone was running against me, but nobody had a clue. I doubt that he even knew. It joined the list of mysteries for that summer. Why Anheuser Hampton didn't stop for The Cop, the Hamilton's not suing the city, why the County Attorney didn't press charges, and, finally, why hadn't I seen it coming, why had I been so oblivious to some serious opponent materializing against me?

But Firestone's campaign committee was deadly serious. Like El Cid propped up on a horse to frighten the heathen Arab hordes, Charlie Firestone's face and name were soon everywhere. In the first two weeks of August, every registered voter in Athens got a post card announcing his candidacy, and then a separate fund-raising letter. Billboards on Gilbert Street popped up, with a picture of Firestone that must have been taken before Lyndon Johnson was pulling puppy ears. Bernie Huss told me to worry, but how could I? Charlie Firestone was clueless in Gaza.

I used that Gaza line in front of Julie and a few other people, but she was the only one who laughed. I also told her, "I'm from Texas. I know how dead men can get elected to office. Happens down there all the time. But this is Athens. We're different."

"For sure, pardner, but even the PC crowd in my department know all about Charles Firestone, and that should tell you something," she said, right after I told her about Prose calling me.

Charlie Firestone was indeed an old-Athens pillar. Youngest mayor in our history, past member of the zoning and parks commissions, retired pediatrician who had inoculated a few thousand Athens babies who were now voters, founder of the Athens "Friends of the Library" foundation, Rotarian, Mason, Shriner, past Chamber of Commerce president, current member of the Iowa Arts Board of Trustees, and deacon at the Episcopal Church. More credentials than God. But, I repeat, clueless in Gaza. Face to face with me, one on one, asked a simple question about any city issue of the past ten years, he'd be blinking. He was well known, well liked, and suffering from every ailment afflicted on most 80+ year old men.

I started calling my old supporters, who all assured me that I would beat Firestone easily. But when I asked them for a public endorsement, they hesitated. I specifically asked if they were supporting me at all, and they hesitated. Their favorite response was: "I want to be fair to both of you, see where you stand on the issues, make up my mind later." Or another favorite, from a downtown businessman who I thought was my friend, with whom I had shared council gossip for years: "I wish both of you could win." When I pointed out the un-likelihood of that happening, all I got was more hesitation. A downtown bank president: "Joe, I encouraged Charlie to run. But I didn't think he would run against you. I thought he would run for one of the at-large seats, not in your district. So now I'm stuck, but I can't support you. Sorry."

My favorite disappointment? Two years earlier I had helped an insurance agent get his seemingly moderate candidate elected to council, one of the two new women. Went to his organizational meetings, prepped his candidate for debates, wrote sample letters to the editor, and then helped his pet projects get funding from the council. When Firestone's first "signature" ad came out in the **TELEGRAM**, this guy's name was near the top of a list of a hundred other Firestone supporters. Him, he's the archetype of betrayal.

The weirdest phone calls? From Betty Norris. The first time, I thought I was hearing from some phone-sex line direct solicitation. Until she identified herself, after a throaty "Joseph, I have some information for you only" introduction that got my attention, I was intrigued by her new voice. Deep and conspiratorial and blatantly sexual, nothing like her voice at the meetings. The fascination didn't last long. Betty wanted to tell me about "sources" that I should know about, information she had about the police department from retired cops who knew "the truth" about the chief. According to her sources, the chief was ignoring existing policies, and changing some policies without council approval. I asked for names. She told me that "they" would be contacting me directly, but they never did. Still, in her notes to the **BM FORUM**, those sources were stone tablets down from the mountain. And those notes were paraphrased and translated into letters to the editor at the **TELEGRAM**. The chief was out of control, and the city manager was protecting him. The police department was issuing clarifications daily. Harry explained the chain of command over and over until he seemed insincere. I was getting stopped in the Hy-Vee, head-on shopping cart collisions, and grilled about why I hadn't told Harry to fire the chief. Julie told some women from her department to go buy some new batteries for their dildos when they cornered her about me.

Then Harry called to tell me that we're all going to be on national television: *"Heart-ache in the Heartland—Cops and a Cover-up."*

"Here's your chance to be a star, Joe," Harry said. "Take my advice. Dye your hair."

August in Athens, no rain since July Fourth, and ABC was coming to town. I called the ABC affiliate in Cedar Rapids, but they told me that it was strictly a national story. The Iowa station hadn't contacted the higher-ups in New York, but somebody with journalism connections somewhere had.

ABC blew into town on Monday and was gone by Thursday morning. I talked to enough people to learn that the network was making Athens part of a larger story about police chases gone bad all across the country, the "issue" of the week. And, truth was, it <u>was</u> a chase gone bad. We needed to take the punches and get it past us, to make sure that ABC knew we were working on a citizen review board and other changes in the department. Hope for the best.

Then I got other calls, and suddenly the story was <u>only</u> about Athens. The public outcry, famous Donald Mason, the black and white dynamic, and especially Becky Hamilton—surely enough meat for 18 minutes of *PRIME TIME* or *DOWNTOWN* or *20/20*. If we hit the media jackpot, we could be 22 minutes of *NIGHTLINE*. Harry Hopkins and Ted Koppel in a hair stare-down. We were warned to get ready for a lot of cameras at our next meeting, so Bernie said she was wearing special make-up. Julie made me wear my blue shirt and a red tie, promising that she would watch the meeting.

Harry and The Chief were interviewed Tuesday afternoon before the meeting, and Harry called me immediately afterwards, "I smell a rat, Joe. They were in my office ten minutes, about the same with the chief. No big deal, I know they can't use more than a minute, probably less, from anybody. But I did learn that they were doing some sort of 'town forum' tomorrow afternoon and wanted to use the council chambers. I told them okay. When I asked them if they wanted me for that, they told me they already had a group. Who was representing 'the city' I asked, and all they said was the somebody from the council would participate."

"Ken Rumble, is that your guess?" I asked him.

"You know the line about the Pope's religion," Harry said. "This is all too obviously a set-up. I told them, if they had anybody, they ought to have the mayor. That's his job, to speak for the council."

"Oh god, Steve Nash on national television," I moaned. "We're going to get sympathy cards from all over the country."

"Steve's a good man, Joe."

"I know. A good, decent man who's a C-list actor even on a small stage like Athens. Can't we get Bernie to do it?"

"Think about that for a second."

"Yeh, right, but Ken will eat Steve alive in front of the camera."

Harry was quiet for a second, "Joe, remember what I said about you being a star. It just might be show-time."

I called the Holiday Inn downtown and got through to the ABC producer's room. I asked to be included in the forum, but he told me that he had already contacted the mayor and they were "going with him." I asked to be added, but he said the panel was full. It was worse than Harry and I had thought. Seven people were lined up: Steve Nash, Ken Rumble, Anheuser Hampton's sister, Donald Mason, some Rumble-ite who had been to every council meeting since the accident and who had told us over and over that we were "not listening to the people," a restaurant owner who was actually a good guy and who would probably be the fairest of the critics—and Betty Norris.

The producer did offer me a deal, "If you can get one of the girl's parents to talk to us, I can bump somebody off the panel and slide you in. We're having a helluva time getting through to them. And they're the key to our story. Their daughter absolutely in the wrong place at the wrong time. And her father a former NFL player, another hook. I know that the guys on Monday Night Football still remember him. So, if we can't get the Hamiltons, we use another story."

"You've got more than one story?" I asked reflexively, not looking for a fight, but you'd have thought that I had just caught him in bed with Barbara Walters.

He stammered at first, something about just doing his job, but finally sighed, in the tone of a man who had been working too long at a job he didn't like, "There's always more than one story."

"So what's the other story?" I wondered aloud.

"Government cover-up, renegade cops, corrupt politicians, citizens against the establishment, anger and fear, bad moon rising in the heartland—we'll film tonight and tomorrow and see what develops."

I sat in the Hollywood after talking to the producer, not even mad at him. He was a smart man doing his job, and he was right— there was always more than one story.

I called Steve Nash and tried to subtly suggest that I represent the council on the forum, but he said he was sure he could handle things. Besides, it wasn't going to be a live broadcast, no pressure, he would be fine. I called Harry and told him I wasn't going to be a star.

"Too bad, Joe, it could have been your ticket out of here."

During my first term on the council, in a galaxy far away, Julie and I had a secret signal I always gave at ten o'clock. She liked to go to bed then, but she told me she would turn on the TV and wait for me to wave at her before she went to sleep. I would bribe Bob Hardy with some Hollywood passes to make sure he had the camera on me exactly at ten o'clock. I would check the clock on the back wall, wait for the camera under the clock to swing my way, and then wave as I looked directly into the lens.

As I left for the meeting the night ABC was there, Julie asked me to wave to her again. I told her that I couldn't promise that I could get the camera on me at ten, but she said, "Joe, I'll watch the whole thing, me and Danny. Wave to us at least once. Danny will like that. And I'll be your best friend."

ABC lumbered in early and was set up before Bob Hardy had the usual city crew in place. When I arrived, Bob was arguing with some assistant producer about camera locations. ABC was blocking the city cameras, and the council chambers had always been Bob's territory. ABC backed down.

The first sign that all my assumptions were wrong? I had expected a huge crowd, but only a few dozen people were in the chambers, most of them there on the usual zoning issues. The Hampton case wasn't formally on the agenda, but we figured that the crowd would materialize in time for the "public discussion." Wrong.

As soon as Steve called the meeting to order, the Reverend Donald Mason entered the chamber, followed by Hampton's sister and a few other of the usual suspects. Then I remembered—the **BM FORUM** had encouraged its people to come to the town forum on Wednesday night, but it hadn't mentioned the Tuesday meeting at all.

When Steve opened the public discussion, Mason stepped up to the microphone and the ABC cameras began purring.

Three minutes later, Mason walked out of the chambers. I looked over at Harry, both of us wondering what the hell had just happened. Mason had been rhetorical and eloquent, urging the council to "cleanse itself" and "let the truth shine forth as a soothing balm for a troubled community." He thanked us for letting him speak for the "voiceless in Athens." It was a sermon, but we had been expecting a closing argument in front of a jury. Then he was gone.

Harry told me before the meeting that he had spoken with Mason's assistant, and that she had assured him that Mason and the

Hamptons were close to settling their lawsuit, but it might not be until the end of the month.

Hampton's sister stepped up next, reading from a prepared statement in front of her, a transcript of an impassioned and spontaneous speech she had made on camera three weeks earlier. Then she was gone.

Then a woman, who I had never seen before, came to the microphone, cleared her throat and began, "My name is Elizabeth Norris…" I'm glad none of the cameras were on me at that moment. I was hearing a voice I had heard over the phone weeks earlier, a voice that was low and sensual. I just stared. Harry and Bernie told me later that they had had the same reaction. "…and I have some questions about the review process you're pursuing now…"

Where was the smell, I asked myself. There had been no warning. And so, the cosmic question: Who kissed Betty and turned her into a princess? The new Betty in front of us was attractive, was dressed like she owned a Versace outlet, coiffured like a movie star, and—what had happened to her thick glasses? Linda Tripp and Paula Jones—those were amateur makeovers compared to the crystallized woman in front of us.

"………and your timetable……"

I was too stunned to listen. Then, intrigued. But the more she talked the more I realized that she wasn't saying anything. She was asking questions that a letter or phone call could have asked, questions of no urgency with answers that could wait. Bernie slipped me a note: *I wonder if she shaved her legs and pits. She obviously took a bath.*

Then I thought I knew what was about to happen. Betty was surely laying the groundwork for her <u>real</u> question. A week earlier, she had editorialized in the **TELEGRAM** about Harry and the County Attorney colluding to protect The Cop. In print, she had demanded answers. In print, she had impugned the character and ethics of the two men. I glanced at Harry. He was remembering the same editorial, and he had an answer for her. In person, all she had to do was ask.

This was going to be fun.

Then she was gone.

I blinked, I nodded, I looked to my right and left. Betty had disappeared. Mushy questions, not even a statement, and she was out the door. Confrontatious Interruptus. Harry was denied.

ABC started packing up its cameras. From Mason's entrance to Betty's exit—ten minutes. I looked at Harry again, but all he could do was shrug. I waited for a note from Bernie, but she was sliding something to Al Baroli instead.

The rest of the meeting took less than an hour, the shortest meeting we had had in months. But long enough for me to figure out most of it, the big damn picture. I told Julie later, and she was impressed that I had finally caught up with her.

Donald Mason had not come to the meeting to address the council. He knew he was about to settle his case and get out of town. He was speaking to a national audience of five million potential clients. Name, face, a few words—his business card. The next night's forum was simply repetition. Like a television ad for a soup or automobile, you might forget the details of the ad but you'd remember the warm fuzzy feeling connected to the brand name. Hungry, think Campbell's. Want a new life, think Chevrolet. Want to sue the bastards, think Mason.

Betty was not there to confront us as she had in the past. She was there for a job interview; she was her own start-up company. Not literally for ABC, but she wouldn't turn them down if they were interested. Focus-focus-focus—it was all coming into focus. Athens was not big enough, nor the lights bright enough, for Elizabeth Norris.

Mason had been predictable, but Betty was a disappointment. If I was right about her, then I had to figure out when it had all changed: When the tragedy of Becky Hamilton had finally become an opportunity to pad resumes.

And the last thing I had to figure out was Ken Rumble. Throughout the ABC filming, he had been silent. I paid attention to where the ABC camera was pointed, and it never went in Ken's direction. It was fairly obvious that ABC had simply needed stock footage of some sort of interaction between the council and the public, to splice into their longer story in which the town forum was to get most of the airtime. Ken was to be the star of the town forum. His time was coming.

I was disappointed in Betty because she had lost something in the past few weeks. If nothing else, she had been sincerely outraged about the deaths of two teenagers in Athens. A passionate rage, like the crowds who had come before us in the council chambers, her rage didn't have to be justified, nor could it be dismissed, as long as it was genuine, as long as the issue was two tragic deaths, not her own life. As unpleasant as she was, I had respected Betty because she cared deeply about something more important than herself, just like Ken did years ago.

Betty had become Elizabeth, but what about Ken?

At the end of the meeting, after processing for an hour in silence, voting without comment, I was falling asleep even though it wasn't even close to ten o'clock. The last item on the agenda was "council time," the flip side of "public discussion" at the beginning. Any council member could bring up any subject that hadn't been on the formal agenda. Ken had two items, and I finally understood him.

"I have two issues that I would encourage the council to give serious consideration. Personally, I have no problem making a decision tonight, but I raise them now to alert the people of Athens to a future council discussion that will require their input," he said, sliding copies to his right. Before my copy reached me, he continued, "First, this council should undertake a review of the city manager and consider whether his contract should be terminated......"

I turned toward Harry in time to see the blood in his neck start going north.

"......and, second, I would urge this council to make a commitment to the Library Board that the bond issue which the majority has avoided———that bond issue should be placed on the ballot of the council election in November."

I almost pissed in my jeans.

Out of thin air, Ken Rumble had uttered the sacred words—the Athens Public Library—and the room went silent. Of course, not really, only for me. The meeting was still going on, but I had stepped out of myself to look around. Was I the only person in the room who knew what Ken was doing? Harry made eye contact and then looked down, his head slowly shaking. I was on my own. I was invisible for the next few minutes.

All the parts were coming together, the old stories about pigeons and cemeteries and what they meant.

You been to your public library lately? Checked out a book? Used one of their computers? Rented a video? I grew up in libraries, on the military bases my father was stationed at, in the schools I attended. Saturday mornings, I waited for the bookmobile to come down our street. Me and my older brothers, loaded down with books to return. Your town has a crappy library, you've got a crappy town.

Athens has the best library in the mid-west. Not as big as the one in Iowa City or Des Moines or Cedar Rapids, but better than those. If you compared city budgets, Athens spent more money per capita on its library than any city in Iowa. And, up to a point, money means quality.

Libraries in small towns always have their supporters, who

211

usually have to kick and scratch to squeeze dimes out of the city fathers (and mothers). Our library was different. I explained it to the TELEGRAM once, and caught hell for a month afterwards for being too glib. That was Joseph Holly for a lot of people, too glib, too ironically detached.

On a national level, I said, Democrats will protect Social Security, Republicans will pump up the Pentagon. In Athens, the public library was both Social Security and the Pentagon, the "third rail" of city politics. It could do no wrong, no request for money was unjustified, and the Library Board was tougher than the Christian Coalition, AARP, the NRA, and Common Cause put together.

It was the only city program that the Iowa Arts crowd and the downtown business crowd could agree on. Library fund-raisers always had the broadest spectrum of political support, and the library was beyond the control of the city council. We approved a lump sum of money, but all policies and expenditures were controlled by an independent Library Board. All well and good, especially in good times, but for the past few years the overall city budget had been getting tighter and tighter. The lunatic state legislature was eliminating tax sources and rolling back tax rates allowed to the cities.

So, the library is always a big issue, and it had gotten bigger two months before Becky Hamilton died. The Board came to us with a request to expand the downtown library building, to double its size, and it would only cost ten million dollars, about two hundred dollars a square foot. Rumble immediately announced he was for the expansion. But ten million dollars is tricky. We would have to sell bonds and borrow that much money, and interest over twenty years pushes the total cost to twenty million, not including new personnel and increased annual operating expenses for a larger building. The Board seemed to have the numbers on its side. Use of the library had gone up fifteen percent in two years, and everybody could see the long lines at the checkout counters. And, as the Board reminded the council, it was not our decision anyway. That much of a bond issue had to go to the voters in a referendum. It would be "the people's decision."

I reminded the Board that the bond issue could only go on the ballot if the council put it there, and we needed more time to study this issue. On every other issue that Rumble was on the short side, he had insisted that more study, more public input, more discussion was needed before we voted. Not this time. The library was the "crown jewel" of Athens. The Board's numbers proved that the people of Athens wanted an expanded library. Why would the council object to that—unless the council was anti-library? End of discussion.

Two months earlier I had had the weird feeling that if I kept talking much longer I would start getting death threats on my answering machine and bloody Dewey Decimal System cards under the door of the Hollywood. I retreated, but Harry offered a seemingly neutral suggestion, "The staff can put together all sorts of financing options. And we can certainly find a way to pay for this expansion and its related costs, but I'd urge the Council to set aside some extra meetings to go over the details."

Time gave me substance to flesh out my intuition and my rhetorical distinction for public debate. The issue was not expanding the library, it was about expanding the building or expanding the service. They were not synonymous.

The Board was right about increased usage of the building, but their own records showed that was based on an increase of people coming through the turnstile counters. Their circulation number for books actually checked out had been stagnant for a couple of years. The cost per square foot for their planned expansion was almost double that of other communities' library expansions. We could never pin them down on their projected increased operating expenses. Their basic attitude seemed to be— "Trust us. We're the experts, and the public loves us." Gradually, enough other council-members, including Bernie, who had initially sided with Rumble, started to have misgivings. We delayed a decision about putting it on the ballot, and Rumble made us pay in the public perception department.

I went to the Library Director and asked him two simple questions. First, does a building twice as large mean twice as much service and books checked out? He was honest—no, it meant a better service but not anywhere near double the service. Second, how would a branch library help service? And that's when I figured it out, as soon as he answered, "A branch would open up services to a different population, people who don't come downtown now, but a branch is not in our master plan for now. Perhaps in the future, after we expand our site downtown."

There was only one logical place for a branch library, on the southeast side of Athens, in the area with the lowest per capita income, where most of the public housing was, what the cops called the Broadway Belt. The Director had said "a different population." Athens had the best-subsidized housing program in the state. Those units were on the southeast side of town. If I were cynical, I would say they were dumped there. Land was flat and cheap, apartments were too far away from the Iowa Arts campus to attract students. Families from Chicago were looking for a haven from gangs and drugs and crime, and Athens offered them cheap housing, but not much else. Without much else to help them, they brought along what they had hoped to leave behind, and we got people like Anheuser Hampton. I was as responsible as anyone else who had ever made a decision about that housing. All it took was a well-fed downtown library asking for more money to make me start connecting all the dots.

I approached other Library Board members. How about a branch? How about expanding service, not a building? "Not in our

Master Plan—later, maybe, sure, a branch <u>and</u> a bigger downtown building—and, besides, a branch would merely duplicate existing services. An expansion downtown is more cost efficient."

Cost efficient at two hundred dollars a square foot?

Where is all this going? Why not go back to the big deer and dead teenagers and the answer to why Ken Rumble was so scared at that vigilante meeting? But this is all connected, Becky Hamilton and libraries are connected. They have to be, or nothing makes sense.

I found an empty store in southeast Athens, ten thousand square feet, on sale for three hundred thousand dollars, plenty of free parking outside. Two hundred thousand for renovations. The additional staff that was planned for the expansion could be used at this new location. Two neighborhood groups in the Broadway area said they would provide dozens of volunteers to help the paid staff. Computer technology would cut down on the need for duplicate inventories. Utilities would be cheaper. Harry had millions in the reserve fund. We wouldn't have to put it to a referendum vote, which would have required a 60% win. This thing could be open in six months, and the net cost would be nineteen million dollars less than for a downtown expansion. Not only would this be the <u>right</u> thing to do, it would be the least expensive, freeing up money for other projects to help that area, like more cops for "community policing," the effort to be a daily presence in neighborhoods to prevent crimes as well as solve them.

The Library Board said it was not in their Master Plan. Ken Rumble said we should listen to the Library Board, the experts. I pointed out that he had second-guessed every other department in city government. He had made a career of it. I pointed out that he had accused all of us of ignoring "the other people of Athens—the young, the old, the poor." It was a line from his last campaign brochure. I reminded him how the rest of the city staff resented the library budget, how they had to beg for a budget increase and still got denied while the library got everything it wanted. I might as well have been pointing out that the emperor was naked. Out of left field, a letter to the **TELEGRAM** asked, "why is Joseph Holly advocating that library cards should cost five dollars instead of being free?"

And then Becky Hamilton died. I didn't see the connection right away, but as soon as Ken made the Library part of the upcoming campaign I put it in the mix with the pigeons and the cemetery. Athens was two cities: educated and common, rich and poor, black and white. Library services in Anheuser Hampton's neighborhood were not part of the Master Plan.

I stepped back into myself. The two pages in front of me each had a single paragraph. Each had the same heading: FOR IMMEDIATE RELEASE TO ALL MEDIA. I lowered my voice, "Ken, let me see if I understand you. You want us to fire Harry?"

"That is not what I am advocating, Joseph. You did not read my memo."

Al Baroli was about to speak, but Bernie reached over and grabbed his hand. Steve Nash asked, "Does the council want these on the next meeting's agenda?"

I ignored Steve, and went straight to Ken, "Your memo is three lines long. I read it twice. Twice, slowly, because I want to make sure I understand you. You want to fire the city manager?"

"Read it again, Joseph."

Okay, I was getting more pissed, and I was tempted to tell Bernie to turn Al Baroli loose, but I went back at Ken, "Do _you_ want to fire the city manager? That's all I'm asking."

Ken Rumble swiveled in his chair to face me, "As is clear in my note, I want us to _discuss_ whether we should terminate his contract. Many people in this community have expressed a lack of confidence in the City Manager's performance. If we think he is doing a good job, then a public discussion of our support will only benefit him."

You had to hand it to Harry. He sat there and kept his own counsel. I was betting that he was reviewing the retirement package in his contract. Take this job and shove it, Harry Hopkins had options.

"Okay, evidently I'm not reading your note and you're not listening to my question," I said. "You said you were ready to make a decision tonight. Thumbs up or down, do you want to fire Harry? You've worked with him for years. Can you make that decision tonight?"

"I want us to discuss this with the public. My decision tonight is to have that discussion. I am not afraid of public input, nor, I might add, am I afraid to let the people choose to tax themselves for an expanded free library. Perhaps something will come out of that public discussion about the City Manager which will influence my support for him."

"Do you want to fire Harry Hopkins?" I repeated.

"Are you afraid of a public discussion?" he replied.

"We're not going to fire the city manager. You know that, Ken. You also know how this will play out in the press, the headlines, and it will all have been an unnecessary controversy. As for the library, you know as well as I do that that issue is more complicated than a simple election, and putting it on the ballot in…ten weeks…doesn't give the Board enough time to make their case to the voters, nor enough time for opponents to get organized."

"The Board has been ready for two years to go to the voters. I have been a consistent supporter of an expanded free library, Joseph. You have convinced a majority of this council to postpone a decision, a delay I have opposed. I support the free library. You do not. The rest of the council needs to make up their own mind."

I had gone beyond being pissed. I went beyond being homicidal.

I looked at Ken Rumble and asked a question for which I already knew the answer, "Why are you doing this <u>now</u>, Ken, in this way?" Funny, how seeing something clearly, how it makes you calm. I looked around the council chambers. Meeting almost over, a few city staff waiting to go home, Bob Hardy in the cable control room, two reporters. The only "citizen" in the room was John Brownstein, pamphlets in hand.

As Ken was about to respond, Harry finally spoke, doing the job that Steve Nash should have been doing, "Before the council proceeds, I need to point out that you can evaluate me anytime you wish. I welcome such a review. But if you want to put the library bond issue on the ballot you need to decide before September 15th. That's the legal deadline for getting any issue on the November ballot."

I was impressed. Harry's voice didn't give him away. Just another day at the office.

Bernie then gave me a sign about the future. "I'm not so sure about an extended debate over the city manager, but I don't see a reason we can't have a special meeting soon to finalize this library thing."

I was screwed. Bernie had been Ken's only other supporter on the library expansion. She was happy with <u>anything</u> being built or expanded downtown. She was now giving the two new members some political cover. And Steve Nash had never really forgiven me for trying to be mayor instead of him. The timid coalition I had put together months earlier looked at the camera and the two remaining reporters in the chambers, and it folded. A meeting date was set, but I knew how the vote would go, and the fall election would have a real hot button issue for the candidates and public to debate. I smiled, almost sincerely, at Ken, who nodded back. Then I turned to face Harry. He knew. He arched his eyebrows, then looked down again.

After the meeting, Harry stopped me before I could walk home.

"Julie called the switchboard and left a message. Said for you to call your brother immediately. She also said something about you not waving to her. You know what that's about?"

"Oh, Christ!" I said, "I was just........." and then I paused. "Nothing, just a thing I forgot."

"You know you're swimming against the current, don't you?" Harry said, sitting behind his desk. He had a corner office in the civic center. Two walls of floor to ceiling windows letting in the orange light from the parking lot, a desk lamp the only light on in his office, the two of us sitting across from each other. You want to know something else about Harry that few people know? He likes New Age music. Go figure. We're there in the semi-dark listening to Enya or something comparably celestial, and I have this conflicted feeling. I'm drop-dead tired, but I'm as calm, as wide-awake, as I've been in months. "You sure you want to run again? Not running is better than losing, you know," he said.

"You don't drink, do you, Harry?" I said, ignoring his question. I didn't want to admit that I needed the council salary, and that I was willing to, had to, take the chance I would lose. I had no choice. And I wanted a drink.

He shook his head. "I come from drunks."

I sat there wondering what else I didn't know about Harry's life before he came to Athens. I looked around his immaculate and orderly office. Without thinking, I leaned forward and turned around a small-framed picture that had always been on his desk but which had always faced only him. A beautiful woman with long hair and a Mona Lisa smile. "You got a girlfriend now?" I asked, turning the picture back around.

He slumped further down in his chair, "My ex-wife."

We sat there a minute, not talking about his past or my present, and then I stood up to leave.

"One more thing," he said. "That giant deer that has been giving us hell all these years……"

"Hartford!?"

"That's the one, your big deer. We got him tonight. Up in Oakland Cemetery."

"You caught Hartford?" I said, energized again.

"No, Joe, we killed him. I've got a crew up there tonight trying to haul him out. He's a genuine load."

You remember that scene from the original Frankenstein movie, when the townspeople are charging some castle to kill the monster, a mob of people with torches? That's what I was thinking as I got to the Oakland entrance. I had turned down Harry's offer of a ride. I was pumped enough, almost running the few blocks from the civic center to the cemetery. The closer I got, the more cars I saw headed that way, the more people on foot, headlight and flashlight beams bouncing off the tombstones and trees. The word was out. Hartford was dead.

Just inside the gates, I surveyed the crowd at the top of the highest hill in Oakland, near the Black Angel. The police had stopped the cars from going deep into the cemetery, so there was a constant flickering line of people racing back and forth from the entrance to the top of hill. Camera flashes were popping like crazy, bright explosions fading to dots that lingered even after their own deaths. The wind was blowing, and I started hoping that it would rain like it did on the Fourth in Weber Park. I wanted those people to go away so I could see Hartford by myself. He and I had some things to settle.

I walked slowly toward the hilltop, passed by people I knew who called out my name, who gave me a thumbs up signal. The closer I got to the top, the less I could see because the crowd was blocking my view. I was about to push my way through when I saw some kids off in the Babyland section. They were tramping across Kathy's grave.

Before I could yell at them, or even start to run over there, an Athens cop materialized out of the dark and ran the kids off. He was a huge cop, somebody I didn't recognize.

I shouldered my way through the mass and stood in the inner circle, staring at a giant, a mammoth, a damn big deer, with dozens of flashlights pointing at it. It wasn't Hartford.

John Brownstein was kneeling in front of the carcass, crying like a baby, being jeered by the crowd. "I wish it was me. I wish it was me," he was sobbing, his voice choked and barely comprehensible, but clear enough for some of the people to mock him with offers of help to reach the same place the deer had gone.

Who were all those people? All the faces I had recognized a few minutes earlier, they were nowhere to be seen. And there wasn't a cop in this inner circle at all.

I stared at John and the crowd, and then I stared at the deer, the massive wound in its chest. The wind was really picking up, but I knew it wasn't going to rain. This crowd smelled the blood on the deer. John stood up and waved his arms at them, trying to be heard above the wind and their taunts. "Go away. Go away!" he pleaded. Somebody threw a paper cup at him. Harmless, except as a symbol. I had to tell these people something, something they needed to hear.

"All of you," I yelled as loud as I could. "ALL OF YOU, JUST GET THE FUCK BACK. AND GO THE FUCK HOME!"

Of all the people there, the two most shocked were me and John Brownstein. The rest of the crowd simply took a collective breath and waited for me to go totally nuts.

"This is not the deer you think it is!" I said, a little quieter. "This is a big buck, but it's not Hartford." I could hear a few people mumble to each other, "Hartford? Who the hell is Hartford?"

"Look, I know the deer you want this to be. But this deer doesn't have enough points on its antlers, and the spread is too small. The

221

deer you want has over a dozen. This one only has ten." I could see some of the men looking at the deer and counting to themselves. It was soon obvious that if it wasn't Hartford, this crowd wasn't interested.

In a few minutes, John and I were left with the dead deer, in a cemetery at the edge of Athens. It made no difference to him that it wasn't Hartford. He was still upset. " It seems like such a waste," he said sadly. I hadn't brought a flashlight with me, but the moon and stars were enough light to lead us back to the gate of Oakland. John offered me a lift home in his fifteen-year-old Volvo, plastered with Green Party stickers. I told him thanks but no thanks. I needed the exercise. Before he got in his car, he turned and grabbed my hand, shaking it, saying, "Thank you," and then he was gone and I was alone.

I got home before midnight, and Julie was still waiting up for me. For the first time in years, she had left a liquor bottle out on the table, evidence of the obvious. I told her the Hartford story, and she told me that I should have called her before I went to the cemetery. She could have told me it wasn't Hartford. I asked her about the bottle.

"I watched the meeting. Your brother called. I think you've earned a drink tonight. Just one, but a good one."

"Is there a problem about my father?" I asked, pushing the vodka back toward her.

Sometimes I hated myself more than others. I knew what my brother was calling to tell me. I had expected it for a long time. At that moment, I wish I could have felt as bad as John Brownstein had felt an hour earlier. I knew how I was supposed to feel, but I was empty.

Jack Hamilton took his wife to Chicago in August. He had gone back to work at the post office at the end of June, but his brother Jerome called soon after that and invited him back to Chicago for his fiftieth birthday party. "This is my last one, brother. I ain't celebrating another damn one of these things," Jerome had said. "But I want you here to hold my hand."

Hamilton asked the postmaster for some more time off. It was awkward, but the postmaster did not hesitate. "Take it," he said. "You know that August is the slowest month for mail in a college town. We'll get by."

His brother had offered his own spare bedroom for Jack and Marcie to stay in, but Hamilton had turned him down. Instead, he booked a room at the Blackstone Hotel on Michigan Avenue. He told Jerome that he wanted to have an excuse to do some walking, and the Blackstone was only a mile away from his brother's house, two miles away from the house in which he and his other brothers had grown up. Jerome had seen through him immediately, "You're just getting sentimental, Jack. But, you think about this, they've fixed that place up. It ain't got the 'charm' it had when you worked there."

Marcie had never heard her husband's Blackstone stories. A three-hour drive to Chicago from Athens was enough time to get the highlights. Marcie drove because Hamilton's legs got too stiff if he did not keep them moving.

Hamilton's mother had insisted that all her sons have a job and save part of their salary every week. He had heard about an opening at the Blackstone coffee shop from a friend. Hamilton was a large fourteen-year-old boy, so he got away with adding two years to his age, old enough to bus tables.

He had walked into the Blackstone lobby and thought he was in a gangster movie. Red velvet cushions, dangling crystal chandeliers whose brilliant light was muted by the dark walls and carpets, a *winding staircase wide enough to march a dozen people up the steps side by side, mahogany counter tops, and elevators with old ebony men on stools. Al Capone had stayed at the Blackstone, and Hollywood had filmed a movie in that lobby, all about gangsters. By the time Hamilton went to work there, it had started to decompose. Fifty years of elbows and rumps on the furniture had left it shiny and threadbare. Chandelier lights were replaced once a month, not as needed. A faint whiff of pine-sol lingered in the restrooms, and strips of tape held a few carpet seams together. But Hamilton loved the place, and he walked to work four days a week until he graduated from high school. When he started to play football, the manager worked his schedule around his practice time, and as long as his work was done Hamilton was allowed to bring some schoolbooks. For his mother's forty-fifth birthday, he and his brothers all chipped in to rent her a Blackstone room for the night, complete with room service.*

He started in the coffee shop, but worked his way through the hotel maze from busing tables and up to parking cars for the guests, where he made the best tips. But he did not like parking cars, he told Marcie, because it kept him out of the hotel. So he accepted an offer to work in the laundry room in the basement, until something else opened up, and he learned too much about the stains that a human body could leave overnight. The laundry room was an inferno, and the starch and lye were hard on his eyes and throat, but it was the best way to meet all the housekeeping girls. He did not tell Marcie about that advantage, nor about the girl who first touched him with her hands silky with lotion usually reserved for the master suites.

From laundry room to kitchen, where he learned how to enrich his own mother's table with the excess bounty of the Blackstone, Hamilton finally graduated to the job he wanted from the beginning——a lobby bellhop. The desk clerk might have been paid more in salary, but Hamilton's knack for small talk, and knowing when to be quiet, inspired a steady tip income to supplement his token salary. Most important, unlike being a desk clerk, being a bellhop did not require the ability to read or write.

Whenever he stood at the desk waiting for a guest to finish signing in, Hamilton would measure that guest by his prior experience in the laundry room. How would the guest room look the next morning? Soon enough, he could break couples down into three categories: married to each other, unmarried but looking for a night of fun, and married—but not to each other. When he was seventeen, Hamilton told himself that he would never cheat on his wife, whoever she might be. Those couples, he thought as he carried their bags into the elevator and then up to their room, those couples never seemed as happy as the unmarried couples nor as comfortable as the couples married to each other.

Hamilton worked at the Blackstone until he went to college. His last night on the job, before the other bellhops took him to a party with a few of the chambermaids, he asked to be left alone for a few minutes. When he was sure they weren't looking, he went to the payphone booth in the darkest corner of the lobby. With a pocketknife, he carved his full name, and the date, in the underside of the wood counter in the booth. With a felt pen, he then colored in the grooves. He told himself that he would show it to his wife sometime in the future.

As they drove to Chicago, Marcie listened to her husband's story and then surprised him with a story about her own motel housecleaning job in Pella, Iowa. Nothing so glamorous as the Blackstone, just a Motel Six, but Hamilton was pleased nonetheless.

"So, where's the phone booth?" she asked as soon as they walked into the Blackstone lobby. Hamilton did not answer.

Everything had changed. The lobby was magnificent, but it was not the same lobby. It was plush and glamorous in its own way, but

Hamilton wished he had not come. He saw a black bellhop, and for a moment he was back in the old Blackstone, but then he realized that there were as many white and Asian faces as black. And the single wooden and glass phone booth was gone.

"Jack..." Marcie took his hand, "......you okay?"

"It's not here anymore," he said. "It was over there," pointing, "but it's not there anymore."

Marcie nudged him toward the front desk and spoke quietly so nobody could hear except her husband, "You promised me a night at the Blackstone, Jack Hamilton. This is the first time I've been here. I'm a virgin. So let's enjoy ourselves and then find a spot somewhere in this building where we can leave both our names."

Hamilton let out a deep breath, "I was just expecting..... ."

Marcie nudged him again, "You spell my name with an ie and not an ey, just remember that." She did not admit that she was disappointed herself that the phone booth was gone.

A firm mattress, deep sleep without any dreams, and a closet with soft wood trim even on the inside, wood that a butter knife could penetrate. Jack and Marcie christened Room 503 the Hamilton suite, theirs until the Blackstone was ever gutted and resurrected again.

They spent the night, but only one. Hamilton called his brother the next day and accepted the prior invitation.

Jerome's birthday was more festive than he had anticipated. Cousins, nephews and nieces, some former in-laws still in good graces with the Hamilton family—it was a good mix, stirred by rum and whiskey for one generation, discreetly blended with marijuana by a younger generation.

Becka Hamilton was not mentioned. Her cousins might have talked about her among themselves, but nobody raised her name in the presence of her parents. The public party talk was mostly about Jerome Hamilton and his increasing girth or his latest failed exercise program. Jerome was a Chicago bus driver, the Ralph Kramden of his family, the most good-natured, and Jack Hamilton's favorite brother.

Nearing midnight, with Marcie and the other wives in bed, the older children gone to a movie, the younger children watching television in a basement rec room, Jerome and Jack Hamilton were left to themselves on the front porch, the closest place Jerome was allowed to smoke near his own house. The two men were stripped down to their sleeveless undershirts, sweating in the hot muggy night, waiting for Jerome's oldest daughter to get home from her janitorial job at the University of Chicago. She was nineteen, but her father still stayed up for her.

Hamilton had not seen his niece Jeresa in three years. She always seemed to be working whenever he and Marcie came to visit his brother, and she never came with Jerome to visit Athens. Watching her walk up the steps this night, Hamilton was disappointed to see that she had more and more of her father's genes. Jeresa was a big girl.

"Hey, Uncle Jack," she smiled and waved as soon as she saw him. "You and daddy out here doing some reefer in the dark?"

"That is <u>not</u> funny, Jeresa Hamilton," her father said, but he laughed in spite of himself. "And you know I don't touch that weed."

"No sir, just the legal weed for you, daddy, just the same old stuff that's gonna kill you before I make you a grandfather. Am I right, Uncle Jack?"

Hamilton nodded, and his brother stubbed out a freshly lit cigarette.

Then, as casually and naturally as breathing, Jeresa pulled her uncle up off the steps and gave him a long hug, saying softly, "I sure was sorry to hear about Becka. It broke my soul not to be able to go to her service, so I hope you'll forgive me for that."

Hamilton collapsed in her arms, but she held on to him long enough for her father to rise and help her lower Hamilton back down to the steps, where he put his hands over his eyes and cried. Held by his brother on one side, niece on the other, both silent, one patting his knee, the other rubbing his shoulders, Hamilton wept until he was dry, and then he sat there with his head down as Jeresa started to tell a story.

"I sure do miss her, Uncle Jack. Not like you, I know that, but a real pain. She wrote me all the time, and I'd tell her things I wouldn't tell anybody else. We kept our secrets. I was older, but she always seemed more, you know, more mature than me. And, damn, she had those legs I always wanted."

Hamilton and his brother both nodded.

"Few years ago something happened that she made me promise not to tell you...," seeing her uncle's confusion, "...not a bad something, and she was gonna tell you as soon as she turned eighteen. But I guess it's okay to tell you now. Back when ya'll were here, when she was twelve and I was sixteen, she and I went down to that hotel you and daddy used to work at..."

"The Blackstone?"

"That's it. I had a boyfriend back then, when I weighed a lot less than I do now, and he worked there. I wanted to show him off to Becka, and she had always wanted to see where you had worked."

Jerome Hamilton was as surprised as his brother. "You never told me about this boy, and you know I told you to stay away from that part of town."

"Daddy, this ain't about me or that boy. Anyway, he's long gone. This is about Becka. See, she went with me, and there were some other boys there, my boy's friends, and they thought Becka was mighty fine looking. Twelve or not, she was fine. So I do a dumb thing..."

"Jeresa, you didn't.... ," her father exploded.

"Dammit, daddy, let me finish. You'll bust a vessel."

"You stop cussing," her father admonished her.

"You stop interrupting, I'll stop cussing."

Father and daughter glared at each other, but then they both rolled their eyes and laughed as Jeresa said, "Ain't either one of us going to stop what we always do, eh?"

"The Blackstone?" Jack Hamilton said, wanting to hear more.

Jeresa continued, and it was obvious that she felt somewhat awkward. "Well, some of the boys wanted to show Becka around the hotel while me and my boy...we spent some private time together..."

Hamilton knew all about employee "private time" at the Blackstone. He had covered for his friends plenty of times.

"So after awhile I come up for air and can't find Becka. My boy don't seem too concerned, but I shake his butt loose and go looking for her. I hear some sort of yelling down a hall off the lobby and I start running. One of those boys is holding a supply room door shut. That door is pounding from the inside and I figure Becka's in trouble in there with the other boys. Well, this boy sees me coming down on him like Jesus on the moneychangers and he lets go the door. And, bam! That door turns to chips and nails and that colored boy is white like a ghost. Becka has done kicked down the door from the inside."

Jerome Hamilton whistled, "That's the Becka I remember."

"Becka's out of that room in a second and before that boy can duck or cover she's put her foot in his private parts and she's off to running past me through the lobby and headed back here."

Jack Hamilton smiled as Jerome slapped his knee.

"I'm standing there thinking she is coming home to raise hell with you, Uncle Jack, or tell my daddy. But then I see two boys stumble out of that closet, one holding his crotch, the other bleeding from the lip, and those boys are looking to find Becka for some payback. I spin and head for the hills, and I see Becka go through the lobby *door as I'm panting after her. Lucky those boys were hurting or they'd been faster, but I don't think they'd caught her even on a good day. Damn, she was FAST. You remember that daddy? How fast Becka was?"*

"Lord, do I remember," he said, shaking his head and lighting another cigarette.

"I get almost home and she's waiting for me, and I know she's justified angry with me about leaving her alone with those boys. But you know what she tells me. She asks me to keep it quiet. Daddy, you and Uncle Jack are waiting for us, we know that, and she tells me not to tell anybody. And you know why? That's the surprise thing to me. Not because she was in trouble and kicked three boys back to the southside. No, she doesn't want you to know, Uncle Jack, because she says that you had promised to take her to the Blackstone sometime for lunch, to show off where you worked, and she didn't want you to know that she had already been there on her own. She wanted you to think that you took her there first. She had promised you that. It all made sense to her, and I was just happy to be out of trouble myself. So, that's the story, and I figure she wouldn't mind now."

Hamilton looked up at his niece, "No, I think it would be okay with her. Thanks for telling me."

"You're okay with it?" she asked.

"I'm okay."

"Well, good. I was thinking about that story tonight as I got off work. Thinking about Becka. Jesus, she was special. And sometimes I wish I could just talk to her one more time. You know what I mean?"

Jack Hamilton nodded, "I know, Jeresa. I think about that all the time. How I wish I could talk to her one more time. Just once. I'd give ten years of my life to talk to her just one more time."

I saw him again the day after I went to see the dead deer. I was in Oakland telling Kathy about her grandfather dying, and there he was off in the distance. I didn't want him to see me because I wanted to get closer, and I was afraid he would go away if he saw me. I hadn't seen him for a long time, and something about the night before had made me wonder where he was. How he was doing. How he had been handling all the public scrutiny. I told Kathy goodbye and eased around behind him. He was motionless, his back to me. I got closer. He was bigger than I remembered him. His shoulders were broader. And he was darker than I remembered. He turned in my direction, surprising me, waved at me, then he walked off. I froze. Alone again, I thought about his face. His daughter's face was nothing like his.

August in Athens, two days before my father's funeral, ABC took our pulse. We were in ICU, on life-support, our loved ones reaching for the plug. If you had come from Mars and just landed in the council chambers that morning, that's what you would have thought.

The place was packed, with Rumble-ites tripping over camera cables. I got there early, sat on the front row corner seat, and had my notebook ready. I had introduced myself to the producer and asked for a copy of the tape as soon as it was available. He laughed, friendly enough, and told me to watch the broadcast. My chances of getting an unedited tape were nil. I kicked myself for not asking Bob Hardy to have a city camera there to tape things. I would have to rely on my graduate school note-taking skills, long dormant. Steve Nash arrived early too, but he again declined my offer to stand-in for him.

The town forum was an hour long. When it was over, I had fifteen pages of notes. I did my best to write down the exact words of Ken Rumble and the newly telegenic Elizabeth Norris. Lots of quotation marks and underlined phrases.

I sat there looking at Ken, trying to make eye contact, but he was on-message like a pro. As much as the forum might seem spontaneous, Ken spoke like he had seen a script the night before. He was good, very good. But I knew too much about his voting record. He talked about the need for more and better trained cops to make "community policing" effective. I knew how he had opposed department requests for additional men and equipment. He talked about how The Chief had changed car chase policies, but that was a factual error. Steve Nash didn't correct him. In fact, in that hour Steve probably spoke less than three minutes. If he was the Athens "establishment," we were out of touch and unconcerned. Good man or not, Steve was headed for the cutting room floor. That was my prediction. All that would be left was the angry Athens of Elizabeth Norris and the beleaguered Athens personified by Ken. Even Donald Mason had trouble snaring airtime from those two.

I wondered if Ken had any friends. I knew he had admirers, fans, apostles, and groupies. I just wondered if there was anything "private" about him. Did he ever relax? In an odd flash, I wondered if he ever had sex. Could he ever let himself get that intimate with anyone else? I had seen him weep at council meetings, feel the pain of "the people," but had he ever had sex without his clothes on? I searched my memory for my first private conversation with him. He had been un-ironic, intense, sincerely concerned about many of the same things that were bothering me. He wanted Athens to be ideal. We seemed to be closer than other communities, why not go farther, do more. But, in all the time he had been in office, he had actually accomplished—nothing. The first two years of my second term, with two of his allies on council, the four of us had done a few good things, but those happened only because his two allies were willing to compromise. Ken remained pure, but irrelevant. Still, his people loved him.

Sitting there in that chamber watching him, I knew I had stopped believing in Ken. He was no different than he had been from the very beginning, with the exception of only one thing—an ideal Athens was no longer his goal. The transformation of Betty Norris had been too transparent. Ken was different. Down deep, like most people who re-tool their image, Betty Norris knew she was a fraud, a hypocrite, insincere. Alone with herself, Betty would see herself. She would know the truth. She might fool other people, but she would never fool herself. But when Ken looked in a mirror, he only saw what his people saw. He never saw himself, just the image of himself. The image was ideal, and its preservation had become the most sincere act of his political life. And for Ken, a political life was all he had.

A summer full of mysteries, and now I added Ken to the list. Had he always been this way, so self-deluded that he fooled us from the very beginning? Or had he become this along the way? And we had missed the moment.

After the meeting, I cornered the ABC producer, "How much time between now and when you broadcast?"

"A month, tops," he said. "Although your Ken Rumble there and the Reverend Mason are pushing us to get it on before Labor Day. I told them, a spot opens up sooner, I'll push to get it on."

Proverbial light bulbs were going on in my head. I knew that we would have killed the Hampton lawsuit no later than mid-September. The confiscated tape would finally force Mason and the Hamptons to settle for a pittance, and then a lot of the steam would go out of the public debate, especially after the public heard about the small amount they accepted. But I couldn't tell the producer all that because the information had only been discussed at an executive session of the Council, and I was legally bound to keep it a secret until it was legally settled.

"Do me a favor," I asked him.

"We're leaving town tonight. And we're not filming anything else. Your 'favor' better be easy to handle, and it better not require us to interview you."

"I just want you to read something," I said, waving my notepad. He looked at me like I had just asked him to pull my finger. Before he could say anything, I continued, "Just give me your office address, and tell your secretary to be on the lookout for a long letter from Joseph Holly in Athens. I'll have it to you in three days. I just want to lay out an alternate story for you, and then you toss it in the trash or whatever, but at least you'll have another story. Deal? You can ignore it, but at least promise that you'll read it. Okay."

The producer was tired, it was obvious, and I assumed he was flying off to another assignment, but he shrugged and stuck out his hand for a shake, "It's a deal."

I went home and wrote a twenty-page history of the summer. Condensed voting records, provided quotes from the forum and quotes from council meetings a year ago. I pointed out the discrepancies between public statements of Rumble and Norris and the factual public "record." I made the case that Athens was not New York City. That the "story" of an incompetent or out of control police department was a square peg and Athens was a round hole, so to speak. I wrote and re-wrote, trying to avoid all metaphors except that square peg thing. I had appointed myself to be Athens' pro bono Public Defender, and I wrote as it if was the last legal brief to the governor before somebody yanked the switch.

The next morning I showed it to Harry, but he was skeptical, "This won't make a bit of difference, you know that, right?"

"I've got to try," I said. "This town doesn't deserve to be turned into the cliché that Ken and Betty are trying to palm off on the rest of the country."

Harry looked at me and sighed, "I'm going to miss you, Joe."

I went home, polished the letter, and mailed it off to ABC. Then I walked to the Hollywood to make arrangements with Gary Sanders to cover things while I went to Texas to bury my father. The first thing he said, "So, how come you think the public ought to pay to check out a book?"

I stared at him, and then said, **BM FORUM**, right?"

"Nope, letter to the **TELEGRAM**. Dang, I knew you were Scrooge McDuck, but charging the little kids to check out all those Mother Goose books—you are cold, man."

"Gary, do you really believe I want to charge to check out a book? Do you?"

"You don't want to expand the library downtown—same thing, according to that letter," but he knew the truth.

"Gary, I never......," but then I stopped. One fight at a time. I was getting too old to maintain fronts on the east and west simultaneously. ABC for now, then my father, and then I could come back and—I was sleepy. I went home to pack.

Texas is a long way from Iowa if you're driving. I-80 west to I-35 and straight south to Fort Worth. Young, single, and with a good car, you could do it in a day. Middle-aged, married, and a thirteen year old Toyota, you take your time. My father was lucky. My brother Carl had the body flown from Des Moines to Fort Worth, where the Greenwood Funeral Home was waiting for him. My mother had made all the pre-arrangements years earlier. She always tried to be in control, even after she was dead.

Julie and I had made arrangements to have Danny stay with another family I knew from the autism support group. If I thought he would have halfway understood what was happening, I would have taken him. But, then again, Julie reminded me how he could sometimes be too much of a distraction. A funeral didn't seem the right time to be dealing with Danny trying to knock over a casket or crashing some other family's visitation down the hall.

We took our time, and for the two days we were on the road I almost forgot about Athens. Almost.

Julie slept a lot, and I would drive a methodical 70 miles an hour, scanning the radio dial looking for the NPR stations along the way. You ever look at somebody when they're sleeping, and you realize that you spend most of the waking day NOT looking at their face? More than look, I guess, I mean stare at them. Study their face. I got a lot of Julie's profile on this trip. And I found myself patting her leg every so often, just making contact.

When she was awake, Julie kept asking me questions about my childhood. She knew most of the old stories already, but she kept asking me how I felt about my father. She wanted me to talk, and she wouldn't let me get away with saying that I had no positive feelings about my father. She wanted me to admit that I cared about him. "And stop blaming your mother for everything cold about you," she prodded. "Your old man was as mean as a snake too."

"But you still think I cared about him," I said, keeping my eyes on the road. "My mother smothered me, and he ignored me. I should care about either of them?"

"Joe, you care about everything else, about people in Athens you don't even know. You love me and adore Danny, and you're a sentimental sap about being a father. But you keep pushing your own parents away from you as if you were afraid to admit that you might even care about them. Just because they disappointed you doesn't mean you don't care about them. Tell me I'm right."

"Julie, you had great parents. Did you ever have a day in which you had any doubt they loved you? A single day?"

She stopped talking, and I kept staring ahead. We were looking for a motel to spend the night and a Cracker Barrel restaurant for dinner. She finally said, "Is there any <u>one</u> thing you liked about your father?"

"He was funny?"

Julie laughed, "God, yes, until he lost his memory he was indeed that. He had that wonderful smirk every time he slipped in some smart-ass dig about his own mother and father. Was he always that funny?"

Funny, how a simple question leads to an answer you're not expecting. My father had <u>not</u> always been funny. He had been surly and cold as long as I lived at home, but I realized, at that moment on the road, that after my mother died and before his Alzheimer's wrecked him, my father was funny. He was almost likeable. Had he always been that way? Was it something only my mother knew? Had I just not seen the obvious? How much empty baggage had I been carrying with me all those years? Those kinds of questions always led me back to Danny.

"You think Danny knows we love him?" I asked Julie. "You think he'll ever miss us?"

"He knows," she said, sliding closer to me.

"You want to know a secret?" I asked her. It was a sunny day, and we were both wearing sunglasses. She turned toward me and looked over the top of her glasses as I took a second to turn in her direction. Great eyes.

"You're gay?"

"No, not hardly," I laughed, "But I do think sometimes that I might be crazy. I'm not gay, I'm just insane."

"Either is okay with me, Joe. But crazy is more interesting."

"I talk to that giant deer that runs around town," I said. "I named him. Fact is, I think the giant deer I see is not the giant deer that other people see. Mine is bigger."

"He's real, Joe. Trust me, he's real."

"There's more," I said.

"I hope so. I want proof that you're crazier than I am, and seeing a big deer is small potatoes in the mental health field."

"I talk to Kathy every week," I said, watching for some reaction. I had never told her. Danny had gone to Oakland with me since he was born, but I'm sure he never told her either. " I don't mean I just think about her. I go to her grave and talk to her, out loud. Been doing it ever since she died. Tell her about you, how you're doing, how Danny is doing, even council stuff. Nothing profound."

Julie pushed her glasses back over her eyes and slid to the other side of the front seat. "I knew that," she said. "You want to know a secret of my own," she said as I scanned the side of the road for signs of a safe exit. "I have a secret too."

You ever get scared about something before you know about it? Some premonition of disaster? At that moment my pulse was skyrocketing and I was blinking like I was about to go blind.

"I sure hope you win your election this fall. We're going to need the money," she said, twirling both her forefingers at me.

"Julie..... ." I began, totally lost, trying to keep the damn car in a straight line.

"I think I'm about to lose my job," she said.

I let out a deep breath and almost smiled. I had expected something worse, but I was optimistic too soon.

"When you talk to Kathy," Julie then said, as I was about to ask about her job problem, "Does she answer you?"

I shook my head, not looking in her direction.

"That's sad, Joe."

I kept my eyes on the road.

"She's tried. You know that, don't you. She's tried to talk to you. She told me, but you always seem too distracted."

And that was the thing I expected, the worst thing.

It was an open casket, and my father looked better dead than he had in years. My last image of him alive had been colored by the blank look in his eyes and the way his jaw hung to one side. About to rest in the Texas dirt for eternity, Daniel Lloyd Holly almost looked handsome, like the picture I had of him from WW II, a rugged captain in his Army Air Corps khaki uniform.

I thought I could do it, do one of those scenes from a movie in which some adult has an interior monologue with himself and his parent. Finally get things off my chest, like Brando talking to his dead wife in LAST TANGO. Achieve some sort of catharsis. But not me. I stood there wondering how much of my father was in me, and in his grandson.

I once asked my father about his earliest memory. He had been born in 1908. Lived through the Roaring Twenties, the Great Depression, fought the Nazis in Italy and the Commies in Korea, retired, worked for the post office, drank too much in his fifties, and was a lousy pinochle player. How far back can you go, I had asked him. He told me about a covered wagon. He was born in Eros, Louisiana—Eros, the first irony of his life—and his family moved to Shreveport when he was four. It was 1912, and he remembered being in one of those Conestoga covered wagons, pulled by horses on dirt roads. Looking out the back as his mother handled the reins up front, looking at his own father on a horse behind them. I told him that he had been watching too many western movies. But I had been wrong. His brothers, older than him, had the same memory. So I stood there at his funeral looking at a man who had lived the twentieth century from start to finish. All he left behind was me and my brother. My uncles and aunts, my mother and daughter, all dead. My son was autistic, my wife thought she was losing her job. And my dead daughter was talking to her.

Like most children, I finally had a complete list of questions for my father, some I should have asked my mother, but I was too late. I looked at his corpse, and it hit me, that I still had time and a chance to save Julie, protect Danny, that I was neither husband nor father to Athens.

My brother and I were the last ones to leave the viewing room. We stood there like orphans on a street corner, and I listened as Carl sniffled and took deep breaths. He was the older brother, and my parents' favorite. I told him that when my mother died, and he set me straight, "Heck, Joe, I'm a lot more likeable than you. Not so sure of myself as you. And I never left home." I knew what he meant, and it had nothing to do with geography.

"So, how's politics?" he asked me, his breathing sounding almost painful. Neither of us looked at each other. "You know that you guys are always in the Des Moines news. Sounds pretty hectic over there."

"Yeh, and we're going to be on ABC next month. Small town dark secrets, that sort of thing," I said, noticing my father's wedding band.

"Barbara Walters interviewing you?" he asked.

"We're not that big-time."

"Too bad," he sighed. "You and her would be fun to watch."

"Carl, you are one very sick person, you know that. If you think that would be fun, you're obviously...."

"And you took me seriously?" he laughed.

I turned to face him. He was an older, shorter, fatter, happier version of me. And I was going to be very sad when he was gone.

"Carl, I guess I've been taking too many things seriously too much too long......"

"You should bring Julie and Danny over to see us soon. Get away from all that stuff in Athens. Take a break after the election, okay?"

"Carl, after the election, a trip to the other side of Iowa in

December is my second choice. No offense, but Julie and I need a warm beach and an ocean. I just wish I had the money to take her."

He leaned closer to my father's body and patted the old man's sleeve. Then he turned back to me. "Would forty thousand help?"

I stared at him, and then down at my father.

"Savings and insurance. You get half of eighty. It's not much, but it'll get you to Florida for a week. Everything should be probated soon, and I'll send you a check. But don't forget that I'm the sole executor. You piss me off, little brother, you get zero." He was grinning as he said it.

"Carl, I thought…," I stammered. "I thought everything he had got sucked up by that home he was in. I never…"

"You never saw how much you and him were alike, Joe. You're both cheap and don't like to spend money. He even told me that he had a private savings account that he never told mother about. Nickels and dimes add up, he told me. But he never thought you needed to know. Of course, it's a good thing mother died first. If she had gotten the money, we could both go see all the fancy Baptist pews she would have bought."

In the national economy, it was sinking in to me, forty thousand was a sub-atomic blip. But for Joseph Holly, it was El Dorado. I looked at my father again. He had taken care of me in ways he would never have anticipated. Money, paying my bills, my primary reason for running for office again—a moot point. The filing deadline had come and gone. I was on the ballot whether it mattered or not, and the campaign had just gotten more interesting.

A deep voice whispered, "Gentlemen, with your permission, we should close the casket and join the others at the grave site."

Carl and I took one last look. My memory about that moment isn't too reliable, but I think I looked at daddy and muttered, "thank you." Carl's no help. He says he didn't hear me, but I'm sure I said it.

I do remember what Carl did after the dirt was piled on top of my parents' grave. He started laughing. Julie was waiting in the limo, and it was just me and Carl, and a black man with a shovel smoothing out the dirt.

Carl had been genuinely close to our father, but he was laughing.

"You want to let me in on the joke," I asked him as we sat there on folding chairs.

"Mother made all the arrangements," he said. "Made the decision to get one plot, with coffins stacked instead of side by side. She was fifteen years younger than him, probably assumed he would go first. But it was her. So I'm sitting here thinking that daddy finally gets to be on top, and he'll be on top for the rest of time. Mother always thought she was in control, but she died first. So now she's on the bottom. She's not going to be happy, not at all."

That black guy had worked for Greenwood for a long time, long enough to have seen all the ways that survivors say goodbye to the dead. Two sons laughing at their father's grave—he just kept smoothing out the dirt.

Driving back to Athens, I made plans for the future. Two days earlier, I had needed the five thousand a year in Council salary. Inheriting forty thousand was like eight more years on the Council, but better. I could run a campaign and say whatever I wanted. You say you want a politician to be truthful with you, but what you really mean is that you want them to be honest with you. Politicians don't know what the truth is. All they've got is an opinion based on some facts. Same facts can produce different opinions. Don't laugh—it is possible to be politically honest. But you probably wouldn't vote for anybody who was.

First things first, I had to find out about Julie's job. I called Robin King, her department Chair. I told Robin to be honest with me, and he told me that things were getting out of hand, but Julie's job was safe for the time being. He had called her into his office at the end of the spring term and laid out the complaints against her. She was ignoring committee assignments, refusing to work on dissertation committees, skipping faculty meetings, and had stopped advising undergraduate English majors. But he also told me, "Those are the formal complaints, and easy to rectify. Trouble is, Joe, Julie's beginning to really alienate people in this department." I had a hard time imagining anybody not liking Julie, but Robin was adamant, "She's always been sarcastic around the hardcore feminists, you know that, but she's also nailed most of us at one time or another. As long as she was funny, most of us let it pass. English departments are supposed to be safe havens for irony. But she's getting—well, she's getting mean. Used to be that she would simply respond to somebody, but then she started seeking out confrontations, and then she goes for days and doesn't speak to anybody. More trouble than that, Julie has started ignoring her students, and as soon as one of them complains to their parents back in What Cheer, Iowa, then she's got real problems, problems that tenure won't protect her from."

I had to ask Robin an awkward question, "Do you think this has anything to do with alcohol?"

"Oh, you and I have both been at parties where Julie had too many, but I've never seen a hint of trouble in this building. I don't think booze is the problem. Joe, it might be none of my business, but are things okay between you and her at home?"

Another one of those questions with more than one answer. "I'll be honest with you. I don't think I've paid enough attention to her in the past few years. I've been too wrapped up in city business, and Danny..." I talked and talked and explained myself, but if I had been honest with Robin I would have told him that I had been looking the other way around Julie for a long time because I had convinced myself that my problems were bigger than her's. My burden was heavier. If I had been honest with him, I would have admitted that I had been a complete and utterly self-absorbed fool. He didn't need to know that, but I did.

Robin listened patiently, and then said, "All I know is that she's been real unhappy lately. Funny thing is, the happiest I've seen her was when she was defending you."

"Me?"

"She catches a lot of grief in this department for things you do on the council. You know that Ken Rumble has a lot of supporters over here, and Julie was always fielding the hardballs thrown her way about something you said or a vote you took, especially when you disagreed with Ken. Used to be that she would set them straight, win an argument and make them look un-informed in the process. I'd seen her do it lots of times and she always gave me a look afterwards that said she was one happy woman, that she enjoyed making your enemies look bad. But, lately, she simply tells them to go to hell or to go—to go screw themselves. She's not funny anymore, she's just angry. If you win re-election, the next four years around here aren't going to be pleasant. And if she doesn't change, well, that's what I talked to her about."

My status as a medium sized fish in a small pond was about to be confirmed or denied, the voters would take care of that, but"that was nothing to lose. I was merely a spectator. And I discovered that spectating was a lot more fun than acting. But, Julie? I had assumed she was my audience all those years. If I lost her, then the drama of my own life would be pointless. I would be on center stage in an empty theatre.

After talking to Robin, I called Harry. He had lots of news. Charlie Firestone had already raised ten thousand dollars in contributions. Ken Rumble had endorsed a petition drive to change the city charter so that the city manager would be subject to a periodic vote of confidence by the public. Didn't matter that no other city in the country with a city manager had such an arrangement for public recall.

Harry also alerted me to the special meeting that the council had while I was gone. One item on the agenda—the library bond issue—and only Al Baroli opposed putting it on the ballot in November.

"You could play it safe, Joe," Harry told me. "It's on the ballot and you didn't formally oppose it. You're not on record. You've just always told the council to be cautious."

"Yeh, but I was too subtle," I said. "You know as well as I do that this thing is a long-term budget buster. It will suck the blood out of a lot of future programs, and it's absolutely the wrong approach to expanding library service to a lot of people. You know that......"

"Joe, all I know is that if the bond issue passes, then I will make it happen. Athens wants a Taj Mahal, I hire the contractors. Athens wants a bigger downtown library, I make sure it gets paid for."

"If it passes—exactly. Bond issues need sixty percent to pass. Thirty five percent of the people in any town would vote against the second coming of Christ. All I need to do is convince six more percent to take a closer look." I went into campaign debate mode for a few minutes until Harry stopped me.

"Joe, you come back from Texas and tell me you don't need to win this election to be happy, you act like you don't care, and now I can hear your blood pressure rising. Make up your mind."

"I just want this town to do the right thing," I said.

"Joe, you want this town to do what you want it to do, just like Ken wants to fire me because in _his_ town that's the right thing."

"Am I wrong, Harry? Am I wrong about the rippling impact

that expansion will have on everything else in the budget? Just answer that question for me. Am I wrong?"

Harry was silent for a moment, and I could visualize him at his clean desk in his well-ordered office, wearing his five hundred dollar suit and listening to Enya. I could hear him take a deep breath and let it out with a sigh. "You're not wrong about the budget, but that doesn't make you right about the library. If Athens wants a single Cadillac downtown instead of a downtown Oldsmobile and a branch Ford, then that's what Athens will get."

I was sitting in the Hollywood box-office by myself, and I knew what had just happened. Harry had gone over to the other side. I hadn't given him enough credit for having political instincts beyond dealing with the Council itself. "You going to use my car metaphor when somebody asks you how you feel about the expansion?" I asked him.

"No, Joe, I am not. I'm merely going to say that the budget will always be balanced, and I will do whatever the Council tells me to do. Cadillacs and Oldsmobiles and Fords— I sell 'em all."

Summer in a small college town like Athens is the best time of the year. Most of the kids are gone, so the pace slows down. That's how it usually was, but this summer had been different. Hot and humid, rain in short supply, and Becky Hamilton was dead.

When I went to see Kathy, I sometimes went to see Becky too. She had one of those markers with her photograph laminated in stone. Not just her face, some sort of sports picture. She was in uniform. It was a good picture. You thought she was looking right at you, a look that said, "Hurry up and take the picture. I've got things to do." Kathy just had one of those flat ground markers, name and dates, a lamb in each corner. I would look at Becky's picture and wonder what Kathy would have looked like at fifteen. Probably some longhaired version of Danny, a lot of Julie.

Sometimes when I was at Becky's grave I had the feeling that I was being watched. A few times, I was in Oakland and saw Becky's father, and I'm sure he saw me, but we never spoke. I was never at his daughter's grave when I saw him. I would be there talking to Kathy and look up the hill past the Black Angel and there he was, this big black man. We made eye contact once, and I waved at him, but neither of us moved toward the other. That was a Sunday afternoon. The times I thought I was being watched were at night. I was starting to let Gary Sanders run the Hollywood in the evening more and more, so I could stay home. But sometimes, especially late Friday nights, I would work and then walk home, going through Oakland on my way. I would talk to Kathy and then go visit Becky. One night, I took a flashlight so I could see her picture in the dark. That was the night I knew I was being watched. I made a mistake, I think now, crossing some boundary I wasn't aware of at the time. It was the first, and only, time I ever talked to Becky. I had the flashlight beam pointed at the ground, muting the glare off the shiny surface of her picture, and I simply said, "My name is Joe Holly. My daughter is here with you, down the hill." Then my flashlight went dead. So I shook it, banged it on my palm, and I heard branches start cracking. There was no wind. I wasn't alone, I knew that, but it was too dark to see anything. I stopped talking to Becky and did something really, really dumb and juvenile. I threw my flashlight toward the sound and stood perfectly still, but there was nothing, not even the sound of the flashlight hitting the ground. I walked home. Julie was asleep, Danny in the bed with her, and I wondered if Becky's father was still awake.

Summer passes, and then Iowa gets one month of fall. September is a wonderful time in Athens. Mild weather, and the kids come back to town. Fall in a college town is like spring everywhere else.

New faces, life is starting over, the cycle begins again. The Iowa Arts orientation program brings in a lot of proud and guilt-ridden parents of eighteen-year-old freshmen. They're all over downtown for that first weekend, and the residential streets are full of double-parked Ryder and U-Haul mini-trucks. The kids think their adult life is finally beginning, but you can tell by the look of the parents, especially the mothers, that they think their life is ending. September in Athens, hope and memory balanced.

September was when I stopped being a participant in Athens politics and became a spectator. The game's a lot different from the outside, not as personal, more fun. Sure, the **BM FORUM** kept blasting Joseph Holly, and the **TELEGRAM** letters accused him of trying to close down the Athens library, but it wasn't a big deal. That Joseph Holly wasn't me. He was on the ballot, but I wasn't. This was hard to explain to somebody else, even to Harry. I wanted Holly to win, but I didn't want him to serve. I wanted Holly to be recognized for all his work, and getting re-elected was the best sort of validation. Harry was right. I wanted the voters to tell me that Joseph Holly had been right.

The primary ballot had eighteen names on it, more than anytime in Athens history, but that number was misleading. Of the eighteen, no more than six had a chance in hell of winning. The rest were—how do I say it—they were there for entertainment. They collected petition signatures to get on the ballot, and they got to speak at the early forums, but they were credible only to themselves. One guy lived over a bar downtown and wanted to eliminate all the parking meters. Several were Iowa Arts students, claiming to speak for the thousands of students in Athens who had been ignored by every Council since the school was founded.

My favorite at-large candidate was the Christian Coalition activist who ran every two years on the same platform: "I can do a better job in my sleep running this town than the incumbents have done awake." This year he even misquoted himself at a forum: "I can do a better job in my sleep ruining this town than the incumbents have done awake." The moderator offered him a chance to correct himself, and he thought about it while the camera zeroed in on him, but he seemed to like his new line, "Nope, the incumbents have ruined this town. I'll stand by that."

Steve Nash was not running, so one at-large seat was up for grabs. Ken Rumble was probably unbeatable for the other at-large seat. That left the district race. I was the incumbent. It was my race to lose. Of my two opponents, I only saw the Green Party kid in September. Six forums, just him and me, while Charlie Firestone's committee raised another five thousand dollars and spent it on full-page ads. It was overkill. There was no way Charlie or I wouldn't be the two finalists for November.

I liked the Green kid running against me. I say kid, he was thirty, but he seemed young. I liked him because he still believed in his ideas; unlike Ken Rumble, who had come to believe only in himself. At a forum, the Green kid would attack some Council decision and I would always ask him how I voted on that issue. Not the group—me. He never knew how often my position was close to his. He never knew how often Ken and I had voted the same. But he knew when Rumble and I disagreed. He knew I supported Harry Hopkins but not the library expansion. And those, finally, were the only issues that counted for his supporters. I just had to figure out—how important were they to everyone else?

There was another issue in the campaign, the invisible 800-pound gorilla issue—the police department. I had the votes to form a Citizens Review Board, despite Harry's misgivings. But only Ken had advocated firing the Police Chief. The Hampton lawsuit had been settled before the primary vote, Hampton's sister kept calling us murderers, all of us except Ken, but I could sense that the hot dry summer in Athens had exhausted most of the public. The long meetings, the downtown marches and confrontations, the letters to the **TELEGRAM**, the angry speakers at the council meetings—fewer and fewer. But I knew there had to be a residual effect. Athens had been shocked by the event, and even I had been disappointed in some of the things about the department that had been uncovered. But the more we studied it and compared it to other departments, only one basic conclusion was justified: we were better than most. The Rumble-ites had initially succeeded at painting the department as something alien to the town. "The People" were better than, different from, the police department. I had felt it too, at first, but in the long run—it wasn't true. We were all flawed.

By September, the Rumble-ites had run out of new facts and new accusations. A potential flare-up was coming at the end of September, when ABC aired its program about the chase. I was ready for that, but I wasn't ready for Al Baroli almost killing a Rumble-ite.

If it had been some other council member, and if there had been any witness other than an Athens cop, and if the kid had not been wearing a Rumble button on his backpack—well, if pigs could fly we'd all be shooting pork chops out of the sky.

When Harry called with the news, I finally understood how much of a spectator I had become. I started laughing, even after Harry told me that the kid was in the hospital.

"Joe, your sense of humor...," Harry began.

"The kid's going to be alright, isn't he?" I asked him.

"Sure, contusions, a broken shoulder, but it could've been worse."

"Could have been isn't what is," I laughed again. "Aren't you seeing what I'm seeing? Imagine the **TELEGRAM** headlines tomorrow, the **BM FORUM** ballistics. Harry, in two days it will all be <u>your</u> fault. In three days you and Al will be part of a conspiracy with the County Attorney. Forget all the facts you told me about. In a week, you guys will have been on the grassy knoll together back in 1963."

Harry finally agreed, "No way we win on this one either, right?"

"Facts be damned. Unless you find one other witness, preferably Jesus Christ himself, we're back to being a bunch of brown-shirts."

Harry sighed, a habit I was noticing more and more from him, "I suppose we'll get through this too, but the timing is awful, right before the election, all that dust stirred up again."

The facts were simple enough, if you believed Al and the cop. Al was driving home from some midnight shopping. He was going to surprise his wife with breakfast in bed the next morning but discovered he was out of eggs. A short trip to the 24-hour HyVee on North Dodge, just a few blocks from his house. Eggs and bacon on the front seat of his Lincoln, he pulled out of the parking lot, turned left, went through an intersection, and hit a kid on a bicycle. The kid was twenty-one, pedaling like crazy. A golden child gunned down by a black Lincoln.

Facts are funny things. Some of them are downright awkward. Like the fact that the kid was being followed by the cop because he had been weaving in and out of traffic on North Dodge ever since he left the Hilltop Tavern. Midnight or not, North Dodge is a busy street. The kid was drunk. More than drunk, he was stoned and drunk, things a blood test doesn't lie about, a blood test administered at the Mercy Hospital emergency room. The cop sees the kid being dodged by cars up and down North Dodge, sees the kid run some stop signs as he's trying to get away. But if you don't believe the cop, then the kid doesn't do those things. So maybe that's not a fact. If you believe the kid, he was going parallel to Al's Lincoln and Al turned into him at the intersection. If you believe the kid, Al Baroli, an Athens council member who has publicly said, "The damn bicyclists in this town ought to be off the streets and up on the sidewalks out of my way," that same Al Baroli pulled up alongside him and then swerved into him, cop's testimony to the contrary. Forget the fact that the cop has already called the dispatcher to report the kid's behavior, and the report is taped and timed. Forget the minor damage to the Lincoln, which could have only been caused by a head-on collision. If Jesus wasn't there, that Lincoln was a deadly weapon in the hands of an angry sinner—Al Baroli.

The morning after the accident, before the ink was dry on the police report, the **BM FORUM** had settled the case. A day later, the letters to the **TELEGRAM** had ruled out an appeal. Al Baroli needed to be recalled. The cop witness needed to take a polygraph test, and if he passed that then he should take another. After all, wasn't he the same cop who was the back up to The Cop who killed Anheuser Hampton? Not really, but that's what a **FORUM** writer thought. But facts also have a funny way of catching up to opinions. A routine council meeting was scheduled three days after the bike accident. I told Bob Hardy to get ready for another long meeting, bring in some extra chairs, make sure there was plenty of tape in the camera. But, with a morning sun that was the last gasp of a September Indian summer in Athens, I opened the **TELEGRAM** and discovered that Jesus had indeed seen the accident, Jesus _and_ a few of his disciples. I called Harry and this time he was laughing too.

Three letters to the **TELEGRAM**, one from an Episcopal minister, two from members of his congregation. They had been at the HyVee deli that night, coffee'ed up and continuing a late night discussion of angels on the heads of pins, or whatever Episcopalians discuss, three wise men who had walked out of the HyVee to enjoy the warm September air, three witnesses to the collision of Lincoln and Rumble-ite. They more than confirmed the Baroli/cop version,

252

they were angry at the letters from the previous day. They asked the people of Athens, "When is this going to stop——this name-calling, this hysteria? When are we going to think before we speak?"

I was outside the game by then, and I realized that <u>some</u> of the people of Athens had finally grown weary of some of the <u>other</u> people of Athens. When it happened, I don't know, but it was there. Some vague discontent with the performance art that had passed for public dialogue.

By the six o'clock news that night, Mike Wagner, at the Cedar Rapids ABC station, had an exclusive interview with all three men. Mike also had a scoop about the lab work done by Mercy. When the council meeting started an hour later, we had a lot of empty seats. I told Al that he had dodged a bullet, but he surprised me. I expected him to gloat, but all he said was, his eyes watery, "Joe, I was scared to death. I thought I had killed the boy."

September was almost gone. The last day of the month, ABC aired the profile of Athens. I was actually looking forward to seeing it. I wondered if Harry and Ken felt the same, and I wondered if Becky Hamilton's father was watching.

Like it was late on Christmas Eve, the streets were almost deserted, like the town was shutting down. People were gathered around their televisions, as if the tube was a fireplace and the winter wind was howling outside. Even the sports bars downtown had their TV sets tuned to ABC instead of ESPN, the jukebox turned off for eighteen minutes. America was about to see Athens for the first time, in primetime.

I watched it with Julie beside me. I even had the VCR recorder set, just in case Danny started to distract us. The phone ringer was turned off. All we needed was Ralph Edwards to say, "Athens, Iowa——THIS is YOUR life."

253

If you had never stepped foot in Athens, never known anybody from here, you would've thought we were in deep manure. The opening credits started with a map of the United States, the camera eye descending down to Iowa and then to the pencil dot that was Athens. Fair enough, a nice touch, except I think they were using the soundtrack from TAXI DRIVER. A lot of foreboding horns, and then the voice-over, "If it can happen in the heartland, can it happen in your town?"

Julie did a mock groan and whispered, "I'm betting that they open with......"

Side by side pictures of Anheuser Hampton and Becky Hamilton. My stomach turned over to see her next to him, but it got worse. From their pictures to video of their funerals, then a wide shot of Oakland, Black Angel right there in the middle, then separate shots of Hampton's tombstone and Becky's, her picture clearly visible. I wasn't even listening anymore. The pictures were jumping around too fast. I saw the Hampton funeral and looked for me and Bernie, but nada, then Becky's funeral. That video was obviously taken from the balcony, a wide shot of St. Mary's interior, palled casket up front, Father Deyo to one side. I zeroed in on the back of Becky's father, his small wife next to him, but the picture jumped again. I was glad I recorded the show, because I had to go back and watch it again. The first time, I simply watched. Athens was a silent movie.

Map, victims faces, funerals, Oakland, Hampton's sister interviewed weeping, Donald Mason interviewed, film of Jack and Marcie Hamilton leaving St. Mary's with their brothers and sisters, but no interview. Scenes from a crowded downtown Athens during a Friday night concert, a department file photo of The Cop, The Chief interviewed—forthright and overly self-conscious about every word; Harry Hopkins interviewed—articulate but emotionless. Film of Hampton's wrecked car, a filmed "dramatic re-enactment" of the actual chase and accident—actors for The Cop and Hampton and Becky, not exactly Oscar level work, but still compelling. Commercials for Paxil, Toyota, Centrum, an upcoming ABC Special, Sprint, and Red Lobster; then back to film from the council meeting where Mason and Elizabeth Norris advertised their availability, an interview with the County Attorney. Scenes from the first council meeting after the accident—anger and frustration down front, a brief sweep of the council, a handsome and grieved Ken Rumble at one end, five stoic colleagues to his right, and then me, my two seconds of Warholian fame, looking as if I was totally confused. Scenes from the Iowa Arts campus, the interviewer standing downtown in front of the Prairie Schooner bookstore and Hollywood theatre, summing it all up, "A tragedy that could have been avoided, two families from opposite sides of the track, two families, two children dead, a community that has yet to heal." Eighteen minutes, stay tuned. up next— "John Stossel tells us how the environmental movement is ruining American capitalism."

Actually, don't trust me about that ABC show. I'm not objective. I watched the tape again later that night, really paying attention to the words instead of the images and music, and I was impressed. A lot of the voice-over narration was clear and factual information about Athens and the accident. We were put in the context of a national problem with out-of-control police chases, and worse examples of chases gone bad were discussed. Statistics highlighted. Immediately getting rid of The Cop was acknowledged, as well as the creation of a police review board. ABC even acknowledged that Hampton was not an angel, and that his family's lawsuit had been settled for a fraction of the original asking price. Overall, Athens was spared a hatchet job, while ABC focused more on the tragedy of two young people dying. The emotion was a bit forced, almost contrived, but I knew what handicap ABC was unable to overcome, as the producer knew when he was here. The Hamiltons had refused to talk to America about their grief. That was the story ABC wanted.

There was one last thing about the program, however, that made me want to call the producer and thank him. I had watched thousands of movies in my theatre career. I understood cinematography and editing. The producer had somehow showed the Athens I loved. All the scenes from downtown, at Oakland, on the Iowa Arts campus, hundreds of people caught unawares—the ABC Athens was where I lived. The rhetorical narration at the end? You watch the program. Turn the sound off. Pay attention to how the conclusion was filmed. Not typical for television. A close-up of the interviewer in front of the Schooner bookstore and the Hollywood, but then you realize that the camera is on top of a building across the street, and the view pulls back and up from the ABC guy, and you look down and see more of the street, the pedestrians and cars, the bicycle racks, the trees, and then the camera takes your eye and shows you the entire west side of Athens, tops of buildings, Iowa Arts campus, and then your eye moves slowly north and you see Weber Park and the forest around it, even the top of the ferris wheel, then a slow arc to the east, until you see Oakland Cemetery, and the camera starts to close in on the markers and mounds of Athens' past. It stops too soon. Only the Black Angel is clearly recognizable. If it had lasted another few seconds, I would have seen Kathy's grave. That ABC conclusion was almost like being back in Al Baroli's airplane flying over Athens, seeing my town from a distance, from downtown and then to the horizon, then back to the cemetery.

I thought I had been alone, watching the tape a second and third time, but I was joined by Julie. She had come back and had stood behind me as I sat in the dark. She put her hands on my shoulders, said nothing, and watched the ending with me again. I wondered if she had seen all things I had seen, all the scenes from downtown where we had walked or sat or eaten or argued or laughed about the people around us. She started to massage my shoulders. "What'd you think?" she asked.

"It could have been a lot worse," I say.

"Did you see me wave to you?"

"You did what?" I said, reaching over my shoulder for her hand.

"Those shots of the campus. My office window. I was waving at you."

"Julie, you're full of crap. Adorable crap, but still crap."

"Well, duh," she said softly, letting me squeeze her hand and pull her around to sit next to me. "So, you didn't see me. I was there, maybe not waving, but I was there."

I re-wound the tape to watch the ending again, but Julie took the remote control away from me. "You can watch it all you want, but there's still only that one shot of you at the meeting, looking like you just ate a small bitter child. Just remember, this wasn't about you." I reached for the remote, but she threw it across the room. "One last thing, Joe. I thought you told me there was some sort of town forum that was supposed to be on this program. The Ken and Betty show. What happened to it?"

"I guess the producer decided that it had nothing to do with the real story, the real Athens. Or, who knows, maybe he just didn't have time to squeeze it in. Who knows?"

She leaned away from me, smiled in a room lit only by the glow of a television, and said, "Joe, humility has never been your strong suit."

Jack Hamilton had gone back to the post office as soon as he returned from Chicago. Marcie began preparing for another year of teaching at Regina. Becka had been dead for three months.

Hamilton's co-workers went out of their way to be kind. One of the newer clerks, however, who did not know Hamilton very well, had complained to the Postmaster about the extra vacation days that Hamilton had been given "off the books." The Postmaster told him to file a formal complaint if it was that important to him. The new clerk had asked, "Will all of us get that much time when we need it?" The Postmaster, a man looking forward to his retirement in a few years, a condo in Arizona, had looked up from his desk and told the new clerk, "Come see me when your child dies."

Hamilton and his wife went out to eat less often than they had in the past. Too many times, a stranger would come to their table and tell them how sorry they were about Becka. It was always unintentional, but the kindness of strangers hurt more than it helped.

Hamilton stopped watching the Athens council meetings, stopped reading the Athens TELEGRAM. He had moved Becka's computer out of her room and into his study. Late at night, he would surf the Internet for national and world news. He looked at the websites of the New York Times and Washington Post, and a few other major media sites. He read dozens of op-ed pieces and stories every night and could go to work and have an opinion about all the big news of the country and the world. When asked about the proposal for a police review board in Athens, or the idea of recalling the city manager, Hamilton simply shrugged. He did not watch the ABC program about Athens, but nobody at the post office asked him about it anyway. After his first day back to work, after the initial condolences, Becka was not mentioned unless Hamilton did it first, which he almost never did.

As Athens watched itself on ABC, Jack Hamilton was reading his daughter's diary. It was not a book diary. It was simply a file on *her computer hard-drive. Becka had been given the computer only a few months before she died, so the file was short. Hamilton had not been looking for it, but the night of ABC's program he had exhausted the daily news and casually turned to the few files which had an icon on the screen: an "address" file, a "schoolwork" file, a "movies to see" file, a "books to read" file, and a "sports" file. Hamilton had no specific goal when he read his daughter's files, except for trying to hold on to something of which she had been a part. If she had been alive, he would have never thought about doing it. But she was not alive. She was gone.*

The address book was full of names he already knew, even her aunts and uncles, but there were a few boys' names which were unfamiliar to him. But the file had names and addresses only, no commentary.

The movie file actually had two lists: movies to see and movies seen. Hamilton was surprised to see so many R-rated movies on both lists. He and Marcie had always asked Becka about the movies she was supposedly going to see, and she always assured them that she was only seeing PG-13 movies. Hamilton and his wife had seen many of the same movies on the list, and he felt a twinge of embarrassment, imagining Becka seeing them as well. Throughout her life, her parents had tried to insulate her from sex and violence and bad language. Kids see too much—too soon—Hamilton and Marcie agreed. They would protect their daughter.

The book file made Hamilton proud. Becka had always been a serious reader, and her list of books included a lot of civil rights history as well as sports biographies. Like the movie file, there were two lists: "read" and "to be read." Unlike the movie file, however, next to each "read" book was a short comment by Becka about whether she liked or disliked the book. Not profound insights, sometimes only a "boring" or "did not finish" or "EXCELLENT" or sometimes

259

even a date when she finished reading. Hamilton told himself that he would look for some of the same books, especially the ones she liked.

The schoolwork file was the longest, and the least interesting to begin with. Lots of essay rough drafts, polished work, outlines, and the mundane exercises of American public education. Slowly scrolling further into the file, however, Hamilton discovered a new heading at the end: PERSONAL. He stopped himself for a moment, and then clicked the shift key one more time. In the few months Becka had had the computer, she had written thirty pages of a daily journal. It was obvious to Hamilton that she had intended it to be private by the way she had hidden it within the schoolwork file.

When Becka was thirteen years old, Hamilton had walked into her bedroom and casually picked up a book from her dressing table. It was her diary, but he did not know it. He had not opened it. He was merely holding it in his hand when she looked around from her desk. Becka exploded. She grabbed the book and went crying to her mother. Crying, and screaming about her father. Mother and daughter had come back into the bedroom and Hamilton apologized for an hour. The next day Becka informed him that she had destroyed her diary, and that she would never trust him again.

The night that America learned about Athens from ABC, Hamilton read all thirty pages of Becka's journal. Read them twice, wanting some profound revelation about his daughter. At first, he was disappointed. Becka was a teenage girl, and her journal was about a teenage girl's life. If strangers had read the journal, they would have wondered if Becka even had parents. Jack and Marcie Hamilton were barely mentioned in the thirty pages. Boys, sports, teachers, movies, music, menstrual problems, gossip, television, and even the weather——all of them dissected and explored more than her parents, often in language that would shock any parent. Only one entry was exclusively about them, and Hamilton remembered the day well: April

*11th of that year. A prolonged battle about dating and boys in general.
Becka had been very upset:* I can't wait until I'm 18 and out of here.
They don't understand me and they don't trust me. Mama can be
such a bitch sometimes. Daddy is so full of himself and thinks he
knows the answer to everything and that I don't know anything about
life. Mama said I was lucky to be so pretty but I shouldn't think it
will last forever. What the hell does that mean? Just because she was
never pretty she thinks pretty girls are bad. And they think things are
the same for me as they were for them, but they're so wrong it's
almost funny. If they only knew how much goes on at school they
would die. But they don't give me credit. They probably wish they
had a different daughter, but they're stuck with me. Too bad for them.

*Hamilton remembered the argument, and then he remembered
how the next day all three of them had gone to a movie together. The
first time in weeks that Becka had gone out with them. He tried to
remember the title, but all that came back was a few stars: Julia Roberts
and some handsome young man, but his name escaped Hamilton.
Becka had loved the movie, and she had left the theatre between her
mother and father, holding an arm of each.*

*Hamilton did not know much more about his daughter than he
did before he read the journal. She cursed a lot, but that did not
surprise him. It was obvious that she was still a virgin, based on her
comments about certain other girls and the actions of a few boys
who had talked to her, and Hamilton was pleased about that. She
was unhappy some days, frustrated and tired on others, but she was
not depressed or suicidal. She talked a lot about going to college and
was excited about moving to a bigger city than Athens. All in all,
considering all the bad things that could happen to a teenage girl,
Hamilton was happy, and he was proud of his daughter. There was
only one comment of hers that confused him, a cryptic one line
reference to himself from a March entry:* Daddy is getting more and

more like that Harry Chapin song all the time. *It was an entry without context, book-ended by meaningless and bland entries about homework and an upcoming cross-country meet.*

Hamilton read the journal again and then printed it out. But, first, he went back to the April 11ᵗʰ entry and changed the word "bitch" to "pain" and the word "pretty" to "popular." Then he put the thirty printed pages in a large manila envelope and set them on the kitchen table for Marcie.

As he lay in bed that night, with Marcie asleep beside him, Hamilton wondered about the reference to "that Harry Chapin song." It was the word "that" which was important. There was a specific song by Chapin that she thought her father was coming to personify. All Hamilton had to do was listen to every Harry Chapin song ever recorded and figure out which one it was. That was all, and he had lots of time.

You want to solve a problem, you first have to know what the problem is, if it's the <u>real</u> problem. Getting elected to office is a problem, and you can do all the right things but still lose. I was running for re-election, but I didn't care if I won or lost. So I would lose. A dead man would beat me. So, winning wasn't my real problem. In fact, "problem" was the wrong word. I should say "goal." I was running for re-election, but my goal was to be honest with myself and the public. I would shift the burden to them. "Here's reality as I see it," I was saying to them. "Do with it as you will. I'm responsible only for being honest." I had to change the terms of the election. It was not about me and the Greenie, or me and Charlie Firestone. The election was about Athens, and I had to figure out a way to lose and win at the same time. Now, <u>that</u> was a problem.

The library was the answer.

The library represented everything that was right about Athens, and was also symptomatic of what was wrong. I wrote my first guest editorial to the **TELEGRAM** and resigned myself to losing. I laid out the case——the library was a service, not a building——and waited for the phone calls.

In a budget of finite means, a twenty million dollar library building expansion was a mistake. It would paralyze future budgets. For twenty million dollars, I diplomatically told Athens, it could expand library service to areas of town that needed it more than downtown. For twenty million dollars, Athens could have more people reading books as well as more police and firemen, more trees planted, more parkland, more youth services, more affordable housing. It could have more of those things, but it couldn't have them while doubling the number of bricks in a building downtown at the same time. We could not have guns <u>and</u> butter.

It was a hard sell, I knew that, but all I needed was one vote past forty percent to oppose the expansion. One extra negative vote would buy us time to have a <u>real</u> public discussion. My mistake in the past had been to merely oppose the expansion, while I had never offered an alternative.

The **TELEGRAM** had been generous. Instead of its usual 750-word limit for guest submissions, it gave me half the editorial page, and printed my picture too.

"Would you buy a used car from this man?" Julie laughed as we read the morning paper. Danny was standing at the stove, tapping it with a wooden spoon, but Julie and I had long ago learned to tune out noise like that. I stared at the picture. It wasn't me. It was Joseph Holly.

"Forget the messenger," I said. "How do you think the message sounds? Reasonable? Convincing."

Julie was in an especially happy mood that morning, two cups of coffee down, and just up from a good night's sleep. "Like Moses down from the mountain, dear."

"You mean I come across too high and mighty? Harry says I do that a lot. But all I want to know is—does this argument make sense?"

"Joe, I've heard you rant and rave about this at home for a year. I know you're right, but you obviously missed my point about you being Moses."

Danny was finally beginning to irritate me, or maybe it was Julie. "So what's your point?"

"Moses came down from the mountain and found his people worshipping golden idols, false images, sex, drugs, rock and roll, and he got mad. He threw down his guest editorial and broke the tablets. And you? You want to know what's all this got to do with you?"

I nodded, looking at Julie and hearing Danny pound his sticks.

"Joe—those people finally got to the Promised Land, but Moses never did."

I went for the obvious. "So I'm a prophet in my own time."

Julie reached over and took the spoon out of Danny's hand and replaced it with a cloth potholder, which he started tossing like it was pizza dough, then she looked back at me, "I can live with a prophet, Joe. I just don't want to put up with a martyr. This house is only big enough for one person to wallow in self-pity, and I was here first."

With friends like these, who needs enemies? September had six forums. Of all the people running in the primary, only one agreed with my position on the library expansion. The Christian Coalition guy. He didn't want to give the library another dime because all it would do is buy more Harry Potter books. He wasn't too fond of Holden Caulfield or Stephen Jay Gould either.

First time the library question was raised at a forum, the moderator asked, "Do any of the other candidates agree with Mr. Holly?" I didn't bother looking for hands in the air. The Coalition guy gave me a thumbs up, and I could feel the rigor mortis in my ass.

Since Ken was the only other incumbent running, and supposedly knew as much about the budget as me, he was asked directly if I was right about the budget constraints. He had the perfect answer, "We can easily expand our free public library. All it takes is a Council willing to make hard decisions about priorities."

Translation: As long as we freeze some departments indefinitely, eliminate staff positions, cut the police department, don't build that much needed satellite fire-station, don't increase funds for human service agencies, and reduce the budgets for streets and roads—sure, we can eat cake. Asked what he would specifically cut from the budget, he was himself, "I want to hear from the people what their priorities are, and I will let them help me formulate a new vision for Athens. It will be the people's vision, not mine."

We never made eye contact in any of the forums, Ken and me. He knew there was no pork in the budget. He never said there was.

He didn't have to. All he had to do was imply it.

Charlie Firestone didn't attend any of those forums, but his campaign manager wrote a letter to the **TELEGRAM**, making sure everyone knew that "Charlie was a founding member of the Friends of the Athens Library and was dismayed by his opponent's hostility toward a free public library." He ignored the Greenie.

The **BM FORUM** had a field day after that: *Joseph Holly—the stealth Christian Coalition candidate?....... Joseph Holly sides with book banning..... . Holly wants more cops and less books......Holly go lightly, but please go!!!!*

The national trend had finally seeped down to Athens. Single-issue politics. Find the hot button and push it. The library was one. The deaths of Anheuser Hampton and Becky Hamilton were another. I was ahead of the curve on death, behind the eight ball on the library.

The Rumble-ites insisted on making the police department an issue in the campaign, and, by extension, the city manager. But, unlike the library issue, they were in the minority. Most candidates were satisfied that the city was making progress on reforming the department and that Harry was not <u>the</u> problem. But the thing about single-issue politics is this—it doesn't matter how many people feel one way, it only matters how <u>intensely</u> they feel about it. And in Athens, intensity was all on the Rumble-ites side.

The last forum of the primary, I finally won the war about death. Too bad it wasn't televised, but the **TELEGRAM** did give me credit in a story the next day. With so many candidates at one forum, we only had time for us to each answer about three generic questions. It was a rotten format, no time for give and take, but I soon became the focus.

The Greenie and the other Rumble-ite candidates had been giving me grief about the city's "insensitivity toward the victims and their families." Ken Rumble admitted, in his role as Council conscience, that we had not been contrite enough."

Remember Lloyd Bentsen nailing Dan Quayle about not being John Kennedy? Bentsen had studied Quayle's speeches, knew that Quayle had used the "new generation" line a dozen times, and he waited. I was waiting too.

"You could have at least apologized," the Greenie said, and Rumble-ites in the audience nodded. "You could have at least said you were sorry, but, except for Mr. Rumble, the council tried to stonewall...," he paused, and I knew he had practiced his delivery for maximum effect, ". . . you stonewalled your. . . emotions. Athens deserved better."

In a proverbial nutshell, the Greenie laid out the indictment: Worse than covering up the facts, we had separated ourselves from the heart of a grieving community. We did not feel their pain. In the audience, the Greenie's words brought it all back for the Rumble-ites. And Joseph Holly was there to defend the indefensible. A woman in the front row was crying.

Silence, not a word from me, as if I was speechless and guilty as charged. I blinked, cleared my throat, started to speak but then stopped. I was trying not to smile. I was as sincere as Judas.

"Let me see if I understand you," I began. "If we had apologized at the beginning, a lot of the anger and...," seeming to struggle for the right word, ". . . the strife. . . ," another pause, ". . . things would have been different?"

The Greenie and Rumble-ites nodded.

"Would it have made a difference if we had said something like...," I paused, seeming to improvise on the spot, pulling out a phrase and then waiting for another phrase to follow, "...*The City Council would like to. . . offer its condolences...to the friends and families of the two young people...who were recent victims of a tragic...accident...involving a city employee. Our words .... ,*"

It was the absolutely most cynical thing I had ever done in my life, and that says a lot, but then I stopped myself. I was a fraud. I was looking in the mirror and seeing what I had become, a performer who hated his audience. I paused too long, and that audience leaned toward me. I wondered if Ken knew what I was doing, if he remembered the words I had memorized. I was about to drown, but I looked back in the mirror I always talk about, and Becky Hamilton's father saved me. Instead of seeing myself, I saw him, that day in Oakland. I saw him standing over her grave, and I finally spoke <u>to him</u>. *"Our words cannot bring them back, but our hearts share this community's grief. We will look at this tragedy as an opportunity to re-think and re-evaluate the relevant city procedures. Our goal is to make sure this never happens again. Once again, we urge this community to come together and work toward a common goal. The Council needs your help, as the families need your prayers."* It wasn't insincere Joseph Holly speaking, it was me. Ten, fifteen seconds? The audience was silent. I knew I had been talking, but not to them. I wondered if the Rumble-ites and the Greenie understood absolution. I turned back to the Greenie, and said sadly, but sincerely, "If we had said that, back then, would it have made a difference?"

Dan Quayle opened his mouth just as Ken tried to save him, "Joseph, those are not...."

"Ken, I'm not talking to you. I'm talking to my opponent. He can speak for himself," I pointed my finger at Ken but kept my eyes on the Greenie. "Would it have made a difference?" I repeated.

"Of course it would," he fell. "All the people wanted was...."

I pulled a videotape out of the bag I had brought with me and placed it on the table in front of the Greenie, "We did say that. The first night. The mayor. And we were, all seven of us, ...absolutely sincere. This is a tape of that meeting. Were you there? Did you listen?"

The Greenie turned red. Ken spoke for him, "Joseph, your theatrics..."

He was at the end of the table, fifteen candidates away from me, but he heard me whisper clearly into my microphone, "Kenneth, were you at that meeting?"

He cut his losses, and I went home. The primary election was three days later, first Tuesday in October. Time for the people to speak.

The people spoke, alright, loud and clear. Ken led the at-large primary field by two hundred votes. A solid lead, considering the low turnout, but much less of a margin than he had four years earlier. I was grimly pleased. At this rate, Ken would eventually lose, but I wasn't going to be on the ballot when it happened. Behind Ken were a Chamber woman, a young black man, and a home-towner named George Bedell.

Voters in my district were also clear enough. I beat the Greenie by 23 votes. Put his votes with mine, add a hundred, and you had Charlie Firestone's total. I made the cut. To beat Firestone in a month, all I had to do was get all the Greenie's to vote for me and hope that Firestone died. Even then, according to Gary Sanders, Firestone was probably still going to be the bookies favorite. Welcome to Texas.

Joe Holly was going to lose, and I'd be disappointed about that, but not enough to do the work needed to help him win. Harry Hopkins wasn't so nonchalant.

"You got any more brilliant campaign strategies, Joe?" he jabbed at me the morning after the primary. "You tell the most educated town in America, and the most affluent town in Iowa, that it can't have a bigger library. You embarrass the Lefties, pontificate to the middle, and promise the Right that you'll spend twenty million on something even if it's not a bigger library? You are a smug sonuvabitch."

"I'm just making your job easier," I said, sitting across from him in his office. The votes had been tallied by nine o'clock the previous night, and I was asleep by ten. I was feeling good that morning. First time in a long time. "Me gone, Ken isolated, Bernie as Mayor, you'll pat the rest of the Council on the butt and they'll follow you anywhere. You'll ignore Ken, and the rest of them will work like hell to have the shortest meetings on record. Am I wrong?"

Harry gave me one of those looks that a hospice patient sees from his friends. False optimism, sincere grief. "Are you just going to drop off the face of the earth?" he finally said. "Hibernate until the snow melts? Forget your friends?"

"Nope, I'm going to go home and take care of Julie and Danny, like I should've been doing all along. Somebody else is going to have to tilt at windmills."

Harry was fidgeting with some papers on his desk, being un-typically antsy. He didn't look at me for a few seconds, then leaned back in his chair and put his feet on his desk—very un-typical for him. "You're wrong about my job being easier, you know that, don't you?"

I nodded. I understood.

"Funny town, this is," he continued. "I describe it to other managers across the country, and they tell me they'd sell their managerial souls to be in my chair. To have our 'problems.' Trade theirs for ours. But they also know how a good council makes their jobs easier. Joe, don't let this go to your puffy head, but you were one of the best this town's ever had. You did a lot of good things that nobody will ever know about—By the way, thanks for getting in ABC's face about that forum. You did Athens a favor by getting that thing killed.... ."

I started to protest, but he shook his head and rolled his eyes.

"Save it. Whether you did it or not, I'll always think you did. And for that, this town should be grateful to you."

"Thanks accepted," I said. I wasn't sure it was deserved, but I'd take it in private. "So keep talking. Tell me how I'm an FDR or JFK, the best thing since sliced bread. I need something to take home."

"You were very good," he said. "<u>Were</u>," he emphasized. "But you shouldn't have run for re-election. You changed in the last six months, Joe, who knows why, but four more years and…I don't know. Four more years and you would have gone crazy, or something."

I looked at Harry, "Crazy?"

"Or something," he mumbled back.

It was time to change the subject, but all that Harry and I had in common was government and politics. The best we could do at that moment was to shift the discussion to something else in that category.

"How am I doing on the library vote?" I asked.

"You've got the sixty percent rule on your side, and people are finally talking."

That's all he said, so I waited for more, but Harry just stared at me, waiting for another question.

"You got any preferences in the at-large race—other than Ken losing, which ain't going to happen. The other three—any favorite?"

"I can work with any of the three," he said. "I'm just thankful that it's them in the finals. If one of Ken's supporters had gotten through, I would have been on the same plane with you."

"You might be anyway," I tried to joke, "if that petition drive for a city manager recall gets enough signatures."

Harry was unfazed. "I have more faith in this town than they do. The charter amendment is probably illegal anyway, but if it ever gets to a serious public debate I'm assuming you'll come out of retirement and defend me, right?"

I maintained the best stony blank look on my face for as long as I could, as silently as I could, until Harry blinked.

"You <u>are</u> an asshole, Joe, you know that, and you can forget all those nice things I said about you. You can tell Julie that you're an asshole too, but I doubt that she'd be surprised."

We both started laughing. Harry had always said he would miss me. I knew I'd miss him too.

"You are so easy, Harry. You know why?"

"And why is that, O-insightful asshole?"

"Because you are the vainest man in Athens. You're great at what you do, you know it, and you assume that everyone should know it too. That there must be something wrong with anybody who doesn't agree with you. Damn smart of me, eh?"

"So, Mister Smart and Insightful Asshole, am I the pot...or the kettle...in this little profile of yours? And, for your Freudian file, you might remember that I'm not the guy who sees a giant deer in this town that nobody else sees."

"Not true. Hartford's been seen by hundreds of people," I shot back, having fun with Harry.

"Joe, hundreds of people in Athens have seen a big deer, bigger than most, running around this town, but nobody has seen the same deer you have. Nobody."

Suddenly, I wasn't having fun anymore. Harry saw me start to slump back in my chair, so he threw me a bone, "Okay, I wasn't going to give you the pleasure, but here's some grist for your Hartford myth, news that won't make the **TELEGRAM**. I made sure of that."

"Harry, the most interesting thing about you is not that you don't believe me...it's almost like you don't want to believe me."

"Save the analysis. Just take this home with you. Last night, something destroyed a metal tool shed up in Oakland. Maintenance man first thought somebody had taken a sledge hammer to the walls and door, maybe a vandal, or some gang work, but nothing was gone. Just sheets of twisted and dented tin all over the ground."

"And?" I asked quietly.

"And there were some very large animal foot prints stamped in the metal. Even the roof panels. BIG prints."

"And?" I asked once more, knowing that Harry was stringing me along, making me drag at his pace.

"And you know how dry it's been around here since July. The ground up in Oakland is rock hard. You know that, right?"

I nodded, then asked, "And?"

Harry took his feet off his desk and swung around to face me, elbows on his desk." And those prints in the metal...well, there are no prints on the ground. Not a trace. But I'm telling you again. The ground is so hard up there now that you could drive a tank over the dirt and not leave a track."

"And you weren't going to tell me this?"

"After the election, Joe. After you lost, and you are going to lose, I was going to tell you. Eventually."

I asked the obvious question, "And why were you going to wait?"

"Your plate's full right now, more than I think you even realize. I just thought you needed to have some breathing room before you started sorting out that deer thing in your head. Go fight the good fight for now, Joe...," he smiled, almost embarrassed, and looked down, "...and don't forget to come see me sometime."

Freedom's just another word for nothing left to lose. It just took me too long to figure out what I couldn't afford to lose. I had something. I had Julie and Danny. I wasn't free.

Iowa Arts was back in session, and Julie was on unofficial probation. Unofficial because all the complaints had been verbal, and Robin King's talk with her was off the record. He told me, "Something has to change this term, Joe, or else the paper trail begins. I want to help her, but I've got to protect this department too. I can't hold her hand, and I'm not a doctor."

I wasn't a doctor either, but I could sure hold her hand. We walked together to her campus office everyday, even though she sometimes told me to go to hell and leave her alone. But we walked, and talked, and I arranged to have lunch with her almost every day. But that wasn't going to be enough. If I missed a day, she would ask me why. As the weather cooled, we would stop at Lou Henri's Restaurant for afternoon coffee on the way home. Then I would drop her off and go get Danny. If she was feeling good, she went with me, but I never knew ahead of time. I had Gary Sanders work more nights at the Hollywood so I could stay home. My father's money was in the Iowa Arts Credit Union. I told Gary about the new cash, and he said he would tell his dead relatives to thank my father in heaven for all the extra hours. I misunderstood for a second. I asked him if he really talked to his dead relatives, and he gave me one of those "Are you serious?" looks.

I wish I had been enough, but I wasn't. I couldn't go with Julie into her classroom or stay with her in the department lounge. I would get progress reports, more good days than bad, but not enough good.

After the primary vote, I stopped campaigning except for going to the forums. I was totally confused. The more attention I paid to Julie, the worse she seemed to get at home. She was angrier at Danny, and she went to bed crying. She mumbled to herself more, and the house got dirtier. I had never noticed how much work a house required. Things Julie had always done and I had never noticed. She stopped dusting and vacuuming, and Danny started wearing dirty clothes. It took me a few weeks, but I developed my own cleaning routine, and the house became livable again. Julie thought I was the funniest man in Athens. Joseph Holly—Mr. Clean. She would watch me, and smile, but not a happy smile. I joked about hiring a maid to help me, a Norwegian teenager named Hulga, blond and blue-eyed nymphomaniac. Julie smiled and nodded. Danny overheard me. He didn't smile at all.

I was losing, but then Bernie Huss, that mannish version of a female, reminded me of the obvious, "Joe, she's a middle-aged woman, and her hormones are probably flying all over the place, like mine and most of the other women I know. Get her to a medical doctor—a female doctor. Get her blood work done. Make her talk to the doctor. Then you talk to the doctor in private if you have to. If there's a pill to help, make her take it. No shame in that. The only reason I haven't killed Ken Rumble and Al Baroli, and sometimes you, is Zoloft. I love prescription drugs, and my portfolio loves drug company stock."

Bernie had come to see me one afternoon at the Hollywood. She seldom came to my place, preferring to hold court in her clothing store or her Iowa Arts office. But she saw the handwriting on the wall about my time left on the council. As she talked, I realized that I had turned cool toward her at the Hampton boy's funeral, and I had never warmed up again. We had exchanged fewer and fewer private notes at the council meetings. But here she was, throwing me a lifeline and revealing something personal about herself in the process.

"We're not that lucky," I said, my skepticism too heavy. "A pill's not the answer."

I was looking through my front windows, proud of the windexing I had just given them. Paul Harris passed by outside, on his way to work at the Prairie Schooner next door. He waved at me and kept going. I drifted off, remembering when Julie had taken me to Iowa City to meet her mother as she was dying of breast cancer. Julie was pregnant with Kathy, and her mother wanted to make sure that Julie got all of her old baby clothes out of the cedar chest for the new Knight baby. Funny how you remember things, right out of nowhere. I was thinking about Julie's mother when Bernie spoke again, "Joe, you are so typically male I should have you stuffed and mounted after you die and put on display."

275

I was clueless.

"All this blather about men being decisive and natural leaders. Complex thinkers, all that crap. Truth is, you think too much. You miss the obvious. Sure, a pill won't solve all of Julie's problems, but you've got to start somewhere. Medicine buys you time, Joe, and that's what Julie needs first. She's depressed, and that's not a metaphor. It's a physiological condition. It can be treated. It's the wall you have to break down before you treat anything else."

I looked at her. Of course she was right. I didn't tell her about Julie and the voices. Bernie had given me a push toward a solution to the easy problems first. And, sometimes I thought to myself, sometimes I thought the voices weren't that bad of a problem. Sometimes, I wish I heard them too. Bernie merely gave me a clear first step. If she had had a bosom I might have leaned into it and cried, but Bernie always had that warp field around her which kept emotional gestures in the next galaxy.

All I could say was, "You're a smart woman, Bernie."

She almost grinned, "Well, you're half right."

A week before the election, I became a political cliché. I tried to be as honest as I could, and I would lose. Praised, and then passed over. It's a wonderful story for the movies. Remember Warren Beatty in BULWORTH? Hell, they shot him, but that movie was still only a liberal wet dream. It never happens in real life. Who knows, maybe they shot John Kennedy because he was going to pull us out of Vietnam. Wouldn't it be nice to think so? Remember John McCain and his Straight Talk Express in 2000? Straight talk, for sure, until he got to South Carolina and was asked about the Confederate flag. Sometimes you wonder who's more cynical, more self-deluded—the candidates or the voters. Political straight talk is always curvy. Always. And at some level, George Orwell was right about political language being "designed to make lies sound truthful and murder respectable, and to give an appearance of solidity to pure wind." I always liked that quote. But I always told people that it didn't apply to Athens. We were different.

A week before the election, the **TELEGRAM** sponsored a televised forum about one issue: the Athens library expansion. It was to be held in the largest meeting room of the library, and I was asked to be the con. The pro side had the Library Board and Charlie Firestone. It was a smart move on their part. Me at one table, six people at the other. I was a visual minority, a not so subtle message about "the community." Even though only one of the six proponents actually spoke, the bodies were lined up. More "people" wanted the expansion than not, and silent Charlie Firestone, I had to admit, looked good on television.

Julie dressed me. Made me wear a tie and sports coat, patted me on the back, and pushed me out the door with some advice, "Don't be yourself—be nice instead. I'll be watching." Danny handed me my notebook, and off I went, thinking I was Ward Cleaver headed for the office. As soon as I got to the library, however, I felt like the office was some sort of Biblical lion's den, and I was Daniel. I wished I had anticipated the feeling before I left home, so I could tell Danny that Bible story again.

A ninety-minute format: fifteen for each side, fifteen for each side to rebut the other side, and thirty minutes for questions from the audience. Expansion advocates first, then me, then the lions. I understood that <u>my</u> audience wasn't in the same room with me. But how many people were watching at home? Enough to make a difference in the election, enough who would agree with me?

First rule of debates—anticipate your opponent's argument as well as you know your own, then look for your own weaknesses as well as theirs. Prep—prep—prep. The Board Chair made the expansion case, but not as well as I had made it in front of Julie the night before. I was surprised. These were smart people. But I also understood their weakness. They were totally committed to a cause which seemed to them self-evidently good and logically unassailable. Athens' Library was the best in Iowa, with the best staff, and the most used—all true. Therefore, money for a bigger library building was a no-brainer. But their case had two simple flaws: The Athens Library was not the town itself; the Library was a service, not a building.

For the first fifteen minutes I sat there and listened to their case, complete with charts and graphs, and I looked at the audience. I knew most of them, and I could honestly say that everyone in the room was a good person. I doubted that many agreed with me, but that was okay. The important thing was that they were there. They cared enough to be there. If the angry crowds that first came to the council when Becky Hamilton died had come with their hearts broken, most of this polite crowd, some of whom had been part of the summer drama, had come with their minds made up. I could live with that. At least they cared enough to come. I knew I was a disappointment to them, telling them something they didn't want to hear, but I was proud of them nonetheless. I wouldn't live anywhere else.

I went through the expansion case point-by-point, statistic-by-statistic, and re-interpreted everything. I attacked the second flaw of their case by insisting that more service and more bricks were not synonymous: "A bigger building is a nineteenth century answer to a twenty-first century question." I thought that was a good line, but I also knew it would irritate some people.

In a debate, the opposition always has an advantage. In a sense, all opposition is rebuttal, not advocacy. So when it came time for the expansion people to "rebut" me they had to rebut a rebuttal, offering criticism of criticism, and that can get tricky if not done clearly. That's what I was expecting, but the Board Chair merely paraphrased his original statement and spoke as if I hadn't been invited to the party. *We hold these truths to be self-evident. We want a bigger building. Give us the money.* Julie had been right. I had to remind myself to be nice.

For my second fifteen minutes, I went after the ankle of the other expansion flaw. The Library might indeed be our "Crown Jewel," but baby needed new shoes. There was more to Athens than the Library, and I wanted to talk about that "other Athens." All I needed to begin was one fact about the library.

"Anheuser Hampton didn't have a library card, and I'm guessing that he died without ever stepping foot in this building." I was guessing for sure, and the Lesser Angel of my Being thought that Hampton's death was not a loss, but I had also thought a long time about how to make the case I wanted to make that night. I had looked in my own mirror and finally seen Hampton's connection to me and to Athens. I surprised myself—I had some Better Angels too. And I had finally put all the pragmatic nuts and bolts of serving on the council into something I didn't think I was capable of building——a vision for Athens.

"Hampton lived in a part of Athens we don't like to talk about, but that's what I want to start with. And then I want us to lift our eyes over Athens and see more than our library," I continued, pausing a split second as I remembered what it was like to be fifteen again, in a tent in Texas, to believe in something. As I talked, I forgot about the camera and tried to make eye contact with as many people in the room as possible. I talked about money and taxes and priorities. I talked about southeast Athens, a foreign country to most of the people in front of me. I talked about public art and subsidized housing, bus replacements, playground equipment and park maintenance as well as more parkland, more police protection and a new fire station, about needs versus wants, about the thread between feeling good and doing good. My only visual aid for the camera? I held up a copy of the three inch thick city budget, Harry Hopkins' love-child, the municipal Bible, held it up with one hand and pointed to it with the other, saying it meant nothing unless we understood how all the pages were connected to the other pages, numbers bouncing off other numbers, mixing metaphors of trophy children pampered and step-children starved, muscles steroided and muscles atrophied, and the body dying. Abstractions supported by a litany of real numbers, chapter and verse cited from the budget, page number and line item. Billy Graham meets Robert LaFollette. I was sincere, but still in control, my speech written first and then spoken over and over until I didn't need the pages in front of me. Proud of my own last second revisions, sensing that me calling the library expansion a "false god" would have been going too far. Too much Graham. Too much metaphor. Too close to the truth. But, lined-out nonetheless. For that fifteen minutes, me and Joseph Holly were the same person again, and then we stopped talking. We didn't see as many lions in front of us as there were before. The questions that followed were thoughtful, and I was glad to see some of the people using my presentation to question the other table. A few questions zeroed in on my budget analysis, insisting that some of the items I deemed essential might not be. That was fair. I didn't have all the answers, I admitted. I just wanted everybody to know that the issue was not as simple as building a bigger Library. The ninety minutes went by, the moderator thanked everybody for coming, and then I spent thirty minutes shaking hands with a lot of people.

My favorite moment of Zen that night? Charlie Firestone shook my hand, praised my eloquence, said that he looked forward to serving with me on the Council. I opened my mouth, but nothing came out.

I walked home. A mild night, I was tempted to go through Oakland, but I knew Julie would be waiting for me. When I got home, she handed me the remote control and said, "Harry called and wanted to know if you had been kissed first."

"Kissed first?'

"He said he'd call back, but I know what he meant," Julie smiled, pointing to the television. "I taped it. You looked great."

The phone rang, and Harry gave me the news, "I hope you got kissed first because you sure got screwed. I just want you to know that Bob Hardy had nothing to do with this. His Government Channel people didn't handle the broadcast. It was all volunteers. Call me after you've seen the tape."

I watched the tape with Julie. Then I walked back downtown and counted popcorn boxes at the Hollywood that I had counted the day before. Still got the same numbers. I counted them again. Then I walked to Oakland and told Kathy about the tape.

My second fifteen minutes, my vision for Athens, me and Joseph Holly at our best—our microphone had been turned off. The television crews were all volunteers, all amateurs, and most of them were Rumble-ites. Harry didn't need to explain.

Jack Hamilton watched the boy get beaten on every play. He looked at his program. The boy was a freshman, a hundred and fifty pounds but already a wiry six feet three inches tall. If he worked hard, ate right, lifted weights, Hamilton knew, the boy would eventually fill out and have the strength to play defensive end and knock down the smaller offensive backs trying to block him. The boy had heart, Hamilton could see that too, getting punished but also getting back up and charging again. The boy had a strong heart and unlimited potential, but Hamilton could see that he had no technique. Basic skills, sensing when a blocker is pushing one way and knowing how to turn that blocker around so he could cut off the run. Hamilton wanted to tell the boy, "If you feel him pushing you to the outside, it means they want to go inside, so stop trying to go around the blocker, go back inside, but always keep an eye on the runner."

Hamilton had learned the hard way when he was fifteen. His coach had benched him during the first game. At practice the next week, that coach had the seniors run at Hamilton all afternoon, and for the next four days. Hamilton ached all night long, and limped in the hallways. It took longer than the coach wanted, but before the season was over, as the coach had promised, Hamilton could see the opposing linemen take a quick glance around to make sure they knew where he was. By the time he was a senior, Hamilton was a hundred pounds heavier, quicker, and a lot smarter.

"I should call the coach," Hamilton said as he watched the Regina High School football game, more to himself than Marcie, who was taking a break from working in the concession stand. Their daughter had gone to Regina Elementary, and Marcie still taught there. When Becka went to the public school junior high and then Athens High, Marcie had been disappointed. But she agreed with her husband that the Athens High music program was where Becka needed to be. Hamilton had also joked about his daughter needing to be in an athletic

282

program that would teach her a little humility. Becka had thrived at Athens High and was the number two cross country runner by the end of her freshman year. "So much for your humility theory," Marcie had kidded him in April, while they watched Becka anchor the Athens mile-relay team to a school record a month before she died.

"I was hoping you would finally call him," Marcie said to him as the first half ended.

"Yeh, I want to apologize for calling him a bastard when I was a kid, tell him thanks for things I should've thanked him for back then."

"Jack?" Marcie said, standing over him, confused.

Hamilton looked up and immediately knew that they had been thinking of two different coaches. Marcie had suggested more than once that he ought to volunteer to help Regina, which only had two paid coaches. Hamilton looked back at the field, nodded, and then back up at Marcie, "Season's almost over."

"They play every year, Jack," she said, leaning down to pull his jacket collar up around his neck. It was a cold night. "And they practice in the spring."

For his daughter's fourteenth birthday, Jack Hamilton had gone downtown to Discount Records and asked the clerk to suggest a CD for a young teenage girl. The clerk had long frizzy hair, thick glasses, and not much respect for any music that a fourteen-year-old girl would like, but he went to the racks and handed Hamilton a CD that Becka raved about the next day. No respect for bubble gum pop rock, but the clerk knew music.

On the afternoon of the first Tuesday in November, after work, Hamilton went back to Discount Records. He wanted to find Harry Chapin. He had first thought about going directly to his daughter's music teacher, but then he thought that might embarrass her.

He went right to the Chapin section of the racks, scanning titles on the back of CDs, but that did not help. He had always known about "Taxi" and "Cat's in the Cradle," but the other titles meant nothing to him. The clerk who had helped him before was still there, his hair still frizzy but also grayer. Hamilton stared. It wasn't that long ago, was it, he thought to himself.

How do I explain what I'm looking for, he thought. He was turning into a Harry Chapin song, isn't that what Becka had written. The clerk waved at him, as if Hamilton was a regular. "How's it going?" he asked, then quickly looked back at his register as he counted cash.

"Do you know a lot about Harry Chapin?" Hamilton asked, making sure nobody else was in the store.

The clerk looked back at him, cocked his head to one side, as if he had been asked a trick question, and said, "Um, I wouldn't have pegged you for a Chapin fan. I mean, no offense, but...." And then he stopped counting, put the money in the drawer, and walked over to Hamilton, talking as he walked, "But I mean...how rude can I get?"

"No offense taken. You're right, I'm not a fan, but I need to find one song in particular. And I don't know where to begin."

"You got a clue?" the clerk asked.

"Not really, but something a daughter might...," and he paused. How to say it? "...something a daughter might say about her father. I know that's not..."

The clerk reached around Hamilton and pulled out a CD, flipped it over to scan the titles, and handed it to him, Tangled Up Puppet. "That's my guess."

Hamilton blinked, but he did not know what to say. The clerk put the CD in Hamilton's right hand, and Hamilton quickly held on to it with his other hand as well, as if it were the only copy in existence.

284

But he was still speechless. "You want to hear it before you buy? I can put it on the store system," the clerk asked, but he did not wait for an answer. He took the CD, ripped off the plastic wrap, and loaded it into a CD player at the front counter. Three minutes and forty-two seconds later, Hamilton understood what his daughter had meant. He had become a song, a tangled up puppet.

"You okay?" the clerk asked, for the third time. "Mister Hamilton, you okay? Hey, Mister Hamilton, you okay?"

Hamilton was sitting on a chair in the corner, but he did not remember how he got there, nor could he remember introducing himself. The clerk put the CD back in its case, the case in a bag, and handed it to him, "Song's on the house." Hamilton started to protest, but the clerk insisted, "Tell your friends…Crazy Ray's got all the answers. But they gotta pay. For you, this one's free, a gift from me and Harry Chapin. Damn!…I loved that man's stuff!"

Small package in hand, Jack Hamilton went to vote at Longfellow Elementary, a few blocks from his house. In the past, he and Marcie had always gone together to vote, sometimes taking Becka with them. This year, Marcie told him that she was not voting. He did not argue with her. They had voted in every election since they moved to Athens, including the school board elections. This would be the first time that Marcie did not get one of those "I Voted" lapel pins.

Hamilton knew all the precinct workers, and they all asked about Marcie. He told them she had voted with a mail ballot earlier in the month. Other obligations today.

It was a short ballot, and Hamilton was soon out of Longfellow. From checking his name on the rolls and then slipping the ballot into the electronic counter had taken less than five minutes. He voted for Joseph Holly in the district race. He had always liked Holly. For the at-large race, he only recognized two names: George Bedell and Ken Rumble. Bedell had knocked on his door a week earlier, handed him some brochures, asked for his vote, thanked him, and then went to Philip Reisetter's house next door. Hamilton remembered, and he voted for him. About to mark Rumble's name, however, Hamilton suddenly remembered Becka's funeral, and Rumble's hand extended toward him, and he paused. He had two votes to give in that race, and he had voted for Rumble in the past, but something stopped him this time. No reason, he told Marcie later, just a feeling.

The library bond issue was on a separate ballot. This was an easy decision for Hamilton. He went to the library a lot, had taken Becka there hundreds of times in the past fifteen years. A bigger library was a good thing. He was willing to pay the taxes. He voted for it. Then he went home, excited about letting his wife hear the Harry Chapin song.

Marcie was waiting for Hamilton after he voted, but so was an elderly small black woman. The two women seemed to be conspiring, that was his first thought. They were sitting close together on a couch in the den, and Marcie was holding the other woman's hands in her own. Marcie stood up as her husband came in the room, and the other woman began to slowly rise, using a cane at the same time she was holding on to Marcie's hand. Hamilton motioned for them to sit down again as he came closer.

"Jack, this is Winnie Mason," Marcie said. The name meant nothing to him. He stared at the woman. How could she stand in the wind? She was tiny, surely less than a hundred pounds, surely not five feet tall. "Winnie is the Hampton boy's grandmother. The boy who drove the car.... ."

Hamilton recoiled, stepping back abruptly and tensing, the brown bag still in his hand. The two women moved closer together.

"She wanted to see us and..."

It all came back, that day in late May, the walk home, the police car waiting for them, him shattering the answering machine, the drive to the Lensing Funeral Home to see Becka, the chill of her skin. It all came back.

And more.

"Jack, would you sit with us, please?"

He sat in the recliner next to the couch, a right angle to the women. They shifted to face him, but no one spoke for a moment. Winnie Mason was trembling. "Mr. Hamilton, I was telling your wife...," the older woman finally began, her bony hands twisting a damp kerchief, "...that I was taking Andy back home. But I wanted to come see you and your wife, and tell you how sorry I was about your daughter. I mean, how sorry I am."

Marcie was patting the woman's back, glancing at Hamilton to see how he was reacting. His face was blank.

"I should have come sooner, and for that I apologize, but my son Donald and Andy's sister...they thought it was a bad idea. They told me that you did not want to hear from me, that you would not share your grief with me. You would not want to share mine. So, I was afraid, but I can't.... any longer..."

The two women had been crying before Hamilton arrived, that was now obvious to him. Marcie was about to begin again.

Hamilton looked at the small woman shrinking even more as her voice trailed off. When she started talking again, he thought about his own mother, a big woman, three women bigger than the woman in front of him now. Becka had her grandmother's eyes. Hamilton stared at the woman on his couch. It occurred to him that he could not remember anything about how the Hampton boy looked although he had seen his picture in the paper several times. Was there something in this woman's face to remind him? But, nothing. Anheuser Hampton was a blur.

"I'm sorry," he interrupted, "but you said something about taking your grandson home?"

287

"He grew up in Chicago. Most of his family's back there, but Donald insisted that Andy be buried here. He even paid for everything. And I was too weak...too deep in myself...to say no. Oh, Mr. Hamilton, Andy was my boy until he was five, until his mama convinced me she could raise him right. I prayed I was doing the right thing, sending him back to her, moving here with my other daughter. I wanted to bring Andy with me, I thought he would be safe here, but I was weak."

"I grew up in Chicago too," Hamilton said quietly, leaning forward in his chair to touch the woman's hand. Marcie smiled at her husband and kept one hand on the older woman's shoulders.

"When he finally came to be with me, I knew it was because he was in trouble back there, but I wouldn't admit he was lost. He came here too late. Athens is my home now, but it was never his. He brought Chicago with him."

"I know about Chicago," Hamilton told her. "Lots of good people there, but a lot of bad ones too. A lot of ways to fall."

Winnie Mason nodded vigorously, "But that's where Andy belongs. Me, I'll take him home, but I'm coming back here. I've got other grandchildren there, and I'll try and bring them to grow up in Athens before it's too late."

"Take him home?" Hamilton wanted to understand.

"I've worked extra at the nursing home where I clean, and I've borrowed from a few friends. I'm having his remains shipped back to a plot I've bought in Chicago. As close to my parents as I could get him, but he'll still be by himself for awhile. I bought two plots."

It was late afternoon, already dark in Iowa.

"Andy was the happiest baby of all my children," Winnie Mason whispered. "But I lost him."

Hamilton stood up and pulled Winnie Mason gently up with him. Marcie sat and looked at them. He put his arms around the old

288

woman, thinking to himself that she was so frail that if he squeezed too tight he would break her bones. The top of her head barely reached his chest. "You must stay and have dinner with us," he told her while he looked at Marcie.

The old woman shuddered and then let herself weep. "Oh, Mr. Hamilton, I just want to tell you how sorry I am about your daughter, and I hope, so dearly hope, that when you pray for her you'll pray for Andy too. You've got to forgive him."

Hamilton hesitated, but finally said, "Your boy doesn't need my forgiveness." He was uncomfortable, and he knew that Marcie understood his dilemma, but he wanted Winnie Mason to feel better, so he invoked a God in whom he did not believe, "But I'm sure that God will forgive him."

The woman leaned back, looking directly up at him, "I hope you do too." Hamilton looked away, and Winnie Mason put her head back against his chest. "I pray every night, pray for Andy, but I wish I could talk to him one more time. I'd trade my prayers for that. Do you know what I mean, Mr. Hamilton, wanting just one more time to talk to him? Just to let go?"

Hamilton nodded without looking down.

Hours later, after a dinner with Winnie Mason, after the three adults exchanged stories about their children, sometimes laughing, sometimes falling silent, Jack and Marcie Hamilton were alone. He told her about his trip to Discount Records, Crazy Ray and Harry Chapin.

"You're sure this is what she meant?" Marcie asked as he put the CD in the player.

"I knew it as soon as I heard the first lines," he said, sitting back, knowing that Marcie was about to cry and he would need to be there to hold her. Chapin's voice filled the room, and Jack Hamilton started talking to his daughter

I was yesterday's news, the sock that gets eaten by the dryer, a political footnote. I was going to my last council meeting. Athens was on its own.

Danny has a new favorite picture. The morning after the election, in color above the fold of the **TELEGRAM**'s front page, was a big picture of me voting, Danny by my side. It was a frigid Iowa morning, so we were both bundled up. Me in my down jacket looking like the Goodyear blimp, Danny wearing a sock cap to keep his ears warm. He's watching the ballot slide into that electronic counter, and I'm looking down at him. You can see the family resemblance.

I voted and went to work, went home, got the results that night, went to bed, and woke up to the **TELEGRAM** headlines: Holly Loses Re-Election Bid on the top half of the page; Library Bonds Find Support on the bottom. I got 47 percent of the votes; the Library got 64 percent. The people spoke. Nobody seemed surprised at the message. Not even me.

But every political junkie in Athens was ecstatic about the results of the at-large race. A feast to be savored. Too bad we weren't like the national elections, with the networks doing those exit polls, asking voters how and why they made a choice. Pundit fodder, and in Athens we were all pundits.

Ken Rumble was re-elected. But barely, and the dissections began. Rumble Squeaks Into Office Again the **TELEGRAM** blared. I immediately knew how Al Baroli would plague Ken for the next two years. Out of nowhere, Al would whisper into his microphone, "Excuse me, Kenny, but could you repeat that. I couldn't hear you because of all the squeaking." Variations on a squeaker theme. And Harry would sit there, holding his cards where nobody could see them.

Me losing was not a shock, but Ken being dumped back into the pack with the other three contenders—that was NEWS. Conventional wisdom before the election had Ken comfortably ahead, the white Chamber of Commerce woman a probable second, with the young black guy a strong third, and the home-towner last. That was the smart money.

Ballots tabulated, Rumble led the pack by a hundred and ten votes while Hometowner edged out Race by a dozen votes and Gender by fifty. Conventional wisdom went back to school. I called Harry and asked him to explain it, but he was as surprised as anyone else. I called Ted Stanton. He was only mildly surprised, but he also thought the voters had made the right choice, "Those two guys were the best in the field. Sometimes the voters do the right thing. George Bedell worked harder than any of them, and he was a native son. And you, Joe.... . the voters figured out that you didn't really want the job. You just wanted to preach to them."

"Hey, loser, come by my office before the meeting tonight. I've got something for you. Sort of a going away present." Harry was in a good mood. I hated to ruin it for him.

"You see the"TELEGRAM this morning? Go get it and call me back."

Ten minutes later, Harry's on the phone, "Just shoot me." The TELEGRAM had published its latest circulation stimulus package: The Most Notable Athenians of the 1990's. A readers' poll, one entry blank per issue, no Xeroxes allowed, only one vote per email address. Twenty notable citizens of Athens, and Ken Rumble was the only elected official to make the cut. Harry made the list too, but not in the top ten like Ken. That made him even madder: Being on <u>any</u> list lower than Ken Rumble. "Has anybody been paying attention out there? Does anybody know that we've done good things in spite of him, not because of him? Next thing we know, he'll be running for President."

"I love you, Harry. Does that count."

He hung up on me.

My last meeting. I went early and had a talk with Bob Hardy, asked him a favor, and then went to see Harry. "Don't say I never gave you anything," he said, handing me a giant gift-wrapped, incredibly heavy something. Six feet long, three feet wide, probably thirty pounds. I damn near dropped it as soon as he handed it to me. "And I expect to see it hanging on the side of your garage when I drive by."

I tore off the wrapping and stared for a few seconds until I realized what it was—a piece of dented sheet metal, part of the roof of the tool shed in Oakland that had been destroyed. "I had maintenance save this for you, special," he said, obviously proud of himself.

I found the footprint. As large as I had imagined.

"Hartford said to say hello," Harry almost giggled. He still didn't get it. But, he knew the metal would mean a lot to me. We had a few minutes before the meeting started, so we sat there and reminisced.

I went to my last meeting. Al Baroli slipped in one "squeaker" comment. Ken Rumble ignored him, but you could see him flinch. He wasn't going to enjoy a lot of future council meetings.

The meeting proceeded without me paying attention most of the time. When it came time for public discussion, shifted to the middle of the agenda, the President of the Chamber of Commerce went to the microphone to thank me and Steve Nash for our public service. Form letter stuff, but part of the ritual, and I was thankful. Then John Brownstein, antlers atop his head, came to the podium and we got ready for another suggestion about controlling the deer population. But John, bless him, almost made me cry.

"I'll miss you, Mr. Holly," was all he said, and then he sat down.

"I'll miss you too, Mr. Brownstein," I whispered, so low that my mike didn't pick it up, but I'm sure he heard me.

Down in front of us that last night were a lot of people who had done business with us long before Becky died. The council was either a problem or a solution for them, and they had to deal with us again and again. It was the nature of government, and I had come to know all of them. Doug Russell, Churchill scholar and Chair of the Historic Preservation Commission, was there to answer our questions about a code revision. Richard "Sandy" Rhodes was in the front row, looking like a Disney-fied version of Ho Chi Minh, but a man who knew more about acidic soils and wetlands than anybody on the city staff, and who was the best environmental advocate Athens had, there to disagree with a staff recommendation, knowing we would give him serious consideration. Doug and Sandy, others, all of them smart, all of them willing to plod through the maze of local government, each typical of hundreds like them.

I wrote to Bernie: *If you could pick your own city council, elections be damned, who would you choose?* Bernie looked at the note, tapped it a second with her forefinger, never looking my way, and scribbled: *Other than you and me?* I nodded. We exchanged names until we had a list: Doug Russell, Sandy Rhodes, Dee Norton, Mary Ann Dennis, Jackie Blank, Adelaide Morris, Jim Clark, Dan Daly, Carolyn Cavitt, Howard Horan, Nancy Seiberling, Leigh Bradford, Mary Neuhauser, Karin Franklin, Don Heistad, Jim Larew, Bob Hibbs, Tom Scott, Tim Shields, Lisa Mollenhauer, Leslie Menninger, Dale Helling, Sandy Jensen, Clemens Erdahl, Connie Brothers, Harry Rueber, Jim Throgmorton, Richard LeBlond, Jay Stein, Bob Leutner, Marian Karr, Ann Rhodes, Peter Fisher, Matt Lage, John McDonald, Julie Tallman, Harry Lewis, Doug Ruppert, Saul Mekies, Carl Bendorf, Linda Baez, Peter Hansen, Denny Gannon, Rick Fosse, Marlene Perrin, Dick Greenwood, Ralph Washington, Carol Spaziani, Jerry Hansen, Dennis Ryan, Tom Hobart, Lavonn Horton, Mike Hoppman, Karen Kubby, John Stimmel, Bob Welsh, John Bennett—and hundreds more. All those atoms. Athens would do alright without me.

Halfway through the agenda, probably another hour to go, I looked at the clock on the wall in the back of the room, dead center above the picture of the man who was going to replace me. All the little details that had obsessed me for years, I was letting them go. I even had a twinge of regret about being so hard on Ken Rumble. He was more good than bad, more right than wrong on most of the issues, and he would eventually go away. A minute before ten o'clock, I looked for Bob Hardy. He gave me a thumbs up. Exactly at ten, the red-light camera swung around to focus on me. Steve Nash was reading some agenda item into the public record, but all across Athens the only person in the picture was Joe Holly. I looked right into the camera, and then I waved at Julie and Danny.

The girl had a decision to make. She was supposed to be home before her parents returned from dinner. But she had had an exceptionally good day, and she felt like running some more. She had run in the morning as soon as she got to school, but just as her legs seemed to get stronger she was supposed to go to her first class. All day long she had thought about running again. Even her last period music class, in which she usually worked off a different kind of energy, even that class had not been enough. She practiced her flute an extra hour, staying after school with a few other band members, but she then decided to run again. Just a few miles, and then she could still be home before her parents got back. Just to make sure they weren't worried, however, she decided to call and leave a message.

"This is your favorite daughter. I'm running late this afternoon. But I should be there as soon as you get back. Mama, tell daddy that I forgive him for being such a jerk this morning. Love ya, bye."

Then she changed into her jogging clothes and went to the track behind her high school. Running in circles was soon boring, so she raced through the gates and went running on the sidewalks. She ran toward the east and then turned back to the west. Sometimes she would wear a Sony Walkman, the music setting a faster pace for her, but not today. It was very warm, and she knew she would be sweating. That was good, she told herself. Her parents disagreed with her, but she thought she needed to lose some weight. More muscle, less fat, that was her goal.

As she ran, she thought about her day at school. It was the end of her first year in high school, and she was surprised at how much fun she had had, after worrying throughout her eighth grade about the future. She was even beginning to think that her parents might have been right about some things. In her English class this morning, her teacher had asked the students to make a list for themselves, not to be shown to anyone else, a list of things about themselves that might surprise their parents. It was an exercise for their journal writing. "Step outside yourself," the teacher had said. "Put yourself in your parents' position. Be them. And then go back into yourself. Do this a few more times this summer. Nobody will know anything except yourself. Be honest." The girl already kept a secret journal, but she knew she had not been too honest. It was more like a calendar of things she had done during the week. But this summer was going to be different.

She ran, and ran some more. As her body reached that point when running was effortless, she thought about her parents. Would they be surprised, overly concerned, that she was interested in an older man, in his early twenties, a teacher's aide for the music program? A man she had not even mentioned in her journal? A man who seemed oblivious to her existence, but whom she watched at band practice every day? Would they be surprised that she liked ancient old people's music, music from the seventies and eighties. Music from when her parents were young. She would sometimes stay after school, and the young man would organize an informal "pop music" singing club. The girl was one of many girls in that group, and she suspected that all of them looked at the young man as she did. She had not told her parents, but she had been thinking about dropping the flute and concentrating on vocal lessons. The young man tutored outside of school for a small fee. He had introduced his students to the radical concept that music also included words as well as notes, that the voice was an instrument. He played jazz vocalists for them, folk singers, but not choral music. "Somebody else's passion, not mine," he had said about the award winning school choir, and the girl knew he had gotten in trouble with the choir director for that comment, which was just another reason to like him.

The girl ran and ran, wishing that the young man was interested in running with her. When she was older, of course; or else her father would do his father routine and go see the young man. The thought of her father confronting the young man made the girl angry for a moment. Her father, she knew, would never let her grow up. But the anger passed. Her legs were getting stronger.

She was heading back to her school, flying, her new jogging shoes turning the concrete sidewalks into another source of energy, her feet hitting the surface and springing up, as if the concrete was pushing her back into the air. Anti-gravity, that's how she felt. She was defying gravity. It always happened sooner or later. She had told her father about it once and he had understood, always smiling, but her mother never did.

As she saw her school come back into view, she slowed down and started to walk. She was still pumping endorphins, but sometimes, like now, she wanted to simply relax and enjoy the feeling.

She heard the sirens behind her and turned around. She saw nothing at first, but then, focusing farther in the distance, she could see a flashing red light. It was blocks away, a tiny pulsating red light, and the screech of the siren seemed to come from it. She crossed the street and waited on the other side, a few feet from a stop sign. Two cars were racing toward the four-way stop, and she assumed they would keep going straight. She was safely to one side, a spectator to a chase. This was exciting, she thought, wondering why the first car was trying to escape. Like a television program, cops and robbers, as real as television.

As the cars approached the intersection, the girl looked around to see if anyone else was watching too, but she was the only witness.

For a split second, the girl realized that the first car was going to turn instead of go straight. Her body had to make a decision, not her mind, which way to move, right or left, back or forward. Her body moved to her right, and a few feet further back, as the first car had already turned the corner, one side rising off the pavement, and the girl saw the driver of the car for the first time, a young boy, both hands on the wheel, eyes wide open.

Her body frozen in a new spot, the girl felt the red lights of the second car flood over her.

Then the cars were gone, disappearing down the street, continuing their chase, and the girl was left standing alone, noticing how the flashing red light had turned the entire sky red.

She was trembling, but the worst was over. She turned and started walking toward her school, but it was further away than she had remembered. She had to get home. Her parents would be upset. But the school kept receding in the distance. The girl closed her eyes. When she opened them again, the school was gone.

She was somewhere else, but it still looked familiar. She was on the street where she lived, and her house was just ahead. She kept walking. Then she became confused. All the houses looked like hers. And she was incredibly cold. The warm day had turned icy. It was absolutely silent.

She went to the first house, but it was not hers. Then the second, but not hers. She went back to the street. Then she heard something. Like a slow drum, almost a muffled thunder.

She was back at the corner where the cars had turned. Something was walking toward her, far off in the distance, a small glow only. The girl stared, but the glow would not come into focus. She waited for it to come to her.

The girl was getting colder. Her jogging suit had been soaked with sweat a few minutes earlier, and the cold air was turning the sweat to ice. She closed her eyes again. When she opened them, standing in front of her was a huge deer.

The deer was looking down at her, its eyes staring into hers. Waves of vapory silver were coming off its back, and, as it breathed, that silver vapor came out of its nostrils too. The deer was dark brown, but its antlers seemed a glowing green, and the silver vapor coming off them made the antlers look even larger.

"You okay?" the deer asked the girl.

The girl did not speak at first, but not because she was surprised at a deer speaking to her. She was simply curious. A talking deer was not strange, but the voice of the deer sounded familiar. More than that, however, she was intrigued that the deer could speak without opening its mouth or moving its lips, with absolutely no motion of speech. But she heard it clearly.

"I'm cold," the girl said.

The deer stepped closer, and the girl could feel the heat coming off its fur. She felt warmer, and she stepped even closer. The deer changed colors, from brown to black and then to dark red. The air turned warm again, and the girl stopped shivering.

"I was going home," she said, motioning back over her shoulders.

"I'll walk with you," the deer said.

They walked toward the girl's school, and then through the school, through hallways that seemed larger to the girl than she had remembered, past rows of lockers, past the music room. The girl had reached for the door, thinking she would retrieve her flute, but the deer kept walking so she had to leave her flute and catch up with the deer.

The girl was feeling better the more she walked, feeling like she felt earlier when she was running. She wanted to run again, but she did not think the deer would run with her. Then, as if she had spoken to it, the deer began running away from her, as if they were playing tag, and she ran after it.

It was easy, catching up to the deer, and she passed it. Or, so she thought. She looked ahead and the deer was beyond her. She looked back. It was gone. So she ran harder, and soon she was beside the deer again, both of them seeming to float.

"You're very fast," the deer said.

The girl laughed. She was running faster than she had ever run in her life. As she ran alongside the deer, she asked, "Do you have a name? Something I should call you?"

"No," was all the deer said.

They stopped running and walked. The girl was not tired, but she was strangely sleepy. As she walked, she reached over to touch the deer's shoulder. She could feel the muscles.

"We're almost there," the deer said.

The girl was standing on a rolling hill. The deer lowered its head and used its antlers to point ahead. In the distance, a woman was waiting. The girl had seen the woman somewhere before. A pale woman, in some sort of flowing robe. The woman raised her right arm, and the girl stepped under it, turning back to the deer.

"I know you, don't I?" said the girl to the deer as the woman's arm folded around her. The deer nodded slowly. Then, as the pale arm became a dark wing, the girl closed her eyes and saw the voice of her father.